D0882596

BY GREG WEISMAN

Rain of the Ghosts
Spirits of Ash and Foam
World of Warcraft: Traveler
World of Warcraft: Traveler—The Spiral Path
Magic: The Gathering—War of the Spark: Ravnica
Magic: The Gathering—War of the Spark: Forsaken

MAGIC™

WAR OF THE SPARK
FORSAKEN

MAGIC™

WAR OF THE SPARK

FORSAKEN

GREG WEISMAN

DEL REY
NEW YORK

Copyright © 2019 by Wizards of the Coast LLC.
All Rights Reserved.

Published in the United States by Del Rey,
an imprint of Random House, a division of
Penguin Random House LLC, New York.

DEL REY and the HOUSE colophon are registered trademarks
of Penguin Random House LLC.

WIZARDS OF THE COAST, MAGIC: THE GATHERING, MAGIC,
their respective logos, War of the Spark, the Planeswalker symbol,
all guild names and symbols, and characters' names are property
of Wizards of the Coast LLC in the USA and other countries.

LIBRARY OF CONGRESS CATALOGING-IN-PUBLICATION DATA
Names: Weisman, Greg (Gregory David), author.
Title: Forsaken / Greg Weisman.
Description: New York: Del Rey, [2019] | Series: War of the spark; 2
Identifiers: LCCN 2019034616 (print) | LCCN 2019034617 (ebook) |
ISBN 9781984817945 (hardcover; acid-free paper) |
ISBN 9781984817952 (ebook)
Subjects: LCSH: Magic: The Gathering (Game)—Fiction. |
GSAFD: Fantasy fiction.
Classification: LCC PS3623.E432545 F67 2019 (print) |
LCC PS3623.E432545 (ebook) | DDC 813/.6—dc23
LC record available at https://lccn.loc.gov/2019034616
LC ebook record available at https://lccn.loc.gov/2019034617

Printed in the United States of America on acid-free paper

randomhousebooks.com

2 4 6 8 9 7 5 3 1

First Edition

Book design by Elizabeth A. D. Eno

To the foremost professors of my undergraduate career: Albert Guerard, John L'Heureux, Thomas Moser, Nancy Huddleston Packer, Ron Rebholz and Juan Valenzuela. Thank you for opening up new planes for me to walk upon . . .

DRAMATIS PERSONAE

Dovin Baan—Planeswalker, vedalken from Kaladesh, former Minister of Inspections of the Consulate of Kaladesh, former Azorius Senate guildmaster, artificer, systems mage.

Jace Beleren—Planeswalker, human from Vryn, Gatewatch member, former Living Guildpact of Ravnica, mind-mage.

Blaise—Human of Ravnica, Orzhov Syndicate servitor, majordomo to the guildmaster.

Ana Iora—Human of Fiora, peasant.

Teysa Karlov—Human of Ravnica, Orzhov Syndicate hierarch, former Grand Envoy and advokist, Matriarch of Karlov line, lawmage.

Kaya—Planeswalker, human from Tolvada, Orzhov Syndicate guildmaster, Gatewatch member, ghost-assassin.

Chandra Nalaar—Planeswalker, human from Kaladesh, Gatewatch member, former abbot of Keral Keep on Regatha, pyromancer.

Rat—Human of Ravnica, Gateless thief.

Atkos Tarr—Vampire of Ravnica, House Dimir assassin.

Tezzeret—Planeswalker, human from Alara, artificer.

Teyo Verada—Planeswalker, human from Gobakhan, Shieldmage Acolyte.

Liliana Vess—Planeswalker, human from Dominaria, former Gatewatch member, necromancer.

Vraska—Planeswalker, Gorgon from Ravnica, Golgari Swarm guildmaster and queen, former pirate captain and assassin.

Tomik Vrona—Human of Ravnica, Orzhov Syndicate syndic, aide-de-camp to Orzhov guildmaster, lawmage, security mage and advokist.

Ral Zarek—Planeswalker, human from Ravnica, Izzet League guildmaster, Storm Mage.

GUILDS OF RAVNICA

Azorius Senate
Dedicated to bringing order to the chaos of Ravnican streets, the Azorius Senate strives to educate the compliant—and restrain the rebellious.

Boros Legion
The zealous Boros Legion is united in pursuit of a peaceful and harmonious Ravnica, no matter how many bodies its forces must step over to achieve it.

House Dimir
The agents of House Dimir dwell in the darkest corners of the city, selling their secrets to those who hunger for power, and their steel to those who need enemies silenced.

Golgari Swarm
All that lives must die, and death brings new life. The Golgari Swarm are guardians of this cycle, feeding the citizens of Ravnica and preparing them to feed the earth in turn.

Gruul Clans
Once, the Gruul Clans ruled over the untamed wilds of Ravnica, but as the city has grown they've been forced

into exile to escape its crushing weight. They're ready to crush back.

Izzet League

With their endless public works, the geniuses of the Izzet League maintain the sprawling splendor of Ravnica . . . when their experiments aren't accidentally blowing it up.

Orzhov Syndicate

The Orzhov Syndicate is ruthlessly ambitious and endlessly acquisitive. Still, the Orzhov offers succor to the soul and the purse, collecting from both with interest, even after death.

Cult of Rakdos

Entertainers and hedonists, the Cultists of the demonic lord Rakdos know life is short and full of pain. The only thing that matters? Having as much fun as you possibly can, no matter the consequences.

Selesnya Conclave

The Selesnya Conclave is the voice of Mat'Selesnya, the mysterious manifestation of nature itself. Guardians of Ravnica's threatened environment, they will stop at nothing to defend it.

Simic Combine

Nowhere is the balance of nature and civilization more important—or more at risk—than in a city that spans a world. The Simic Combine stands ready to maintain Ravnica . . . or *revise* it to the guild's own unique specifications.

EPILOGUE

ONE

KAYA

Numb.

She felt numb.

Maybe that was necessary right now, as she helped Arlinn Kord carry off the desiccated corpse of a man she barely knew, a Planeswalker named Dack Fayden, who'd sacrificed his Spark and his life to save Ravnica—*to save the very Multiverse*—from the dragon Nicol Bolas.

Now Bolas was dead, too. Like Fayden, he had ultimately lost his Spark to the Eternals he himself had created, and Kaya and all of Ravnica had watched him dissolve, disintegrate into ashes that blew away on the wind.

It had been a stupendous victory—and a costly one. Kaya was certain she should *feel* it more, both the exaltation of triumph and the pain of the losses that earned it.

Instead—as she and Arlinn lowered Dack's body onto an

empty wooden board between the cadavers of Domri Rade and a viashino named Jahdeera—what passed for her emotions seemed, what—

Shrouded? Is that it?

Or was the metaphor simply suggested by the thin white sheet of spidery silk that the Golgari priestess, Matka Izoni, was rapidly weaving over all three corpses?

Kaya barely knew any of them. Rade had been an idiot and a turncoat. Jahdeera had followed him blindly. But Dack had been an actual hero, part of the team that shut down the Planar Bridge, stopping the flow of Eternals pouring into Ravnica from Amonkhet. From there he could have planeswalked anywhere. Instead, he chose to return and fight the good fight. To fight—and then to die for having made that choice.

If I can't feel anything for him . . . then who exactly is wearing that silken shroud?

Kord turned around to fetch another corpse, but Kaya decided she'd had enough of that grim work.

All around her, a joyous victory celebration had erupted—punctuated by mourners crying over their very personal losses. Each extreme created contrast for the other. The elven girl climbing over the wreckage of Bolas' fallen statue, and the human boy swinging from the branch of the fallen world-tree Vitu-Ghazi, seemed all the more carefree when set against the goblin mother and child desperately mourning over what remained of their husband and father, whose lower half had been crushed beneath the foot of the God-Eternal Bontu.

The sinking sun passed between two buildings and a sudden ray of light caused Kaya to squint, caused her eyes to water. It was the closest thing to tears she had managed since this whole thing had begun.

Maybe the real tears will come later. Catch me unawares and lay me out.

She found herself hoping so. She didn't like feeling dead inside. She'd had enough of death for one lifetime—which was more than a little ironic, considering her profession. Kaya was—or had been, until very recently—a ghost-assassin. Her magic allowed her to send spirits to a final rest. Death was quite literally her business. But until today, she'd never felt quite so dead herself.

Dead and dead tired. With the battle over and the adrenaline rush receding, Kaya, the reluctant Orzhov Syndicate guildmaster, could once again feel the full force of the thousands upon thousands of Orzhov debtor contracts that weighed down her soul.

Ah, it's tempting, so tempting, to simply declare all those debts forgiven.

But she knew such an act would destroy the Orzhov, and she *feared* that if even one guild fell, the delicate balancing act that was Ravnica would topple with it. The world-city literally (and magically) depended on its ten guilds operating, if not in harmony, then at least in balanced opposition to one another. And Kaya had not worked so hard to save Ravnica only to be the cause of its downfall by a different means. So the debts would not be forgiven, and for now, at least, she would continue to carry their weight.

She wanted, *needed,* to see a friendly face. By this time she had many close friends on Ravnica. Ral and Tomik. Hekara. Lavinia. Even Vraska. And yet the two people she felt closest to, most wanted to see, were two teenagers she had only just met this very morning: Teyo and Rat.

My entourage.

She smiled.

There! That's an emotion. Not much of one, I'll grant you. But it's something. Chase that!

She started moving through the crowd with a purpose, trying

to find the young shieldmage and the even younger thief. Not that Kaya was all that old. She wasn't even thirty years old, herself. But relative to those two, she felt like one of the Ancients of Keru.

Why was she so attached to them? How had it happened so quickly? All right, sure, each had saved her life today—multiple times. But during this "War of the Spark," as folks had already dubbed it, her life had been saved by two or three dozen different individuals, and she herself had saved easily three times that number (whatever that number might be). No, it was more than that, she felt sure.

It's their purity. What they have is what I'm missing.

Teyo was so naïve. But there was a hidden strength beneath that naïveté. A strength he had only barely discovered—and still didn't truly believe he had.

And Rat? Araithia "Rat" Shokta's life had been . . . impossible. Truly. Impossible. It was a miracle she had survived it. Yet the true miracle was that she hadn't simply survived it, she had embraced it and had maintained an optimism that was even more impossible.

They were two pure souls. Relative to them, Kaya felt a bit like a vampire, a creature of darkness desperate to feed off their bright light. That thought scared her a bit, and she literally stopped in her tracks. But she took a deep breath.

It's a metaphor, Kaya. You're not actually taking anything from either of them. In fact, there are gifts you can give them. Things that might make them happy. Or at least make their lives a bit easier. Before you say goodbye.

Buoyed by that, she started forward again and soon spotted them together. Well, of course they were together. The sixteen-year-old Rat had adopted the nineteen-year-old Teyo the moment he had arrived on Ravnica.

As she approached the two kids, Teyo spotted her and said to Rat, "Don't forget, you still have the two of us."

Kaya immediately knew what they'd been discussing, as Rat nodded sadly and said, "Except you're both Planeswalkers. You'll leave Ravnica eventually."

Kaya wasn't sure she *could* leave Ravnica. She'd been told that all those Orzhov contracts had bound her to the plane. But if she did . . .

She said nothing for now. Still weighing her options, she linked arms with them both and walked on.

With her entourage quite literally in tow, she joined a group of Planeswalkers and Ravnicans, most of them friends of hers (or at least comrades in arms), just to be around people. They were debating something. She couldn't focus on what, and honestly didn't much care.

The angel Aurelia approached. She was carrying something with an almost devout air that brought Kaya back into the moment. At first she couldn't tell what the thing was. Then she saw it was a man's breastplate, charred and blackened. She didn't immediately grasp its significance. Each of the ten guilds had so many rituals and traditions. (She barely understood all the Orzhov's traditions, and she was theoretically their leader.) Maybe Aurelia's Boros Legion worshipped this holy piece of armor and trotted it out after every victory.

Then Chandra Nalaar said, "We should bury that on Theros. I think Gids'd like that." And Kaya knew. This breastplate was all that remained of Gideon Jura, a Planeswalker who had given his life to save Ravnica and the Multiverse. If anyone had been a hero of this War of the Spark, it had been Gideon.

Ajani Goldmane, the leonin Planeswalker, responded to Chandra: "What he'd like is to know it's not over."

"It's not over?" Teyo asked, horrified.

Ajani chuckled and placed a reassuring paw on Teyo's shoulder. "I do believe the threat of Nicol Bolas has passed. But we cannot pretend Bolas will be the last threat to face the Multiverse. If we truly wish to honor our friend Gideon, we need to confirm that the next time a threat rises, the Gatewatch will be there."

The Gatewatch.

She'd never heard of it before today. And yet it seemed that this group, this team of half a dozen or so Planeswalkers, had been protecting the Multiverse for months, from Bolas and multiple other threats, as well. They had led the charge today, and they had suffered for it. They had known what was coming, and they had come to face it anyway. And if they *hadn't* come, there was no way anyone on Ravnica would have survived. Of that, Kaya was quite sure.

Goldmane, another member of the Gatewatch, was saying, "We just need to renew our Oaths."

Jace Beleren, the Gatewatch's de facto leader (less *"de facto"* now, with Gideon dead), replied, "Ajani, we all renewed them earlier today. Don't you think once a day is plenty?"

Ajani scowled. His grip on Teyo's shoulder involuntarily tightened, causing the kid to wince slightly. Kaya reached over and delicately removed the paw. Teyo breathed a small sigh of relief, and Rat giggled.

"Perhaps . . . perhaps *I* could take the Oath."

Who said that?

Everyone had turned to look at Kaya.

Holy Ancients, I think it was me!

Chandra looked at her hopefully and said, "Really?"

Ral looked at her dubiously and said, "Really?"

Kaya looked inward and asked herself, *Really?*

Well . . . yeah.

She *felt* it. She felt something. A desire to be a part of something larger than herself. To prove to herself she wasn't just a thief and an assassin. Or even just a woefully unprepared guildmaster. She could be someone that the Multiverse called on when there was trouble. She could be . . . Gatewatch. She liked that feeling and decided to run with it.

Uh, assuming they'll have me . . .

"I'm not a perfect person . . ."

"Trust me, none of us are," Jace interjected.

Vraska snorted.

Kaya ignored them both. "I've been an assassin and a thief. I've had my own moral code, but the first tenet of it was always, 'Watch your own ass.' I have the ability to ghost my way through life, to allow nothing to touch me. That's the literal truth of my powers, but it somehow became my emotional truth, as well. But my time on Ravnica as assassin, thief, reluctant guildmaster and perhaps even more reluctant warrior hasn't left me unaffected. Fighting beside you people has been an honor. The scariest and yet the *best* thing I've ever done with my somewhat bizarre life. What the Gatewatch has done here today—" She glanced down at the armor in Aurelia's hands. "—what you *sacrificed* here today . . . well . . . this'll sound corny, but it has been truly inspirational. If you'll have me, I'd like to be a part of this. I'd like you all to know that if there's trouble, you can summon me, and I will stand beside you."

"We'd like that," Chandra said.

"Aye, girl," said Ajani, grinning his leonin grin.

The remaining members of the Gatewatch—Jace, Teferi and Nissa Revane—all smiled and nodded their assent.

So Kaya took a deep breath and raised her right hand to take the Oath. Perhaps as a symbol of what she had to offer, she turned that hand spectral, so that it became transparent, flowing with a soft violet light. Then she thought about what she should say. She had heard the Gatewatch's six members—Gideon included—give their own Oaths earlier that day, when victory over the dragon was far from assured. Each one had said something different, but there had been a consistent theme. She said, "I have crossed the Multiverse, helping the dead, um . . . move on, in service of the living. But what I've witnessed here on Ravnica these last few months—these last few hours—has changed everything I thought I knew. Never again. For the living and the dead, *I will keep watch*."

There. That didn't sound too bad.

Feeling kind of proud of herself, she turned and smiled at Teyo and Rat. Rat grinned back. But Teyo was distracted by the descent of a dragon—not Bolas, of course. It was Niv-Mizzet, the Firemind, newly resurrected as the Living Guildpact, the literal embodiment of the mystic treaty that bound Ravnica's ten guilds together. He and Jace, the *former* Guildpact, exchanged a few words about the transfer of power.

But Kaya paid little attention. She was watching the elf Nissa Revane, who leaned her head over one of the many cracks in the plaza's pavement. She closed her eyes and breathed deeply. From between the battle-broken cobbles, a seed sprouted and rapidly grew into a plant with large green leaves.

Nissa nodded to Chandra, who somehow instinctively knew what the elf wanted her to do. The pyromancer carefully plucked three of the bigger leaves from the plant.

Then everyone watched as the two women and Aurelia lovingly wrapped Gideon's armor in the leaves.

Aurelia handed the armor to Chandra, who—flanked by Jace and Nissa—led a solemn procession toward the celebrating (and mourning) crowd. A forlorn Aurelia watched them go but did not follow—while most of the Planeswalkers did.

Kaya *started* to follow, but Ral touched her on the shoulder and gestured with his eyes for her to wait. Tomik did the same to Vraska, who nodded and called out to Jace that she would catch up to him.

With Teyo and Rat beside her, Kaya soon realized that she was standing amid a not-quite-impromptu convocation of representatives from all ten guilds, a realization immediately confirmed by the Firemind: "As the new Living Guildpact, I have consulted with representatives of every guild."

Kaya couldn't help noticing that *she* had not been consulted, though she was—more or less against her will—the current Orzhov guildmaster. She raised an eyebrow at her aide-de-camp Tomik, who nodded. She wondered if *he* had been consulted, or if Niv had gone directly to Tomik's former boss Teysa Karlov, who had her own designs on the Syndicate.

Niv continued: "We have agreed that certain individuals, those who collaborated with Nicol Bolas, must be punished."

Vraska, the gorgon Queen of the Golgari Swarm, bristled at that, her eyes brightening with magic: "I won't be judged by the likes of you."

Lavinia, acting head of the Azorius Senate, spoke sternly but without threat: "You *have* been judged. And your actions on this day have mitigated that judgment."

Ral, the new Izzet League guildmaster, stepped up, employing a conciliatory tone that was fairly out of character for him. "You are not the only one Bolas misled and used. Kaya and I share that particular guilt. We may have realized our error sooner than you did, but we have no desire to quibble with an ally. Not with an ally willing to prove her allegiance to Ravnica and her own guild."

Vraska looked no less suspicious—no less on guard—but her eyes ceased to glow. "I'm listening."

Aurelia, the Boros Legion guildmaster, said, "Hundreds, maybe thousands of sentient beings died on Ravnica today. Such acts of terror must not go unpunished. There are three who did everything in their power to aid and abet the dragon: Tezzeret, Dovin Baan and Liliana Vess."

Teyo said, "But didn't Liliana—"

Vorel, the Simic Combine biomancer, interrupted him: "Vess changed sides too late. Only after being the direct cause of most of the carnage."

"All three are Planeswalkers," stated Lazav, guildmaster of House Dimir. "They are out of our reach. But not out of yours."

Kaya didn't like where this was heading: "What exactly are you asking?"

The Firemind brought the point home. "Ral Zarek has already agreed to hunt Tezzeret. Vraska, as penance for past sins, we assign you Dovin Baan. And Kaya, the ten guilds wish to hire you to assassinate Liliana Vess."

PART ONE

SURVIVORS

TWO

LILIANA VESS

Liliana Vess stumbled through the swamp, the Caligo Morass, heading vaguely toward the ruins of her childhood home.

Because where else is there to go?

Night had fallen. The moon was low in the sky, providing little light. Little light shone inside her mind, either. Her thoughts were jumbled and jagged, a dark maze, truthfully a disaster area.

Like the ruins of Tenth District Plaza on Ravnica.

She remembered being on Ravnica. She remembered whispering, *"Kill me now."* She remembered wiping her tears away, tears that in the moment she was grateful to have the capacity to shed. Then she remembered rejecting all those emotions as self-pity. And even now, she pushed them down—pushed down the most human part of herself—deep, deep down into her psyche.

Stay down. They'll do you no good here.

No, she wouldn't pretend she left Ravnica out of guilt or shame. She left because she was under threat.

That was it. Self-preservation, pure and simple.

The Gatewatch and the other so-called heroes of Ravnica were destroying Bolas' Eternal army. And she had known those same heroes would soon come for her, as she was the most visible of Bolas' minions—if also the most coerced.

They have no idea the hold Bolas had over me. They can't pretend they would've acted differently.

Momentarily defiant, she kicked at a stone like an angry child. She missed and, losing her footing, hit her shoulder hard against a sagging tree. When she pushed off it, a small branch caught the hem of her dress and tore it.

There, are you happy? You ruined your dress. If you needed something to cry over, cry over that! But don't you dare cry over . . .

No. She wouldn't make excuses for herself. She didn't have to be a human being, but whatever she was, she'd at least be honest with herself, about herself. She had made a choice: to kill others for Nicol Bolas in order to save her own life.

It was the smart choice. No one said it was the right one.

She struggled forward. Why had she come here? She distinctly remembered closing her eyes and planeswalking away from Ravnica. What she didn't remember was making any conscious decision to come to Dominaria. For reasons she could not begin to explain, she had returned to the lands of the House of Vess, where she had been born and raised . . .

And where my life first went to the Nine Hells!

Bracing herself against a sagging tree that leaned out over the water, she suddenly realized she was holding Bolas' dormant Spirit-Gem in one hand. She stared at it. It was a smooth egg-shaped stone, with a silken sheen. It was silver. No, gold. She couldn't tell what color it was. It seemed to change as she turned it in her fist. And it was heavier than it looked. It had always floated or hovered between Bolas' horns. For years, she had assumed it was simply a decorative element, no more, no less. But the dragon had used it to absorb the Sparks he had harvested from dying Planeswalkers.

The Sparks I harvested for him.

When the dragon disintegrated, why hadn't the Gem disintegrated with him? How had she gotten it? She had absolutely no memory of picking the thing up back on Ravnica.

And why would I pick it up? As a souvenir of my wonderful times with Nicol Bolas?

She thought about throwing it deeper into the swamp . . . but didn't even seem to have the energy for that.

Just drop the thing. Let it sink into the water.

She didn't, of course. It had potential value, held potential power, and Liliana Vess did not throw power away. She collected it. Everyone knew that. Everyone believed that.

Except maybe Beefslab.

Gideon Jura hadn't believed that. He had believed . . . in her. Or in any case, he had believed in her potential. In her potential to be more than the sum total of the self-serving, power-hungry reputation she had so actively curated, promoted and cultivated.

Of course, all that proves is that Gideon Jura is a fool. Was *a fool.*

His memory loomed large for Liliana now. He had said, *"I can't be the hero this time, Liliana, but you can."* He had said, *"Make it count."* He had said those things while dying. While dying in order to save her life. She had always been so cynical about Gideon's faith in her. What had she ever done to earn it?

What had he ever done to prove himself a good judge of character?

So yes, after he was gone, after he couldn't possibly know what his death would count for—*or cost her*—she had tried to honor his sacrifice by taking Bolas down. By *successfully* taking Bolas down.

That's right, I did it, Gideon. Not you. Me. Liliana Vess destroyed Nicol Bolas. Did you see me do it for you, Beefslab? Did you see?

Now all *she* could see was Gideon's last horrible, beautiful smile. That and his ashes blowing away in the wind after taking her curse upon himself. She remembered the ashes, and she remembered that smile, but for the life of her she could not remember Gideon's face, the face of a man she had come to think of as a brother.

It's no different with Josu. Why can't I remember their faces?

She kept moving through the slough, trying to place each foot more carefully on solid ground.

There is no solid ground. That bastard Gideon and that bigger bastard Bolas have stolen the very ground beneath my feet. Who am I now? Who is Liliana Vess?

She hated them. Both of them. Almost equally. Almost.

And what of Jace?

He had tried to kill her earlier in the day—tried to kill her when she was still serving Bolas and using his Eternals to kill Ravnicans, using his Eternals to harvest Planeswalker Sparks for the dragon. But when it was all over, Jace had reached out to her telepathically, reached out not with anger—but with concern. After all she had done, after she had allowed even Gideon to die in her place, she couldn't face his sympathy. His fury, she could have dealt with, could have understood. But his sympathy nearly destroyed her right then and there.

He had no right to offer me that!

She shouted a question to the fen: "I'm making no sense at all, am I?" Even her voice sounded slightly off. Pinched. Or maybe just unreal. False. She wasn't Liliana Vess now, at least not a Liliana Vess she recognized. She stopped and looked down at her reflection in the still water. "My hair's a mess. When did I tear my dress? I actually look . . . dirty." It wasn't like her not to maintain her appearance. She tried to cast a spell to clean herself up. The magic didn't work. She couldn't focus enough to *make* it work. That wasn't like her, either.

So maybe I'm not Liliana Vess. Maybe I'm just a forgery. Or a Jace Beleren illusion. The dirty, ugly, wicked witch he always imagined lurked under the surface of the woman he couldn't bring himself to resist. That's what I was to him—am to him—isn't it? And what is Jace Beleren to me?

He was a man she used and manipulated, for sex, for power, and to win her freedom from the demons that had held her in thrall.

And that's all *he was, right? RIGHT?*

No. Somewhere in that deeply buried humanity, she knew that was a lie. There was a part of her that truly loved him.

Assuming that's something I know how to do.

Liliana laughed out loud at that. It was a cold, dead sound to her.

Was love ever *one of my goals?*

No, again. She had worked for decades to maintain her youth, to augment her power, to win her freedom. Love had *never* been on the agenda. The horrifically comic irony, of course, was that she now had everything she'd ever wanted—and the cost had proven too high for her to live with herself.

As if there's some alternative?

And just then, she tripped again. Only this time, she fell into the deep water. She went down, submerging completely. She was sinking, drowning. And a part of her welcomed it.

There's your alternative. Stay here. Beneath the water. Don't fight it. Let yourself go.

She recognized the irony: She was half prepared to kill herself after working so desperately—and killing so many others— in order to preserve what she was now on the razor's edge of relinquishing.

So maybe this is the end I deserve. In the swamp, within a day's walk of my father's home.

But if she was to die, she wasn't going to do it facedown in the muck. Her dress was soaking up the water, weighing her down. With some effort, she managed to turn herself over. The moon must have risen some. She could see a bit of its light shining down through even this silt. She closed her eyes then. She was still holding her breath, but she knew she'd have to release it soon enough. She'd involuntarily exhale air and inhale fluid, allowing her lungs to fill. She'd lose all buoyancy and sink. Maybe in a few centuries, an archaeologist would find her bones and admire their perfect proportions, *her* perfect proportions. The archaeologist and her colleagues would then argue over their discovery's age at death. But she would defy all scientific divination. She would remain a mystery for the ages. This appealed to her.

I could live *with that*, she thought and smiled.

She opened her eyes one last time for one last glimpse of moonlight. Then, for just a second, she thought she saw something or someone pass above her, watching her from the shore. A figure in white? Or perhaps . . . a figure surrounded by a white aura of invulnerability . . .

Gideon! It's Gideon!

She fought, she swam, she struggled her way to the surface to see him, to find him, to have it out with him, once and for all. To make him tell her. Who. She. Was. Her dress dragged her down; she had no air. None of it mattered. Not if she could see Beefslab alive again. She surfaced, gasping for oxygen, fighting her way to shallower ground until she could stand and look around for him. And for one insane moment she thought maybe she spotted that white figure between the trees. Dirty water dripped down from her sopping matted hair into her eyes, and she blinked twice to clear them. "Gideon?" she whispered.

But, no. There's no one there. Of course there's no one there.

THREE

TEYO VERADA

As the guild conference continued, a tense Teyo scanned twelve even tenser faces. By this time, he could identify every one of these leaders, down to each's guilds and titles. It was funny. He had recently spent four days in Oasis, and he couldn't remember the names of anyone he'd met there. But after *less* than a day on Ravnica, he'd learned an entire political geometry and could tick off most of the names of those it comprised.

The dozen world leaders—*for, in fact, did they not collectively rule this world?*—had clearly waited for the Gatewatch to move out of earshot (perhaps not having counted on Kaya actually *swearing an oath to* the Gatewatch just before the meeting commenced) in order to discuss a policy of assassination.

Teyo didn't like it. He hadn't encountered Baan or Tezzeret and had no reason to doubt they had cooperated with the dragon

And certainly not Gideon Jura. He's dead. You know that. 〕
him disintegrate away before your eyes. He died saving you.
you . . . for this.

Gideon's Revenge. Well, he'd earned it. And she was up ɛ
her feet. She might as well keep moving. So, drenched anc
erable, she continued—for no good reason—on toward h
taking little notice of the gathering ravens . . .

and deserved punishment. But he had seen no evidence of it, either. Even Abbot Barrez, who ran the monastery where Teyo was raised with a burlap fist, would not punish an acolyte without proof or a confession. Maybe the guilds had both, but then why such a need for secrecy? And what about Liliana Vess? Yes, she had controlled the Eternals for Bolas, and many had died as a result. But many more would have died if she hadn't turned on Bolas, hadn't destroyed him. At the very least, she should have the opportunity to explain, shouldn't she?

But the leaders of Ravnica would prefer to send Kaya to kill her in secret?

It didn't sit right. It didn't. But he'd been put in his place by Vorel when he had attempted to raise the issue. So clearly, now wasn't the time or place to cite his objections. It made a difference that he had Kaya's ear. He could—he *must*—talk to her about this later.

Kaya, meanwhile, was pointing out a less philosophical problem: "It's been hours since Vess left Ravnica, longer still for Baan, and longer than that for Tezzeret. Don't you see the problem?"

Vraska said, "They're not Planeswalkers. They don't understand . . . the rules."

"Enlighten us," said Aurelia.

Ral said, "A Planeswalker can follow another Planeswalker in his or her immediate wake."

"But the key word," Vraska emphasized, "is '*immediate*.'"

Kaya nodded. "After this much time, there's simply no way for the three of us to track our 'targets' down, assuming we even agree to the hunt."

The Firemind eyed Ral. "What about Project Lightning Bug?"

Teyo had no idea what "Project Lightning Bug" was, and from the looks of nearly everyone else, he wasn't alone in that. He exchanged glances with Rat, his usual source of information about this world, but she just shrugged.

Ral shook his head. "The project was keyed into the Beacon, which I effectively destroyed earlier today. Baan and Vess left after that. And even if we could still recover the data on Tezzeret, it would only tell us he went to Amonkhet. We know from Samut and Karn that he planeswalked away from *there* hours ago. He could be anywhere in the Multiverse by now."

Niv-Mizzet scowled and said, "This is simply a problem requiring an innovative solution."

That caused Boruvo to scowl. "Spoken like a true Izzet guildmage, not the Living Guildpact tasked with representing *all* our interests."

The Firemind huffed out a cloud of smoke from his nostrils. "I never promised to acquire a new vocabulary to smooth ruffled plumage. When you feel Selesnya is not fairly and faithfully represented by my office, *then* you can complain."

Without a doubt, this last statement did not "*smooth ruffled plumage.*" In fact, it launched a volley of objections from nearly all sides.

Teyo found he couldn't follow it all. He suddenly felt exhausted. He'd been awake for two straight days—one on Gobakhan and one on Ravnica—days filled with more excitement, exertion and stress than any two *years* of his life. He yawned involuntarily and barely managed to raise a hand to cover his mouth.

Gan Shokta, already cross from yelling at the Firemind, barked out, "Are we boring you, boy?"

"No, sir, I—"

Rat stepped forward, "Where are your manners, Father? Teyo deserves better than that. You know he saved your life today. Twice."

But Gan Shokta took no notice of his daughter, leaving it to Kaya to intercede. "We're all exhausted."

Niv-Mizzet concurred, with a glance toward the procession of Planeswalkers that were working their way back toward them now. "We will reconvene in the morning."

He looked to Lavinia, who nodded and said, "Meet at the Azorius Senate House. One hour after dawn."

There was a general—if somewhat begrudging—murmur of agreement.

The Firemind turned to the gorgon next. "Perhaps, Queen Vraska, you should avoid relating this discussion to my predecessor."

Teyo had seen Vraska and Jace kiss earlier. Now the gorgon's face revealed that she was conflicted about keeping things from a man she clearly cared so much about.

Ral Zarek seemed to notice that, too. "Perhaps," he suggested, "you'd be better served staying away from Beleren this night—"

"How and with whom I spend my nights is no business of yours, Zarek."

"Of course not. But you don't want to give the mind-mage the opportunity to read your thoughts."

"Jace wouldn't do that. Not to me." And as if to prove her point, she defiantly walked away, crossing broken pavement and passing multiple mourners and celebrants, to join Jace Beleren— and to take his hand.

This seemed to signal an end to the conference. As the quorum broke up, Kaya turned to Teyo and Rat, saying, "Why don't you both come back to Orzhova with me. Just for the night. We can wash. Eat. *Sleep.*"

Teyo looked to Rat. He thought maybe she'd prefer to follow her father, who was stalking off without her. And if she decided to spend the night with the Shoktas, he thought maybe he should go with her.

But Rat said, "Sounds keen."

And Kaya misinterpreted his hesitancy. She put a hand on his shoulder and said, "I know you must be eager to return to Gobakhan."

"No hurry, really." He found himself stifling another involuntary yawn.

"I get it. Too tired to think about planeswalking right now."

"I don't even know *how* to think about planeswalking. I've only ever done it the one time—and that was by accident."

"No worries. I *promise* we'll get you home in the morning."

But Teyo was less concerned about getting home than he was about Rat. He was watching her when Kaya made her promise, and he could see Araithia's violet eyes lower sadly and lose a little bit of their light . . .

FOUR

JACE BELEREN

They had walked the length of Tenth District Plaza and then walked back again. Chandra still carried the breastplate in her hands, and everywhere they went, Ravnicans of all shapes and sizes, guilds and genders bowed their heads to honor Gideon Jura. It was right to honor him—for what he did *and* for what he represented. It was Gideon who had held the Gatewatch together.

Without him . . .

Without him, Jace wasn't sure if the Gatewatch even existed anymore.

We'll always be loyal to each other—but to the Multiverse?

The cost just seemed too high.

How can it be I never noticed that Gideon was my best friend?

Vraska was a short distance away, conversing with Niv-Mizzet and other guild leaders. He didn't envy her or Niv. He was *glad* his days as the Living Guildpact were through.

"Are we agreed?" Ajani said. "Tomorrow morning we go to Theros to honor our friend."

Jace, Chandra, Nissa, Teferi, Karn, Saheeli, Jaya, Ajani and Huatli all nodded or murmured their assent. Jace wondered briefly why Huatli wanted to go. She'd only met Gideon that morning.

But who am I to tell her no? He deserves all the damn honors he can get. He deserves a lot more than that, but I suppose that's all we have left to give him.

He glanced up to the top of the Citadel where Gideon had died. Died saving Liliana, so that Liliana could save the Multiverse.

With some reluctance, he said, "Listen. I'm . . . worried. About Liliana."

"You've got to be kidding me," Chandra snapped. "I still don't understand why I shouldn't be hunting her down to kill her for taking Gids away from us."

Jaya Ballard's look darkened. "Is that who you are, child? A killer?"

"I'm not a child. And I've killed plenty."

"In cold blood?" Ajani asked.

"My blood's not cold on this subject."

Teferi rubbed his chin. "I'm still not clear on what happened. *Did* Liliana Vess take Gideon's life?"

"No," Jace said. "Not exactly. At least I don't believe so."

Karn's voice rumbled out, "What *do* you believe?"

"We all saw Liliana turn on Bolas," Jace began . . .

"A day too late," Saheeli said. "*Thousands* died at her hands before that."

"Yes," Jace said, "But I can guess why. You all saw it. She was dissolving before our eyes. Turning on the dragon was *literally* killing her. Yet she was the only one who could possibly stop Bolas. I believe Gideon saw that, realized that."

Nissa spoke quietly, more to herself than to the rest. "So he gifted his invulnerability to her . . ."

"And in exchange took on whatever curse was killing her."

"She allowed that?" Chandra asked bitterly.

"Maybe. I don't know. What I do know is that I reached out to her—telepathically—after it was all over. I could feel her pain, her conflict. Her lack of understanding of her own feelings."

"You always had a soft spot for the woman, Jace," Ajani growled.

"Really? You think so? Didn't you all accuse me of being too hard on her?"

Chandra looked away. She had in fact made that charge against Jace many times. "Maybe you were right about her. Maybe we were wrong."

"Maybe. But . . . Look, I don't relish being her advocate. It's not exactly a job I've trained for. I just think the situation with her may be more complicated than we know. Can't we at least acknowledge that?"

Chandra whispered, "I once loved her like a sister, Jace. And she betrayed us all."

They were all silent for a time. Jaya was still studying her protégée Chandra as she said, "What exactly do you propose, Jace?"

"I . . . honestly don't know. Maybe . . . maybe we should try to track her down, at least hear her out. I think she's . . . broken."

Chandra looked up at Jace then. "She can join the club."

Jaya took Chandra's hand in hers and said, "We don't have to decide anything now. There's nothing to be done tonight. We don't even know where she went. And we have something important to do in the morning."

"Aye," Ajani said. "We can decide what to do about Liliana Vess *after* the memorial." He looked at Jace. "Agreed?"

"Of course."

Huatli said, "Perhaps we all just need some rest. Some time to sort things out."

Teferi said, "Not here."

Chandra agreed. "No, not here. I'm sick to death of Ravnica. You're all welcome to come stay with me on Kaladesh."

"I have somewhere I need to go," Karn stated.

Teferi said, "Somewhere that will still be there tomorrow. I think we could all benefit by staying in each other's company for one night."

Karn hesitated . . . then nodded.

"To Kaladesh then," Ajani said. "Just for the night."

Out of the corner of his eye, Jace saw Vraska break off from Niv and the rest, beelining straight toward him. "I'm going to stay," he said. "Let's meet right back here at dawn. And we'll all planeswalk to Theros together."

There were a few more nods, but no other words were spoken. Jace watched them all planeswalk away; Jaya and Chandra disappeared in brief conflagrations of flame; Karn vanished with a sharp metallic sound; Ajani gave off a golden light and was gone; Teferi seemed to transform into a blue whirlwind that swept him away. By the time Nissa, Saheeli and Huatli had departed, Vraska was with him, taking his hand.

She said, "As I recall, we had a date planned."

"That's right, Captain. Tin Street. Coffee. A bookstore."

"You like memoirs, reading about interesting people."

"I do. And you like histories, I think."

"I do."

They started walking.

For a time, they were silent, simply glad to be in each other's company. He could tell she had something on her mind, something that troubled her. But she said nothing, and he chose not to pry—psychically or otherwise. He knew she had her secrets but was convinced that none of hers could possibly be as big—and truly awful—as the secret he himself was keeping. Keeping from her. From everyone.

Jace knew he needed to decide what kind of man he wanted to be. For years, he had been hampered—*stunted*—by huge gaps in his memories, which had made him secretive, difficult. Now that he had all his memories back, he wanted to be a better person and hoped he could be that better person with Vraska.

He remembered their kiss—their *first* kiss—after the battle.

He stopped suddenly and turned to face her with a questioning look. She seemed to understand and nodded her consent. So cradling her face in his hands, he kissed her again. She tasted so sweet. It was a kiss that eased the burdens on his soul. And he hoped, maybe, the burdens on hers, as well.

She smiled at him. He smiled back.

They started walking again. Neither spilling their secrets.

After a while, he asked, "Didn't we just pass Tin Street?"

"We did," she said.

"And yet we're walking this way."

"We are," she said.

"So no coffee?"

"No."

"We are headed to . . ."

"My quarters. If that's all right with you."

He could feel himself blushing.

She squeezed his hand in hers, and they walked on.

FIVE

LILIANA VESS

Was she trying to ignore them? The ravens. She knew exactly what this ever-gathering conspiracy of birds meant. She knew exactly *whom* they meant. But she was trying very hard to pretend otherwise, as she continued her increasingly pitiable trek across the Caligo. And the reason why was simple enough . . .

I don't want to see him.

Clearly, he didn't much care what she did or didn't want.

He never had.

More and more ravens began to pursue her. They'd fly ahead, cluster unkindly upon a single tree, occupying every branch. And as she passed, the birds would depart en masse and descend upon the next tree, only by that time there'd be still more of them. And more at the next tree. And more at the next.

"You're not exactly subtle," she grumbled, knowing he could hear her even if she never spoke the words aloud.

It was almost getting ridiculous. In a flurry of black wings, the ravens launched themselves (himself) off one tree and descended upon another that could barely bear the weight of them all (him all). This got her to stop. And the reason why was simple enough . . .

I'd actually enjoy *seeing that tree trunk snap in two, and watching all those damn birds (him) get as drenched and miserable as I am.*

The tree bent dangerously. The birds cawed nervously, shifting on the branches with their clawed feet. Liliana Vess waited. Then she had an idea.

This could be fun.

She reached out a hand and reached out with her magic, pulling the life force from the sagging tree, from its thin trunk and too many branches. The tree died, but she kept going, hoping to make the wood brittle and corrupt.

It's working . . .

It worked. The tree snapped, and the ravens were forced to scatter.

But it only took one.

A single raven descended, morphing into her second greatest nemesis: the Raven Man. He was just how she remembered him from her childhood. His precisely trimmed white hair and beard, his immaculate—if slightly dated—mode of dress. His shining golden eyes. "Still dapper, after all these years," she said to him in a tone that belied the compliment.

He isn't just *how I remember him. He's* exactly *how I remember him.*

An illusion then. Or maybe he was a very precise shapeshifter. Either way, she knew that what she saw was no more real, no more *him,* than the birds had been. After all these years, she still didn't know what he *really* looked like. Or who he truly was.

I probably don't want to know.

He said, "I wish I could return the compliment. But you've never looked worse in my eyes."

"I could use a good inn with the proper amenities. Can you recommend one in the neighborhood?" She was trying to sound like Liliana Vess.

But I'm not pulling it off.

He confirmed that for her with a sad shake of his head and an expression that clearly was meant to say, *You sound as pathetic as you look.* Instead, he said, "I've come to whet your almost blunted purpose. Why do you wallow in self-pity, here? You have all the power you ever dreamed of, and now you are free of your demons *and* the dragon!"

"*But not free of you!*" she screamed, suddenly shaking.

"No," he confirmed. "But I am not your enemy. I have never been your enemy. All I've *ever* wanted is to guide you toward becoming the best, truest and most powerful version of yourself that you may be. I can still do that. I know where to send you next. There's even a nice inn there. Where you can clean up. Feel more like yourself. All you have to do is listen."

All I have to do is listen. Listen and obey.

Still, it was tempting. She *had* achieved all her goals—if in the worst possible way. The four demons that held the contract on her soul had been slain. The dragon that took over that contract had been reduced to dust. She was free. She was powerful. And although another quick glance at her reflection in the water revealed that, yes, she could definitely use a hot bath, she was still young and beautiful. Missions accomplished; goals achieved. The obvious drawback being that she had never, *never,* thought beyond those goals.

What do I do now?

The Raven Man was once again offering her purpose and direction. He tried to play it off as if he were a benevolent father figure, and she his beholden apprentice. Not like she was a loaded cannon, and he a man taking aim.

Whom would he make me hurt this time? That is, whom besides Liliana Vess?

She knew that in her current state, she was particularly vulnerable to his machinations and manipulations. She also knew that the Raven Man simply wanted to use her, like the demons had used her. Like Bolas had used her. But she knew that the Raven Man had the potential to be worse than her other enemies . . .

Because he *was the bastard who started me down this damned path in the first place.*

SIX

RAT

The plush robe currently folded in a neat square on her lap was the softest, most elegant item of clothing Araithia Shokta, the Rat, had ever been anywhere near. She couldn't stop petting and stroking it, as if she half expected the thing to start purring.

Rat was sitting in a preposterously cushy armchair across from a decidedly relaxed Mistress Kaya, who had emerged from her shower, ensconced in a duplicate robe. She sat upon her long, folded legs in another armchair, and stretched languidly. Rat thought she was one of the most beautiful women she'd ever seen.

They were in a tower of Orzhova, the Cathedral Opulent, inside the salon of the Orzhov guildmaster's suite of rooms, which were sumptuous to the point of decadence, to the point of Rat spontaneously giggling every couple minutes or so over having found herself amid such lavishness.

"Pretty sweet digs for a Rat," she murmured.

"Hm?" Mistress Kaya murmured back, still languid.

"Thanks for letting me—*us*—stay the night."

"Of course. You can stay as long as you like."

Hearing that, Rat tried not to let her smile fade—for her friend's sake.

Presently, a grinning Teyo emerged from the lavatory, coming down the hall toward them, wrapped in yet another robe, with a towel around his shoulders. His hair was soaking wet and dripping, and he carried a neatly folded pile of his battle-filthy clothes.

Pointing back at the room from where he'd emerged, Teyo gasped out: "That. Lavatory. Is. Amazing!"

"I'm glad you like it," Mistress Kaya said with a smile.

"No, you have to understand. That . . . 'shower' is a thing of pure genius. We don't have that on Gobakhan. Baths, yes. But showers? Do you know how much sand gets in your . . . in your . . . in your everything after a diamondstorm, or even just a small sandstorm, or even just a walk across a dune? Showers would change lives. And the, um, toilet. The big towns, like Oasis, have those, but they're still so . . . so . . . I mean, this indoor plumbing is still the greatest magic I've *ever* encountered. Ever!"

His enthusiasm was kinda adorable.

An amused Mistress Kaya turned to Rat and said, "Your turn."

Teyo said, "There are clean towels on the shelf for when you're done. A whole pile of them. They're very white and very large and very soft."

"Best towels ever?" Rat teased.

"I know you're making fun of me," he said. "But yes. Best towels ever."

She giggled again and walked past him down the long hallway to the lavatory.

She went in and closed the door. The ridiculously large bathroom was still steamy from Kaya and Teyo's turns. Carefully placing her robe on the closed toilet seat, Rat quickly stripped off her clothes and turned on the water. Teyo was easy to tease, coming as he did from a seemingly backwater plane, but honestly a shower like this was a rare luxury for this child of the Gruul Clans, as well. She reached a cautious hand in under the faucet and found the water was already hot. She was about to step inside when she glanced down at her own unwashed garments strewn as they were across the floor. She glanced over at the neatly folded robe and thought about the neatly folded clothes in Acolyte Teyo's arms and was suddenly embarrassed.

As she quickly folded her things and stuck them on a shelf, she mused over how she'd felt *embarrassed* more times in this one day than she had in all the rest of her years combined. She was rarely embarrassed in front of her mother or godfather and had *never* felt embarrassed with Hekara.

And who else or what else can embarrass the Rat?

But around Mistress Kaya and especially around Teyo, she was quickly learning that uncomfortable emotion. Yet it felt so . . . normal, she relished it. Araithia had missed out on a lot of *normal* in her short, odd life and didn't mind taking the bad with the good. And Mistress Kaya and especially Teyo made her feel very good.

She stepped into the shower and let the water flow over her face and hair. She closed her eyes and soaked in the sensations. She hadn't thought about it until now, but she was sore from all the fighting, and the hot water streaming onto her various muscle groups felt very, very good.

She was nervous, however, about taking too long. So she opened her eyes to look for the soap.

There are multiple kinds of soap!

All right, yes, she completely understood why this room had so excited Teyo.

Despite her best mental efforts, she found her thoughts drifting to the coming separation. Teyo would return to Gobakhan, and Mistress Kaya would depart on her mission to kill Miss Vess, which was a depressing notion on all sorts of levels. Rat wasn't thoroughly convinced that Miss Raven-Hair deserved death. On the other hand, Rat wasn't thoroughly convinced—as Teyo seemed to be—that she didn't, either. In any case, her unformed opinion was decidedly moot, since she couldn't exactly follow Mistress Kaya to wherever Miss Vess was hiding. She couldn't follow Mistress Kaya or Teyo anywhere. All she could do was let them go.

Let them go without making a fuss.

Suddenly a hand reached in, turned the spigot and shut the water off.

"What is wrong with that boy?" grumbled a woman's voice from just outside the shower stall. "Was he raised in a barn? Who just walks out and leaves the water running like this?"

Wiping the soap from her eyes, Rat peeked out and saw Madame Blaise, chief servitor to the Orzhov guildmaster, picking up her pile of clothes and griping, "And whose are these? They're all twisted with vines. How am I supposed to clean this?" She sighed heavily and walked out with Rat's things, leaving the door to the bathroom wide open.

Rat never even thought about saying anything to the servitor. She heaved her own heavy sigh, waited until she heard Madame Blaise's footsteps tread far enough down the hall and then turned the water back on briefly to quickly rinse all the soap from herself.

The fact that the door was wide open wouldn't have bothered her normally, but Teyo was loose in the suite, so she quickly grabbed the robe, which was thankfully still on the toilet seat, and threw it on soaking wet. Only afterward did she close *and lock* the door, take the robe off again and towel herself dry.

She emerged a couple minutes later, dressed in the now damp robe and not feeling quite as enthralled by the lavatory as Teyo was—or as she had been previously. Going down the hallway, she could hear Mistress Kaya and Teyo attempting to explain things to Madame Blaise.

"I promise you, madame, I did not leave the water running. That was Rat."

"I promise you, young master, we have no rats in the Cathedral Opulent, and certainly none that can *turn on a faucet.*"

"No, no, see—"

Rat padded into the salon as Mistress Kaya said, "Madame Blaise, our friend Rat—our *human* friend Rat—was taking a shower."

"There was no one in the shower, mistress. I checked."

For fun, Rat walked right in front of Madame Blaise and offered up a little wave, which of course the woman couldn't see.

Rat looked over at Mistress Kaya, and the two shared a grin. Then she glanced over at Teyo, who was staring at her and swallowing and pulling his robe more tightly around himself. He was blushing, and Rat's face felt hot, too. She pulled her robe tightly around herself, as he had done. She felt a little better, but he was struggling with some difficulty to look at absolutely *anything* in the room *except* Rat. It got her thinking . . .

Does he think I'm . . . pretty? Me, with my big teeth and my Rat face and my stupid, crazy hair that I have to cut myself? No, that can't be right. He's just kind enough to be embarrassed for me.

Mistress Kaya was saying, "Rat lives with a unique condition that renders her invisible."

Madame Blaise eyed her mistress with a little suspicion. "Mistress is entitled to her whimsies, but there's no need to weave tales or play tricks on a faithful servant in order to make her look foolish."

Kaya laughed. "I swear to you, Blaise. I'm perfectly sincere, perfectly serious. Our Rat has lived her entire life under an admittedly bizarre . . ."

"Curse of Insignificance," Rat prompted.

"Curse of Insignificance, yes. Thank you, Rat. This curse makes her invisible, even unhearable, to nearly everyone. Teyo and I are two of only four people who can see her naturally."

Madame Blaise looked appalled. "Why, that's, that's . . . awful. The poor, um, *girl*?" she asked, unsure.

"Yes, Rat is a girl or young woman. About . . ."

"Sixteen summers," Rat said. "Or sixteen winters. Sixteen springs or autumns, too, I guess."

"She's sixteen," Mistress Kaya said.

"And she's been this way since birth?" the kindhearted servitor said, wiping a tear from her eye.

"Yes," Kaya said, her tone falling to match madame's.

"It's not that bad," Rat said. "It's just my life. We've all got whatever whats we deal with. This is mine. Oh, please, mistress, don't cry!"

Kaya sniffed and wiped away a couple of tears of her own, murmuring, "I'm not; I'm not." But she kinda was.

Teyo, sounding desperate to help, said, "We've found that a few people can learn to see Rat if they're told exactly where she is, and they concentrate on the spot."

Madame Blaise straightened up, even straightened her uniform, before stating, "Then I will be one of those people. Where is the dear?"

Mistress Kaya put an arm around Rat's shoulder and said, "She's right here under my arm."

The servitor leaned forward and stared. Squinted. Strained. Finally, with a sigh, she stepped back and shook her head. "I'm sorry. I just don't see her."

"It can take practice," Rat said, shrugging.

"Rat says it can take practice," Mistress Kaya repeated for Madame Blaise's benefit.

"Well, then I will practice. But for the time being—now that I know the poor thing exists—I will make allowances. To begin with . . ." She held up the neat pile of Rat's clothes. ". . . I will clean her clothes. I have a perfect spell for that, they'll be done in less than a minute. Once I extract all this foliage."

Rat quickly spoke to Kaya: "Please tell her not to remove my vine belt. It was a gift from my godfather. He knows I get hungry sometimes, and I like to nibble on the berries that grow on it."

Mistress Kaya relayed the message. Madame Blaise raised the folded clothes up very close to her face to examine the belt. "I see," she said. "Selesnyan magic. How clever. Well, I still wouldn't have her eat these berries without giving them a good washing first, but I can manage that without harming them, I believe. Give me just a few minutes. I'll bring these clothes right back, and *all three of you* can change for dinner. Oh, and I will set an extra plate in the dining room for Mistress . . . Rat?"

SEVEN

TEZZERET

He was admittedly weary. The white sand shifted under his feet as he trudged along, and he fought the high wind with every step, making every step annoyingly taxing, especially with the damaged Planar Bridge in his chest leaking energy that slowly seared the surrounding flesh. He hadn't *walked* anywhere in ages, and the organic muscles in his calves burned. But it had been the smart choice to hike the final distance on foot, and he didn't regret it.

Since leaving Amonkhet, Tezzeret had planeswalked multiple times, bouncing from world to world, to ensure that tracking him would be as difficult as possible. And if he *was* tracked, he didn't want the trackers popping into his fortress without warning. No, let them follow his last planeswalk out to the far shore where he'd landed, and let them wear themselves out as he was doing before they reached him. If nothing else, he'd be able to see them coming.

After all, he didn't want just *anyone* stumbling on him or his operation. Especially now. Now that said operation truly and finally belonged to him and him alone, servicing his agenda and no one else's.

Certainly not the dragon's.

Tezzeret had served Nicol Bolas faithfully, because Tezzeret was a realist and a pragmatist. He had served Bolas because Bolas was too powerful for Tezzeret to beat.

Now—thanks to a gloating Tibalt, who'd witnessed the end—Tezzeret knew Bolas was dead. Tibalt had probably confronted him to feed on Tezzeret's pain over his master's death, but Tibalt departed disappointed, as Tezzeret couldn't be happier about it. After all, Bolas was the only entity in the Multiverse with the power to stop his former minion. With the dragon gone, there remained no one who could stand in his way.

He had reached the final canal. This was close enough. He raised his right arm, his perfect etherium arm, and shot up a simple flare. The response was immediate. Illusory clouds parted like perfectly carved pieces of a jigsaw puzzle, and four gargoyles emerged, winging their way toward him. They were animated stone, enhanced, like himself, by etherium.

Well, to be accurate, the trio of smaller gargoyles appeared to be all-but-solid metal. Any living stone that remained was hardly visible to the naked eye.

The fourth and biggest gargoyle was Brokk, whose five glowing eyes shone out even from this distance. His body was reinforced, augmented and decorated with etherium, but he still retained his stony bulk and strength.

With a single powerful flap of his wings, Brokk soared past the trio, landing first and bowing low. "Master," he intoned in his voice of gravel.

The second gargoyle was close behind. It landed and genuflected silently, while its cargo—the homunculus Krzntch—practically rolled off the gargoyle's back. The diminutive sky-blue biped, with her stubby etherium arms and legs and nearly spherical body, quickly prostrated herself at Tezzeret's feet. "Boss," she said in her high-pitched squeak.

The final two gargoyles, knowing their duty, flew past Tezzeret and circled, coming around to land flat on the ground in front of him, facing the way they'd come. He took two steps forward and stood upon their backs.

"Any orders?" Brokk asked.

"Quite a few. But they can wait until we're home. Go."

"As you command, Master."

Krzntch, who moved rather speedily for a creature of such near-perfect roundness, quickly hopped back in the saddle of her gargoyle, which took off, leading the way. Tezzeret's gargoyles followed, carrying their master. Brokk took up the rear, on guard for any potential threat.

Erect and on his feet, Tezzeret soared toward the carved-out cloud entrance to his fortress, smiling a smile of grim but authentic satisfaction. He no longer felt weary. The dragon was gone, and it was like a weight had been lifted. Lifted off his back and placed upon the backs of billions of others. A minion no longer, he was finally the man in charge.

EIGHT

RAL ZAREK

Ral couldn't help wondering what rock Tezzeret was hiding under now. With the master dead, the minion was vulnerable, and Ral was eager to put that etherium-armed freak down, once and for all.

Those were, he realized, fairly violent thoughts for the bathtub.

The water was hot; the air, steamy. The suds . . . well, the word *luxuriant* came to mind.

He and Tomik had retired—or retreated—to the apartment they shared in Dogsrun, a genteel neighborhood of quiet streets tucked away from anything resembling the life-pulse of Ravnica, which was how they both liked it.

Tomik had gotten washed first and then surrendered the bathroom to his partner. And Ral had made the most of it, washing off the grit, grime and, yes, *guts* of two days of the worst fighting of his life.

They had won, but the price had been very, very high. Too many Izzet Leaguers had died. Morfix had died. And Tibor, Kongreve and Mastiv, as well, just to name a few that Ral would particularly mourn and miss. Plus thousands of Ravnicans had perished, and who-knew-how-many Planeswalkers?

Gideon Jura had died. Ral had barely known the man, but had come to truly admire him over the course of the world's longest day. He couldn't imagine what his close friends in the Gatewatch were feeling.

The truth was, Ral felt almost blessed. After having spent the last month feeling almost cursed, he realized he had come out of the whole horrible conflagration largely unscathed. Yes, today had literally been a global tragedy, and yes, he had lost friends. But frankly, no one he was truly close to. Kaya had survived, and so had Lavinia. Vraska hadn't simply survived but had actually been redeemed in his eyes. By Krokt, *Jace Beleren* had survived and had emerged as someone that Ral actually respected and valued. Even Hekara and Niv, who had both perished, had both been miraculously resurrected!

And more important than any of them, there was Tomik in the next room. If Ral was being honest, all of Ravnica could have burned to a cinder, as long as Tomik remained beside him.

When did this happen? When did this man become my whole world?

Not that he was upset over the situation. A part of him was grateful that he was even capable of loving anyone this much. After Elias, he'd convinced himself that the whole *idea* of love was a fraud. He'd never been so glad to miscalculate anything in his life.

The bathwater was starting to turn tepid. Ral could have heated it up easily, but he figured he was suitably cleaned and sufficiently pruned by this time. And he wanted Tomik. *Hungered for him.* Now.

He stepped out of the tub and toweled dry. He wrapped the towel around his waist, ran a hand through his spiky hair and left the steamy bathroom.

He found Tomik sitting at the kitchen table, his nose buried in about sixteen law books simultaneously.

"What in the world are you about?" he asked Tomik, laughing. "Are you seriously studying? Tonight? After . . . *everything?*"

"I'm trying to find a way to free Kaya from her Orzhov obligations. Trying to find a way for her to planeswalk away from Ravnica without, you know, *dying.*"

"I thought you wanted her to stay. I thought you preferred her over Teysa Karlov as your guildmaster?"

"I do. I think Kaya could be very beneficial to the Syndicate. Move us onto a better path. But she's my friend. *Our* friend. She has to be able to choose. She shouldn't have to stay if she really doesn't want to."

"Nephilim Spawn, you're good. Are you *sure* you're Orzhov?"

"Stop it," Tomik said, shaking his head and rolling his eyes.

"You stop it," Ral said, coming up behind Tomik and kissing the top of his head, the back of his head, the back of his neck. He paused and said, "I love Kaya, but her problems can be solved *tomorrow.* Come to bed."

"In a minute. Ten at most. I think I'm onto something."

Ral stood up straight and grumbled, "Tomik, I'm wired *and* exhausted. Come to bed, now, please, before I pass out. I want you. In fact, I cannot emphasize enough how much I *need* to be with you right now."

"Five minutes."

"All right," Ral said as languidly as he could manage. Then he removed the towel and dropped it on the kitchen table in front of his man. Without looking back, Ral turned and walked toward their bed. Either Tomik would turn around and watch him walk away . . . or Ral Zarek was very much losing his touch.

"Two minutes," Tomik squeaked.

Hah! Gotcha! "Lover, I could be dead to the world in two minutes, easy."

Ral heard the chair push away from the table and Tomik's bare feet scrambling across the hardwood floor. "Coming . . ."

NINE

RAT

At dinner in an immense and formal Orzhova dining room, Rat ate as if she were storing up for winter. But between bites, she was her usual motormouth self.

"Madame Blaise is such a darling, don't you think? She's tried three times to see me already. I mean it's not working, but she's really putting in the effort. Most people tend to give up after ten seconds or so. So I really appreciate the attempts, you know? I also really appreciate this plum tart. Mistress Kaya, are you sure you want to leave the Syndicate?"

"Quite sure."

"But why?"

"I never signed on for this job, Rat. It's a responsibility I don't want on a world that isn't mine. And that's on top of the fact that this guild doesn't really want me here, either. I've survived one coup attempt already. I don't relish the opportunity to *not* survive the next."

"Fair enough," Rat said, taking another bite. "Still, I think a plum tart like this might be worth a coup or two. Your chef-servitor has a lot of talent. And I know, 'cuz I have stolen a lot of plum tarts in my day. And I mean *a lot* of plum tarts. Peach tarts, too. And apricot. And grtleberry, and, well, pretty much every tart you can name. I'm like Queen of the Tarts. No, wait, that did not come out the way I meant it to."

"I think not," Mistress Kaya said wryly from the head of the table. "You're blushing."

"Am I? Again?" Rat snuck a quick glance across the table at Teyo, who was leaning his chin on his fist, watching her and smiling. "It seems I blush quite a bit around you folks. Never used to happen to me, I swear. But then again, I've never spent this much straight time with anyone who could see me. Not since I was a little girl. Not even Hekara. Not a whole day like this— 'cuz, you know, Teyo's been with me since early morning. Hekara always had a show to perform or an errand to run for Lord Rakdos. We—she and I—we've spent tons of time together over the years, but never a whole day. Not that this was like a *fun* day. Although, is it horrible if I admit I've had a lot of fun today, you know, in and amid all the tragedy and everything? Is it the fun that makes things more tragic, or the tragedy that makes things more fun, you think?"

"Both," Kaya said bittersweetly.

Rat's head bobbed up and down. "Exactly. I guess that's how we measure things, right? No light without shadow. No shadow without light. No highborn guildmasters without a lowborn Rat to liven up their table, you know?"

"Every table should have such a Rat," Kaya said.

"Well, then maybe I'll stay. You know I've been Gateless my whole life, always on the fence, deciding between joining

Gruul, Selesnya or Rakdos. Maybe I should consider Orzhov, as well."

"You'd be welcome as long as I'm guildmaster."

Rat swallowed and looked away.

But that's the problem isn't it? You don't plan on staying *guild-master for long.*

Rat suddenly knew why she was talking so much. Oh, sure, it wasn't exactly out of character for her, but for once she wasn't rambling idly. She was maintaining all this verbiage to stop her-self from crying. She knew what was coming, coming as soon and as certain as the morning light. She could give herself a good cry then, once she was alone.

And it's easy for the Rat to be alone in this city. Even if a few thousand people are walking right past me.

But not now. She'd keep her chin up and her mouth moving so that Teyo and Mistress Kaya didn't know what she was feeling. So they didn't make any decisions based on how good their hearts were. (And Rat knew they had good hearts. Too good.) She didn't want to influence them that way. It might just kill her if she thought they were deciding what to do with their own lives based on their pity for the Rat.

I'm a funny little story they can tell someday. Assuming they even remember me. But either way, it's much better than becoming someone or something they resent, right?

She saw Teyo stifle a yawn and knew both he and Kaya had to be exhausted. It would be bedtime soon. Very soon. She could hold out until then, keep things keen and fun and decidedly non-tragic until then. Of course she could. She just had to keep talking.

She blurted out: "So are you really going to kill Miss Vess?"

Mistress Kaya looked stunned. Then she frowned and said, "If we can figure out a way for me to leave Ravnica without dying, then . . . yes."

"But," Teyo said, appalled, "she saved us all. Kaya, you know she did."

Mistress Kaya's frown grew more pronounced. "Do you know how many people died at the hand of her Eternals, Teyo?"

"*Her* Eternals or the dragon's?"

"Does it matter? She didn't have to use them against us."

"Are you so sure of that?" Rat asked, sincerely curious.

"Everyone has a choice, Rat. One's alternatives might be spectacularly unpleasant, but that doesn't mean the choice doesn't exist."

"Yeah," Rat said quietly. "I see that."

Teyo shook his head, unconvinced.

Mistress Kaya's frown receded and her expression waxed more sympathetic. "Teyo, I don't necessarily expect you to agree. You've spent your life training to save people; I've spent mine removing dangerous individuals from the lands of the living. This is my work, not yours. You've said your piece, and I'm sorry, but you're not a part of this decision."

Now Teyo was frowning. Rat pretty much regretted raising such a serious topic and was about to launch into a gossipy recounting of Mister Zarek and Mister Vrona's progress from bedmates to soulmates when Madame Blaise entered, walked up to Mistress Kaya, leaned down—bending very properly at the waist—and whispered, "The Triumvirate requests an audience, mistress."

"Now? Here?" Kaya whispered back.

"I told them it was late and that you were at dinner, but they insist on paying their respects."

"The Triumvirate? Wishes to pay *me* respects?"

"So they say, mistress."

"I'd lay odds *true* respect isn't on the dinner menu, but—fine—send them in."

"Yes, mistress." Madame Blaise straightened and departed.

Teyo leaned over the table and asked, "Who are these folks again, and why are they so important?"

Mistress Kaya said, "The Triumvirate have considerable power and influence in the guild."

Rat pitched in, "You see, Mistress Kaya assassinated the Obzedat, the Ghost Council that used to run the Orzhov Syndicate. That's how she became guildmaster."

"Though that was *not* my intent," Kaya clarified.

"No," Rat said. "But that was the result. And the Triumvirate do not like it. With the ghosts gone, the three of them have gained considerable power, which they should be *grateful* to Mistress Kaya for. But instead they resent her, which seems pretty unreasonable to me."

"There's much that's unreasonable about this guild," Mistress Kaya said, but their conversation was cut off as the Triumvirate entered one at a time, each announced by Madame Blaise, and each accompanied by a small thrull on a leash that did nothing—as far as anyone could tell—except make its master look more important.

"Pontiff Armin Morov."

The pontiff was a human, the Patriarch of the Morov family hierarchs. He was quite old, with graying skin, a withered right hand and absolutely no hair, looking very much as if he were already well prepared to join a reformed Obzedat.

"Tithe-Master Slavomir Zoltan."

The tithe-master was a dangerously handsome vampire, with—for an undead bloodsucker—a curious obsession with increasing his material wealth.

"Milady Maladola."

Milady was an angel, a long-ago defector from the Boros Legion who now acted as the Orzhov's chief warrior-executioner, a position she profited by mightily.

Each chose a seat, neither close to their guildmaster nor close to one another, forcing everyone to shout in order to be heard. This seemed to be a favored strategy with the trio, as they had done the same thing when Mistress Kaya had first attempted (unsuccessfully) to rally their forces into the fight against Nicol Bolas.

Pontiff Morov began, "We are so relieved to see that you are safe and whole, Guildmaster."

"Yes," Tithe-Master Zoltan continued. "It seems your concerns over the dragon Bolas were perhaps overstated."

Shifting a bit in her seat, Milady Maladola cleared her throat and said, "Or if not overstated, yet there was some wisdom in holding back a portion of our forces as we did. The other guilds committed everything, and if there's further trouble—from anyone—we are in a prime position to respond as needed."

Mistress Kaya glowered. "I am very grateful to Chief Enforcer Bilagru for rallying as much of *my* guild's military might as he did. And I am grateful to you, Executioner, for your eventual participation, as well."

The fact that Chief Maladola had, at the last minute, personally joined the fight against the dragon's forces seemed to come as some surprise to the angel's two fellow Triumvirs.

Tithe-Master Zoltan asked, "You did battle, milady?"

Pontiff Morov hissed, "That's not what we discussed."

Chief Maladola looked briefly uncomfortable but then stood up and leaned forward, her hands braced on the table, her arms stiff and straight. "I exercise my duties as I see fit," she said, daring either of them to disagree. Even her thrull seemed to sense its mistress' cold rancor, as it began growling at the pontiff's thrull until the chief executioner gave a fast, brutal tug on its leash.

Tithe-Master Zoltan made an attempt to smooth the waters. "Of course, milady. As you see fit. What's important is that we present a united front. Against *all* of Orzhov's potential enemies." His glance from the angel to their guildmaster was less than subtle, and Chief Maladola took the hint and took her seat.

Mistress Kaya said, "Are you implying *I'm* a potential enemy?"

"I'm sure that was the farthest idea from the tithe-master's mind, mistress," Morov said unctuously. "You are an integral part of said united front. Hence our need to pay our kind respects tonight. We would not want you to feel unattended or un-*observed*."

"How good to know."

"Isn't it, though?" Zoltan said, with a deferential nod that wasn't truly deferential at all.

"Still, you must be fatigued, mistress," the angel said. "We must leave you to your meal and your rest."

"Thank you."

Thus, with a few more pleasantries (spoken less than pleasantly), the Triumvirate took their leave. Earlier in the day, their thrull leashes had become embarrassingly tangled when they had tried to depart. Careful this time to avoid a repetition, there was a wealth of *After you*s spoken before they actually exited.

Once they were gone, Kaya violently slammed her pewter goblet down on the table. "They say just enough to let me know we're at war, yet not enough for me to take action against them. Gods and Monsters, I hate being guildmaster! If killing Vess means *someone* will be forced to figure out a way for me to ditch these obligations, then I'd kill a hundred Lilianas!"

This brought another scowl to Teyo's face but for Rat mostly served to confirm that Mistress Kaya would leave the Orzhov and Ravnica as soon as she was able.

Guess there's no point in me joining Orzhov with her leaving it. Besides, Orzhov really isn't my style . . .

An uncomfortable-looking Teyo grabbed a plum from a fruit bowl and pretended to study it. He glanced up at Rat and down at the fruit and up at Rat and down at the fruit.

"What?" Rat asked.

Looking up again and then away, he mumbled—*yes, adorably*—that the plum was the same color as Rat's eyes. Then he quickly took a bite.

"This plum!" he said rapturously (and with his mouth half full).

"Best. Plum. Ever?"

"Best. Plum. Ever. It's so much sweeter and juicier than any plum I *ever* ate on Gobakhan."

Gobakhan. Teyo would return to Gobakhan tomorrow morning, and Kaya would leave her guild and Ravnica just as soon as she was able.

It's inevitable.

Madame Blaise entered once again, and once again she approached Mistress Kaya to whisper in her ear, but before she could say anything, another voice called out, "Well, look at this keen feast and all this keen company!"

It was Hekara, in her keen new blood witch regalia, leaning against the doorjamb.

Madame Blaise straightened to her full height and spoke with some umbrage: "I told you to wait in the hallway."

"And wait I did," Hekara said. "Two seconds or more. Then I came to save you the trouble of announcing me."

"It's fine, Blaise," Kaya said, allowing a smile to begrudgingly replace the anger she still felt toward the Triumvirate.

Madame Blaise nodded curtly and departed—but not before Hekara performed an impressive series of backflips that resulted in her standing with her arms up atop the dining room table, with one foot in a bowl of savory pudding. *"Ta daaaa!"*

Teyo mumbled, "Your foot . . ."

Hekara smiled down at him. "'S'okay. Did it on purpose. I'm a tad peckish, just now." She sat herself down on the table and contorted her body so that she could lick the brown pudding off the bell on her slipper. "Mm. So good." She untwisted herself and said, "I'll finish the rest later."

"She will, too, you know," Rat said. "It's kinda disgusting and wonderful all at the same time."

But Hekara talked right over her, saying, "When I leave pudding footsteps across Ravnica, it's like I'm sharing my meal with the world. And then when I *do* settle down to eat, it's like I'm enjoying a side of Ravnica with my entrée."

Hearing their crossed words, Mistress Kaya said, "Hekara, Rat is here. In this room. I know things have . . . changed. But Ral Zarek can see her if he focuses. I'm sure you could, too. She's sitting here"—Kaya gestured with her right hand—"in the chair to my right."

Rat didn't have to be slightly telepathic to see Hekara's upper lip twitch as she said, "Sure. Rat's my girl. I can focus on her. I can see Rat." But being slightly telepathic, Rat could feel how . . . *antsy* the topic made Hekara. With obvious reluctance and not a little fear, Hekara turned toward Rat's chair. "Now, all I have to do is focus, right? I know how this works. I've seen her father do it all the time. And I should have a head start, 'cuz Rat's always been my best mate. And I've always been able to see her. That is until I died, right? Died and got resurrected as a blood witch. And she's still my Rat. And I'm still her Hekara."

But the more she talked, the more nervous she became. Rat couldn't bear it any longer and said to Mistress Kaya, "Don't make her. Tell her I left the room."

"But—"

"Please. Please."

"I'm sorry, Hekara. Rat seems to have left the room."

Instantly Hekara's entire frame seemed to relax. "I'm sorry I missed her." Rat got a distinct sense that Hekara *knew* she was being let off the hook—and that she was grateful for it. Her new inability to see Rat now worried the blood witch—or *scared* her. After all, if Hekara had lost that, what else might she have lost when she died?

"Yeah, I'm sorry I missed her," Hekara repeated more quietly to no one in particular. Then she whispered sadly, "I do miss her. She's my Rat."

"I'm your Rat," Rat whispered back, knowing Hekara wouldn't hear.

Rat knew from experience that even folks who did manage to see her for a time forgot what she looked and sounded like a few minutes—if not seconds—after they lost focus on her. In fact, when Rat stayed away too long, even her own mother started to forget her—though Ari Shokta had never admitted this out loud to her daughter. Hekara would soon forget Rat ever existed in her life. *So Hekara won't be sad about missing her Rat for very long.*

It suddenly occurred to Rat that joining the Cult of Rakdos was out of the question now that Hekara was no longer in her corner. No Rakdos. No Orzhov. Just Gruul and Selesnya as her only options. Until, inevitably, they weren't options, either. Because without Hekara, Rat had no peers or friends native to Ravnica (who were staying on Ravnica) who were consistently able to see her. Just her mother and her godfather. Until, inevitably, they forgot how to see her, too.

Hekara didn't stay long. Mistress Kaya had spoiled her mood. She cartwheeled away, leaving Teyo to try to cheer Rat up by saying things clearly intended to get her to tease him.

Mistress Kaya remained silent, and Rat could tell she was mulling over Rat's isolation and loneliness. She was sympathetic. She and Teyo both were.

But Rat was adamantly determined not to burden either of them. She put on a happy face, talked a bit more about fruit tarts, and intentionally put a milk mustache on her face for Teyo to shyly point out, until—*finally*—Madame Blaise appeared to escort all three to their bedchambers for the night.

TEN

VRASKA

Their victory had been sweet, but this was sweeter.

Vraska and Jace made love. It had been a long time coming, something they had both wanted since being shipmates aboard the *Belligerent* on the plane of Ixalan. Something they had delayed because fate had never been kind to either of them and Nicol Bolas had still loomed large on their horizon.

Now the wait made every kiss, every touch, all the more tender. And with her permission, he had telepathically connected what they felt for each other, what they were feeling of each other. Every sensation was reflected back and doubled.

This is very intense. Very intense. Very . . . Very . . .

In that moment, they were one mind, one body, one soul.

Collapsing down atop his chest, she kissed him over and over. He held her tight. She came close to saying . . .

But, no. Not yet. I can't. Not yet.

He said, "I think I've fallen in love with you."

She laughed out loud and said, "I love you, too."

So yes, yet.

She laughed again. They kissed again.

Eventually, feeling drowsy, she rolled off him—*and they spooned!*

Is this what normal folk do? Just hold each other like this? Just enjoy each other like this?

His breathing became regular behind her. She loved the fact that Jace felt comfortable enough to fall asleep with his arms encircling her body.

Besides, he must be exhausted. I know I am.

And yet she didn't sleep. Instead, she enjoyed the afterglow of their lovemaking. Her mind wandered through their history together. Their time aboard ship. The hunt for the Immortal Sun. The various psychic revelations that had cemented her feelings for him—and his for her. It was so strange, since the two of them were so different. And yet so much alike.

Unfortunately, her mind kept wandering—to less pleasant concerns. Ultimately, to the one concern that almost always filled her thoughts: the welfare of the Golgari Swarm.

She was the Golgari's queen now, and—though no one was more surprised than Vraska—she seemed to have inspired much loyalty within her guild, certainly among the teratogens (those of the Swarm who were neither human nor elf), especially among the Erstwhile and the kraul. Storrev and Azdomas were more faithful to her than she deserved.

But Vraska was also well aware that the devkarin elves—led by their high priestess, Matka Izoni Thousand-Eyed—wanted her gone. Gone so that Izoni and the devkarin could once again take cruel control over the Swarm. It was little consolation knowing the rest of the Swarm didn't trust or even like the devkarin, because Vraska knew it would be unwise to underestimate their power.

Particularly when she also had nine other guilds with which to contend. Nine guilds currently insisting she once again do the work of an assassin, something she had hoped she'd given up forever.

Not the killing, per se, but the idea of being ordered *to kill at the beck and call of others. What by Krokt do I care about Dovin Baan?*

"Zino for your thoughts." Jace was awake. Had her dark musings pulled him from slumber. Were they still psychically attached?

How much does he know? How much did he learn?

With a gentle hand, he turned her face toward his. "I was dreaming of Vryn," he said sleepily.

"Yes?" she whispered, relieved.

"Now that I have all my memories back, I have to admit I'm . . . eager? Yeah, eager . . . to planeswalk there."

"I don't blame you. It's your homeworld. How could you not want to see it again?"

"It's a little scary, actually."

"Aww." She stroked his stubbly chin.

He stroked her tendrils, which got her going a little. Again.

"Would you go with me?" Before she could respond—or object—he quickly added, "I know you can't leave the Golgari for long. But perhaps a short trip? A week?"

She looked into his eyes. The candlelight reflected in them. She found herself reflected in them, too. She thought he looked at her as if she were all there was to see. She kissed his soft, soft lips and said, "A week sounds lovely."

"*You're* lovely," he said.

He rolled on top of her. She liked the feel of his weight upon her. She liked the feel of the other things he was starting to do, as well.

This feels right. So right. Jace and I. A couple. Better than I could have dreamed.

They began again . . .

ELEVEN

DOVIN BAAN

Dovin Baan was in hiding. Hurt—*blinded* by Lazav's throwing knives—Baan had instinctively planeswalked away from Ravnica to his old boarded-up domicile on Kaladesh. It was, he had to admit, a move driven by desperation—if not flat-out panic.

But almost immediately his fearsome intellect had kicked in. He knew Lazav, Chandra Nalaar, Saheeli Rai and Lavinia had seen him planeswalk away. And they had seen his condition at the time, which was to say, they had seen a rare moment of *unpreparedness* in him.

They'd soon guess at the truth, calculate that he would planeswalk home.

Moreover, Baan knew he was not safe on Kaladesh. It seemed insane that the Kaladeshi weren't grateful for his efforts on their behalf, and yet he would not be a fool who denied the obvious truth: He was unwelcome on his own homeworld.

And if that weren't enough of a problem, there existed—with the Immortal Sun no longer under his or one of his surrogates' control—a combined 11 percent probability that Nicol Bolas might have failed, might have fallen. And if the dragon fell, then Nalaar, Rai and Beleren might soon chase Baan here to Kaladesh. To this very room.

Dovin Baan had made this stop to regain his wits and to take a breath. But he would not risk stopping long.

TWELVE

RAT

Rat didn't stay long.

Though Madame Blaise still couldn't see Rat, the servitor had assigned her new young (invisible) mistress an extremely luxurious bedchamber. Rat took a moment or two to explore the amenities she would not, in fact, be enjoying.

But within minutes, she had entered the darkened corridor and was kneeling before Teyo's door to pick the lock to his room. She entered quietly. He was out like a light, snoring softly.

Adorable, adorable.

Rat crawled onto the bed beside him. He was dead to the world and had no idea she was there. For some reason, she found this strangely reassuring. Rat was so accustomed to her curse, it rarely bothered her. But tonight had been different. Frankly, it had been brutal—brutal because she *had* been noticed. Now it was a relief to be once again unobserved.

Without waking him, Rat kissed Teyo goodbye—on the cheek—and departed first his room, then the dark corridor and ultimately the entire Cathedral Opulent.

In no time, she was on Tin Street, where multiple celebrations of the day's victory were in full swing. Folks toasted the dead, the heroes, each other. The nervous, relieved laughter of survivors filled the air. As dozens of inebriated Ravnicans passed her by without a second glance—or a first glance, for that matter—Rat found a shadowed doorway, slid to the filthy ground in her newly cleaned clothes and had herself a good cry.

THIRTEEN

CHANDRA NALAAR

Chandra was trying to sleep—and failing miserably. She was lying in her mother's bedroom, in her mother's bed, as her mother, Pia Nalaar, slept soundly beside her.

It wasn't like she wasn't tired—exhausted, even. They were all exhausted. There probably wasn't a soul on Ravnica that wasn't exhausted after all they'd been through today.

But sleep simply wasn't coming. Her brain just wouldn't turn off.

Giving up, Chandra rose and dressed as quietly as she could manage. Her mother stirred but didn't wake. Chandra watched her breathe for a time, then snuck out, feeling vaguely guilty about it, as if she were a teenager breaking curfew.

Moving down the short corridor, Chandra paused outside her own bedroom. She *called* it her bedroom, and certainly it was the room Pia had designated as hers, but the pyromancer could probably count on both hands the number of times she'd actually slept there. This wasn't really her room. This wasn't really home to her. Not yet, anyway. Maybe not ever. Not that there was somewhere else she could or did consider *home*. There was Keral Keep, but she dreaded the thought of returning to her role and responsibilities as its abbot. She'd had a bedchamber in the Embassy of the Guildpact for a while. Bolas and Tezzeret's Planar Bridge had ripped the building apart. And honestly, it had been so long since she had spent any significant time there, she hadn't even bothered to look through the wreckage to see if she could find anything she might want to salvage.

Pushing the door open just an inch, Chandra peeked into the chamber. Nissa and Jaya were both asleep in Chandra's bed. Chandra watched Nissa slumber and remembered, after the battle, telling Nissa she loved her, and Nissa saying she loved Chandra, as well. It hadn't meant what she had once hoped it would mean. Not to either of them. It couldn't anymore. They had been mourning Gideon, and Nissa had wiped Chandra's tears away. Chandra wanted to cry now. But she was drained, numb. She didn't like feeling numb in Nissa's presence. She nudged the door closed again and moved on.

She made her way through the living room, where Teferi slept on the couch beside a standing, dormant Karn, which frankly didn't look all that different from a standing alert Karn. Or perhaps he really *was* alert? She seemed to recall someone—Jaya, maybe—telling her that Karn never slept. Perhaps he was merely pretending to be dormant in order to make his organic friends more comfortable. If so, she'd let him pretend.

She nearly stepped on Ajani, who for lack of another available bed was curled up on the floor in the corner like the world's largest domesticated cat. It was a full house, despite the fact that Saheeli Rai had taken Huatli home with her. Chandra felt stifled among all these people though every single one was her friend. She had to get outside and feel the cool night air on her face. She opened the front door as quietly as she could manage and departed.

But there was no cool night air. It was a hot, sultry evening in the city of Ghirapur. Chandra had all this pent-up energy she needed to vent, all this fire she needed to channel somehow. Her face set, she headed for Dovin Baan's home.

When he had planeswalked away from Ravnica, Baan had been hurt, blinded, in trouble. Off his game for maybe the first time ever. Chandra figured Baan would have—for once—followed his instincts and gone home. The odds of him still being there all these hours later were pretty slim. But if there was even a chance Chandra might get to bring him to justice for all the damage Baan had done on Kaladesh and Ravnica, she had to try. In any case, it was better than staring at the ceiling in her mother's bed.

When she arrived at Baan's home—with the windows boarded up and the boards completely covered with the kind of graffiti that would have annoyed Dovin Baan to no end—Saheeli Rai and Huatli were already there.

"Couldn't sleep," Chandra said.

"Neither could we," Saheeli replied, nodding.

"Thought Baan might have come back here," Chandra said.

"Had the same thought," Saheeli said, still nodding.

"Probably not there anymore."

"Probably not."

"You want to break in or should I?"

"I'll do it," Huatli said, taking a step back and immediately kicking the door open. She entered first, blade drawn. Saheeli followed, releasing one of her little golden filigree mechanical hummingbirds into the air. Chandra was right behind them both, with a ball of fire hovering half an inch above the palm of her right hand. She levitated and expanded the flame-ball so that it lit the room.

The hummingbird zipped around everywhere, through every

door, in and out, until finally it came back, landed on Saheeli's shoulder and shook its tiny head at its mistress.

"He's not here," Saheeli stated.

"Probably hasn't been here in the four months since he fled Kaladesh," Chandra said grumpily.

Saheeli slid an index finger over the surface of a cabinet and examined it. "Then why is there no dust?"

This perplexed Chandra for a moment—and then her jaw dropped. She said, "You don't think that . . . that all this time . . . while he was infiltrating Azorius, building all those thopters and taking over the guild to serve Bolas . . . you don't think he was planeswalking back here every week or so . . . *to clean?*"

Saheeli and Chandra's eyes met. Then in unison they nodded and said ruefully, "Of course he was."

For some reason, this conclusion drove Chandra crazy. The ball of fire grew perceptibly larger.

Huatli said, "Over here."

She had moved across the room to the kitchen. They joined her.

She pointed at the counter and said, "He's been cleaning here, too. And recently. You can smell it. But I suppose being blind made it slightly more difficult. He missed a spot."

They leaned down to look. There was a dark spot on the counter.

"Blood," Huatli stated firmly. "Blood recently shed. He may be gone now, but he was here today. Tried to cover his tracks, so we wouldn't know—or at least couldn't confirm—he'd been on Kaladesh."

She sniffed the air and moved on. She found another drop of blood on the floor. And another on the windowsill. "He went out this window."

Saheeli said, "He had to. He had to know he was no more welcome on Kaladesh than he would be on Ravnica. Instinct might have brought him home, but his intellect would have told him he couldn't stay."

Chandra whispered, "But he *climbed* out or walked away. As opposed to '*walking* away, if you get my drift."

They clearly did.

Huatli opened the window and exited. Saheeli and Chandra followed.

Huatli was a decent tracker and found a drop of blood here and a drop of blood there. But within a hundred yards, she'd lost Baan's trail completely. She muttered something about needing a dinosaur to track him any farther at night.

Saheeli apologized for the lack of the breed on Kaladesh.

Huatli heaved a long sigh. "We'll not find him now. It's just been too long."

Chandra said, "But we know he was here within the last few hours."

"And still that's too long for us to draw any sound conclusions. It's possible Baan has gone into hiding somewhere on Kaladesh. And it's equally possible he already planeswalked away to planes unknown. Until someone we trust runs into him or hears word of him, I don't think we can know."

A frustrated Chandra clenched her fist and extinguished her fireball quite suddenly, leaving the three women in darkness.

It was either do that or let it expand to burn the whole city to the ground.

Peering through the night, Saheeli said, "Well, it was worth a try."

"Do you think you could sleep now?" Huatli asked, suppressing a yawn.

"Yes, maybe," Saheeli said as she lifted the hummingbird off her shoulder and put it away.

Chandra said good night to them both and walked off, heading back—for lack of a better option—to her mother's home.

FOURTEEN

TEYO VERADA

"I thought I told you to lock your door."

"What door?" Teyo asked blearily. "There's no door."

"Teyo, wake up."

The abbot was shaking him out of a very sound sleep. Morning sun was shining in through the window. The abbot shook him again. He looked up.

Not the abbot. Definitely not the abbot.

It took Teyo a few seconds to even recognize Kaya. To even remember where he was. What *world* he was on.

But it all began to come back to him through the haze of his still-tired brain.

"Why didn't you lock your door?"

"I did," he muttered low. Then, clearing his throat, he repeated, "I did. I know I did."

"Well, I found it open. And Rat's door was unlocked, too. She's gone."

"Wait, what—"

"Rat is gone."

Instantly Teyo was fully alert. He sat up in the bed and asked, almost demanded, "Where did she go?"

"I don't know. But I'm already late for the meeting at the Senate House. So *you* need to find her."

He nodded.

Nothing happened for a beat, until an exasperated Kaya said, "Teyo, get a move on. I'm worried about her. She needs you. She needs us."

Now, without a doubt, her tone reminded him of Abbot Barrez. He scrambled out of bed and immediately began donning his outer garments, but he was also shaking his head. "Kaya, you know why she left. She left because *we're* leaving."

"I'm well aware of that. Nevertheless, I want you to find her and bring her back."

"So that we get to say goodbye?"

"So that maybe none of us have to."

FIFTEEN

JACE BELEREN

As planned, the Planeswalkers gathered atop the Citadel of Bolas, where Gideon Jura had died. As Jace climbed the steps of the pyramid with Vraska by his side, he spotted Kiora and Tamiyo. And Samut, Saheeli Rai and Huatli. The angel Aurelia was there, too, though she wasn't a Planeswalker and couldn't possibly join them on their journey. She held the leaf-wrapped breastplate of their fallen friend.

Vraska had come to see Jace off, but she had already told him she wasn't going with him to Theros, and now she explained it to the others: "I'm sorry, but I barely knew the man. And I have Golgari business to attend to." She glanced then at Aurelia, who nodded subtly—but not subtly enough for Jace to miss it. He made a conscious choice *not* to ask what Golgari business Queen Vraska had with the Boros guildmaster. Instead, he reiterated to his new love that he would return to Ravnica and be back with her soon.

Kiora also offered her condolences, but explained that she, too, would not be going with them. It seemed she was persona non grata on Theros. "Ajani can explain it to you," she said. "Although maybe today is not the day to bring it up."

"Where will you go?" Tamiyo asked.

"Home. To Zendikar. But first, I want to say . . . It's been . . . That is . . ." She trailed off, looking inward. She glanced up at the others, shook her head rather hopelessly and planeswalked away, vanishing in a fine mist.

Almost immediately—and practically simultaneously—Chandra, Nissa, Teferi, Karn, Ajani and Jaya planeswalked in from Kaladesh.

Jace looked around, shrugged and said, "I figure that's pretty much everyone."

Aurelia said, "I wish I could go with you. I would have liked to have seen the world that forged Gideon Jura."

Jace knew she had loved Gideon as much as any of them and watched as the tears of the angel fell upon the leaves that enfolded Gideon's armor.

Jaya said, "I'm going to beg off, too."

Ajani said, "What?"

And Jace said, "Really?"

A stunned Chandra just stared and whispered, "Jaya?"

"I'm sorry, Chandra. But when you've been alive for as many centuries as I have, well . . . sometimes you simply cannot face one more funeral for a friend."

Teferi eyed her a bit suspiciously, but Chandra nodded. She seemed to accept the explanation, though she still seemed disappointed in her mentor.

"I guess the rest of us can go," Jace said. He kissed Vraska one more time and whispered, "I'll be back soon. And then Vryn."

"And then Vryn," she whispered back.

And with that, Jace, Chandra, Nissa, Karn, Samut, Teferi, Ajani, Tamiyo, Saheeli and Huatli departed Ravnica for Theros, leaving Vraska, Aurelia and Jaya behind.

SIXTEEN

TEYSA KARLOV

Teysa Karlov, scion—and now Matriarch—of the most prominent family in the Orzhov Syndicate, was in her chambers.

Well, of course I'm in my chambers. I've been confined to these same five rooms for the equivalent of an eternity!

She was having a pleasant little chat with her executive assistant—her *former* executive assistant—Tomik Vrona. She was saying, "Tomik, please. I know all about the assigned contracts. Your man Zarek is to hunt Tezzeret. The gorgon is sent after Baan. And our Kaya has been hired to kill Vess. She's being sent *off plane* to kill Vess."

Tomik stuttered out a response: "I—I wasn't . . . *aware* you were so well informed."

"Because you chose not to inform me?" She sighed. "My friend—and I like to think we are still friends—I have multiple sources of information. I'd never have survived this long without such sources."

"No, I suppose not."

"In any case, I'm sure you can see the opportunity Kaya's assignment presents to us."

Tomik scowled but said nothing.

"The perfect opportunity . . ."

Still no response seemed forthcoming.

"Tomik, dear, it's the perfect opportunity to take the Orzhov away from its decidedly reluctant guildmaster. This isn't another coup. It's what Kaya wants, after all."

"No, mistress—" He stopped and corrected himself. "—*milady*. I will not condone taking advantage of this situation to remove Mistress Kaya from her position."

"She doesn't need to be removed if—"

"If what? If she dies by trying to leave Ravnica while all those debtor contracts are still in force? I won't allow that to happen, either. Nor will anyone be tearing those contracts away from her magically. We both know that could kill her, too. And neither of us will do *anything* that could harm our lawful guildmaster."

"So now you see her as your one true lawful guildmaster? I remember when you saw me in that role."

"I remember that, too, Milady Karlov, but things have changed."

"Yes. Apparently, they have." She paused before saying, "Your lack of vision disappoints me, Vrona. You have left me quite . . . cross."

"I'm sorry about that. Truly. But as you probably know, my time is short this morning. I must go." He rose nervously and made his way to the door. He glanced back once and looked like he wanted to say something. But he shook the thought off and exited, shutting the door behind him.

Almost immediately, Lazav seemed to melt out of the shadows behind her. She could feel his presence there without turning to look. He said simply, "You see now?"

She nodded and said, "Plan B, then."

SEVENTEEN

TEYO VERADA

Teyo was currently under attack.

Fortunately, he was cornered. This might be a problem for most people, but for a shieldmage—*even a mediocre acolyte like Teyo Verada*—it made things a bit easier. With his back to the ninety-degree intersection of two walls of brick and mortar, he had been able to activate both his eastern and western vertices, creating two large rectangles of solid light. Since his eastern vertex had always been stronger, he created a small circle of light beneath his right ear to give him balance. Plus, he could lean back, using the two walls to brace the two shields, which he enhanced with his heart, spirit and mind vertices, thus increasing their strength. There was no way the three attacking Gruul warriors would be able to get to him.

So he felt safe enough. For now.

But I'm stuck. This is not *helping me find Rat.*

Before entering Gruul territory, Teyo had traveled first to the Selesnya Conclave, only getting lost twice along the way. Consulting briefly with Emmara Tandris and Rat's godfather Boruvo, he'd been told not to worry, for Rat often disappeared for weeks at a time. But Teyo had worried, and thus his journey had continued.

He had informed the trio now attacking him—two humans and a goblin, wearing fur tunics and a considerable quantity of decorative bones—that he sought the daughter of two of its finest warriors, Ari and Gan Shokta. But the three weren't impressed by Teyo's name-dropping. It seemed they were from a different clan than the Shoktas, and since the war that had united the Gruul Clans was now over, they weren't in the mood to suffer another clan's friend.

Teyo's one hope struck him as wishful thinking. There had been a young viashino nearby, who had not joined in on the assault. When he'd heard who Teyo was looking for, he had turned to head down a tunnel—rather lazily, Teyo thought. As the boy maintained his shields against the regular pounding of three Gruul hammers, he was crossing his vertices that the viashino might be bringing help.

He'd never be certain if the viashino was indeed his savior. But sure enough, Ari Shokta and her clan leader, the cyclops Borborygmos, both arrived on the scene, armed and ready for battle. But there was no fight. Borborygmos roared something unintelligible (to Teyo, at least), and Teyo's three assailants made a few feeble threats before taking off at a run.

Ari Shokta approached, and Teyo instantly dropped his shields. She grabbed him up into a fierce bear hug that put his ribs at greater risk than they had been during the attack. "Teyo, my boy," she said. "It's good to see you." Despite the pain to his nearly caved-in sides, this warm greeting was a welcome change. The first couple of times Teyo had encountered Ari, she had been decidedly suspicious of her daughter's new friend. But Teyo had somehow managed to be instrumental in saving the entire Shokta family—not to mention Borborygmos and the other nine guild leaders—from the God-Eternal Kefnet, and that act had impressed Ari enough to change her opinion. She liked that Teyo could see her daughter and seemed to feel he was worthy of Araithia's company. Looking around, Ari said, "Where is our Araithia?"

Teyo's shoulders sank. "I was hoping you knew. She left us during the night, and I haven't been able to find her."

"I haven't seen her since the end of the battle," Ari said, then turned to shoot a questioning look at the cyclops, who shrugged and muttered something Teyo couldn't make out but was clearly meant to impart, *Don't ask me.*

Ari turned back to Teyo and looked at him sympathetically. "Don't worry, Teyo. This is not unusual. Sometimes Rat doesn't come around for weeks at a time."

"That's exactly what Boruvo said."

Hearing the centaur's name, Borborygmos growled low and Ari scowled darkly, reminding Teyo he shouldn't be mentioning Rat's godfather—the Gruul defector—in these domains.

"Sorry, sorry," Teyo said. "But I am worried. I've been worried about her ever since we learned Hekara can no longer see her."

"That . . . was a blow, indeed. But trust me, my daughter is extremely resilient. It's a blow she will recover from. Still . . ."

"Yes?"

"I'm glad you seek her, Teyo Verada. It is good."

Teyo nodded, not feeling worthy of her confidence. He knew where he needed to seek Rat next . . . and he dreaded it.

EIGHTEEN

CHANDRA NALAAR

One stone on top of another, on top of another, on top of another, on top of the armor of her Gids. By the time they arrived, it was already night on Theros, and they built the cairn together. Each of them had scoured the landscape under the light of a beautiful full moon to find just the right stone for the purpose, the right stone to suit each Planeswalker's unique vision of Gideon Jura. So some were big, and some were small. Some flat, some round. All of them, hard and strong. And . . .

Can stones be cheerful? I think mine is.

Chandra was sure they'd found the perfect spot, surrounded by nature, alongside a babbling brook, reeds blowing back and forth in the breeze—but in view of the city of Akros where Gideon had grown up. She had been here once briefly with Gids, not too long ago. It had been night then, too, and he had pointed out the Therosian god-heaven of Nyx and all its constellations. It seemed to her now as if the constellation Heliod watched them from above, and not without some approval of their efforts.

There were no trees nearby, which seemed to offend Nissa. From a pouch on her belt, she pulled out an acorn and buried it about six inches deep and a yard behind the cairn. Ajani knelt beside the brook and with both paws scooped up a little water, which he poured over the buried acorn.

Nissa then closed her eyes, whispered a request for permission . . . and then, in a matter of seconds, RAISED A MIGHTY OAK to mark Gideon Jura's "grave."

Everyone paused in silence to admire that for more than a few minutes.

At last, Ajani said, "Shouldn't one of us say something?"

Nissa frowned at him and looked at the oak, as if to say, *I've just spoken volumes.*

Ajani nodded his acknowledgment of her eloquence but still clearly felt like some actual verbiage was necessary. He looked at Chandra, who shook her head in one quick back-and-forth movement. Suddenly she felt overwhelmed; she had no words.

Choking up, Jace said, "I'll miss my friend."

That simple eulogy took Chandra's breath away. She bit her lower lip hard enough to taste a little copper tang of blood.

Huatli then stepped forward, announcing, "I have composed a poem in Gideon Jura's honor."

Chandra exchanged looks of semi-horror with Jace and Nissa. *Huatli barely knew Gids, and she wrote him a poem?*

But Saheeli Rai caught Chandra's eye, and her expression seemed to say, *Give her a chance.*

Huatli began. She had called it a poem, but she sang it. And, well, at least she *could* sing. She had talent. It wasn't embarrassing to hear. Her voice was a clear alto—soothing and warm without putting one to sleep. It acted as a gateway, opening Chandra and the others to the moment, to the meaning . . .

Another hero falls, another vict'ry won,
And yet we who remain are left torn and undone.
The man we mourn is not the champion they cheer;
He's more than just a name to celebrate each year.

He held our hearts in outstretched hands;
He battled back our fears.
We owe him more
Than can be shed with tears.

Our greatest hero falls; our enemy's undone.
And yet this triumph's cost was far too hard-won.
They gained a symbol and salvation from the end;
We live with knowing that we sacrificed our friend.

He held our hearts in outstretched hands;
He battled back our fears.
Now all we have
To offer is our tears.

His strength, his soul, his grace, they'll never truly know,
But we'll recall the man, e'en as his legends grow.
To them, we'll leave the tales of struggles and of trials,
But we'll remember all his bright and handsome smiles.

How is this possible? She didn't know him . . . She doesn't know us, know me . . . How is she capturing our Gids? How is she . . . singing . . . what my heart feels . . . how is she singing my guilt?

He held our hearts in outstretched hands;
He battled back our fears.
We'll miss him more
Than we can cry in tears.

Huatli's song touched Chandra deeply; she leaned on Nissa and cried. Honestly, it was a relief she *could* cry. She was actually happy she could cry; the numbness of the night before was gone—at least for the time being.

He held our hearts in outstretched hands;
He battled back our fears.
We'll miss him more
Than we can cry in tears.

When the song ended, Saheeli commented, "That's quite unlike the other, um, poems you've shown me."

"I felt Gideon Jura required something different."

Chandra breathed in the cool night air, looked toward the horizon and sighed out, "Gideon would like this. Even Liliana might like this." Instantly she caught herself. "Sorry," she said, quickly. "I didn't mean to say that. Didn't mean to bring her up. Not here. Not now. It just . . . slipped out."

Jace tried to reassure her. "It's all right. I think we're all still a bit conflicted about Liliana."

Nissa cleared her throat. She tended to talk as little as possible, and she had never really liked Liliana, so when she actually started to speak, what she said came as a bigger surprise than the fact that she was speaking at all: "Gideon would not be conflicted. Gideon would try to save Liliana. Gideon would try to redeem her."

NINETEEN

LILIANA VESS

The ravens flew away—at least for the time being.

How long have I been standing here?

How long had she been trying to hold off the Raven Man's advances and his *oh-so-sincere offer of assistance*? She'd managed to put him off for now. (Whomever he was.) Resisted him. (And whatever he wanted to use her for.) But that didn't mean she knew what she wanted instead. What she wanted out of her life.

Or do I simply want out *of my life? Which is the correct question? What do I expect out of life or what do I demand from death?*

For years, Liliana had been so focused on freeing herself from the demons—and dragon—that had held her contract, she had never given any real thought to what she would do *after* attaining her goal.

And I damn sure never gave a moment's contemplation to what attaining my goal might cost.

She looked down. She'd been standing in chill water up to her ankles. Her feet were numb.

Well, fine. Now they match what passes for my soul.

She walked on, continuing rather pointlessly toward the ruins of her family's mansion.

My life is a ruin, an empty shell like that mansion.

Then the whispers began . . .

Oh, no, please, not them. Not them, too . . .

First the Raven Man, now the Onakke spirits that inhabited the Chain Veil kept in the small pouch tied to her belt. The spirits whispered to her, more insistent now than they had been since she'd first obtained the Veil.

Since the contract was abrogated . . . it's freed them some-how . . .

Not simply more insistent, they were now more . . . *present* in her mind. *Vessel,* they whispered, for that was what they called her, what they considered her to be: something empty that they sought to fill.

And they're not wrong about the empty part . . .

The root, they hissed, *has finally come to full flower. Give yourself up to us,* they hissed, *and still your troubled heart.*

It's tempting. Tempting to abdicate all responsibility to the spirits. Even if abdication is just a euphemism for a kind of death.

For at this moment, the stark truth was that a growing part of Liliana was more and more willing, even *desperate,* to die. The near-drowning she had all but allowed was just the opening salvo of a war she was losing.

A war I had better lose on my own terms for the sake of the gods-forsaken Multiverse. I can't allow myself to be used again.

A darkness was building within her and around her. And she was frightened where it might lead.

Frightened of what I might do next. As it seems I'm capable of anything now. Capable of being a monster equal to Bolas himself . . .

She'd have to hold them off for a bit longer. Give herself time to find a way. Give herself time to tread that final distance.

I can do this. It's better. Better for the Multiverse and better for me. I killed Bolas and Gideon to save myself from being the dragon's slave. I should be willing to kill one last person to save myself from becoming the Onakke or the Raven Man's minion.

"Silence," she said aloud and meant it. The word and the intent behind it was enough to temporarily hush the voices of the spirits.

For an hour? For a minute? If I'm going to end things to save myself from becoming their tool, I better do it quick.

She knew she was close to home. She could crawl in among the shattered dreams of the place. If she did it there, it would seem like a kind of justice. This was where she first caused pain. Where she first decimated the people she loved the most.

Home.

She came over a rise.

What in Urza's name?

She now had a clear view of the ruins. Only they *weren't* ruins. She had to literally rub her eyes in disbelief. It couldn't be . . .

It's only been a few months since I was last here . . .

The mansion, the Vess mansion, was still some short distance away. But from where Liliana stood atop the rise, it seemed to have been completely refurbished. In fact, from the look and sound of things . . .

Nine Hells, there's a damn party *going on inside.*

TWENTY

KAYA

The representatives from the Orzhov Syndicate—
Guildmaster Kaya, flanked by Chief Enforcer Bilagru and
Advokist Tomik Vrona—were among the last to arrive for the
conference at the Senate House, where most of the participants
had already assembled before the statue-slash-corpse of the
sphinx Isperia (the former Azorius guildmaster).

Taking the late Isperia's place was Lavinia, accompanied by a
Senator Nhillosh, who took some pleasure—though Lavinia
clearly took none—in introducing his new acting guildmaster as
the Azorius Senate's Grand Arbiter Pro Tem.

Lavinia grumbled, "I preferred being an arrester."

Nhillosh *tsk*'d at her: "That would now be thoroughly
inappropriate . . . Grand Arbiter Pro Tem." The title repeated as
an afterthought and, almost certainly, as a dig.

Standing as far from the two Azorius delegates as possible

was Isperia's killer—or perhaps executioner—Queen Vraska herself, with her Erstwhile aide Storrev, representing the Golgari
Swarm. The gorgon queen wore a grim expression, but at least
her eyes weren't glowing and ready to turn anyone else to stone—
for the time being.

Kaya was glad to see Guildmaster Ral Zarek, there with
Chamberlain Maree, to represent the Izzet League. But he, too,
looked inward, his visage dark. And even the presence of Tomik
failed to raise a smile.

The blood witch Exava was there for the Cult of Rakdos; the
biomancer Vorel, for the Simic Combine; Gan Shokta, the Gruul
Clans; Guildmaster Aurelia, the Boros Legion, and Spearmaster
Boruvo, the Selesnya Conclave.

There were a handful of Planeswalkers there, as well, all gathered around Living Guildpact Niv-Mizzet: Jaya Ballard, Vivien
Reid and the Wanderer. Kaya was surprised to see them. She had
assumed that Jaya in particular would have gone to Theros for
Gideon Jura's memorial service.

I thought the two of them were close.

Kaya stood a short distance away, trying and failing to ana-
lyze their motives for attending. Jaya looked troubled. Vivien
looked tense. And the Wanderer? Kaya had no idea. Between the
Wanderer's long white hair and her low and wide-brimmed hat,
Kaya couldn't even manage a decent look at her face.

The last to arrive was an apologetic Aurelia—the real Aurelia,
who caught sight of the *previous* Aurelia and glared at her, until
she shrugged and morphed into the decidedly unapologetic
Lazav of House Dimir.

"Why do you play these games?" Kaya asked him.

"I'm a scamp," he replied drily. "Where's your entourage hiding?"

"I sent Teyo to find Araithia," Kaya responded—then instantly
regretted giving up even that much information to the spymaster.

"Why does the Orzhov seek my daughter?" Gan Shokta demanded.

"The Orzhov doesn't. I seek her—because I'm worried about her."

The big man waved off such concerns, not dismissively but with pride: "Araithia Shokta requires no guildmaster's concern."

An impatient Niv-Mizzet interrupted. "Let's get down to business. Queen Vraska. Guildmaster Kaya. Guildmaster Zarek. Do you accept your assignments?"

None of the three rushed to answer, and instead Chamberlain Maree stepped forward. "Before they respond, Firemind, I must question the wisdom of sending three new guildmasters away from Ravnica at such a crucial time."

"Must you now?" growled the Firemind, less than pleased that this goblin he had raised to her current position would dare to question *his* wisdom.

Ral stepped in. "I believe it is necessary. Ravnica needs to know it can trust its leaders to defeat would-be conquerors and bring its enemies to justice. Those of us—like Vraska, Kaya and myself—who collaborated, even briefly, with the dragon Bolas have much to prove. That's why I volunteered to hunt Tezzeret. He opened the Planar Bridge that allowed the Eternals to kill so many sentients on Ravnica. Beyond that, I truly believe Tezzeret might become a major threat to our world, if not the entire Multiverse. Besides, we have a history. We've fought before. For me, this is personal."

"Not for me," Vraska said. She'd been staring at Isperia with some satisfaction before turning to those assembled. "I'm no apologist for Dovin Baan, but I don't much care about him one way or another. Nor do I have any desire to leave Ravnica or the Golgari. Still, I'm aware of what you all think of me and my actions. To be clear, I killed Isperia for personal reasons—not for Nicol Bolas. But I'm also aware that, personal motives aside, I did exactly what the dragon wanted and needed from me."

The Firemind stated, "And the result was the destruction of our alliance, which resulted in my temporary death and nearly resulted in Bolas' victory."

"That's debatable," Kaya said.

Vraska nodded her thanks.

Vorel stated, "What's *not* debatable is that if you don't cooperate, the Golgari will be crushed by the combined might of the other nine guilds."

"That's *extremely* debatable," Kaya stated back.

Ral waded in, as well. "And extremely unlikely. The Living Guildpact would prevent any such conflict."

Niv puffed two rings of smoke from his snout and seemed to consider this. "Yes," he finally said, "I would have to prevent that. But much damage might be done to the Golgari before I found the right moment to step in. However, if Queen Vraska succeeds in killing Baan, all past crimes and offenses will be forgiven, and the other guilds will leave the Golgari in peace. You have my word."

"And I put so much faith in *that*," Vraska replied cynically. "But fine. I will spend, say, a week or so planeswalking away from my guild and my homeworld to hunt down Dovin Baan."

"You shouldn't have to if you don't want to," Kaya said.

Vraska seemed to appreciate the sentiment, but she shook her head. "It hardly matters. Like you, I'm an assassin as well as a guildmaster. Killing Baan is just another job for me. He picked the losing side, and the winning side wants him dead. If Baan must die to further Golgari interests, so be it."

The Firemind turned to Kaya. "What say you?"

"Before she answers," Jaya said, "are we truly agreed that Liliana Vess must die?"

There was a kind of collective groan that emerged from the group, as if to say, *Not this again.*

"Not this again," Vorel grumbled out loud, rolling his eyes.

"*She* killed Bolas. None of *us* did." Jaya turned to look Niv-Mizzet in the eye. "And that includes you, Firemind."

"All that proves," Aurelia said, "is that she could have killed Bolas from the beginning. Instead, she waited. Waited until thousands were dead. And most of them at the hands of Eternals *she* controlled."

"Apparently, she needed Gideon's help."

"Then she should have asked for it. And maybe if she had, Gideon Jura would be alive today."

"Beyond that," Lazav mused, "can we suffer the continued existence of someone with uncertain motives and enough power to destroy Nicol Bolas? What might she do next?"

Jaya took this in and nodded. "So no dissenters?"

No one spoke. Not even Kaya.

Jaya nodded again and said no more.

Niv-Mizzet turned back to Kaya. "Mistress, we believe you are the best qualified to assassinate Vess."

"Really?" Kaya sounded dubious. "Because I'm usually hired to kill ghosts, spirits and the undead. Liliana is none of these."

"It's likely you'll have to kill quite a few of the undead to get to the necromancer Vess. In addition, you have no relationship with Liliana. No baggage. No conflict. Like Vraska, this would just be another job to you."

"That's all well and good, but we still haven't addressed the pragmatics. How am I to *find* Liliana? How are any of us supposed to find any of our targets? As we discussed yesterday, all traces of their journeys will be long gone by now."

"Not *all* traces," said the Wanderer from beneath her hat.

Niv agreed: "This is true. Use logic. Deduce where each would go."

Vivien opined, "A necromancer like Vess might feel most at home on Innistrad or perhaps—"

"She's on Dominaria," the Wanderer stated with certainty.

Jaya responded with equal certainty, "That's the last place she'd go, believe me."

"Nevertheless, that is where she went. I followed her there from here when she planeswalked away."

"You followed her?" Ral asked. "Why?"

"The *'why'* hardly matters," Gan Shokta stated. "I'm just glad she did."

The Wanderer nevertheless responded. "For all the reasons stated above. I believed she might still be a danger and wanted to know where she'd go to ground. The answer is Dominaria."

"Where on Dominaria?" Jaya demanded.

"Not a place I recognized. It was a swamp or morass with an old house visible in the distance. She actually stumbled into the water and nearly drowned. I didn't go to her aid, but she managed to surface. If I didn't know what she was capable of, I'd say it was almost pathetic."

Jaya stared at the ground. "Then she's as desperate as Jace believed." She looked up. "Liliana has returned to her childhood home."

Kaya eyed Jaya. "Since you bring up Jace, I have to ask why you're even here. You hardly seem enthusiastic about this project, and I thought we were leaving the Gatewatch out of it."

Jaya corrected her: "You're Gatewatch, not me. You took an oath. I never have. But if you must know, I'm worried about my protégée Chandra Nalaar. Last night, I followed her to Baan's home on Kaladesh."

"Was he there?" Vraska asked.

"No. He'd been there but had since left. But *my* concern is Chandra and the current conflict tearing at her soul. At this moment, Chandra is deeply troubled. Baan's bad enough. Vess is a whole 'nother story. Her relationship to Chandra was complicated and runs deep. In her current state, I would like these decisions to be taken out of her hands."

Kaya asked, "So you aim to protect her by stopping us from killing Liliana or Baan? Tezzeret, too?"

"Tezzeret needs to die for a hundred reasons. Baan won't be missed, either. If I thought I had a chance to talk you lot out of killing Liliana, well . . . But clearly that's off the table. If the only way I can 'protect' Chandra right now is to advance this agenda, then I'm willing to escort you to Liliana's former home on Dominaria. But I won't stay for the kill. I don't want Chandra looking at me and seeing Liliana's assassin."

"That takes care of Vess," Vraska said dismissively. "But if Baan is on Kaladesh, I'll need assistance, too. That's not a plane I've ever visited. I have no connections there, no way to track him."

Vivien stepped forward. "I can help track him, if Jaya brings us to his last known location."

Jaya sighed heavily. It was clear she didn't relish getting in deeper and deeper. Still . . . "Agreed. On the condition that all three hunters leave Ravnica before Jace and Chandra return from Theros."

"I'm all for that," Vraska said quickly.

Ral said, "I'm all for it, too, but—"

The Wanderer turned to him and said, "I can help you find Tezzeret."

"I don't see how. He was last seen on Amonkhet and left there nearly a day ago."

"It's the Planar Bridge technology in his chest. There's been some damage to the device, causing it to leave longer-lasting traces through the Blind Eternities than those of a typical Planeswalker. Traces I can follow."

"That . . . would be appreciated," Ral said, looking half stunned, half intrigued. "But if I might ask, what's your interest in this hunt?"

"I, too, have a history with Tezzeret. Knowing him, need you ask more?"

Ral was silent, at least for the moment.

Kaya said, "I have another problem. I'm bound to this plane by thousands of Orzhov debtor contracts. Don't get me wrong. I don't want to be guildmaster of Orzhov, and Orzhov doesn't want me as guildmaster. Leaving Ravnica would be a relief. But leaving would also kill me, which is something of a drawback."

Gan Shokta nodded. "Dying *would* interfere with your ability to kill the necromancer," he said without irony.

"Right. *That* was my exact concern," Kaya replied, dripping with irony, which he didn't seem to notice. "Of course, I've thought about—fantasized about it, really—releasing all the debtors from their debts in one fell swoop . . ."

Tomik looked panicked. "That would destroy the Syndicate!"

They both looked around the room. Gan Shokta, Boruvo, Exava—even Ral—seemed to like that idea.

But Niv-Mizzet stated, "Destroying the Orzhov would destroy Ravnica's delicate magical balance of power."

Aurelia glared at him. "Is it Ravnica's power that concerns you—or your own?"

The Firemind glared back as flames roiled around his cheeks.

Tomik said, "Wait, wait. I believe I've found a solution. A better solution."

They waited.

He gathered his thoughts and began: "I studied as a lawmage for years under Teysa Karlov, and early this morning those studies paid off. I believe I have found a legal loophole that would allow Kaya to magically, legally, voluntarily and *temporarily* hand over the debtor contracts and the day-to-day operations of the Orzhov to . . ." He paused and bit his lip nervously.

"To whom? Out with it," Vorel demanded.

"Well . . . to me. I'd become acting guildmaster, and that would allow Kaya to planeswalk away from Ravnica—*for short periods.*"

Ral and Kaya both protested simultaneously: "Tomik, no!"

Looking a little hurt, Tomik addressed them both. "Don't you trust me?"

Lazav laughed. "Ral's worried about two guildmasters sleeping together."

Ral glowered at Lazav—but neither confirmed nor denied his assessment.

Kaya said, "I trust you, Tomik. But you *really* don't know what you're getting into."

"I can handle it. You know . . . temporarily."

"Well, if you're sure you want to take this on, I'm willing to give it a try."

"And that," said the Living Guildpact, "settles that. But let me make one last thing crystal clear to all three of you: *We will require proof of kills.*"

TWENTY-ONE

TEYO VERADA

In theory, Teyo was still looking for Rat—except he no longer had any idea where to look. With considerable dread, he'd descended the five hundred steps to Rix Maadi, past the jugglers and the knife throwers and the caged horrors and the ventriloquists, one of whom was performing with a dummy named Teyo Veridiot. The original Teyo had braved Rakdos, fought off the hellhound Whipsaw and even talked with Hekara, but there had been no sign of Araithia Shokta.

He barely knew Ravnica, and Rat knew its every nook and cranny. He'd gone to all the places he could think of to go, while remaining very aware that his search had barely scratched the surface of the world-city.

So he wandered, keeping his eyes open, without much hope of success. Meanwhile, his thoughts wandered back to Liliana Vess. He couldn't fathom the guilds' apparent lust for killing the woman without ever hearing her side of the story. And as much as he liked and respected Kaya, he couldn't understand her willingness to accept their assignment. Still, he didn't despair of talking her out of it. She was a reasonable person, and reasonable people generally saw reason in the end.

He looked up at Ravnica's single sun. Accustomed to the twin suns of Gobakhan, Teyo thought that Ravnica's star looked, well, *lonely* up there in the sky. He sighed heavily.

Ravnica was a city of wonders—even after all the death of the previous day. There were Orzhov Collectors and their thrulls. Azorius Arresters on patrol. Rakdos Cultists cartwheeling through the streets. Boros Skyknights soaring overhead. And the Gateless, like Rat, just trying to survive. There were mourners and celebrants. There were drunkards and scholars. Minotaurs and elves. Goblins and centaurs. Hundreds of folks must have passed Teyo by without giving him a look.

You could probably fit the entire population of Gobakhan into these few city blocks . . .

Yet it seemed easier to get lost among these crowds than it was to get lost on the dunes where he was raised. Ravnica fascinated him, had done so almost from the moment of his arrival. But now there seemed a coldness to it that left him feeling hollow and alone—like a single sun floating through the sky.

Was it only Rat that allowed me to believe in its splendor?

Eventually, he found himself on the Transguild Promenade where he had encountered her after his very first (and only) planeswalk from Gobakhan to Ravnica. This was where she had picked him up off the cobblestones and adopted him. Where she first terrified and enthralled him.

By the Storm, Araithia, where are you?

There she was. Sitting on the railing, just as she had been the day before. In fact, her pose was so similar—right down to the berry she plucked off her belt and popped into her mouth—that for a second Teyo wondered if she was merely a memory.

But it was Rat. In the flesh. And as he had been thinking about their first encounter, it was clear the same thoughts were occupying her mind, as well. Clear because she was going over it—out loud.

"He was right there, wasn't he? Covered in sand and coughing like he was gonna spit up a hairball or something, you know? And me, I was just sorta watching him. Kinda curious about wherever where he had teleported from and maybe wherever where he'd go to next. Didn't occur to me right off that he was a 'walker. Why would it've, right? And then, whoa, when he called out to me for help—looked right at me and said, 'Please . . .' Well, you could've knocked me right off this rail with a feather. Right off the promenade, even. Maybe off the whole Multiverse. He saw me. He saw me."

Since normally, no one else could hear her, talking out loud to herself was a common practice with the Rat. He'd come to love her high-speed rush of words. He could have stood there listening for hours.

She said, "When I think about it now, he must have been adorable from the very first moment, right? But I don't think I noticed that right away. Or maybe I did somewhere deep, you know?"

Teyo, blushing a deep red, quickly cleared his throat and made his presence known: "Rat?"

She turned toward him fast with an expression of pure panic. She tried to hide, jumping off the railing and curling up small. She held her hands in front of her eyes, like a child playing peek-a-boo.

If she can't see me, does she really think I can't see her?

He walked right up to her and took her hands in his. "You are really bad at hiding."

She allowed him to pull her up to her feet.

"Yeah, well . . . no experience at it, right? Not a skill I ever needed to acquire, me being me and all. Though me being me, I *have* acquired a lot of skills, you know?"

"I know."

"A lot."

"A lot."

"I'm sorry," she said. "Just taking off like that. But see, I'm no good at goodbyes. Another skill I never had to acquire. Never had a lot of folks to say goodbye to. Still don't, really."

"Maybe it's not time for goodbyes. Kaya sent me to find you. She insisted on it."

" 'Not time for goodbyes'?" Rat said, scrinching up her nose suspiciously.

"That's what she said. You have to come back with me."

"I don't know, Teyo. I mean . . . I can't watch you both leave. Not . . . not after Hekara."

"I understand. And I think Kaya does, too. But she sent me to find you, nevertheless."

"It is kinda curious-making. I wonder what she has in mind . . ."

"One easy way to find out."

She looked away.

He waited.

She shrugged and echoed, "One easy way to find out." She put her arm through his, and they headed off together.

Before they were even off the bridge, Rat said, "Wow, you really feel strongly about not killing Miss Raven-Hair."

He only looked briefly surprised before saying, "Yes. I do. Kaya's Gatewatch now. She took an oath to protect people, not to assassinate them."

"But what if killing Miss Vess does protect people?"

"How can we know that without at least listening to what the woman might have to say for herself?"

"That's a good point."

"So you'll help me convince Kaya?"

"I think so," Rat said.

Teyo nodded and smiled.

But Rat wasn't quite done: "Unless she convinces me first."

TWENTY-TWO

TOMIK VRONA

Tomik felt a bit self-conscious. Chamberlain Maree, the Fire-mind and the Wanderer were all standing by waiting as Ral took his leave. Ral had once been so . . . paranoid about letting anyone find out about the two of them. Now he walked up to Tomik and kissed him full on the lips in front of the goblin, the dragon and the Planeswalker.

Truthfully, it felt like he was proving some kind of point to the three observers, and Tomik didn't particularly appreciate being a symbol or a tally mark or a moral victory or whatever.

Then Ral broke the kiss and saw the scowl on his lover's face. Ral's own face fell immediately. "I'm sorry," he said. "I'm sorry." He kissed Tomik again, tenderly this time, and Tomik's ire quickly melted away. Ral had been damaged goods when they met. But he had come such a long way.

"Be careful," Tomik said.

"*You* be careful," Ral returned quietly, nervously.

Tomik sighed. "Please tell me you're not still worried about conflicts of interest or—"

"It's not that. It was never that. Or at least it hasn't been that for a while, anyway."

"Then what? You're not mad I'm helping Kaya?"

"No."

"That's all I'm trying to do."

"I know."

"Then what?"

Ral chuckled a little to himself. "I'm just being stupid. Please don't make me reveal my stupidity out loud."

"That's exactly what I'm making you do."

"Tomik—"

"I'll conjure it out of you one way or another."

"Tomik—"

"What are you afraid of?"

"That once you get a taste for power—"

"You think I'll be corrupted by it?"

"No! Will you let me finish a sentence, please? I mean if you're going to force me to spill my guts, the least you could do is let me spill them all at once."

"Sorry."

"Once you understand the true power of a guildmaster, I'm afraid you'll realize what a fraud I am. I'm afraid you'll realize you don't need me anymore."

"Wow. You really are being stupid."

"I told you so."

"Besides, *you're* the one who's a guildmaster. I'm just a temp."

"You are many things. But certainly not that."

They kissed again. It was excruciatingly delicious.

Ral broke off and turned to face the others.

Niv-Mizzet, with Maree watching, said, "Don't screw this up, Zarek."

Ral stared up at the dragon and ruefully replied, "I appreciate the encouragement." He turned to the Wanderer. "Ready?"

She nodded.

He turned back to Tomik and smiled, a little sadly.

The Wanderer planeswalked away—presumably to Amonkhet—in a violent slash of white light. Half a second later, Ral followed in an explosion of electrical sparks.

Without a word, the Living Guildpact took wing and flew away. Chamberlain Maree walked off. Tomik was left alone to say a little prayer for his man.

TWENTY-THREE

VRASKA

Vraska had wanted to go away for a week. But not like this. Not for this. Not with these people.

Vivien Reid and Jaya Ballard waited—respectively patient and impatient—to planeswalk with Vraska to Kaladesh to initiate what could be a prolonged hunt for Dovin Baan.

And they were sneaking away, now, before Chandra Nalaar and Jace could return from Theros.

Jace'll return and find me gone. Not a great way for us to start our lives together.

A week on Vryn with Jace had sounded lovely.

An unspecified period of time hunting the vedalken was considerably less appealing.

But such was the life of a queen. A highly compromised queen.

She was giving last-minute instructions to her two staunchest allies within the Swarm, Storrev the Erstwhile and Azdomas, leader of her kraul honor guard.

"You'll be in charge," she told the latter. "I vest you with my authority until I return."

The insect clicked in his throat to acknowledge the command. "I will do my best to be worthy of this trust, my queen. But please . . ."

"Do not stay away too long," Storrev said in her hushed, whispered voice. "Matka Izoni and the devkarin . . ."

"Will attempt to take advantage of my absence. Believe me, I know. And I'll return as soon as I possibly can."

For more reasons than one . . .

Storrev bowed her head, and Azdomas clicked.

Vraska turned to her two planeswalking companions.

Jaya said, "Ready?"

"Ready."

Jaya vanished in a brief conflagration of red flames. Vivien departed in a burst of ghostly green light. Vraska latched onto their mana-trails and followed, fading into shadow.

If I can find him, Baan's as good as dead.

TWENTY-FOUR

RAT

Madame Blaise bowed her head and said, "Welcome back, Master Teyo. Am I correct in assuming that Mistress Rat is here, as well?"

"Mistress Rat"? Me? A mistress? So strange.

"She's right beside me," Teyo said.

Madame Blaise squinted toward the empty space to Teyo's right and said, "Welcome back, Mistress Rat."

Since Rat was to Teyo's left, he said, "The *other* side, madame."

"Ah, yes, of course." She turned her squint in Rat's direction.

Rat nudged Teyo and said, "Tell her I'm not that tall. She's looking clear over my melon."

Teyo raised his hand and placed it atop Rat's head. "Rat's about this tall, madame . . ." He lowered his hand to Rat's eye level. ". . . and her eyes are about here." Then as an afterthought, he added, "They're violet."

For a brief second, a knowing smile might have flashed across Madame Blaise's face. Not on her mouth so much, but in her eyes. But it was soon gone as she lowered her gaze and squinted again, trying hard to focus on the girl in front of her. Ultimately, she sighed and said, "I'm sure her eyes are lovely, but as yet I cannot see them. Still, I shan't give up. I'll spot her one of these days." She quickly corrected herself, "I'll spot *you* one of these days, mistress."

Maybe. But that assumes I'll be sticking around Orzhova. Which doesn't seem too likely, whatever what Mistress Kaya has in mind for me.

Just then, that mistress stalked in with Chief Bilagru.

An eager and anxious Rat ran up to her. "Mistress Kaya, why did you tell Teyo to bring me back?"

The guildmaster held her off with a slightly raised hand as she finished with the giant: "During my absence, I expect your full allegiance to be with Acting Guildmaster Vrona."

"Of course, mistress."

"He'll require your protection—as much from internal threats as external."

"Don't I know it. No fears on his account, mistress. I'm somewhat fond of the boy. In fact, he's the reason . . ." He trailed off, unsure how to respectfully continue.

Mistress Kaya helped him out. "He's the reason you're loyal to me now," she said with a smile.

Chief Bilagru growled something deep in his throat.

"That's fine," she said.

"So you are going after Miss Vess?" Rat asked, barely able to contain herself. "And the plan is still to drop Teyo off on Gobakhan first?"

Teyo stared at the ground, but Mistress Kaya looked Rat in the eye and said, "Yes."

This meant Rat was now facing exactly the kind of goodbye

she was hoping to avoid with her two friends, her *only* friends. "Why did you bring me back?" she whispered, looking away.

"Rat—"

"I'd said my goodbyes last night. You may have slept through them, which might've been kinda rude of me. But this was far more unkind, mistress, to make Teyo drag me back if you were both simply going to leave me, anyway."

Mistress Kaya stroked a kind hand against Rat's cheek. "Rat, I wouldn't do that . . ."

The girl looked up with a vague notion of hope—just as Madame Blaise announced, "Mister Tomik Vrona."

Kaya glanced at Rat and said, "Just be patient for a moment longer."

A somewhat exasperated Rat nodded helplessly.

I hate *being patient. But what choice do I have?*

"I've prepared the ritual," Mister Vrona said.

"How involved is it?" Mistress Kaya asked.

"It's surprisingly simple and involves very little blood."

"It involves blood?" Teyo asked, appalled.

"Very little," Mister Vrona repeated.

"Let's just get it over with," Mistress Kaya said.

"Follow me."

Mister Vrona led Mistress Kaya out of her suite—with Chief Bilagru, Madame Blaise, Teyo and Rat tagging along behind—to a small conference room (that the chief barely fit into), where three identical scrolls were spread across a table. Beside them were a pen, an inkwell and a ceremonial kris with an ebon handle and a wavy blade of loxodon ivory. Mister Vrona picked up the kris and said, "Your left hand, please."

Mistress Kaya frowned slightly. "Do you plan to remove it with that?"

"Nothing quite so drastic."

She lifted her left hand. He gently steadied it and then quickly jabbed the tip of the kris into the tip of her middle finger. He then moved her hand over to the inkwell, allowing exactly three drops of Mistress Kaya's red blood to mix with the black liquid within.

As soon as he had released her hand, Madame Blaise stepped forward and, with three whispered words, healed the tiny puncture mark on her mistress' finger. Kaya raised an eyebrow, and Madame Blaise said, "Well, what kind of a servitor would I be if I couldn't heal something as simple as that, I ask you?"

"Thank you, Blaise."

"My pleasure, mistress. My honor."

While this little exchange of niceties was going on, Mister Vrona had repeated the finger jabbing on his own left middle finger with three drops of his own blood mixed with the ink, as well. Using the pen, he stirred the inkwell then, one by one, signed each of the three parchment scrolls.

He handed the pen to Mistress Kaya. She reached for it, but he pulled it back slightly, saying, "I've seen the way you sign things. You'll need to add more of a flourish. Your name is short, and if you sign it simply as you usually do, it won't be sufficient. The spell requires more . . . *traction* on the parchment to do its work."

"Seriously?"

"Quite."

She nodded and took the pen. She approached the first scroll with some hesitation. "I should read these, shouldn't I?"

"Probably," he said. "But I doubt it would help you. The contract incantation is written in the best Orzhov legalese. It would take years of study as an advokist to truly decipher its ramifications. Fortunately, I've had years of study as an advokist, so if you trust me . . ."

She nodded absently but still didn't sign.

"Is there another problem?" he asked.

"Yes, you've got me overthinking my signature now. Goddess, it's one word, four letters. What exactly do you expect?"

"You could employ your last name."

"No. I really can't." Before he could speak, she held up a hand. "It's complicated. But trust me; for now I may only go by Kaya."

He waved his hand in the air. "Then . . . just get a little fancy with it."

"Please just sign, mistress," a semi-desperate Rat said. The prolonged wait for the answers she sought was making her antsy.

Mistress Kaya nodded again and leaned over the first scroll. She signed, finishing off the final *a* with a circle surrounding the entire name. "Will that do?"

"Yes, mistress," he said.

She quickly signed the other two contracts in the same fashion. By the third, she had gotten quite good at it. Mister Vrona took the pen from her and placed it on the table beside the kris. He then took her left hand in his, picked up the inkwell with his right hand and poured the ink-blood mixture over both their left hands while chanting something low and ancient. Instead of spilling, the liquid was absorbed into their skin. The writing on the central scroll disappeared from its parchment and began to manifest like tattoos on their left hands and all the way up their arms.

As the writing faded from—or was absorbed back into—their epidermises, Mistress Kaya inhaled deeply and straightened up to her full height, a broad smile manifesting on her face. Simultaneously, *Master* Vrona's shoulders stooped; he cringed and groaned.

"It worked. I'm free," Mistress Kaya said. "The debtors' contracts, they're . . ." She turned and looked at him and her smile rapidly faded.

"Yes, I feel them. I have them. The burden is somewhat worse than I had anticipated."

Mistress Kaya shook her head. "I tried to warn you."

"Yes, you did."

"Well, let's undo this. We'll find another way."

"No, mistress. I can handle it."

"Tomik, you're my friend. And I wouldn't burden my worst enemy with this."

"It's only temporary. I can tough it out." He straightened up to *his* full height. "You'll see. I'll make you proud."

"That's not the issue."

"It'll be fine."

"Are you certain?"

"Quite certain, mistress."

"Am I to call you Master now or can we both just use our names?"

"Tomik would suit me fine . . . Kaya."

"Thank you. Thank you for everything."

"I'm happy I can be of service. I was raised to be a servitor, you know."

Madame Blaise shook her head and murmured, "A servitor as acting guildmaster. Who could have predicted such a thing?" She approached him, took his left hand and performed her bit of healing magic on his finger.

"Thank you, madame."

"I'm happy to be of service, Master," Madame Blaise echoed.

"I'll see you off now," Master Vrona said.

"Mistress Kaya, please . . ." Rat pleaded, with her voice, her eyes, her entire posture.

"All right, follow me," Mistress Kaya said and led her growing entourage back to her suites, where, taking Rat by the hand, she lowered the young girl into an overstuffed armchair and sat down on the matching chair across from her.

"Now, child. Listen—"

"I'm listening. I've been ready to listen for hours and hours and hours."

Teyo said, "I only found you and told you there was something to hear an hour ago."

Rat glared at him.

He started to laugh and then covered his mouth.

"All right, all right," Mistress Kaya said, smiling. "Here's the thing—"

Suddenly the room was filled with red flames, and Miss Jaya Ballard appeared amid them. Bilagru reached for his weapon, but Mistress Kaya rose and waved him back as the blaze was sucked right back into Miss Ballard, and she stumbled forward weakly. Teyo had to catch her and help her onto a settee.

Rat leapt to her feet in a fit of frustration.

You have got to be kidding me! Not now!

Mistress Kaya said, "Jaya, are you all right?"

"Fine, fine. I've planeswalked back and forth and back today from Kaladesh."

"You must be exhausted."

"It's . . . a lot. But give me a minute—or ten—and I can lead you to Liliana's home on Dominaria."

"We're not going straight to Dominaria. We need to go to Gobakhan first. To bring Teyo home."

"No," Miss Ballard said firmly. "No detours. I want—*I need*—to get this over with."

"It's not up for debate, Jaya. Teyo's never planeswalked with intention before. I promised him I'd help him, and I mean to keep that promise."

Teyo frowned and looked tense. Rat could feel his concerns and, momentarily forgetting her own, said, "He's afraid his abbot may not welcome him back."

Teyo gaped at her with wide eyes.

"Well, am I wrong?"

"No."

"Okay, then."

Mistress Kaya tried to reassure him. "That's why the three of us will be there to explain things for you."

Miss Ballard, not seeing Rat, asked, "*Three* of us?"

Now it was Rat's turn to gape with wide eyes: "*Three* of us?"

With clear satisfaction, Mistress Kaya smiled at Rat and stated, "*Three* of us." Once again, she took Rat's hands in hers. "I know you're very lonely . . ."

"I wouldn't say—"

"And I know you manage your . . . *condition* the best you can. But it doesn't change the fact that you spend most of your life in a kind of solitary confinement. And with Hekara's situation changing, well, it's just not fair."

"Aw, everyone's got whatever what they've got to deal with, I guess."

"They do. But something about whatever what *you* deal with reminds me a little of myself when I was just a little bit younger than you are now. Besides, I owe you. You saved my life—more than once—yesterday. More important, I flat-out like your company."

"Who in the Nine Hells is she talking to?" Miss Ballard asked.

No one answered or explained.

Rat wiped at her eyes and said, "There's some pity involved in this. I kinda never wanted to be an object of pity, you know?"

"Do you want to hear my plan or not?" Mistress Kaya asked wryly.

"Oh, I want to hear."

"Okay. So. Here's the thing. Normally, Planeswalkers can't take anything or anyone organic across the Blind Eternities to another world."

Miss Ballard eyed her suspiciously, "What do you mean 'normally'?"

"I'm the exception. I can safely take *one* person or creature by ghosting into my spirit form and simultaneously extending my necro-magic to include my passenger—much as I do when I extend my magic over my dagger or my clothes."

"You cannot," Miss Ballard and Rat said, almost simultaneously, though with very different tones.

"I can, though. I first did it by accident with my cat Janah, who jumped into my arms at the precise moment I was about to planeswalk. Cat. Rat. Same principle."

"I can . . . go with you?"

"If you want, but I have to warn you the process is exhausting and dangerous. Still, if all goes well, I should be able to bring you back to Ravnica after the job to kill Liliana Vess has been completed."

Rat glanced over at a frustrated Teyo and swallowed hard. She wasn't really on board with the killing of Miss Raven-Hair, who had after all killed Bolas. On the other hand, a lot of Ravnicans died because of her, and by the code of the clan she was raised in that meant Miss Vess deserved death. But the part of Rat that felt a kinship with Selesnya wasn't quite as sure.

On the fourth hand, my Rakdos side thinks the trip'll be a blast, you know? And more than that, I get to stay with my friends.

Mistress Kaya asked, "Still worried whether I'm motivated by pity?"

"Is it horrible that I don't care?"

"No."

"Then I can live with whatever what motivates you."

"Good. But for the record, sympathy and empathy are not the same as pity. Not really. And again, I think you're damn useful in a crisis."

"I like being useful."

"I know."

Miss Ballard cleared her throat. "I take it there's someone else here that I can't see."

Madame Blaise, of all people, attempted to explain. "It's Mistress Rat, a close friend of Guildmaster Kaya's. She's invisible and unhearable to most people, though I'm told if you know where she is—presumably right in front of Mistress Kaya at the moment—and focus, you might be able to see her. I've been trying, however, and haven't succeeded yet."

"Uh-huh," Miss Ballard said, already sounding somewhat

grim. "Kaya and . . . Rat. You should think twice about this. I've seen *ghosts* die in the Blind Eternities. This is a dangerous game you're playing at. Or talking about playing at."

"I'm not playing," Mistress Kaya said, "but she's right, Rat. This is extremely risky. I want to make sure you understand that."

"And Ravnica's so safe?" Rat asked.

"It's safer now than it was yesterday, particularly for you. You know how to operate here. As Ral would say, you have the place wired. That won't be true on other worlds like Gobakhan and Dominaria. And that's assuming you make it to either or both alive."

"Are you taking the offer back?"

"No."

"Then I'm going with you."

With both of you.

Teyo asked, "Do you need to tell your mother first?"

"Nah. She's used to not seeing me for weeks at a time."

And if I don't survive, she'll eventually forget all about me. And maybe that would be for the best. No sense in her suffering over my loss. Not such a great loss anyway, right?

"We can go right now, if you want," Rat said.

Mistress Kaya looked to Miss Ballard. "You up to a planes-walk?"

Miss Ballard rose stiffly. "I suppose. But I've never been to this Gobakhan. I can't lead you there."

"I haven't been there, either. So Teyo, you'll have to show us the way."

Teyo looked panicked. "I—I don't know how. I've only ever planeswalked once before, and I've *never* done it on purpose. I have no idea how to get to Gobakhan."

"You do, though," Mistress Kaya said. "Just think of home, summon your, um, *geometry*—and decide you're going back. It'll work, and we'll be right behind you. Trust me."

"I trust you," he said, sounding very much like he didn't—or didn't trust himself not to mess it up.

"Rat, come here. Put your arms around my waist."

Rat did as instructed, and Mistress Kaya wrapped her cloak around them both tightly. Then she put her arms around Rat's back and pulled her close. "Go, Teyo," she said. "Just think of your home on Gobakhan."

Rat turned her head to face Teyo, who closed his eyes. Then he seemed to explode into white translucent spheres and cylinders and cubes, his body reduced to its elementary geometry. The shapes rapidly *pop, pop, popped* away, and he was gone.

Miss Ballard followed suit in flame.

Mistress Kaya warned, "Keep your eyes shut tight and whatever happens, *do not let go*! Understand?"

"Uh-huh," Rat said breathlessly.

Then with a nod to Madame Blaise, Chief Bilagru and Master Vrona, Mistress Kaya's entire body turned violet and incorporeal, with the field of her magic extending through her to encompass Rat, as well.

A second later, they'd left Ravnica behind . . .

TWENTY-FIVE

JACE BELEREN

Jace planeswalked back to Ravnica, directly into Vraska's royal bedchamber.

He had been hoping to find her there—and hoping there were things they could do there together—but wasn't exactly surprised to find that the Golgari queen wasn't confining herself to her chambers in the middle of the day.

He exited the room and nearly walked right into Storrev.

"Excuse me, Master Beleren," she whispered. "I was not aware you were here."

"I just got back."

"And will you be staying with us . . . long?"

"That's up to your queen, I suppose. For the time being, I have nowhere else to go."

"Ah, yes, your embassy was destroyed."

"It was. And in any case, it's not my embassy anymore. What-ever's left of it—save for a handful of books—belongs to the Fire-mind now."

"Of course."

"The queen?"

"Yes?"

"Where is she?"

"Wherever it suits her, I imagine. I do not question the move-ments of my sovereign."

"Storrev, you're taking a simple question and making it com-plicated. I think you know my feelings for Queen Vraska. And her feelings for me. I simply want to see her."

"I am aware of all these things, Master Beleren."

Jace waited, but the Erstwhile said nothing more. Beginning to get cross, he said, "You're intentionally obfuscating. Another thing I don't doubt you're aware of is my abilities. Perhaps you think they won't work on the undead, but you'd be wrong on that account. Tell me where Vraska is, or I'll *take* the infor-mation from your mind. And it will not be pleasant, I assure you."

"You may do as you must," she said stoically, "but I will not willingly betray the confidences of my queen and mistress."

"Confidences she's keeping from me?"

"You are better suited to answer that than I, Master."

Jace glared at her.

She whispered, "Would you prefer if I stood still for the . . . procedure?"

Jace shook his head. When push came to shove, he couldn't bring himself to telepathically force intelligence from the loyal Storrev.

I don't want to be that *guy anymore.*

"Then may I go?" Storrev asked.

Jace nodded.

"Thank you, Master Beleren."

She glided off, and Jace watched her depart.

He had his suspicions about what Vraska might be up to, and if he was right, he'd have an extremely difficult decision on his hands . . .

TWENTY-SIX

LILIANA VESS

The ravens were starting to gather again as Liliana approached ever closer to the House of Vess, which had clearly been repaired and restored immaculately.

Who did this? Who gave permission for this . . . desecration . . . of the symbol of my ruin?

Though her despair had hardly gone away, her immediate curiosity held it off for the time being, and she was consciously grateful to have an excuse to think about something else.

Keep going . . . get to the bottom of this . . . Move . . .

She sensed a magical force at work, which she couldn't quite identify.

Another riddle . . .

Once again, the Onakke spirits in the Chain Veil made their propositions: *Unleash us, Vessel. We will punish all trespassers, as we punished the souls of Ravnica . . .*

No . . . don't say that . . .

Instantly all the guilt and shame and self-disgust came flooding back, practically overwhelming her. She had never been one to wallow—or even linger—on such emotions.

Now it's all I can see . . .

It was still tempting to let the Veil and its spirits use her as their vessel—not to punish any trespassers but simply to abdicate all future responsibility for her life.

They could hardly do a worse job . . .

"Milady," a voice hissed at her from the shadows.

Now who?

Liliana turned and saw an old woman waving to her from within a copse of dying skeletal trees. "Milady, over here."

A person, just a person . . .

Distracted once more, Liliana crossed to join the woman. She was dressed as a peasant but had a thick gold collar around her neck. "Who are you to address me?" Liliana said haughtily, just to see if she could still present such a façade.

Hopeless, hopeless vanity . . .

"My name's Karina, milady. Karina Témoin. And I'm only trying to help you, save you. Don't go any nearer to that mansion, I beg of you, child." As she spoke, the golden collar began to glow. Liliana could feel waves of heat flowing off it into the night air. The collar was searing the old woman's throat. Yet, with a grimace, she fought through the pain to offer her warning: "It's not safe, young stranger. You must run away before you're caught by my mistress. The mistress of that house." She pointed at the mansion and then stifled a cry of pain. Liliana could smell the woman's flesh burning under the collar. Karina sank to her knees.

No. Stop. Don't do this for me. I can't carry any more weight . . .

Half expecting the woman to disintegrate before her eyes, Liliana began to get angry. She grasped at the emotion and, her face darkening, knelt beside Karina and demanded, "Who is your mistress?"

Give me a target . . .

Karina Témoin shook her head, gasping for breath.

Give me a target . . .

Liliana repeated, "Tell me now, Madame Témoin. Who is the mistress of the House of Vess?"

Give. Me. A. Target.

Karina managed to gasp out, "She is the Curse returned, child. She is the hated Liliana Vess."

PART TWO

HUNTERS

TWENTY-SEVEN

RAT

There was a second, a split second, when Rat—eyes shut tight—thought, *This isn't so bad.* but a splitsecondlater everythingchanged . . .

AraithiaShoktacrossedtheBlindEternitieswrappedinMistress Kaya'scloakandMistressKaya'sarms.Asinstructed,she*kept*her eyesshuttightandheldonfordearlife.Buttheexperiencewas unlikeanythingshe'deverknownorbeenthroughbefore.Rat*felt* asifherbodywasbleedingintoKaya's,andshe*knew*hermindhad psychicallymergedwiththeMistress'forafewseconds(afewseconds thatseemedlikeablindeternity).ForRat,thesensationwasboth unpleasantandreassuring.Shelearnedfromhercompanion'sown psychethatMistressKayatrulycaredaboutRatandwasafraidfor her.ShealsolearnedthatKayahad*lost*hercatwhileplaneswalking, whichwasconsiderablylessreassuring.Theybecame,inthose moments,onebeing,oneentity.NotMistressKayaandAraithia

ShoktabutKayaandRat,RatandKaya,withnospacebetweenwhere
oneendedandtheotherbegan.Theunitywasunnerving,enthralling,
exciting,terrifying,thrillingandhorrible.Itwentonforeverastheir
mindsandbodiesstretchedacrosseternityinanendlessdanceof
partnerlessoneness.*Anendlessdanceofusasme.*Rathadlostherself
andfoundvherotherself.ShewasaguildmasterandGateless,an
assassin,athief,acountess,avagrant,insignificantandrenowned,
neverallowedtoescapethecurseofher(orherortheir)birth.Andjust
whenitseemedthatthisnewlifeformhadbecomepermanent . . .

RatandKaya abruptly manifested into real space, real time,
as Rat and Kaya. They practically threw each other apart, and
both wound up on their hands and knees, breathing hard and
retching, though neither actually vomited.

Rat tried to stand but found she couldn't. The journey had
drained her completely. Apparently, Mistress Kaya was in a similar state.

I hate her!

*What? No, I love her! What she's done for me. What she risked
for me. What she's shown me. No one's ever . . . Ever . . . Ever
what? That feeling . . . It . . . It's rushing away . . .*

Everything was so confused. Rat had a splitting headache.

'Cuz, you know, my head—our *head*—*just split. We were one.
Now we're two again. Goddess, I'm so confused. Wait, "Goddess"?
What Goddess?*

Kaya's memories—Mistress Kaya's memories—were quickly
fading, receding from Rat's consciousness. Perhaps all of her secrets were likewise fading from Kaya's mind. It felt like a great
loss, as when she had thought Hekara dead. Kaya was dying
away from her. Dying out inside her. All that proximity, that
complete inclusion, that oneness with someone who cared for
her, loved her, was being extinguished. Rat felt tears forming in
her eyes . . .

She rolled over onto her back, blinked several times and

looked up. A blurry wet Teyo, looking and feeling terribly concerned, was leaning over her. His mouth opened and closed several times soundlessly. Or maybe she just wasn't ready to hear him yet. Eventually, after a few more blinks had blinked away whatever what had made him look blurry and wet, he said, or eventually she heard, "Rat—*Araithia*—are you all right?"

She nodded, or at least meant to.

He spoke again, more slowly: "Are . . . you . . . all . . . right?"

"I think so," she managed. She heard her voice. It sounded strange. Not at all like Kaya's.

Well, of course you don't sound like Kaya!

"Can I help you up?" he asked.

"In a second."

"I'm fine, too. Thanks for asking." It was Miss Ballard's voice. Rat managed to turn her head and saw Jaya Ballard lying beside her and groaning. She said, "I haven't planeswalked this many times in one day since before the Mending."

From Rat's other side, Mistress Kaya croaked out, "Sounds exhausting." Rat turned her head the other way. Kaya—her Kaya, her . . . —was lying on her side with her eyes closed, chuckling to herself. "And how are you, Teyo Verada?"

Rat looked up again. Teyo said, "Fine. I'm fine." He sounded embarrassed about it.

"And is this Gobakhan?"

"It had better be," Miss Ballard said.

"Yes," Teyo said. "We're in the garden of the Order. My Order. I mean the Order of the Shieldmage. I'm an acolyte here. Or at least I was. So, you see, it's not *my* garden, though I've spent a considerable amount of time working in it . . ." He was running at the mouth, talking very fast.

Who does he think he is? Me?

Rat said, "You can help me up now."

He knelt quickly and slipped his arms under her shoulders,

propping her up into a sitting position. He was starting to lift her to her feet, but she said, "Easy. This'll do for now, thanks."

He said, "Right, right," and held still for her. She made an effort to breathe. To feel herself breathing again as the Rat. As just the Rat.

She looked around. They were indeed in a garden, a carefully tended garden of root vegetables and succulents, of grapevines and a handful of fruit trees. It wasn't exactly of Selesnyan quality, but it was clear that someone or many someones had worked very hard to maintain it. Teyo included, apparently. The sky was a cloudless pale blue. Twin suns were low on the horizon. It was early morning . . . or maybe late afternoon.

Wait, twin suns?

"We're on Gobakhan, aren't we?"

"Yes."

"We're on another world!"

"Now you know how I felt."

"This is amazing!"

"I promise you that Gobakhan is not nearly as amazing as Ravnica. I fear you'll be bored here quite soon."

"I doubt that."

"It's true. Ravnica is full of wonders. Gobakhan is dull as sand. Like me, I suppose."

"You're like Gobakhan?"

"Yes. Too much like Gobakhan."

"Does that mean I'm like Ravnica?"

"To me, you *are* Ravnica."

She punched him, but she was still weak. He didn't even say *ow*.

"Am I full of wonders?" she asked him, looking away.

"Full of wonders."

She punched him again. "Full of something, anyway. The both of us."

"I'm only getting one side of this conversation," Miss Ballard said, "and I still want to tell this boy to get a room."

"Stop being so grumpy," Mistress Kaya said. "Try to remember your first planeswalk."

"My first planeswalk was not nearly so pleasant."

"Then try to remember your first pleasant one."

Despite herself, Miss Ballard chuckled. "Fine," she said. "I will endeavor to be less of a curmudgeon. How was your first intentional planeswalk, boy?"

Teyo looked adorably embarrassed again. "I'm not sure I should say."

"Why not?"

"Because the three of you all seem so beaten down by it."

Mistress Kaya said, "How was it, Teyo?"

He laughed. "Exhilarating? Thrilling? I don't think I have the words. But I'd like to do it again."

"I'm not going anywhere for at least a few hours," Miss Ballard said, with a curmudgeonly wave of an arm.

Rat was studying him. She said, "You're worried about what comes next. What our reception will be like."

Somewhat reluctantly, he nodded.

She looked around. "It'll be all right. This is where you were raised. And you came out okay, so there must be good folks here."

"Yes . . ."

"I mean, you know what my crazy life is like, and I can always go home and find welcome."

"There are people there who love you."

"So there must be people *here* that love *you*."

He looked down and bit his lip. Clearly, he wasn't sure that was true.

She took his hand and squeezed it. He looked up and smiled at her gratefully.

There are people here who love you now. One person, at least . . .

"Teyo?"

All four of them turned. A young minotaur, dressed exactly as Teyo was dressed, stood five yards away, staring at his fellow acolyte.

"Hi, Peran," Teyo said sheepishly.

"By the Storm, what happened to you? *We all thought you were dead!*"

TWENTY-EIGHT

LILIANA VESS

Karina Témoin continued to urge Liliana Vess to flee Caligo before Liliana Vess caught and collared her. The more she spoke against her mistress, the hotter her collar became.

What does this mean?

"Your words . . . they trigger this punishment?" Liliana asked, with more fascination than horror.

That's fairly sophisticated spellwork.

Karina nodded and winced in pain. "I'm not supposed to speak against the mistress. But milady, please, you must not stay. I wouldn't wish this life on my worst enemy."

I know the feeling.

"Not even on Liliana Vess," Liliana Vess said.

Because I might . . .

"Well." Karina grimaced. "Maybe I'd make an exception for that one." The collar glowed brightly, and the woman bit her hand hard enough to draw blood in order to stifle her cry of pain.

More pain in service to Liliana Vess.

Suddenly Liliana realized what an unfeeling excuse for a human being she was. "Stop talking," she urged the servant. "Here, let me help you." Liliana grasped Karina's bleeding hand in hers, pulling mana from the blood and willing that energy up to the woman's neck and throat. It seemed to soothe the burn.

Well, look at that. I'm good *for something.*

Karina's eyes went wide. "You're a healer, milady?"

A healer. Please. Though I studied to be a healer once . . . less than a hundred yards from here, more than a hundred years from here . . .

"Something like that," Liliana responded. Of course, all she had done was redirect the woman's own life force to address the more significant source of pain. It was a zero-sum game. But it had served its purpose. And Liliana felt *somewhat* better herself—somewhat better *about* herself—for having done it. "Where can I take you?"

Let me do one good thing . . .

Karina shook her head, clearly about to urge Liliana to run away again.

No!

Liliana said, "Don't speak. I understand. But I can't leave you here in this condition. There must be somewhere I can take you, madame."

One good thing . . .

The woman looked on Liliana with pity and some little gratitude.

The first and last person to do that in a few decades.

Finally, Karina nodded her head toward an outbuilding a few hundred yards from the mansion. Supporting the old woman, Liliana helped her along. It continued to actually feel good to help her.

I must be pathetically needy.

As they drew closer, Liliana attempted to still her thoughts and asked, "The servants' quarters?"

Karina nodded again.

They entered. It was a kind of bunkhouse. There must have been nearly a hundred souls living in these cramped quarters. Most were asleep. A few were preparing to sleep. A few more were getting up to do whatever service was required of them. Every single one wore a gold collar exactly like Madame Témoin's.

These aren't servants. They're prisoners.

"Tell me what happened here," Liliana commanded.

A passing servant looked instantly panicked and shook her head violently to warn Karina off from speaking.

Another said, "Who is this woman?"

"I think I've seen her in town," said a third.

Of course, none of them thought for a moment that she might be Liliana Vess.

Karina said, "I found her stumbling through the swamp. She was headed for the mansion."

"Then let her," said an old man who was pulling on his boots.

"Just tell me what happened," Liliana repeated. "Certainly you can relate plain facts without saying anything that would result in punishment."

Karina seemed to consider this. Then she nodded. "Yes. If I choose my words carefully, I should be all right."

"Please. I don't want you to hurt yourself for my sake."

I have enough guilt, thank you very much.

Karina shook her self-bitten hand. Now that her neck burns had eased, it was clearly smarting. But she managed to ignore it. "Let's see," she began. "I believe it started just after word came of the destruction of the Cabal's lich knight."

"Yes," Liliana said as neutrally as she could manage, "I've heard of him. I'd . . . heard of his demise." Liliana knew that the *"lich knight"* referred to was Josu. He had been her first victim. She had loved her brother dearly and had sought to save his life, but instead she had cursed him with madness and had been forced to kill him herself. The Cabal later raised him as a lich, and Liliana had been forced to kill him all over again. But as he had died for the second and final time, he had told her she was a curse upon their family.

A curse upon anyone or anything I ever care about—even (especially) upon myself.

"For a brief time," Karina was saying, "life in Caligo was good. But nature must indeed abhor a vacuum. Or at least evil does. Will-o'-the-Wisps began appearing every night in unusually high numbers. I'm sure you know the story . . ."

"Story?"

"From *The Fall of the House of Vess.* Everyone knows it."

Liliana swallowed hard and said, "It's been some time for me. Could you refresh my memory?"

Karina laughed ruefully. "I certainly can. I know the tale by heart, I do. My old nan read it to me on stormy nights when I was young. To keep me in my bed."

"Did it work?"

"On me, yes. Others weren't as cautious."

"Or as wise."

Karina nodded her thanks and then looked toward the ceiling, summoning up the passage, which she then recited from memory: *"On dark nights you can still see the light of the Vess girl's lantern out in the Caligo, seeking her lost brother. Those who follow are doomed to join her endless search."*

Liliana wondered who had authored this *Fall of the House of Vess* and how she or he had gotten everything so wrong and so right, simultaneously.

Karina said, "Everyone knows this passage, and no one was foolish enough to follow the Wisps. But this time we didn't have to follow them. They converged at the cemetery, and *she* appeared."

"Who?"

"The Curse of the House of Vess."

"Liliana?" Liliana asked with renewed fascination.

"Liliana," Karina confirmed.

Other "servants" began to back away.

The old man with the boots warned Karina, "Watch your tongue, you old fool."

"I speak no treason by simply relating what happened," Karina said in a secretive whisper that indicated less confidence than she pretended to. "Besides, I think the mistress likes for folks to know who she is." The fact that Karina's collar wasn't heating up seemed to confirm her conclusion—for now. "Liliana's first servants were the raised dead. Long dead. Thankfully, no one we loved or even recognized as having died in our lifetime was abused in this way."

"Thankfully," Liliana echoed. "I assume there was a fight."

"Of course. But Liliana Vess' zombies were capable of surviving blow after blow without the slightest damage—"

"You mean they took the damage and kept coming?"

"No, milady. I meant what I said. They were invulnerable."

Invulnerable zombies?

"We were all forced to surrender. Collars were placed around our necks, and we were forced to serve, to rebuild the mansion, farm the lands. Everything."

"I don't understand. Why does this 'Liliana' need living thralls if she has undead servants. Did she release them back to their graves?"

"I have no idea where most of her undead minions went. A few still guard her person, but the rest just disappeared."

"I see. She has a few with her now? Right now?"

"Half a dozen or so. Right across the grass in the main house."

Liliana reached out then with her magics but could sense no undead activity in the area. None. Period.

This is all very strange.

Karina said, "Now will you go, milady?"

Liliana didn't answer. She thought about Karina's story for a long time. Finally, she said, "I want to meet this 'Liliana Vess.'"

TWENTY-NINE

RAL ZAREK

Ral Zarek and the Wanderer slowly crossed the ruins of the city of Naktamun on the plane of Amonkhet. They saw no people. No Eternals. No remains. Only ash and fallen stone. Crumbling pyramids and broken obelisks. Had a single building been left intact and standing?

Bolas did this. This is what he had in store for Ravnica, if he had beaten us, if he had won.

Feeling a brief wave of relief—or maybe gratitude—Ral turned his mind back to the task at hand, the hunt for Bolas' minion Tezzeret. "Anything?"

From under her hat, the Wanderer said, "I think we're headed in the right direction, but I need to find the exact spot from which Tezzeret planeswalked away."

"Then you passed it," a third voice said. They turned to look.

It was Samut, the planeswalking warrior of Amonkhet. She said, "I can show you. Follow me."

She turned and climbed over a block of sandstone. They followed.

"How'd you find us?" Ral asked as he climbed up behind her.

"Hazoret, the God-Survivor, sensed your arrival and your intent. She sent me to guide you." She climbed over more crumbling stone with Ral and the Wanderer close at heel. Placing one foot wrong, he turned his ankle slightly, and the weight of the Accumulator on his back nearly threw him off balance. He corrected quickly and cinched the device tighter. He had a battle to fight, and he couldn't risk being off balance for a moment.

The Wanderer hadn't been too far off course. Soon enough, Samut stopped and said, "Here. This is where Karn, Ob Nixilis, Dack Fayden and I confronted Tezzeret, disrupted his Planar Bridge and sent him scurrying away."

"Yes," the Wanderer said, "I sense his path."

"I sense nothing," Samut said. "It's been too long."

"Not for me."

"How is that?" Samut asked—or rather, demanded.

The Wanderer said nothing.

"It's a fair question," Ral said. "I'm putting my cause, perhaps my life, in your hands. That's a significant amount of trust for a man like me to offer up without *some* reciprocation."

She sighed heavily. Or at least he presumed that she sighed. He could never see her mouth move, as she kept her face carefully hidden behind her hair or her hat—or both.

"It is my nature," she said finally. "My nature, my gift, my curse. You are both Planeswalkers. Except perhaps for the first time you 'walked, it is a *choice* you make to travel between planes. I am the Wanderer. For me, planeswalking is my natural state. You choose to leave, but I must choose to stay."

"I don't understand," Samut said.

"In order to planeswalk, you must decide to do so," the Wanderer said, her voice growing impatient. "In order for me *not* to planeswalk, I must choose not to. In order for me to remain on any one plane, I have to concentrate on *not* planeswalking."

"Even now?" Samut asked, stunned.

"Even now, I am expending some effort in order to remain here with you. It's nothing heroic. Nothing I'm not used to. But if I lose focus on this world for even a moment, I am gone."

Ral stared at her, longing to meet her hidden eyes and see what secrets they might hold. The ramifications of her existence were . . . *astounding* and not a little horrifying. "How do you sleep?" he asked.

"All I know for sure is that I wake up on a different plane every time."

"Wow" was all he could say.

Samut was slightly more coherent: "And all this planeswalk-ing . . . doesn't it exhaust you?"

"No. Not physically, that is. It is considerably more draining for me to attempt to stay in one place for any period of time."

"So yesterday," Ral said, "when the Immortal Sun was in play . . . ?"

"It was . . . an odd sensation. I didn't have to work to stay. The Sun held me on Ravnica, whether I wanted to be there or not. But I felt vaguely nauseated all day long. Fortunately, the battle provided some distraction. I absorb kinetic energy, and that helped settle my stomach."

"Wow," he said again. He knew he must sound like an idiot, but no other word seemed appropriate.

"In any case, my condition makes me uniquely attuned to the Blind Eternities. I feel every ripple across it, and I can sense a Planeswalker's path for far longer than either of you. Far longer than any typical Planeswalker."

"Is there really such a thing," Samut whispered almost to her-self, "as a *typical* Planeswalker?"

"To me there is," said the Wanderer. "To me, you are all of a piece. All of you *except* Tezzeret. The technology—the Planar Bridge technology specifically—that he has built into his person makes his trail even more unique, obvious and long lasting than the rest of your lot. Moreover, as you said, the bridge is damaged. Leaking. Given that, his path is simplicity itself for me to follow."

So that's how she's tracking him. Doesn't exactly explain why she's tracking him. Does she truly believe in Ravnican vengeance? Or does she have her own agenda? What history does she share with Tezzeret? Will I be forced to compete with her for the kill?

"I am locked on his path now," she said, turning toward Ral. He could almost, almost, see her face. It was almost tantalizing. "Are you ready?" she asked.

Truthfully, they had only arrived on Amonkhet twenty minutes or so ago. Planeswalking again this soon would weary him.

And what were the odds that their next stop would be Tezzeret's final destination?

But the idea of getting on with it also had its appeal. He turned to Samut and thanked her and her deity for their help. She bowed her head in acknowledgment.

Then he nodded to the Wanderer.

She planeswalked away, and like any *typical* Planeswalker, Ral Zarek followed her lead and her trail, leaving Samut, Naktamun and Amonkhet behind.

THIRTY

VRASKA

Ever since Jaya Ballard had led them to Dovin Baan's home on Kaladesh (before returning to Ravnica to help Kaya), Vivien Reid had been tracking the vedalken for Vraska.

The two of them were making their way through the city of Ghirapur, following in broad daylight the barely noticeable blood trail that Baan had left behind in the dead of night. Jaya had warned Vraska that there were no gorgons native to Kaladesh, so Vraska was expecting the same kind of response she'd always received on Ravnica. Fear. No one liked to encounter a monster loose on the streets. And Vraska had long ago been trained to regard herself as a monster. The label had defined her for so long, from her earliest childhood memories, that at some point she had begun behaving like a monster. A killer. An assassin. A traitor. The kind of creature that would achieve her goals by any means necessary, no matter who was hurt along the way.

She had her hood up over her head and pulled down low over her brow, hoping it would hide her tendrils and eyes, hoping it would hide *what she was*, long enough for her to find Baan, kill him and get out.

Last thing I need is to start a panic.

Focused as she was on these bitter thoughts, she nearly tripped over a young girl, of maybe seven or eight years, who was playing some version of kanala—a game of marbles and chalk—on the ground. Vraska had clear memories of playing kanala as a small gorgon, though she had *more* memories of her *exclusion* from the pastime, even by her own Golgari peers, especially by the devkarin elves and humans, who had been taught their superiority to all other members of the Swarm on their mothers' knees—if not in their mothers' wombs.

The crouching girl, a glass shooter of swirling blue trapped between two fingers, looked up at Vraska with big brown eyes. Immediately Vraska realized that from the girl's low angle, she could see right up into Vraska's hood. Any second, she would see what Vraska was and scream. It took tremendous willpower on Vraska's part *not* to summon up the golden light behind her eyes, all her willpower to thwart the knee-jerk impulse to turn this playing child to stone for the simple crime of being in the gorgon's way.

On the other hand, she was perfectly prepared to draw her cutlass and threaten the girl into silence.

None of which was necessary. The child stared right into Vraska's eyes and tilted her head. She reached out a hand with such simple innocence that Vraska found her own hand leave the hilt of her sword in order to help the girl to her feet.

This human child with dark hair, dark skin and dark eyes smiled up at the Queen of the Golgari and said, "You're different."

Vraska swallowed. For a moment, she felt as if *she* were seven or eight years old, holding her breath to see if she'd be rejected one more time.

The girl said, "You're so pretty."

She held out both arms, and Vraska picked her up. The girl reached out to remove Vraska's hood. The gorgon shook her head, and so instead the girl reached her hands into the hood and stroked Vraska's tendrils ever so gently.

The girl smiled.

Vraska smiled back.

Vivien broke the spell. "Are you coming?" she asked impatiently.

The guilds' chosen assassin hardened and nodded. Still, she was careful enough lowering the girl back to the ground. The girl held up the blue shooter as an offering, a gift.

Vraska whispered, "That's too precious, child. You should keep it."

The girl said, "I have three. And it's pretty like you."

Vraska held out her hand, palm up, and the girl dropped the marble into it. "What's your name?" she asked.

"Vraska," Vivien Reid said curtly, summoning her hunting partner, not answering the girl's question.

Ignoring her, the gorgon said, "I am Queen Vraska of the Golgari. What is your name, child?"

"If you're a queen, can I be your princess?"

"Yes. Yes, please."

"Then I am Princess Aesha."

"It is lovely to meet you, Princess Aesha."

The girl giggled.

"I have to go now," the queen said.

The princess nodded.

"Goodbye, Princess."

"Goodbye, Queen."

Vraska moved on, risking one last glance over her shoulder. Princess Aesha was already crouching over her kanala circle (or whatever they called it here) with another blue marble, taking aim. Vraska was already a memory or maybe already forgotten.

Still, the gorgon found herself smiling.

She came up alongside Vivien, who eyed her sardonically. "Making friends?"

Vraska felt suddenly invulnerable to any such cynicism. "Yes," she said. "That was Princess Aesha. We have sworn eternal loyalty to each other."

"Is there such a thing?"

"For at least a few minutes more, I will choose to believe there is." Vraska held up the blue marble. "See? She gave me her pledge."

"Mmm-hmm." She almost smirked.

Still following the scattered drops of blood, Vivien turned a corner. Vraska slipped the marble into her jacket pocket. Then patted it to make sure it was secure. She stayed even with Vivien, but her mind was still on Aesha. She wasn't fooling herself. The child was innocent, open. Not everyone on Kaladesh would have reacted as this princess had. Still, it was another taste of life free of Ravnican prejudice. She had had this on Ixalan, where she was a *respected* ship captain.

All right, fine, it was a pirate ship. But piracy's a respectable trade on Ixalan.

She and Jace had been happy there. Maybe happier than Vraska had ever been in her entire life. She thought about returning to Ixalan with him—or the two of them exploring Vryn together. Or going just about anywhere in the Multiverse—as long as it was *not* Ravnica and *with him*. She could never be free on Ravnica. Even as a queen, she would always be the monster there, the assassin, the killer.

Isn't this hunt ample evidence of that?

Vivien stopped at the edge of a river. She grasped her bow and nocked an arrow.

Vraska stayed her hand. "What are you doing? Who are you shooting at?"

"In a way, Dovin Baan." Shaking Vraska off, she let the arrow fly. With a dull thud, it struck the ground on the opposite bank. A glowing green spirit wolf emerged from the arrow and immediately began sniffing and snuffling among the wildflowers on the far shore.

It stopped and raised its head to howl. A soundless howl that still told the story.

There was a footbridge fifty yards upriver. They crossed and made their way back along the riverside. The spirit beast was just fading away when they arrived. Vivien pulled the arrow from the ground and used it to point at another drop of Dovin's blood near some trampled weeds. She said, "He crossed the river here last night. This way."

And they walked on. Into the countryside. Then they doubled back toward town. Then they zigzagged for twenty minutes.

Then Vivien stopped. She looked around. She studied the turf, the vegetation, the stones. She shook her head. "There's no further evidence or sign of Baan. I'm fairly certain he must have planeswalked from this spot."

"*Fairly* certain?"

"Certain, then. And it's been too long to follow his aether-trail. At least too long for me."

She looked at Vraska, who shrugged, silently acknowledging that she could do no better.

Vivien said, "Perhaps the Wanderer could be of some assistance after she gets back from helping Zarek."

"And how long will that take?" Vraska said, frustrated.

Now it was Vivien Reid's turn to shrug.

I want this over with, damnit.

"What will you do?" Vivien asked.

"What can I do? I'll return to Ravnica, where the Golgari require their queen."

After all, Ravnica is where the gorgon Vraska belongs.

THIRTY-ONE

DOVIN BAAN

Dovin Baan was *still* in hiding. He had departed his home on Kaladesh quickly, taking off into the night. The handful of souls on the street at that hour took no great notice nor gave a second thought to the blind vedalken in the hooded cloak.

Fortunately, Baan had an eidetic memory, allowing him to maneuver blindly through any location he had ever seen. For a time, Baan did everything he could to make his trail from home fairly obvious, so that any Planeswalker from Ravnica with half a brain would believe he was still in hiding on Kaladesh. Then Baan did everything he could to make following his trail next to impossible, so few would guess he had eventually planeswalked away.

Of course, even if they did guess, they'd never guess where

Baan planeswalked to: a safe house he kept on a most unlikely plane. He was fairly confident no one would think to look for him here.

But just in case someone did, Baan was ready.

Blind or not, there is much Dovin Baan can still see.

THIRTY-TWO

TEYSA KARLOV

N ow she met with all three together . . . after having already met in turn with each member of the Triumvirate separately, carefully playing on their fear and mistrust of one another to create unseen fissures in their relatively new alliance. That work done, it was now time to bring her message home.

"I believe we can agree," she said, locking eyes with first Morov then Zoltan then Maladola, "that we simply cannot have Kaya—a debt-forgiving outsider—as our guildmaster."

She received a nod of confirmation from each.

"Therefore," she continued, "we must take advantage of her being offworld to . . . slide the guild out from under the control of her proxy, Tomik Vrona."

Now Morov shook his head and wondered aloud, "I do marvel, milady, how your own assistant has slid out from under your thumb. Was that good management, I ask?"

Teysa smiled. "Perhaps you'll recall, my dear Pontiff, that my late grandfather Karlov and the Obzedat has had me confined—trapped, really—within these apartments under house arrest. A condition the Triumvirate has maintained since their passing, restricting my ability to manage guild problems . . . like Vrona. And since our previous failed attempt to oust Kaya, recent events have forced Tomik to spend much time elsewhere, thus escaping my influence and my *management*."

"This cannot be denied," Zoltan said to the other two, having been primed to believe that allying with the Karlov heir would elevate him above his two partners.

"Indeed not," said Maladola sharply, who'd been warned that Morov sought to limit the prestige of her sacred office.

Hence, Morov, caught off guard by the lack of support from his allies—and fearing, per *his* private consultation with Teysa, that the other two might team up to edge him out of power—was forced to concede, "Well, *erm*, yes. I . . . see your point. It is a situation we could perhaps rectify in good time."

"That would be appreciated, of course," Teysa said. "But even I must acknowledge we have more serious issues before us at this moment."

Looking relieved that she was not yet insisting on her freedom, they all nodded like parrots, spouting words like "Quite" and "Assuredly" and "Without a doubt."

Hiding her smile behind a stern and serious façade, Teysa continued: "We've all been very diplomatic up to this point, but let's speak frankly now. If we intend to plan another coup—for harsh as that word sounds, it is exactly what we need—then we must be confident of the full support of the guild in this coup's aftermath. Agreed?"

"Quite" and "Assuredly" and "Without a doubt."

"Meaning we'll need the power of the Triumvirate's offices *and* the Karlov name that I alone can provide. We'll need the influence I have—*and the pressure I can wield*—over the lesser families. The Morovs excepted, of course, as I'm sure, Armin, that your unquestioned authority over your cousin Lazlo and your great-aunt Esperanza will be enough to keep them in our corner," Teysa added diplomatically—while unsubtly reminding Armin that he wasn't the only Morov in town.

This time the pontiff offered up the "Quites" and "Assuredlys" and "Without a doubts" all on his own.

"Unfortunately, none of our influence and preparation will be worth an Izzet tinker's damn if, from the moment we succeed, the four of us begin infighting. It seems essential that we agree on the new guildmaster, that we choose her or him from among our party now."

This, as intended, caught all three off guard. No "Quites" or "Assuredlys" or "Without a doubts" were heard.

"Let me start by removing myself from consideration. All I want for my cooperation in this endeavor is a legal and binding magical guarantee of my freedom. To be signed here and now, in this room today. I do not believe that is an unreasonable request."

Relieved that they would not have to fight Teysa Karlov for guildmastery, the "Quites" and "Assuredlys" and "Without a doubts" returned in full force.

"I appreciate your indulgence, truly. You'll find the documents are prepared and ready on that table." Teysa snapped her fingers, and four identical scrolls magically unrolled, while four identical pens magically dipped themselves in four identical inkwells and then hovered in the air, waiting. It was a flourish of unnecessary magical nonsense designed to maintain the great Triumvirate's sense of their own illustrious importance, while simultaneously maintaining the momentum of her play—and her ploy.

It worked.

Ever the dashing gentleman, the vampire rose first and signed.

Not to be outdone, the angel followed suit.

Morov seemed slightly more reluctant, and Teysa briefly wondered if she had overplayed her hand with him. But it soon became clear that his reluctance had more to do with the effort it would take to launch himself out of his soft-cushioned chair than any other more pertinent scruple. So Teysa set a good example by milking the need for her cane as she hobbled over to sign her scroll. Morov, demonstrating how much more vibrant he was than the young-seeming Karlov heir, groaned like the old man he was and pushed himself onto his feet, strode to the table and signed with his unwithered hand.

Good. That's done.

"Thank you," Teysa said, once all four had resumed their seats. "Now, which of you three will lead the Orzhov into what I'm sure will be a grand new era of orthodox prosperity?"

The Triumvirate regarded one another with daggers for eyes. She had successfully made each one so suspicious of the other two, the outcome seemed inevitable. Still, she prompted it.

"Come now, my friends. Even as we sit here, Acting Guildmaster Vrona manages our diplomacy, our manpower, our *assets*. Certainly, we can at least come up with a temporary solution to our leadership issues."

Maladola took the bait. "Since with these contracts just signed, you have agreed to waive any permanent claim to power, *you* could be our temporary solution, Teysa. You could replace Vrona as acting guildmaster until the three of us have had the opportunity to settle this question among ourselves."

"No, no," Teysa protested. "I will not be your whipping boy. I will not be the straw man for you three to tear down as a show for the oligarchs and the rank and file."

"My darling Teysa, that is not our intent," said Slavomir. "If you remain neutral, we will support your rule for as long as necessary."

Morov weighed in with a caveat: "As long as you agree to step down when the time comes."

Teysa waved her hand at the table and the scrolls upon it. "I have no choice on that front, as you very well know, Armin. But I *can* choose not to expose myself to this treachery. You seek to catch me up, to use me as your pawn in whatever game you three are playing. I cannot yet see to the bottom of it. But I can tell you that Teysa Karlov is no one's pawn."

All three issued strong denials. In fact, since Teysa had previously pledged her allegiance to each in turn, they all were beginning to love this idea. To *adore* it. Each one believed that Teysa Karlov would act as an apparently independent temporary guildmaster, while secretly and subtly forwarding her or his agenda until enough power had been consolidated to overthrow the other two, at which point Teysa would be contractually obligated to step down and hand the guild over to her secret ally.

The meeting went on for twenty more minutes as they "wore her down," until with tremendous bitterness, suspicion and reluctance, she finally, begrudgingly acquiesced to their wishes.

"I will hold you to your promises today," Teysa said.

"Quite" and "Assuredly" and "Without a doubt."

Sitting back in her seat, Maladola said, "With the issue of ascension out of the way—"

"*Temporarily* out of the way," Teysa cut in edgily.

"Temporarily, yes. The question now becomes how to proceed. Should we assassinate Vrona?"

Seeming to calm down, Teysa also sat back and shook her head. "I've checked every bylaw, every statute, and I'm confident that won't work," she said. "His spirit will remain acting guildmaster even after death, and when Kaya returns, she'll simply get everything back. We'd have gained nothing and shown our hand."

Morov scowled: "If we can't kill him, then what?"

Teysa looked to Zoltan and said, "If we can't kill him . . . we enthrall him."

THIRTY-THREE

CHANDRA NALAAR

Jace had already left, as had most of the others.

But Chandra was still on Theros with Nissa, Ajani, Teferi and Karn, the latter of whom—despite being the living embodiment of stoicism—was (by his standards) impatient to get back to his mission to help the Mirran Resistance, or what was left of it, by scouting the plane of New Phyrexia.

"I have spent too much time away from this quest," he stated.

"I'd like to help you," Ajani said.

"Or at least hear more about what you have in mind," Teferi added.

Ajani nodded. "Such an endeavor *will* require careful planning."

Teferi said, "I would be honored to host all of you at the home of my daughter Niambi in Femeref on Dominaria, while we devise a workable strategy."

"That would be much appreciated," Ajani said.

Karn remained quiet for a good five seconds . . . then nodded curtly and said, "Yes."

Ajani shook his head and said, "There is a certain irony for me in having this discussion here of all places." Before explaining, he looked around and breathed in the night air. "Elspeth Tirel, my dear friend, was leader of the Mirran Resistance for a time. But once the New Phyrexians had solidified their power, she was forced to flee here. And here on Theros is where she died. I used to hate this plane." He glanced down at Gideon's cairn. "It's funny how one's view of things can change. Perhaps there are worse places to lay down one's burdens. Perhaps."

They stood in silence for a few moments.

Then Teferi turned to Chandra and Nissa. "Will you be joining us?"

Nissa shook her head slightly.

Chandra said stiffly, "Other things . . . require my attention first." The numbness was setting in again.

Ajani started to speak. Heading him off, Chandra quickly said, "But we will answer your call if you need us." It seemed to satisfy him, though Nissa shot her a look that indicated she didn't necessarily appreciate being included in that commitment.

"Chandra, will you be returning to Ravnica?" Teferi asked. "Do you think you'll see Jaya?"

"Yeah. Probably."

"Then you'll tell her where we've gone?"

"Sure. I mean, yes, I promise.

"Many thanks. Goodbye, ladies. Until we meet again." He planeswalked away.

Karn nodded slightly and followed.

Ajani gave Chandra a big hug and said, "If we need you, we'll call. But if *you* need Ajani Goldmane . . . ?"

"I won't hesitate," she said, forcing a smile for his sake.

He returned her offering with a decidedly unforced smile. Then he said goodbye to Nissa and departed Theros.

Without looking at the elf, Chandra said to her, "I assume you'll be returning to Zendikar now."

"Yes. You are welcome to come with me. If you like."

"I have unfinished business on Ravnica, but I'll come soon. I promise." She was making a lot of promises.

They approached each other awkwardly. For all her usual heat, Chandra felt like her heart was now encased in ice. She kissed Nissa on the cheek, also awkwardly.

"Goodbye, Chandra," Nissa said.

As no words would come out, Chandra just nodded in reply.

Nissa planeswalked away.

Chandra stood there, trying to breathe. Eventually, she placed a hand upon the uppermost stone of the cairn. "Goodbye, Gids," she whispered. "I'll miss you more than you'll ever know."

And with her heart of ice intact, she planeswalked to Ravnica in flame.

THIRTY-FOUR

KAYA

The acolytes had gathered quickly—in response to Peran's shouting—to marvel at the sudden reappearance of a back-from-the-dead Teyo Verada. Ultimately, they were joined by Abbot Barrez, a human with dark-brown skin, close-cropped steel-gray hair and a close-cropped steel-gray *manner*, accustomed to command. He had arrived on the scene and had with exasperation ordered his charges "to *help* these poor women—not leave them lying on the ground of *my* garden."

Thus the entire ensemble began making their way down the garden steps to the monastery. Teyo aided the weary Rat, who was considerably shorter than the boy, forcing him to stoop to support a portion of her weight as she gingerly descended. Kaya, who was just behind them and was herself being supported down the stairs by a dwarven acolyte named Theopholos, wondered what the sight of the bent and halting Teyo must look like to all who couldn't see Araithia Shokta.

Can they see the care and concern on Teyo's face? Or does he simply look foolish?

She got a bit of an answer when Peran, who was helping Jaya navigate the twisting staircase, looked back over his shoulder at Teyo and said, "Are you injured?"

"No. I'm fine."

Rat giggled.

Another acolyte, whose name Kaya hadn't caught, ran ahead and opened the great wooden door to the monastery. As she crossed the threshold, Kaya saw that every external surface, whether wood, adobe or stone, was studded with a veritable armor of gemstones. Diamonds, apparently.

Theopholos lowered Kaya onto a hard wooden bench in what appeared to be a spare and empty chapel. She had finally begun to catch her breath. Planeswalking with Rat had been more difficult than she had remembered it being with Janah (*either Janah*). Still, despite the resulting exhaustion, Kaya—free of the Orzhov contracts that had been weighing down her soul—felt more relaxed and revitalized than she had in weeks. She didn't really want to go back to Ravnica unless she could be permanently freed of her Syndicate responsibilities.

Of course, I owe it to Tomik to return. Right? Yes, right.

Teyo was tending to Rat, who was now lying across another bench, and shooing off a couple of acolytes, who nearly sat down on her. Eventually, he noticed the abbot staring down at him. He swallowed hard and said, "Master."

The abbot scowled and shook his head before speaking. "I find myself sadly unsurprised that instead of dying, Teyo, you simply wandered off while all who cared about you dug desperately in the sand to find your body."

"No, Master, it wasn't like that. It's very complicated and . . .

and . . ." He trailed off, despairing at the idea that the strange truths he had to tell would ever—*could ever*—be believed.

"Mistress Kaya, say something," Rat pleaded, her concern for the boy evident on her face. His look of gratitude to her was equally touching. Teyo was smitten by Rat, and she was smitten by him. Not that either had done anything about it. (For very different reasons, both had real confidence issues.) Kaya thought about the way she had, at their age, gone after Janah, making her intentions clear in no uncertain terms. It certainly had sped things up. But she wondered if all that speed had cost her the love of her life in the end.

Worth it? Yes, worth it.

But to the matter at hand, Kaya cleared her throat to get the abbot's attention. "Abbot Barrez, is it?"

He looked at her sternly. "It is."

"I know this may sound unbelievable, but Teyo here did not wander off. Without intending to, he planeswalked . . . he traveled to another dimension, another world. And it was fortunate for all of us that he did. We were engaged in a battle against a great evil, and Teyo was invaluable to the cause, saving many lives. He saved my life many times over."

"Mine, too," Rat popped in, though only Teyo and Kaya could hear her.

Teyo shook his head, saying to Rat, "I don't think I ever saved *your* life. Though you saved mine more than once."

"I'm trying to help," Rat said and punched him, weakly.

Of course, to the abbot and the acolytes and even to Jaya, it seemed as if Teyo were contradicting Kaya.

Abbot Barrez said, "I'm relieved you make no such pretense, Verada."

Jaya said, "He's being modest. He did save Kaya's life. And mine, once. And many others with his shields of light."

The abbot scoffed. "Now I know you're all lying. This boy's geometry can't even save himself. And you expect me to treat this truant as a hero? I wonder, Acolyte Verada, where you found these strange women to lie for you—and to lie for you so badly."

"I am *not* lying," Kaya said darkly.

"No, of course not, Madame Jaya."

"I'm Kaya. She's Jaya."

"And where, pray tell, is Madame Maya? Couldn't she be found to join your troupe of players?"

Jaya had had enough. Grasping Peran's arm, she pulled herself up to her feet and said, "I do not appreciate your tone, Abbot Barrez."

"I'm sure you don't—"

"Silence, you fool," she whispered dangerously, allowing flames to dance around her eyes and the one free hand that wasn't grasping the minotaur to maintain her tenuous balance. "I have been many things, but never a liar—nor an actress. But I was the Matriarch of Keral Keep on the plane of Regatha, and I hope I was never quite so leaden-brained a spiritual leader as you are proving yourself to be."

"Keral Keep? Regatha? Can't you make up better names?"

Jaya appeared to be on the verge of incinerating the man when a desperate-looking acolyte came running into the room, shouting "Master—" Spotting Teyo, his eyes went wide and his chin dropped almost to his chest. "Teyo?"

Barrez asked, "What is it, Arturo?"

Arturo stared at Teyo, then slowly turned to stare at the abbot. "What?"

"Spit it out, boy!"

"Oh, uh . . . it's the Western Cloud, Master. It sends us a diamondstorm!"

THIRTY-FIVE

JACE BELEREN

When Jace arrived at her offices in New Prahv, Lavinia was in mid-conversation with a semi-desperate Chamberlain Maree.

"Please, mistress," Maree was saying—or begging, really. "The Firemind understands that your docket is full now—"

"Quite full."

"Yes, but we're all very aware you're looking for a substitute, a more permanent solution for the Senate. All I ask—all Niv-Mizzet asks—is that once a new Azorius guildmaster has been found, you commit to resuming your position as Deputy to the Living Guildpact."

"I'm sorry," Lavinia said. Then seeing Jace smiling at her, she stiffened and said, "Actually, I'm not sorry, Maree. I know Niv-Mizzet is running you ragged, forcing you—in Ral's absence—to serve as acting guildmaster to the Izzet, while simultaneously serving as Acting Deputy to the Living Guildpact. I know he wants the embassy rebuilt—probably by last week—and I can guess that he has some sixteen other projects he's desperate to initiate, as well. And I . . . suppose . . . I . . . *sympathize*." That last word, Jace thought, seemed to stick in the former arrester's throat. "But not only will I *not* commit to becoming the Firemind's deputy, I will commit to *never* taking on that role again."

"Lavinia . . ."

"That's my final word, Maree. You'd best move on and find yourself another option."

Maree sighed, nodded, bowed and exited—walking past Jace without offering him even a glance.

"And what boon do *you* seek, Jace Beleren?" Lavinia asked, turning toward her former boss. "As you can see, I'm quite busy."

"I can imagine," he said. And he could. As Grand Arbiter Pro Tem of the Azorius Senate, Lavinia was striving to reform the Azorius after the twin blights of Baan and Bolas, while simultaneously searching for her own replacement, someone who could take her place without tearing the Senate apart.

"Why are you grinning?" she asked him crossly.

"Because I find your predicament amusing."

"In what possible way?" she said, exasperated.

"Being Living Guildpact never sat easily on my shoulders, yet you never had any sympathy for me. It's simply amusing to see the tables turned."

Lavinia scowled. "Were you always such a fool? Of course I had . . . sympathy for you." As he suspected, that word *sympathy* still gave her trouble. "But my . . . sympathy was never going to excuse you from your responsibilities. My . . . sympathy didn't mean you shouldn't do your job."

"I think that's the nicest thing you've ever said to me."

"Forgive me. I'm very tired."

"I can't help wondering if you aren't the *perfect* choice to stay on as Azorius guildmaster. Ravnica could do worse than to have rulers who never had the ambition to rule."

"Are you trying to make me angry." It was not a question.

Jace laughed. "I'm really not. I'm very fond of you, you know."

"Azor's Gall, Jace, don't say that out loud. It's like a curse, coming from you."

"Now, that may be the *cruelest* thing you've ever said to me."

Because it feels a bit like the most accurate thing you've ever said to me, damnit.

She sighed heavily. "Why are you here? What do you want?"

He sighed, too. "I want to know what's going on. I can't locate Vraska's mind-signature anywhere on Ravnica. Vraska's lieutenants among the Golgari aren't talking, so I was hoping I could get a straight answer from you."

"Well, you won't get a lie from me, if that's any comfort."

"It's the least I expected, Lavinia."

"It's the most you'll get. As you no longer have an official role in Ravnican affairs, I won't be spilling guild intelligence to you."

"Lavinia—"

"I know you could read my mind—but I also know you won't."

In fact, Jace had been tempted to do exactly that—right up until she made that declaration. Which is probably exactly *why* she said it.

Who's the mind reader now?

"No, of course not," he said.

"Then be on your way. I have work to do."

"You could say it before I leave. Who knows when we'll see each other again?"

"What are you talking about? What do you expect me to say?"

"What you've resisted telling me for years."

"Get out of my office?"

"That you're very fond of me, too."

"Out!"

He took that as a minor victory and left.

But victory or no, the mind-mage was frustrated. Looking inward, he nearly bumped right into Chandra as he was leaving the building and she was coming in.

She said, "Oh, Jace. I'm looking for Jaya. I have a message for her from Teferi. I thought maybe she might be with Lavinia—"

"She's not."

"Oh. And you haven't seen her, either?"

"No . . ."

"Okay. Hm. I wonder if she left Ravnica . . ."

He considered for a moment and then said, "Chandra, I think something's going on. With the guilds and with some of the Planeswalkers, including Jaya and Ral and Vraska."

"What kind of something?"

"I don't know yet, but, well . . . given the way *everybody's* striving so mightily to keep me in the dark, I'm worried it has something to do with Liliana, and I think we had better get to the bottom of it."

"How?"

"Well, for starters, I need to find a jerk whose thoughts I don't mind reading."

THIRTY-SIX

VRASKA

Queen Vraska sat upon her throne, conferring with Storrev, Azdomas and the huge fungal troll Varolz.

Storrev's voice, which seemed to come like a whisper of cold wind from the land of the dead itself, said, "It is as we feared, my queen. There are rumors of rebellion among the devkarin."

"And," Azdomas stated between clicks, "these rumors center on Matka Izoni."

"Though she herself has said nothing treasonable."

"Kill her," grumbled the troll from low in his throat.

Storrev lowered her head, and Azdomas clicked three or four times, confirming in their unique ways what Vraska herself had already concluded as a truth: "I'd love to. But if the queen executes the devkarin's high priestess without cause, then her followers will certainly rise, splitting the guild and leaving it vulnerable to the other nine ruling powers on Ravnica."

Varolz shrugged. "Yeah, but if Queen Vraska *don't* kill Izoni, we all be facin' a coup one day soon. One day real soon."

And this, too, is a truth.

Vraska brooded on the dilemma.

Storrev whispered another question, "If I might ask, Your Majesty. What of Baan? If that task is completed, perhaps we could count on more support from your allies in the other guilds. It would help if or when Matka Izoni did make a move on the crown."

Vraska shook her head and said, "Baan's gone to ground on some plane or another."

But just saying that aloud gave Vraska an idea . . .

THIRTY-SEVEN

TEYO VERADA

The warning bells began to ring. Belatedly.

The abbot asked Arturo, "Where are the villagers? How close?"

"They're coming up the hill, Master. But the storm is coming up too fast."

"All right, acolytes, get out there. All of you. Get to work. Alternate with the vested monks and make sure there's a shielded path for the villagers to ascend. I don't want an inch of exposure for those poor souls, is that clear?" commanded the abbot in his clipped, sharp crisis-speech.

The acolytes nodded and murmured their assent.

"Then move!"

They sped out the chapel door.

The abbot turned to Teyo, saying, "You, too, Verada. You can prove what a hero you've become."

"Yes, Master."

Next, Abbot Barrez turned to Kaya and Jaya to order them around, as well: "Stay inside, both of you. You'll be safe from the diamondstorm."

"What in the Nine Hells is a diamondstorm?" a still-winded Jaya demanded, sitting back down on her bench.

The abbot shook his head and muttered, "Where did he find these two?"

Teyo quickly turned to Rat and said, "You stay inside, too. This chapel is fortified with diamond-encrusted walls, inside and out. They can withstand most anything."

From the doorway, the abbot barked, "By the Storm, Verada, now!"

Teyo hopped to.

Outside, it was instantly clear that the Western Cloud had sent the diamondstorm in too fast. Humans, dwarves and minotaurs—males and females, adults and children, the entire population of the nameless village at the foot of the nameless mountain upon which the Monastery of the Order of the Shieldmage sat—were moving at a deliberate pace up the trail to achieve the safety of the Order's five reinforced buildings. For years, Abbot Barrez had been trying to convince the villagers to reinforce their own homes with diamonds, but eking out their meager livings in this water-starved climate took up all the peasants' time and energy, and evacuating to the monastery at the first sign of a storm was a deeply ingrained custom. A custom that worked just fine with enough warning and with sufficient lead time that such warning offered.

But a storm this fast provided neither.

The wind was high and loud. The sand was already in, and visibility was already close to nonexistent.

Enhancing his voice magically in order to be heard above the roar of the wind, the abbot called out: "Form the line! We have hapless fools to save!"

Teyo took a position between Brother Armando and Brother Abedo, downhill from Theo, uphill from Peran and Arturo—his three cellmates and the best friends he'd ever had.

Well, until I met Rat.

It was almost funny how close he felt to her already. They had known each other only . . .

Had it really only been two days?

That seemed incredible. And yet . . .

"Shields up!" called out the abbot. "Find your lore!"

Teyo knew the drill. He began chanting, forming a triangle each from his eastern and western vertices.

"Four-pointers, Verada! You need diamonds to stop diamonds!"

Teyo nodded silently. He could no longer see the abbot for the sand. He chanted, expanding his left-hand triangle into a diamond. But his right hand lagged behind, as usual. He was out of balance, as usual. Even now, at the beginning.

C'mon, Teyo, you did much harder stuff on Ravnica. Much harder! By the Eastern Cloud, you formed a giant hemisphere strong enough to hold off a God-Eternal. You must be able to make two decent four-pointers!

He created a small circle of light beneath his right ear to provide the balance he naturally lacked. It worked a measure, and he was able to create the second diamond. And just in time. The diamonds were incoming. A few micro-stones sliced across the top of his scalp, reminding him to keep his shields high.

But, as the abbot taught, if all a shieldmage could protect was himself, he was a pretty poor shieldmage.

"By the Storm, Verada, if all a shieldmage can protect is himself, he is a pretty poor shieldmage!"

"Yes, Master."

He expanded his diamonds, working to join his lore with the geometries of Brothers Armando and Abedo. Once again, his eastern vertex was up to the task. He was flush with Armando.

But his western vertex was a mess. There was a great gap between his diamond and Brother Abedo's trapezoid. And he hadn't yet been able to combine his two diamonds into anything at all, leaving more gaps between them.

"Find your lore, acolyte!" Brother Abedo shouted. "Be the geometry!"

"Yes, brother," he breathed between chants, certainly too low for Abedo to hear over the storm. The diamonds were bigger now, the size of marbles, slamming into Teyo's light and shapes. He felt every single one and knew this was only the beginning. He was faltering. Already.

He heard Peran shout, "Villagers abreast!"

Two minutes later, Brother Berluz repeated the call.

Then Arturo: "Villagers abreast!"

Then Armando: "Villagers abreast!"

They'd be up to Teyo in a matter of seconds and he flat-out wasn't ready for them.

Suddenly Abbot Barrez was shouting, "Hold position! The line is broken above!"

Brother Armando repeated the call, "Wait! Wait! Hold position! Stay put! The line is broken above!"

The abbot was now right behind Teyo, grinding his failures in deep, sand-scouring his meager efforts. "This is appalling, Verada. You've only been gone two days! Have you really forgotten all the lore I wasted my time teaching you in such a short time? What's this at your ear, a balance circle? Is that orthodoxy? Are you a child?"

"No, Master. Yes, Master. No, Master. No, Master." He dissolved the circle at his ear, which instantaneously weakened his concentration, his lore and his geometry. His shields cracked.

"Verada, you're as useful as a fire-djinn doing laundry."

"Yes, Master."

Barrez called out, "Abedo, compensate for this worthless student! Expand your lore!"

"Yes, Abbot."

"Keen! So is this really what you did all day before you came to Ravnica? It's very exciting. I can see why you were so eager to return. You know I think I already have sand in places that I didn't know sand could get into, right?"

Rat!

He couldn't see her but she must have been just behind him. "What are you doing here?" he hissed into the storm. "I told you to wait in the chapel!"

"I know, I know. But I wanted to see whatever what a diamondstorm looked like. It sounded so sparkly. And you know I like sparkly things. But it turns out you can't really see much of anything, except maybe a little burst, a little *peeoo*, every time a diamond hits your shield. It's funny. There are diamonds scattered all across the ground. They're kinda not worth anything here, I imagine. But I've already pocketed a bunch. *A whole bunch*, really. There's this Orzhov fence named J'dashe. She's dead now, but I bet I can sell her ghost a nice handful of these stones for a pontiff's ransom—*if* I can get her to acknowledge my existence, somehow. But if I *can* do that, I better let her think I stole 'em all. Otherwise, she won't believe they're worth a rotten plum—"

"Rat, Rat! You're putting yourself in terrible danger!"

"Ah, no, I'll be just fine. I'll stay behind your shields."

My shields? My shields aren't worth a rotten plum! She needs to stay behind Brother Armando's or even Arturo's. Except they can't see or hear her. They won't know she's there. They won't be able to keep her covered, and they won't even know they're failing.

So it had to be Teyo. He'd have to make sure she was protected, even as diamonds the size of rotten plums began slamming against his pitiful constructs.

Well, then, fix them. Fix them for her!

He didn't chant. He leaned in. Leaned into the wind. Leaned into the pounding of diamonds and the rush of sand. He forgot all his orthodoxy, whatever orthodoxy he might have had. But he remembered Araithia Shokta and his need to safeguard her. He might be a poor excuse for a shieldmage, but he would not be a poor excuse for her friend.

He fortified his shields with his heart vertex and his gut vertex. He pushed against the wind with his mind vertex, and simultaneously returned the circle of light to his right ear. His shields expanded. In length. In breadth. And for good measure, in depth. He pushed the diamond forward, giving his geometry volume.

On either side of him, Brothers Armando and Abedo could be heard to gasp. To gasp over the roar of the diamondstorm.

Brother Armando called out to the villagers, "All right, move. Now. The line's repaired. Villagers abreast!"

Teyo reached out behind him with his lore and felt the flow of the villagers moving up the path. "Villagers abreast!" he called out. "Go with them," he said to Rat.

"Nah. I'll stick with you, Teyo. Gotta make sure you stay safe. You're still my responsibility. I adopted you, remember?"

He chuckled inwardly and said, "I remember, Araithia."

She was silent for a beat, then she said, "Stop that," and punched him in the back. He barely felt it. But it felt good.

Brother Abedo soon yelled, "Villagers abreast!"

And a bit after that, Theo repeated the call.

Brother Armando said, "Abbot. Abbot! You have to see this!"

The abbot shouted, "See? See what? In this storm? Armando, you're too close to Verada! He's rubbing off on you!"

"By the Cloud, Barrez, come look!"

Rat said, "Whoa, is Brother Armando supposed to talk to the abbot that way? I thought only Miss Ballard could get away with that."

Teyo didn't respond, but he was pretty shocked. He knew that Brother Armando and the abbot went way back, but he'd never heard any of the brothers curse at Abbot Barrez. Ever.

Not in front of the acolytes, anyway . . .

The abbot approached, calling out, "All right, what is it?"

Armando didn't answer. For a long minute, all Teyo could hear was the wind.

"Where's your shield, Armando?" And then, "Where's your shield, Abedo?"

"Apparently, I don't need one," Armando said.

"Same," Abedo called out.

There was more silence. Teyo was confused. Why would the brothers drop their geometry? *How* could they drop their geometry?

"Is he doing this alone?" said the abbot in a whisper. If his voice weren't still magically enhanced, Teyo never would have heard it.

"Yep," said Rat. "It's all my boy Teyo."

What?

Teyo reached out with his senses along his geometry. His construct was longer than he could have imagined. It stretched to either side past both the vested monks. It had depth and solidity like nothing he'd ever created before. Like nothing he'd ever seen demonstrated before.

How am I doing this?

"I'm thinking it's your Spark," Rat said, reading him a bit, as she usually did. "You've got that thing all the 'walkers all have. Whatever what that fuels your soul and your magic. It's what Bolas was stealing from the Planeswalkers and why it made him so powerful. You have it. You always have, I guess. When you're not getting in your own way, that is. I mean, sometimes, Teyo, you just think too much, you know? Not me, though. No one's ever accused the Rat of thinking too much. Of course to accuse me of something, you'd have to know I'm here. That's why I'm such a great thief, right? Never once been caught. And never once will—"

The abbot spoke then, running over the end of Rat's explanation. "Teyo," he said. "I'd almost forgotten . . ."

It was all he said for a long time.

By this time, the villagers had all passed.

One by one, he heard Peran, Berluz, Arturo and Armando call out, "Villagers clear!"

A few minutes after that, Teyo made the same call. Still, he waited for Abedo and Theo's confirmations before he felt he could reduce his shields, tighten his geometry.

Eventually, the storm began to fade. Only then did the abbot speak again, his voice no longer enhanced: "You did well, my boy. Very well. Now you must leave this monastery and never come back."

THIRTY-EIGHT

RAL ZAREK

The Wanderer had Tezzeret's "scent."

She'd been helping Ral track his target on a cosmic chase from Ravnica to Amonkhet to Innistrad to Kamigawa to wherever the hell they were now. Like most of the worlds on their search, this was a plane Ral had never visited before.

Ral sat down—all but collapsed down—on a flat rock. "Where are we?"

"Ixalan," she responded. "But Tezzeret's moved on. He barely stopped a moment here. We should go."

Ral hated to show weakness, but—exhausted from more planeswalking in a day than he'd ever done in an entire month—he said, "Listen, I get that you and I are built differently. But I need to catch my breath. I'm pretty well fried." He pointed toward the setting sun. "To be honest, we may have to spend the night here."

"That's sunrise, not sunset."

"Then we may have to spend the *day* here. Or at least an hour or two. I'm sorry."

"It's fine," she said, though she sounded at least a little annoyed.

"You're really not tired?"

"No, but the longer we stay in one place, the more tired I'll become."

"Sorry."

"You said that already."

He laughed. "Sorry to repeat myself. Look, would you sit down or something? I don't need you looming over me."

She looked around and then sat down on another rock opposite him. "Better?"

"Yes, thank you."

"You're welcome."

"Can I ask you something?"

"Can I stop you?"

"You don't have to answer."

"I'm well aware of that."

"Why are you helping me? Do you have a history with Tezzeret?"

"I do."

He waited. She didn't elaborate. So he prompted, "And . . ."

"And I think it would be a good thing for the Multiverse if he were dead."

"Because . . ."

"Because he's an extremely dangerous individual. I'm not sure you realize just *how* dangerous."

"I realize it. I've got a history with him, too."

"You have a history with the man who worked for Nicol Bolas. That man was dangerous enough, I suppose. But that's not the Tezzeret I fear."

"You fear him?"

She hesitated, paused. Long enough for the silence to grow awkward. Just when he was about to break it, she said, "I fear what he might become untethered from the dragon."

Ral watched her. She barely moved. He found he was somewhat desperate to see her face beneath the shadow of her hat brim. But he didn't even know how to ask. Any way—every way—he could think to phrase the request sounded flat-out rude in his head. He said, "So we put him down now. For the greater good of the Multiverse."

"For the greater good of the Multiverse."

"And a little personal satisfaction?"

"And significant personal satisfaction."

"Would you let me see your face?" He hadn't meant to ask that. He had just blurted it out.

"No," she said simply, flatly.

"Why not? Why do you hide it? Why do you go to such extremes to hide it?"

"Do I?" She swept her hair to the side and raised her head. Beneath the brim of her hat, she wore a mask of gold that covered her entire visage and even kept her eyes in shadow.

He rolled his eyes. "Yes, I think you do. I haven't been this desperate to see a woman's face in, well, ever. You've turned it into a mystery. Mystery creates fascination. I take it that was your intent."

"Far from it," she said. Now she sounded amused.

"Well, then?"

"I don't like seeing the faces of those who react to seeing my face." She said it simply. Stating a fact.

"Are you that beautiful?"

"I think I was once." She sounded wistful.

"But now?"

Again, she paused for quite some time. Eventually, she said, "You understand how intrusive you're being, don't you? You think because you have no sexual interest in women, that it gives you the license to speak to us and about us with objectivity. A false objectivity. You say to yourself, *It's not an approach. It's not a line. It's not a judgment or evaluation, so what's the harm?* You say to yourself, *I'm just a safe haven. A non-threatening vessel into which any woman can spill her secrets.* But all you're really doing is sating your own curiosity at our expense."

It was his turn to pause. His face twitched, and he exhaled. "I think you're generalizing. But there may be some truth in that."

"'*May*' be? '*Some*'?"

"Definitely some. But only some."

"Mm-hmm. Still want to see my face?"

"Still fascinated. I'm not quite sure why. Perhaps it's just the common desire to want or wonder about what we can't have."

She didn't respond.

"There are scars, aren't there? Significant scars. And you don't like seeing the faces of those who see them?"

Her only answer was to release her hair, which swept down across her mask; she tilted her head down so that her hat brim put all in shadow. Even the mask was rendered unseeable. He took this as confirmation of his theory.

"How did you get them?"

"Ask me again why I'm helping you find Tezzeret."

"Ah."

They were quiet again for a time. But now the silence didn't seem awkward.

She said, "You have scars?" It was a question that sounded like a statement.

"Significant scars," he replied. "But the most significant aren't visible to the naked eye."

"Tezzeret?"

"No, not him. Don't get me wrong; I hate the guy's guts. But he hasn't hurt me in that way. Not the way he hurt you."

"Assuming you've gleaned the truth and didn't just spin a tale for yourself to satisfy your insulting inquiries."

That stopped him. "Not . . . not sure what to do with that."

"Live with it."

He did for a bit. Then he said, "So it wasn't exactly a *tale*. More like *hints* of a tale yet to come."

"Or hints of a truth I'm unlikely to elaborate upon. Ever."

"Right."

"Right."

"What were we talking about?"

"*Your* scars."

"My scars."

"None from Tezzeret?"

"No."

"In which case?"

"Uh . . . Some are from Bolas. Most are from a lifetime on the streets of Ravnica. And there was this artist I thought I loved. Death by a thousand cuts. You get the idea."

"I do."

"We maybe understand each other a little."

"A little. Maybe."

They lapsed into silence again. A comfortable silence this time. Still tired, Ral let his butt slide down off the rock and onto the sand, leaning back against his Accumulator, which in turn leaned against the abandoned stone. They were on a beach at the edge of a jungle. Morning had broken, and unseen birds were soon squawking up a storm. Palm trees swayed in the warm ocean breeze.

"I like this place," he said.

"It's as good a plane as any."

"I suppose you've *wandered* to all of them, just for comparison's sake."

"The Multiverse is infinite, but I've visited a few hundred, at least."

"*A few hundred?*"

"Easily."

"Stayed long on any?"

"Not a one. Though there are many I've visited over and over. If you counted all the days and nights I've spent on . . . oh, say, Innistrad or Dominaria, for example, I'm sure it would add up to years. Or something along those lines. I've probably spent a few months in total here on Ixalan, one day or one night or one hour or ten minutes at a time."

"Krokt, I don't envy you."

"Then you're not half the fool you appear to be."

"Oh, thanks."

"You're welcome."

He grinned and shook his head ruefully. There was something pleasantly circular about their conversation.

"Are you rested now?" she said, clearly trying *not* to sound impatient.

"Honestly, no."

"All right."

"Is this really a strain for you?"

"Your company?"

"Hilarious. No. Maintaining this plane?"

"No. Not yet. For now, for hours really, it's just a question of maintaining a bit of focus. I'll let you know if it becomes problematic."

At which point, a giant lizard with a mouthful of knives for teeth came abruptly *crashing* through the jungle toward them. They barely dodged out of the way to either side.

In fact, if they had both dodged to the *same* side, one of the two Planeswalkers likely would have wound up breakfast. But because the creature had to make a decision as to which entrée was more appealing, it gave them time to find their feet. Time for the Wanderer to draw her sword. Time for Ral to switch on his Accumulator.

"Things just got problematic," she deadpanned breathlessly as both backed away from the monster slowly.

"*By the Dune-Brood, what is that?*"

"Dinosaur. Regisaur."

The beast decided Ral was on the menu and strode toward him. He hit it with a small burst of electricity that stopped it in its tracks.

It raised its head and *ROARED* to the heavens!

Ral fired off a substantial lightning bolt just on the side of the dinosaur closest to the ocean. That did the trick. The bolt scared the monster, and it retreated back into the jungle.

The Wanderer eyed him: "Rested enough now?"

He laughed in release and told her yes.

She immediately planeswalked away, and he followed her aether-trail.

Seconds later, they were on a new plane.

Ral sat down—all but collapsed down—on a flat rock. "Where are we?"

"Esper. On Alara," she responded.

"And where to next?"

"Nowhere. I can lead you no farther. Tezzeret is here."

THIRTY-NINE

TOMIK VRONA

Tomik was in his small, cluttered and cramped office. At the moment, it felt more cramped than usual, as the new acting guildmaster was conferring with the massive giant Bilagru. The ceiling was high enough for the chief enforcer, but the width of the windowless, bookcase-lined room barely left him an inch on either side to house his bulk. Tomik knew he could probably move into Kaya's large—and largely untouched—guildmaster's suite of offices, but he felt more comfortable staying put. Despite the seeming disarray, he had a system and knew exactly where everything was. And the thought of packing up and moving was less than appealing. Plus, he didn't fancy the idea of letting this temporary position go to his head, of growing too accustomed to the luxury of the job—even if the only luxury involved was the luxury to have more space to *do* the job.

Tomik and Bilagru were reviewing a summation report on collections and repairs. The Eternals had, the day before, caused some damage to Orzhov holdings. The funds to fix things were readily available, but—as the giant pointed out—there were other items in the budget for Restoration, Refurbishment, Renovation and Infrastructure that had been waiting for money to be allocated for considerably longer. Some that had literally been waiting for decades or more. One item that had been waiting for over a century and a half.

Tomik studied the problem and then said, "I don't want to fall behind as the Obzedat famously did. Too greedy and too detached from life to care whether things worked properly. So let's allocate funding to the Eternal repairs and simultaneously to . . . say . . . two-point-five percent of the master R-R-R-I budget, starting with the oldest line items first. Then every quarter we'll fund any new required fixes and two-point-five percent more of the old list."

"I like that," Bilagru rumbled.

"It'll still take a decade to clear the decks, but we'll catch up eventually and not fall any further behind."

"Practical. Efficient. And it chops up the mess the Ghost Council left us with into easily digestible bites. Plus, it didn't take you five years, twelve committees and six prayer councils to figure it out."

"Thank you."

The giant smiled down at his acting guildmaster. Bilagru seemed to genuinely like Tomik, and Tomik knew he genuinely liked the chief enforcer.

With that topic settled, Tomik signed an order and moved the R-R-R-I from one large pile of papers in his inbox to an only slightly smaller pile of papers in his outbox.

The giant noticed the differential and said, "Things seem to be going well so far."

Tomik shrugged. "Well, it's only been a few hours since Kaya left. I could hardly have screwed things up too badly in that amount of time."

"You'd be surprised," Bilagru said ruefully. "And in any case, I appreciate even a few *minutes* without trouble."

"As do I."

"Knock, knock."

Tomik and Bilagru turned toward the open door (though Tomik had to lean far to the side to see past the giant's bulk).

Leaning casually against the doorjamb was the vampire Slavomir Zoltan, tithe-master and member of the Triumvirate. "I was hoping I might be granted a brief private audience with our new acting guildmaster."

"I'm not leaving him alone with you, Tithe-Master."

"Now, Chief Enforcer, you cut me to the quick. What have I ever done to make you so suspicious?"

"You want a list?"

"What have I ever done *to you* to make you so suspicious?"

"I've never given you the opportunity," Bilagru rumbled. "I'm not starting now."

"It's all right, Bil," Tomik said. "I believe Zoltan knows he can't accomplish anything by killing me."

"Who said anything about killing?" Zoltan protested.

"There are other things a vampire can do besides killing," the giant stated.

"Again, no one wants to kill anyone."

"I'm prepared for that," Tomik said. He reached down and opened the top front drawer of his desk. He removed a chain of ridiculously thick silver links and put it around his neck. A large silver pendant hung from the end. He tapped it twice. "This is a powerful ward, which will prevent our tithe-master from biting or turning or mentally influencing me. I'll be fine."

Bilagru growled something low and unintelligible, but he turned for the door, saying, "I'll be right outside if you need me."

Slavomir slipped inside quickly to get out of the giant's way.

Bilagru had to stoop and turn sideways to exit, and he still barely fit through the portal. Once he was in the hallway, he rose to his full height, completely eclipsing any other view. "I'll be right outside this door."

"Admirable but unnecessary," Zoltan said as he stepped up and slowly shut the door, listening for the click of the latch.

He turned back to Tomik and made a little flourish with his hand. "Alone at last," he said.

"Alone at last," Tomik repeated nervously. He'd been fairly confident only a moment before. No longer. "Please, have a seat."

Slavomir Zoltan eased his way forward. He moved a chair slightly, but instead of sitting on it, he sat on Tomik's desk. At close range, the vampire was dangerously handsome. He had dark-auburn hair, green eyes and a fetching smile. His collar was open, revealing just a hint of matching auburn chest hair. "I've been thinking," he said, "that the Syndicate would benefit from you and I having a close working relationship."

Tomik swallowed. Or tried to. His mouth was suddenly quite dry. He said, "Anything that *truly* benefits the Syndicate is worth considering, Tithe-Master."

"Agreed. But please, Tomik. Call me Slav. There's not much point to the formality of titles when we're alone like this." Slav stood up and started to come around the desk. "They only create distance. And as we both agreed, we shouldn't allow distance to come between us."

Did I agree to that? Were we even talking about that? He smells nice.

Slav moved languidly and yet an instant later he was close enough for Tomik to get a little frisson from their proximity. Tomik breathed out, "Careful of the ward. It'll burn you."

"That particular ward protects from any vampiric threat. That's not my intent. Not at all." He placed his left palm flat against the pendant. Flat against the pendant and Tomik Vrona's chest. He held the hand there for quite some time. Time enough for Tomik to look into those sea-green eyes. Time enough for Tomik to get lost in those eyes.

"Such lovely amber eyes you have," Slav whispered. "Like morning light." Then he removed his hand from the ward and held it up to show Tomik. It was unburned, unscarred, the skin perfectly smooth. Perfect. "You see? No threat. I'm not using my vampiric abilities at all."

"No?"

"No."

"I just want us to be friends."

"Friends?"

"Oh, at the very least . . ."

FORTY

RAT

Teyo and Rat found Mistress Kaya and Miss Ballard in the chapel among the crush of village refugees.

The former acolyte spoke so quietly that both women had to strain to hear him over the murmuring of those assembled. "I no longer belong in this old life. I'm ready to leave, and if you don't mind, Kaya, I'd prefer to travel with you and Rat."

"Are you sure?" Mistress Kaya asked. "You know where I'm going next, what I'm going to do."

Before he could answer, Brother Armando entered and called out to the crowd, "Storm's died out. You can all go home now."

Amid the sighs of relief and the gathering up of precious belongings and babies and the like, Teyo said, "I'm sure."

Mistress Kaya said, "I understand. I don't blame you."

"Neither do I," said Miss Ballard. "Your abbot is a complete prick."

"Please don't say that," Teyo murmured, looking away.

Rat, for once, said nothing. She knew, of course, that Abbot Barrez had asked Teyo to leave. After the diamondstorm ended, the abbot had taken Teyo aside . . .

Rat, picking up and pocketing diamonds the size of kumquats along the way, followed to eavesdrop . . .

Although you can hardly call it eavesdropping since Teyo knew I was there, right?

The abbot led them back up to the garden where they'd first arrived. It had diamond-encrusted windbreaks to the east and the west, but the storm had somehow still managed to shatter the trunk of a citrus tree. Abbot Barrez frowned over it and sighed heavily.

Then he turned to Teyo, speaking as if he was already midway through a conversation he'd been having with himself. "You were so young you probably don't remember, and I'm so old I foolishly forgot. But let's see if we can put this together, together. When your parents died, and I found you amid the wreckage of your village, do you recall what you were doing?"

"Uh . . . crying?"

"Well, yes. But what else?"

"I don't know. I was so little. I remember you had a shield up protecting me. A circle, I think."

"No. *You* had the circle up. That's what saved you when everyone else died. And the *reason* you were crying was because you hadn't saved anyone else except yourself."

"What? No."

"Yes, my boy. From the time you were four years old—if not before, I didn't know you before—you could summon up geometry with no lore, no chanting, no training, no orthodoxy whatsoever."

Rat whispered, "I told you. It's your Spark."

"That's impossible," Teyo said.

"Indeed, it is, yes," replied the abbot, "and yet that is nevertheless the absolute truth. Teyo Verada, you have always been a natural shieldmage, a prodigy, a savant. I brought you here to encourage you. I *promise* you that was my original aim. Once. But you felt so guilty for not saving your parents and your sister . . ."

"If all a shieldmage can protect is himself, he is a pretty poor shieldmage."

"I don't think that applies to a four-year-old, son. At least it shouldn't have. Wouldn't have—if I hadn't gotten everything wrong."

"I don't understand."

"You were afraid to create geometry after that. You had it in your head that they died because you raised that circle. Not that you lived because of it, but that they *died* because of it. I tried to explain that distinction to you, but, well, you were four, and you couldn't understand. You had no confidence, no *belief* in yourself. None at all. While *I* believed sincerely that what you needed more than anything was discipline and structure. Orthodoxy. By the Storm, I was dead wrong."

"No . . ."

"I was stifling you, Teyo. I didn't understand any other way; I had never been taught any other way, but that's no excuse. As time passed, and my lessons—all the personal attention I gave you—never seemed to improve your skills, I grew . . . frustrated. I was more disappointed in you than the other acolytes *because* of your earlier promise. I was harder on you than them because of it. It seems so clear now that all I did was . . . bully you . . . for my own failings as a teacher. Needless to say, you did not respond well to being bullied."

"Yikes, who would?" Rat interjected.

"Over time, I believe I even convinced myself that your circle had been a mere fluke. I knew better. Deep down, I knew better, but I wouldn't admit it to myself, let alone to you. I was very wrong. I'm very, very sorry."

Rat had been frowning at Abbot Barrez, but she suddenly found herself feeling bad for the old guy. She leaned in to—needlessly—whisper to Teyo, "Your abbot's not so bad, all in all. I mean we all make mistakes, you know?"

"Yeah," Teyo said. "We all make mistakes."

"I appreciate that. It's generous of you to see my failings that way."

"But why does he want you to leave?"

"Um . . . Master? If all this is true, then why must I leave the monastery?"

"Because the other acolytes aren't like you, my son. If Peran or Theopholos followed your example, they'd fail. If Arturo attempted to compete with you—as you know he would—he'd get himself killed."

Teyo nodded absently.

"You've still got us," Rat said.

Abbot Barrez seemed to concur: "I judge you're in good company now, with people who believe in you and bring out your best self in a way I failed to do."

"See, he agrees with me."

"I'm forced now to trust your story of another world. I've no experience of such things, but I don't need to be a stubborn fool forever. Travels with these friends of yours might do you some good. And if you're fighting evils and saving people, well . . . I take no credit, but I couldn't be prouder of you."

It's like what my godfather always says about me: He has no right to harvest this honor, yet Teyo has made the abbot proud.

"You? Proud of me?"

"It's nothing I've earned. But yes. Today, you made me very proud, Teyo. And taught me a necessary lesson in humility."

"Sorry."

The abbot chuckled, but there were tears forming in his eyes. "Please, do not apologize to me. I hope that one day you can forgive me. I hope one day you will return to Gobakhan to protect your people. Your natural skills would make you one of the finest monks of the Order. But for now the best and most necessary advice I can give my former student is to ask him to leave."

On the way back to the chapel, Rat had been a little worried Teyo might be upset about having to go. So worried, she only scooped up a few of the biggest diamonds off the ground.

"Well, *I'm* happy you're coming with us," she said.

He looked down at her, and instantly she knew he was happy, too. "So am I, believe me. Happy and relieved. From the moment he asked me to go, I felt relief. I was surprised—and maybe a little hurt—but I felt . . . liberated. Does that make sense?"

"Sure it does. You're Gateless now, like me. I mean, sometimes I feel like I should finally join a guild and settle down, but mostly—if I'm being honest—I like the freedom of being Gateless, you know?"

"It suits you, Araithia."

"Stop that," she said, punching him in the arm.

"Ow. Why is it that every time I call you by your real name, you hit me?"

She thought about this and thought she might know the answer, but: "I have no idea. It's like a reflex. If you don't want to get hit, then stop doing it."

"I will not."

"Now, you see? All that fine talk from the abbot has gone to your head, Mister I-have-a-Spark-and-am-better-than-all-the-rest."

He said nothing. Just smiled at her.

She felt a tremendous urge to wipe that smile off his face. To *kiss* it off his face. She wondered if he ever felt that urge with her. She thought she'd better punch him again—but just then the fading sunlight had glistened off a stone the size of her fist. "Ooo, sparkly," she said and had run to pick it up . . .

Now she and Teyo and Mistress Kaya and Miss Ballard were preparing to leave the chapel. Find a quiet lonely place to planeswalk away, someplace where their departure wouldn't completely panic the villagers or monks.

Miss Ballard said, "Let's get going. I want this over with."

Just outside, however, they were intercepted by Theo, Peran and Arturo.

"You're really going?" Peran said.

"I have to. I'm sorry."

Theopholos shook his head. "You realize that with you gone, I become the abbot's worst student. He's gonna sand-scour me. It's not fair."

Teyo thought about this then smiled. "If he does, remind him with all humility that you used to share a cell with me and that my bad habits probably rubbed off on you."

"Why would I ever say that?"

"Because he'll go easier on you, if you do. Trust me, Theo, it'll work."

Rat giggled.

The young dwarf looked less than convinced, but he nodded.

Teyo turned to Arturo. "Try not to show them up too badly."

"I can't help it. I'm just that good."

"You are. And we all know it. That's why it's not necessary."

This seemed to give Arturo food for thought. But he didn't have time to chew on it. The minotaur wrapped all four of them in a great bear hug.

Bull hug?

The other three all grunted as every bit of air was simultaneously expelled from their lungs.

Without releasing them, Peran said, "We'll miss you, Teyo. The cell won't be the same without you."

Arturo smirked. "Yeah, it'll be cleaner, and we'll have more room."

Rat punched Arturo on the arm. He took little notice, though he did start rubbing the spot and looked a bit confused.

Now Teyo smirked: "Hurt your arm?"

"A diamond must have gotten by my shield. Guess in the heat of the storm, I didn't notice until now."

"I'm sure it was something like that."

Miss Ballard cleared her throat impatiently. She'd been tolerant of these goodbyes—up to a point. Rat supposed that point had come.

After one last set of quick farewells, Teyo led the three women around the back of the chapel.

Mistress Kaya asked, "When did you become so wise, Teyo Verada?"

"Sometime in the last ten minutes, I think. I'm sure it's temporary. I'll be an inexperienced fool again shortly."

"And that may be the wisest thing I've ever heard anybody say."

"Again. It's temporary. Best not to grow accustomed to it."

Behind the chapel, all four looked around for possible spectators. Seeing none, Miss Ballard said, "Time to go."

"Wait!" Teyo said. "How do I follow you?"

"Well, he was right," she sighed. "He's an inexperienced fool again."

"Jaya!" Mistress Kaya reprimanded.

"I'm sorry. I am. I'm just very tired. And I don't like anything about this mission of yours."

"I agree with you there," Teyo said, eagerly turning his judgmental eyes on Mistress Kaya.

"This isn't a pleasure trip for any of us," Mistress Kaya said to them both. Then to Teyo: "I understand you're nervous about following someone else's planeswalk. But you were nervous about leading our last planeswalk, too, and that turned out just fine."

Rat could tell, could read, that Mistress Kaya was determined to be a better teacher to Teyo than what she had witnessed of Abbot Barrez.

She tried to reassure him: "You'll both see and feel Jaya's trail, okay? Simply will yourself to follow it."

He nodded, still nervous.

Mistress Kaya waved Rat in, once again embracing her within her cloak and her arms, and once again warning her to keep her eyes closed and her grip tight.

Rat heard the flames of Miss Ballard's planeswalk. Even with her eyes closed, she felt the brightness of Teyo following. And she definitely sensed his absence from where she always kept track of his feelings in her mind.

Always. Since yesterday.

"Here we go," Mistress Kaya said. Rat felt Kaya ghosting her body and expanding her aura to include her traveling companion. And then . . .

MistressKayaandRatwereagaincrossingtheBlindEternities, againmergingintooneentity,neitherMistressKayanorAraithia ShoktaanymorebutjusttheonecreatureKayaandRat,Ratand Kaya.Soontherewasn'tevenroomforanandbetweenthem,as everythingbecameKayaRat,RatKaya,notitlesnow,noroles, noseparateidentitiesatall.Theywonderedwhatcolortheir eyeswere,brownorviolet,violetorbrown.Oneofeachmaybeor twoofboth?Woulditmatter?Woulditevermatteragain?There wassomethingsorightaboutthejoining,theneveraloneness ofitall,butitwasstillfrighteningatthesametimetohaveno independence,nosingularity,noIorsheonlyusandwe.But almostasquicklyasthe'walkhadstarteditcametoasudden—

KayaRat abruptly manifested as Kaya and Rat. Once again,

they practically threw each other apart, rolling onto their backs and gasping for breath.

Rat opened her eyes. Teyo, supporting Miss Ballard, was kneeling over her.

"You okay?" he asked.

"Oh . . . yeah . . . it's . . . getting . . . easier . . ." Rat wheezed between heaving breaths.

"Liar," Mistress Kaya croaked.

"Exaggerator," Rat corrected.

Miss Ballard said, "We've landed in the Caligo territory of Dominaria." She sounded only slightly less destroyed by the journey than Mistress Kaya and Rat did. "I've brought you within a mile of the ruins of the House of Vess."

"It's . . . appreciated . . ." Mistress Kaya began, still trying to catch her breath.

"And it's all I intend to do."

"We . . . understand . . ."

"So I'll leave you here."

"You can . . . take a moment . . . to rest . . . The mission won't be . . . taking place . . . anytime . . . soon . . ."

"I can see that. But I've stayed away from Ravnica too long already."

"Aren't you . . . exhausted . . ."

"Let's just say I'm feeling my age. Every century of it. But I'm going nevertheless." She sounded determined, but she didn't actually move. Finally, she said, "If this boy will help me to my feet."

"Of course." Teyo helped her up and steadied her. When she nodded, he stepped away.

She sized him up for a moment. "Aren't you tired? You've planeswalked twice today and fought off a gemstorm—"

"Diamondstorm."

She waved off the correction. "And that's after spending all day yesterday at war against Eternals. You're new to this. You should be exhausted."

He nodded. "Probably. Probably will be. I'm still charged up from, well . . . *everything.*"

"Ah, youth," she said. She nodded toward Mistress Kaya and instructed him: "Watch over that one . . . and the one I can't see, as well, until they've recovered."

"I will," he said. "I promise."

"I believe you, Teyo Verada. Your abbot might not tell you this, but you're one of the good ones."

Teyo looked so stunned at the compliment, Rat had to laugh. He glared at her.

"She's laughing at you, isn't she?" Miss Ballard asked.

"Yes."

"Good. It'll keep you honest and humble."

"Yes, she does a very good job at that."

"I'm a natural," Rat said, grinning. "A savant."

Teyo shook his head at the prone girl.

Mistress Kaya, still lying on her back on the ground, said, "He doesn't need much help from Rat or anyone. I think honest and humble is his natural state."

Miss Ballard faux-whispered, "Yes, but don't tell him that. It'll go to his head, and he'll lose his way."

"If he loses his way," Rat said, "I'll find him and bring him back."

Teyo smiled and turned to Miss Ballard. "Thank you for your help," he said.

"I hope I wasn't *too* much help," she replied with a growl. Then she inhaled deeply and ignited. A second later she was gone without a trace.

Teyo turned to Mistress Kaya and Rat. "Now . . . can we talk about *not* killing Liliana Vess?"

"No," Mistress Kaya said.

FORTY-ONE

VRASKA

She stood outside the apartment door.

Frankly, after the idea had struck her that Baan would go to ground somewhere he felt safe, everything else fell quickly into place.

After all, where would a Planeswalker like Baan feel safest? Obviously, where no one would *ever* think to look for him. And where was that?

Ravnica.

He was one of the most hated individuals on this planet. And he didn't have to stay on this planet. Therefore, he'd never come back to this planet. Therefore, that's exactly where he'd go upon leaving Kaladesh.

And once Vraska had gone down that path of logic, the rest was child's play. It was ridiculously easy for her Golgari sources to track Baan down. To learn of the purchase of this safe house made months before most people in the world-city had ever heard of Nicol Bolas. Almost before most people in the Azorius Senate had ever heard of Dovin Baan.

She took a step back and kicked in the door.

Baan, a tidy white bandage wrapped around his head to cover his missing eyes, stood behind the kitchen counter in the one-bedroom apartment eating turnips with a knife and fork.

He put down his utensils, tilted his head, sniffed the air and said, "I thought if anyone could find me, it would be you. But I'll admit I did not expect the Golgari queen would come herself. I'm honored."

She scanned the room for signs of booby traps. There was nothing. Or nothing obvious, anyway. She knew Baan was a man of subtlety and strategy, however, so she didn't relax her guard.

"Did you really not think I would come?" she asked. "If so, I'll be quite disappointed in your legendary powers of deduction."

He bowed slightly, acknowledging the lie.

She took a step forward.

Waving a hand before his face, he said, "I might remind Her Majesty that a gorgon's power cannot petrify a blind man."

Drawing her cutlass, Vraska said, "Her Majesty has other ways to kill."

"Of course. And you *could* kill me. But I know your weakness, Queen Vraska."

"Do you now?"

"Indeed. Her Majesty's weakness is Her Majesty's love of the Golgari."

"That's not a weakness; it's a strength."

"Weakness and strength are not mutually exclusive. So in exchange for my life, I offer you my services."

Vraska scoffed: "Why would I—or the Golgari—require the services of a fallen Azorius guildmaster?"

"Because I can tell you how to secure the Golgari crown and render Matka Izoni impotent." He reached behind a pile of turnips and held up what appeared to be a small jar of live spiders.

FORTY-TWO

CHANDRA NALAAR

"She's back on Ravnica," Jace said.

"Who?"

"Vraska. I can sense her mind again. But I want more information before I see her."

"Why?"

He started to speak but couldn't find an answer. His face sank. *Or maybe he found an answer and doesn't like it.*

He said quietly, "I . . . I want to know if I'm being lied to without having to read her thoughts."

"Okay," Chandra said; her voice still sounded numb and dead to her own ears.

"I should just trust her, I suppose."

"She's a hard woman to trust, I imagine."

"Then she's found the perfect match."

Chandra managed a smile and gave Jace's arm a reassuring

squeeze. She knew intellectually it was what he needed, though the action felt dishonest.

I want to help him. I just don't feel it.

But it seemed to buoy his spirits a bit.

She said, "If we're not going to Korozda, where are we headed?"

"Fire and Blood."

"Is that a tavern?"

"More of a block party. A multi-block party. Rakdos and his minions have been celebrating his victory over Bolas for almost twenty-four hours."

"*His* victory?"

"Yes, it's funny how the story changes depending on the story-teller."

Within minutes, they could hear the chants of a substantial crowd: "BLEED AND BURN! BLEED AND BURN! BLEED AND BURN!"

A few minutes more and they could see the glow of what Chandra could sense was a massive bonfire peeking over the intervening buildings.

"It's just around the corner," Jace said.

"That's as far as you go, Beleren." The blood witch Exava melted out of the darkness. "You're not welcome at this celebration."

Now Jace smiled. "And why is that?"

"You're no fun."

"I can be fun."

"Also, I don't like you and neither does the Defiler." Exava turned to Chandra. "You, on the other hand, are more than welcome at the party." She tried to sell it: "It's a real chance to cut loose. Sample some true freedom. Admit it, wouldn't you love to burn down a few city blocks of this plane?"

That does sound appealing. A fire big enough to defrost my heart . . .

Chandra forced herself to ask, "Have they been evacuated?"

"Why would we do that?"

Why is it still tempting? Damnit, what's wrong with me!

"I'll pass," she said.

"Your loss," sighed the blood witch.

Jace said, "I don't need to crash your little soiree—"

"*'Little'*?" Exava sounded outraged.

"—But I do need a few questions answered."

Exava glowered for a moment, then her face broke into a smile. It was not the kind of smile that made one feel happy . . . or safe. She said, "Then you've come to the right place. I have many answers for you, Jace."

"We've only come to talk. There's no need for things to get nasty."

"Oh, reason not the need. Nasty's where I live." She snapped her fingers. Nothing happened. Chandra and Jace both looked around, but nothing seemed to have changed. Yet Exava's expression was borderline triumphant.

"What aren't I seeing?" Chandra whispered.

"I don't know . . ."

Around the corner, the crowd continued to chant "BLEED AND BURN!" punctuated by a handful of shrieking screams of pain that indicated the mantra wasn't just symbolic. But when the noise briefly died down, Chandra thought she heard the sound of running water. She looked down at her feet. She and Jace had been standing on a sewer grate, and a dark liquid was swiftly rising around their feet.

"I have blood on my boots," Chandra said flatly.

"Oh, crap," Jace muttered, looking down.

Exava cackled and twisted both hands in a circular motion, and two blood elementals twisted up out of the flow and reached their liquid limbs toward the mouths of her two foes.

"Drown in blood," Exava hissed.

Chandra wasted no time. She let loose searing torrents of flame from either hand, evaporating the elementals—and maybe singeing Jace just a bit. In any case, he winced and shielded his face with his near hand.

Should feel bad about that. Why don't I feel bad about that?

Exava winced, too. Winced and then screeched in fury.

But now Jace snapped *his* fingers, and the blood witch abruptly went limp. Her arms fell to her sides, and her face went blank.

Jace said, "I told you we only came to talk. But to be honest, I was kinda hoping you'd pull something like this. Now I really feel no compunction about reading your mind. It's a feeble excuse, I'll admit. But also . . . I don't like you, either, Exava. And you're way less fun than you think."

His eyes glowed briefly blue. Then they returned to normal, and Exava simultaneously fell into a heap on the cobblestones. Jace and Chandra turned and walked back the way they came.

"Well?" she asked. "Did you find out where Vraska went?"

He hesitated . . . briefly. But then came to a decision and said, "The guilds sent Vraska to Kaladesh to kill Dovin Baan."

Chandra's cold heart suddenly felt a little heat. "No, no, no, if anyone's gonna kill Dovin Baan, it's me."

Jace's eyebrow went up. "You're not a killer, Chandra."

"We've been through this. I've killed. You know I've killed."

"I know we've been through this, and I also know you're not a cold-blooded killer."

That's the only blood I have now, Jace.

She groused, "Well, if anyone deserves death, it's Baan. Anyway, he definitely needs to be brought to justice. For what he did to Ravnica *and* Kaladesh."

"Agreed. But you're not thinking about the ramifications: Baan's not the only target. The guilds have ordered hits on Baan and Tezzeret and . . . *Liliana*."

"Oh."

"Yeah. Look, no one knows more than I do that Liliana is no innocent. But she did kill Bolas, and—"

"Nissa said Gideon would want us to redeem her."

"Or try at least."

"What are you going to do?"

"I need to talk to Vraska. I'm *ready* to talk to her now."

"Go. Find her."

"What are you going to do?"

"For starters . . . get a drink. Or two. Or a dozen."

"Really?"

"I need to think. I haven't done much of that lately. It's probably time."

Suddenly Jace seemed reluctant to leave Chandra alone.

"Are you okay?" he asked her.

"No," she said. "Obviously, I'm not okay. But I'll figure things out. Go. Find Vraska. Try to be happy."

He had started to go, but as she said that last sentence, he stopped in his tracks. "That sounded like a goodbye, Chandra."

"It was."

"A 'have a good life' kind of goodbye."

"Well, it *wasn't*. Jace, I'm not suicidal, if that's what you're thinking."

"I wasn't thinking that at all, actually, but now—"

"Oh, please. Don't read in. I promise you. I just need time."

"You sure?"

"I'm sure. And I'm sure I'll see you soon."

He looked concerned.

Concerned enough to read my thoughts?

"Okay," he said finally. "Take care."

No. The new Jace wouldn't do that.

"You, too," she said.

He split off. Chandra walked on. The heat of their minor skirmish with Exava was quickly fading. The ice was forming again. She felt torn and yet distanced from both options she was trying to choose between.

Do I chase Baan to bring him to justice—or maybe even to incinerate him myself?

Or do I chase Liliana and try to save her? Have I even begun to forgive her for costing us Gids?

She should go home to her mother's place and to her mother's arms on Kaladesh. She should really try to put Ravnica and all that went with it behind her.

But that's not gonna happen. That's never gonna happen.

She had lied to Jace about wanting to get drunk, because she thought it was a socially acceptable response to all she'd been through recently and would free him to go see Vraska. It hadn't worked, hadn't allayed his obvious concern for her. In fact, it had backfired. It was too out of character for Chandra.

It's just not my style and everyone knows it.

She spotted a tavern called the Titan's Keg. She went inside. It was full of giants. She slipped between a couple of them and walked right up to the bar. With some effort, she managed to climb up onto an immense barstool.

The tapster, an ogre who amid any other crowd would have seemed gargantuan, asked, "What'll you have, little lady?"

Can't tell if he's being condescending or literal . . .

"A hard cider," she said. "No, a bumbat whiskey. Or two. Or a dozen."

FORTY-THREE

TEZZERET

A storm was building. Tezzeret immediately sensed it was the work of Ral Zarek; he could practically *taste* Zarek's power.

"The storm mage is coming," he said to Brokk and Krzntch.

The homunculus squealed, "What would you have us do, boss?"

"Are the traps set? Both the old and the new?"

"Yes, Master," "Yes, boss," the pair replied in unison.

Tezzeret's fortress was chock-full of snares and booby traps. Some that he had installed and others, which he had left in place, that pre-existed his taking possession of the structure. The Seeker's Sanctum, as it had once been known, had once been occupied by the Seekers of Carmot, an organization he'd been exiled from as a youth. Refusing to recognize his genius, the Seekers had said that poor Tidehollow scum like him had no place among their number. He had later learned that the Seekers were a front for Nicol Bolas, and when the Elder Dragon's attentions were elsewhere, Tezzeret had returned to the Seekers—and had slain them all, down to the very last Fellow of the Arcane Council. He had even killed the Hieresiarch, leader of the Seekers' Inner Circle. It had all been ridiculously easy. He had struck quickly and savagely, and most of the Seekers of Carmot had barely had time to put up a fight. The few who had, fell before him quite routinely. The only Seeker who had escaped Tezzeret's vengeance was Seeker Adept Silas Renn—and only because Renn wasn't present when Tezzeret arrived. He'd defeated Renn in battle years earlier, but he hadn't quite finished him off. He'd love to do that now but hadn't been able to locate the smirking bastard. It grated on him that Renn was still alive. It made him . . . *angry.*

Well, I'll just have to take that anger out on Zarek. Should get at least a little pleasure from that.

Tezzeret had been preparing his next moves—his post-Bolas stratagems—for nearly a decade. So there was simply no way he'd allow Ral Zarek to interfere with his plans now . . .

FORTY-FOUR

KAYA

Kaya had remained virtually prone on her back for next to an hour. Between planeswalking twice in a day and planeswalking with Rat, she was thoroughly exhausted.

Rat had seemed to recover slightly faster and was soon sitting up, removing diamonds from her pockets to calculate the value of her haul.

Watching her, Teyo had asked, "Are those *really* worth something on Ravnica?"

"Oh, yeah," Rat had said, her eyes sparkling as much as the diamonds.

Kaya had added, "The cargo of a single pocket would be worth a fortune on almost any plane but Gobakhan."

Why in Keru's name didn't I pick up any myself? There's a lot of freedom in that many stones.

"I'll split 'em with you," Rat had said, probably reading her a bit.

"They're yours, Rat. I'm not going to take—"

"I'd need help fencing them anyway, you know? We might as well split the profits." She had looked up at Teyo then. "Three ways."

Kaya had nodded. "All right. A three-way split. A third each for me and both of my partners."

Rat had squealed unintelligibly, punched Teyo in the arm and said, "You hear that? We're her partners!"

"Ow. Could you at least hit me in another spot? I think my arm is turning permanently purple right there."

"Sorry," she had said, still grinning broadly.

Honestly, it raised Kaya's spirits. She had feared Teyo would miss Gobakhan, but he seemed happy—even relieved to be traveling with her and Rat.

Well, I know why he's happy to travel with Rat. I probably know it better than he does. For now.

And Rat was just, well, *blossoming* on this journey. Kaya had also worried that at least a part of Rat might be jealous of her solitude. Certainly, Kaya knew Rat was lonely and craved relationships. But adjusting to *constant* companionship can be quite a strain. (It was a bit of a strain at times for Kaya, and she had never been nearly as isolated as Araithia Shokta.) But Rat seemed to soak up the camaraderie, perhaps making up for lost time.

More than that—and to Kaya's sincere delight—she found *she* was truly taking pleasure in their company. If someone had told her even a week ago that she'd relish time spent in the constant company of *two teenagers*, she'd never have believed it. And yet, it was a joy to be with them both. There was such a lack of . . . *jadedness* about them. Of course, Teyo's innocence was easy to understand. Just a few hours on Gobakhan had revealed the place to be—at least from Kaya's point of view—a true backwater of a plane. But given Rat's condition, the girl would have earned (even in her short sixteen years) every cynical impulse that might have struck her. And yet, Araithia Shokta was the furthest thing from cynical.

Between the two of them, I think they actually give me hope for the Multiverse.

She had found herself laughing.

Teyo had looked at her questioningly.

A smiling Rat had just gone on counting her diamonds, saying, "We love you, too, mistress."

Kaya had said, "Please, Rat, if you love me, can't you call me Kaya?"

Rat had looked up—almost panicked. "No, mistress. No. Can't do that. It's hard enough for me to not call Teyo, Mister Verada."

Teyo had given her the eye. "It is not."

She had giggled then. "No, it's not. Saying Mister Verada just now sounded kinda silly. You're just Teyo, I guess. Like Hekara was just Hekara."

"Then why can't I just be Kaya?"

Rat had shaken her head. "That's not how we met. I'm sorry. I don't mean to be disrespectful, but I just can't do it."

"Yet," Kaya had said.

A musing Teyo eventually said to Rat, "So we both love Kaya, huh? Does that mean all three of us love each other?"

She had punched him in response.

"Ow."

I swear the boy must like getting hit.

Now Kaya, Teyo and Rat were carefully heading toward the mansion, with Rat in the lead, acting as an advance scout.

Kaya whispered a warning: "Remember, Rat, this is a different world, and you may not be as invisible here as you are on Ravnica."

Without looking back, Rat offered up another of her shrugs and said, "Gobakhan was a different world, too, and I was just as insignificant there as anywhere I've ever been. Not that I've been

many wheres. But *still*, you know? Anyway, I'll be right back."
She scurried on ahead, leaving Kaya alone with Teyo.

The boy had been silent ever since they had set out. More than
once, he'd started to speak—only to swallow the words. It happened again, and Kaya—though she had a pretty good idea of
what was coming—said, "Okay, Teyo, spit it out."

He looked a little surprised. He had grown accustomed to Rat
reading him. But hadn't expected it from Kaya.

She prompted him to get it over with: "You've made it clear
you're not thrilled with this mission."

He shook his head. "I'm sorry, Kaya. Please know I'm happy to
be traveling with you and Rat, but this . . . It doesn't seem right.
We've come to kill Liliana for collaborating with the dragon, but
she switched sides."

"And she's the one who actually killed Nicol Bolas."

"Yes, exactly. I mean, maybe she's worthy of redemption. Or
maybe she *should* stand trial for her crimes. But simply to kill
her . . ."

"Teyo, I know you're not a killer. By Keru's Grave, you never
even killed an Eternal. And I want you to understand that I'm not
going to let you become a killer now. This job, this mission, it's
on me. I appreciate you and Rat having my back—in fact, I'm
pretty much counting on the two of you protecting me—but *I'm*
the assassin here. And this employment is not new to me. My
usual targets have been ghosts and the undead, entities that
needed to move on and leave life to the living. But I've also known
plenty of the living that needed to die, and I haven't been shy
about killing them, either. Though I've never done it lightly. I
have a code. It hasn't always been terribly consistent, but I make
decisions in the moment, and there are few of those decisions
that I regret. At least, not on this topic."

"But Liliana . . ."

"Liliana Vess killed hundreds, if not thousands, of Ravnicans
and Planeswalkers before switching sides. I'm not saying she

doesn't have her excuses. I'm not even saying she wasn't coerced. But in the end, she made choices. Choices she has to live with. Choices she'll have to die for."

From the trees, Rat hissed, "Over here."

Kaya looked at Teyo, who looked back and then nodded. They moved to catch up to Rat together.

"There's the mansion," Rat said. "But it's not the way Miss Ballard described it."

That was true. Jaya had described a ruin. Something that was barely standing. The House of Vess was nothing like that. It was in good repair, elegant and recently painted. Torches lit the entryway, and noblemen and -women were entering what seemed from outside—*sounded* from outside—to be a rather boisterous party.

Teyo whispered, "Are we sure this is the right place?"

"It's the right place," Rat said. She pointed toward another group of people. Servants, apparently, wearing gold collars, who even at night were working to repair a broken gutter. Others brought food and even flowers inside for the party. "I went up close to the servants and eavesdropped. They're not really servants. They're pretty much prisoners, controlled somehow by those shiny collars they wear. First time I've ever seen something shiny or sparkly that I didn't want. Oh, and I heard them whispering about their mistress . . . it's Liliana. Miss Raven-Hair herself."

Kaya looked to Teyo and said, "So Liliana Vess fled the carnage on Ravnica and returned to her home on Dominaria, where she imprisoned the locals and set herself up in grand evil style. I think that confirms she's one of the living that needs to die."

Teyo said nothing, but he nodded minutely.

Kaya turned back to Rat, "I assume Liliana's at the party."

"Sounds that way. Stay put. I'll find a safe way into the mansion." Once again, she scurried off, leaving Teyo and Kaya alone.

Kaya said, "I don't want you to think I enjoy this."

"No, I don't think that. I don't want *you* to think I'm going to fight you on this. I see your point of view. But is it all right if it makes me sad?"

"It's very all right. If this ever gets easy or pleasant for either of us, then we've definitely taken the wrong path." He offered up a sad smile, and she grasped his shoulder. "We'll keep each other honest," she said. "Agreed?"

"Yes. Agreed."

They waited a bit longer. He sniffed the air and scowled.

"What is it?" she asked.

"Something seems . . . familiar, *smells* familiar. But I can't quite put my finger on it."

"Maybe it's just a tree or plant common to Gobakhan and Dominaria."

He looked around the swampy environs. "That seems unlikely. Wait, I thought this place was called Caligo."

"This place *is* called Caligo. This *plane* is Dominaria."

"Oh, I had that backward."

"It's understandable. You've had a lot thrown at you over the last couple of days."

He exhaled. "Well, that's true. Do you know when I first met you, I thought your name was Jaya. I thought *she* was Kaya."

"Yes, as your abbot pointed out, it's awkward for us to travel together."

Teyo paused and then said, "He's not as bad as you think."

"I hope not."

They were silent again until Rat returned. "There's something you both need to see."

She waved for them to follow her, and they did. She took the long way round the back of the mansion until they came upon a plot of land, a garden not unlike the abbot's garden at the monastery. As with the repair work on the mansion, Liliana's servants—her *prisoners*—were working the garden even at night.

There were three women there, each methodically weeding or planting or something. (Kaya didn't know much about gardening.) Eventually, two of the women picked up baskets of what appeared to be cucumbers and headed off, leaving the last woman to work the soil alone.

Hidden in the trees, Kaya turned to Rat and asked, "Why are we here?"

"The woman. The last servant there. Look."

Kaya took another look at the collared woman. Her back was to them at the moment, but Kaya was now fairly certain she was pulling a weed, then inching back half a foot or so before pulling another, and so forth. "I don't understand. Is it something about the weeds?"

"Wait. Wait for her to turn."

When the woman came to the end of the row, she turned around to start back down the next. She lifted her head to wipe her brow, and the moonlight shone down upon her face.

The face of Liliana Vess!

PART THREE

KILLERS

FORTY-FIVE

TEYSA KARLOV

Zoltan arrived to give his report, but even before he opened his mouth, Teysa knew the vampire had failed.

"It didn't work," he said simply.

"And why is that? Don't tell me your legendary powers of seduction have failed your guild."

"They have. As to the why . . . you can blame the Izzet guild-master, Ral Zarek."

"Was he there? I thought—"

"He was there in every way that mattered. I failed because our Tomik truly loves Zarek. Unshakably loves him. That love makes Tomik Vrona unseducible. Invulnerable. And strong. Very strong."

Teysa scowled. "You sound like you admire him."

"Don't you?"

"I admire his competence, not his naïveté."

Zoltan shrugged. "Vrona doesn't seem naïve to me."

Teysa was quiet for some time. Finally, she sighed and said, "Plan C, then."

FORTY-SIX

VRASKA

While Azdomas, Storrev and Varolz looked on, Vraska sat on the floor, playing with Kyteringa, a young devkarin girl, whom Vraska had rescued from the Eternals. Or she had at least participated in the girl's rescue. When Golgari and Planeswalker forces had allied to save civilians trapped by the Dreadhorde, the elven child had been lowered into the gorgon's arms by a Planeswalker named Yangling. But for some reason, Kyteringa viewed Vraska as her sole savior and had, in a very short time, bonded with and grown quite fond of the queen, who was now teaching the child kanala, using the blue marble gift as their shooter.

"You're already very good," Vraska told the girl.

"Did this marble really come from a princess?"

"Yes. Princess Aesha of Kaladesh. The prettiest and wisest

princess of that entire world. Almost as pretty and wise as you, Princess Kyteringa."

"I'm not a princess!"

"Are you sure?"

"Queen Vraska!" All eyes turned toward the door as Cevraya entered, accompanied by a young elven male—young for an elf anyway—whom Queen Vraska had never met in person. Still, it was easy enough to identify him from the skull mask he wore, which marked him as the devkarin huntmaster, Myczil Savod Zunich.

Cevraya was a Golgari shaman, a devkarin elf, who had been passed over as Matka in favor of Izoni. Cevraya was no great fan of Vraska's, but their common distaste for Izoni Thousand-Eyed had created a truce of sorts between queen and shaman.

Zunich, on the other hand, was the son of Vraska's predecessor as guildmaster, the devkarin Patriarch and undead lich Jarad vod Savo, whom Vraska had put to permanent petrified rest as the first step of the coup that had made her queen of the Golgari. It was a minor miracle that Jarad's son wasn't beside his father in the Statuary, as Vraska would normally have included him in her purge. But Zunich had been deep in the Undercity, hunting a leviathan, at the time. In fact, he'd been down there for a couple of months and hadn't even heard of his father's (second) death and Vraska's ascension until long after both had been achieved. Deciding not to open closed wounds, Vraska had declined to demand his immediate execution and had instead ordered Azdomas to have Zunich watched. The kraul had observed no signs—or even words—of treason from the huntmaster any greater than him haughtily abstaining from joining a toast to the queen in a Golgari-frequented alehouse. So Vraska had (for the time being) decided to let Zunich live.

With an eye to the girl and a hand extended to indicate the need for calm, Vraska used a measured tone to speak: "What is it, Cevraya? How can your queen be of service?"

Cevraya took the hint and lowered her own voice—which hardly hid her urgency. "It is a matter of some gravity, Your Highness. Izoni has made an attempt on the life of Myc, of Myczil Zunich here. The Matka's trying to consolidate her power among the devkarin."

"That's a serious charge," Vraska stated, keenly aware that Kyteringa was listening, too. Listening and frozen.

"Serious and accurate, Queen Vraska," Cevraya said. "Izoni Thousand-Eyed sent her poisonous spiders after Myc, fearing that the devkarin would rally to the only son of Jarad vod Savo, rather than to her."

Patting Kyteringa on the shoulder, Vraska stood and looked Zunich in the eye. "You'll be safe here in my court—with me and those loyal to me."

Zunich scoffed: "Please. I know you killed my father."

"Your father died long before I turned him to stone."

"True enough. And I won't pretend he was the same elf who raised me after that first death. But that doesn't mean I'm glad to see his petrified form among your collection. Nor does it mean I'm prepared to trust you, 'my queen.'"

Vraska could practically see the sarcasm drip from Zunich's tongue. Kyteringa, though not fully comprehending the circumstances, clearly understood Zunich's hostility toward her hero. The girl stood abruptly, holding the blue shooter at the ready—as if prepared to shoot it at any enemy of her queen.

Zunich turned his attention to the girl. He crouched down to her level and said, "You shouldn't trust her, either. She killed your father, as well as mine."

"Liar!" the girl shouted back in his face, her hand shaking angrily, the marble ready to launch.

Vraska wrapped her hand around the girl's to head off any potential eye injuries. Kyteringa looked up into the gorgon's eyes, and Vraska looked kindly, if sadly, down into hers. "He's not lying, Kyteringa. I did take your father's life. There are things I did to safeguard *all* the Golgari that I'm not proud of. But I would *never* hurt you."

The girl looked confused. Vraska squeezed her hand gently and smiled sadly down on her. Kyteringa said, "Never?"

"Never, Princess. Never."

The elf child didn't smile back. But she nodded.

Vraska then turned her head to meet a rising Zunich's gaze. He flinched, knowing that looking into her eyes could wind up being a permanent condition. But to his credit, he did not look away.

In a clear voice, she said, "However I came by the crown and whatever the grievances that drove me to seek it, I now intend to be a queen of and for *all* the children of the Golgari. I swear to you Myczil Savod Zunich, to you Cevraya, to all assembled here, to anyone and everyone on Ravnica who will listen, that I, Queen Vraska, *will* protect devkarin children as I would teratogen. Human, elf, kraul, troll, Erstwhile, gorgon or *any* of our guild shall find a haven of safety among the Swarm." Her words rang with true conviction, as every word she spoke was the absolute truth.

Then she sighed and said quietly to Zunich, "But I won't hold you a prisoner, Huntmaster, if you cannot trust me or feel secure in my company. I know you have relatives among the Selesnyans, and if you feel safer among them . . ."

Cevraya grabbed ahold of Zunich's arm and urged, "Your heart is Golgari. Do not deny it, yourself or the Swarm. You know I have always been your friend, even when your father was not one. I believe in Queen Vraska, believe that you'll be safe among her host, at least until I can deal with Matka Izoni."

"And when would that be?" he asked dubiously.

"It won't be long," Cevraya assured him. "Word of Izoni's treachery is already spreading."

Still, he hesitated.

With one hand still gripping Kyteringa, Vraska addressed him most pragmatically: "Huntmaster, if *I* wanted you dead, I'd look you in the eyes, as I did your father. My victims are on full display for all to see. I do not send spiders to do my killing."

And this was also perfectly true. For Vraska, of course, didn't want Zunich dead. She wanted him loyal.

As if to prove her point, Vraska's eyes began to glow. Zunich held his ground, ready to die. And when the glow faded, he nodded to the queen, realizing that she could've killed him at any time.

He said, "I know my father was not the same man after becoming a lich. We had grown estranged long before you . . . took the actions you did, as I did not always agree with—or even respect—the policies of his reign."

"This is known," Cevraya offered.

"It is," Vraska confirmed. "It is why I see no conflict between us. It is why—as unlikely as it may seem to you—I'd like us to be friends."

"One step at a time, perhaps," he said cautiously.

"And what is that first step? Will you accept my protection?"

Zunich looked from Vraska to Cevraya to the girl Kyteringa. The latter seemed to be waiting for him to let her know if the queen could still be trusted.

"Yes. I will. And thank you, Queen Vraska." This time, no sarcasm dripped.

"I am glad of it," Vraska said, smiling. She could feel the elven girl's hand relax in hers. "Now, perhaps you'd care to join myself and Princess Kyteringa in our game of kanala?"

He chuckled and removed his mask. "I haven't played kanala in years . . ."

"I can teach you, Prince Myczil!" said the girl with some glee—and maybe a slight crush. "The queen says I'm already very good."

So the happy princess sat. And the satisfied queen sat. And the thawing prince sat. And the relieved advisors watched the proceedings with no little pleasure.

And Vraska thought, *Baan was right. Much can be done with a simple jar of spiders.*

FORTY-SEVEN

RAL ZAREK

Ral and the Wanderer approached Tezzeret's fortress under cover of a mighty lightning storm, generated by the storm mage himself.

"How do you know this is the place?" asked the Wanderer. "All I see are clouds."

"I know clouds. Those are not clouds."

The Wanderer had agreed to watch Ral's back, but he had made it clear she should leave the killing of Tezzeret to him.

She had said, "I don't care who gets the credit, but if I see my chance, I'm going to take it."

"As long as you don't get in *my* way."

"You're overconfident."

"I've fought him before. I think I'm just the perfect amount of confident."

"You fought the minion of Bolas before. This Tezzeret is a different beast."

As they trudged through the sand, Ral contemplated her last statement and concluded that the Wanderer was probably right. The Tezzeret who fought to execute the plans of another—even one such as Bolas—would be a very different beast from what Ral would face tonight. This beast would have two advantages. He was in his own lair, his own home turf. And on top of that, he was a cornered animal. Ral was coming to kill him, so Tezzeret wasn't fighting for Bolas anymore. He was fighting for his own life.

Well, good to know. But I'll be fighting for my life, too. And for my life with Tomik.

That was a truth. For the first time ever, Ral had something real to live for, something beyond mere survival. He had reached the pinnacle of his ambition as Izzet guildmaster, and even more important, he had Tomik. Someone to love and someone who loved him. Tezzeret was the last roadblock to achieving everything he'd ever dreamed of. He wasn't going to die fighting this beast, this cornered animal. He was going to put the creature out of both their miseries.

But first he'd have to get past the beast's perimeter defenses.

The faux clouds parted and an entire squadron of what appeared to be pure etherium gargoyles—led by an immense gargoyle of etherium and stone—soared out of the gap to attack their master's enemies.

The Wanderer called out, "Well, you were right about the clouds! But I'm not going to be able to do much against these creatures unless or until they get within a sword's length!"

"No worries," he said. After all, *he* had none. With a twist of his wrist, the sky began to crackle above him. Lightning flashed amid the real clouds overhead. Ral clicked on his Accumulator and listened to its hum, waiting for the pitch to peak. When it did, he fired off two spectacular bolts from either hand.

The large, lead gargoyle barrel-rolled out of the way, but both bolts found a target in two etherium gargoyles that exploded and shattered, burst into flame and melted, what was left of each crashing into the beach thirty yards ahead.

He fired off two more bolts while simultaneously inviting the storm to join in. Lightning struck from the clouds above, creating a circuit with half a dozen of the creatures, their etherium conducting the electricity between them as they fried and burst.

And so it went. Ral absolutely devastated the gargoyle attack force. Only two, the lead gargoyle and a second, managed to come within a radius of ten feet of either Planeswalker.

This second, who had deftly dodged a bolt from Ral, broke formation to attack the Wanderer. But the Planeswalker's sword literally split the creature right down the middle, with either half crashing into the sand behind her.

The lead gargoyle dive-bombed Ral and might have ended things right there, but the Izzet guildmaster threw up a virtual net of electricity that forced the monster to break off its attack. Ral closed his fist, hoping to ensnare the gargoyle, but it soared straight upward and avoided the trap.

Within minutes, *all* but that lead gargoyle had been destroyed. And except for the one cleaved in twain by the Wanderer, all had been destroyed by Ral Zarek. Left without his attack force, the lead gargoyle retreated, flying back between the split in the faux clouds and disappearing into the darkness of that gap.

Ral expected the gap to close. He thought he'd probably have to blast their way inside. But the gap remained open.

The Wanderer said, "That looks like an invitation."

"Yeah."

"Which means he's ready for us."

"Or thinks he is."

"Remember what I said about overconfidence. Don't let this victory go to your head."

"I'm not. It was far too easy. I don't think Tezzeret thought for a minute those gargoyles could stop us. He was *trying* to make us overconfident. He failed. The hard part of this mission hasn't even begun."

They trudged on toward the gap with no further interference. Five minutes later, they entered Tezzeret's fortress.

FORTY-EIGHT

TEYO VERADA

Kaya, Rat and Teyo had come to Dominaria to kill Liliana Vess, even if Teyo was expressly against the idea, and Rat hadn't exactly supported it. But even the assassin Kaya was given pause when they saw Liliana wearing a servant's collar while working in the garden of her ancestral home like an automaton.

Kaya looked around for any other eyes that might be on Liliana and, finding none, said to the others, "Stay alert." Then she drew one of her daggers, quickly crossed the moonlit distance from the trees to the garden and stopped before her prey. Teyo and Rat followed.

Liliana just kept pulling thorny weeds from the soil with bare bleeding hands and seemed to take absolutely no notice of the three of them whatsoever. It was more than a little disconcerting.

This must be what Rat feels like all the time.

Maybe it was just curiosity—the need to know what by the Eastern Cloud was going on—but Kaya didn't stab the necromancer. Instead, she tried to talk to her, whispering, "Liliana. Liliana Vess." Receiving no response, she asked, "Liliana Vess, what are you doing?"

No response.

Kaya grabbed the woman's bloody hand, preventing her from pulling another weed. This at least caused Liliana to look up. Her expression was blank. "Liliana," Kaya said. "Can you hear me?"

No response.

Kaya released Liliana's hand. Immediately the gardener went back to her gardening.

Teyo found himself sniffing Miss Vess. He thought maybe he smelled smoke upon her clothes, as if she had been standing beside a bonfire—or maybe in a room of burning incense. The smell reminded him of something, but he still couldn't place it.

"Well, I'm confused," Rat whispered.

"So am I," Kaya grumbled, "to say the least."

Rat looked at Teyo, who shrugged and mumbled something that might have sounded a little like "I dunno."

Rat tapped her chin and pondered the situation. "If Miss Vess here is a prisoner, then who is the Mistress Vess who imprisoned her?"

Kaya nodded at the salience of the question and added, "And how could this Mistress Vess possibly be powerful enough to take down the only person powerful enough to destroy Nicol Bolas?"

Rat said, "Maybe I can find out," and she scurried off once again. For a moment, Kaya looked worried for her, looked as if she might call Rat back. But she shook off her worries, fairly confident—as Teyo was—that Rat would go unnoticed and potentially learn something valuable.

Kaya still had a dagger in one hand. Taking a risk, Teyo nodded toward it and asked, "Are you going to kill her? It would be easy enough now."

As he assumed, the idea of killing Liliana in this state was somewhat distasteful to the ghost-assassin. "No. Not now. Not until we learn more."

It gave Teyo hope that he might finally be able to talk Kaya out of killing Liliana altogether.

Then he had another thought. "Maybe the problem's the collar . . ." He reached out and attempted to remove it.

"Teyo, wait!"

As he fumbled with the latch, the gold collar heated rapidly. Liliana screamed in pain and grabbed for her throat, even as Teyo was forced to let go before his hands were scorched.

Kaya gave him a look that would have made Abbot Barrez proud.

Well, the old Abbot Barrez, anyway.

He felt like a fool. Right up to the point where Liliana reached out and grabbed *him* by the collar, growling out, "What in Urza's name do you think you're doing?"

FORTY-NINE

JACE BELEREN

Jace found Vraska in her quarters, but even as he arrived, she was buckling on her cutlass and preparing to leave.

"You're back," she said.

"I'm back."

"I'm glad. I'm in a hurry right now. But I shouldn't be gone long. You can relax here for an hour. Then you can tell me about Theros." She was already halfway out the door.

"Uh-huh . . ."

Vraska wasn't telepathic, yet something in that *"Uh-huh"* tipped her off to the fact that Jace was troubled. And he guessed that she could guess what he was troubled about. She stopped and turned . . . and waited.

He spoke quietly, calmly. "I think I pretty much know everything you've been keeping from me. I understand why the guilds didn't consult myself or Chandra or most of the Gatewatch, even, about their plans to kill Liliana, Tezzeret and Baan, but . . ."

"But you want to know why I kept you in the dark."

He nodded. "Vraska, one of the things that I love about . . . well, *us*, is that we don't play games. I'm not saying you can't have your secrets—whether it's Golgari business or just something . . . that you feel belongs to you. But you had to know—"

"I knew." She walked up to him and took his hands. "And I was conflicted about what to tell you. Because I know *you're* conflicted . . . about Liliana."

He exhaled. "It's complicated."

"It's all right."

"Still . . ."

"Still, you deserve to know my thoughts. Here's the hard truth: The guilds weren't about to grant Liliana clemency, so by not telling you, I thought I was protecting you." Her eyes suddenly went wide. "Krokt, I just heard myself saying that out loud, and I now completely realize how awful that sounds. Condescending and awful."

He let go of her hands, but he forced himself not to turn away. He felt certain the old Jace would turn away to pout, passive-aggressively. So the new Jace faced her and stated, "We can't be this way, Vraska."

"No, no, you're right."

"We've got to be able to trust each other enough to be honest. Whether the news is good or bad."

"I know, I know. It's just . . . I also know you still have feelings for Liliana."

"I told you it's complicated."

"I understand that, and I'm not jealous. I trust your feelings for me. I do, I promise. And I also promise that I never would have accepted the job to kill Liliana personally. I could never ask you to be with someone who would stoop to killing her 'rival.'"

Jace protested: "Liliana is no rival to you!"

Vraska took his hands again as she made the correction: "I wouldn't kill someone you once loved. No matter how complicated the whole thing is. I'd never want you to have to look at me and see her killer."

He had an impulse to thank her, but that didn't seem right.

She sighed. "Here's the thing. Another hard truth, I suppose. Liliana was personally responsible for the deaths of one hundred and sixteen Golgari. Those are my people, Jace. And I'm their queen, sworn to protect them. So frankly, I *agree* with the other guilds that she needs to die."

He swallowed hard. His head sank.

"Now, I'm sorry," she said as she raised his chin with one gentle touch, "but I have Golgari business. I really have to go. But I will try to be back soon, and I very much hope you'll be here when I return."

She kissed him then, barely brushing his lips with hers. He found he ached for her. But before he could say anything else—*do* anything else—she was gone, leaving him with much to think about, *again*.

FIFTY

RAT

Rat made her way inside the mansion. It was easy. As usual, no one took any notice of her—despite the fact that she kept a running monologue going at all times: "Oh, that's some fine work on the renovations. Precision craftsmanship. So elegant. And if Miss Ballard is right, it was all done so quickly, too." Smiling, she paused to address a tray-holding servant who couldn't see or hear her: "Look at that molding! No one appreciates good molding anymore. I wonder how much of it was original to the mansion, you know?"

But Rat quickly lost her smile; truthfully, she felt awful for the Mistress Vess' collared "servants."

"It's just flat-out not right. I don't even like it when I see the Orzhov treating thrulls this way. And these are humans, no different from me or Teyo. I swear if someone tried to put a collar on Teyo—or, you know, Mistress Kaya—I'd get Gruul-level ornery on their asses, you know? I'd be like, *Mother, can I borrow your axe?*" This last bit was spoken to a girl about her own age replacing and lighting a candle in a sconce.

Rat got up close to the girl. "Oh, you look so frightened. I can feel the fear coming off you in waves. I mean you're just lighting a candle and your hands are shaking so hard you can barely bring the match to the wick. What would she do to you if you messed up this one little candle? Listen, I know you can't hear me, but maybe sorta in your brain I can reassure you a little. You see, we're here. And we may not know exactly what's going on yet, but I promise you that Mistress Kaya, Teyo and me, we're not gonna let this stand. We'll find some way to fix this. Can't promise your life'll be perfect afterward, right? We all got our troubles. Whatever whats we have to deal with. But we *won't* leave you wearing a collar. I promise; I promise; I promise." She thought this as hard as she could at the girl.

But there was too much fear for Rat's minor psychic thing to cut its way through.

Better just get on with this then.

She moved into the large expansive dining room. More "servants" were here, bringing some kind of whipped confection for dessert. Still more "servants" were in the corner, playing music for guests, who seemed to take no notice whatsoever of the collared prisoners making their lives pleasant.

Like this whole place was staffed by a legion of me.

One laughing guest at the far end of the feast said, "Mistress Vess, you set a remarkable table."

Rat scoffed loudly: "Except *she* didn't set it, did she?"

No one paid her any mind, so she focused on the woman accepting the compliment.

"You honor me, Lord Valois," said "Mistress Liliana Vess" with a slight dip of her well-coiffed head. In contrast with her elegance, two large and fairly hideous zombies guarded the necromancer from behind her chair. Rat noticed that the collared servants who came anywhere near their mistress or her body-guards seemed to be doing everything in their power to be especially efficient. Efficient and invisible—*insignificant and Rat-like*—desperate to avoid notice.

Rat scurried around to the head of the table for a closer look. This "Mistress Vess" had dark hair and was somewhat pretty . . . but otherwise looked nothing at all like the true Miss Raven-Hair. Even covered with dirt from the garden, the real Miss Liliana was beautiful, in a smoky, dangerous sorta way. This woman wasn't anything like that.

Nothing special at all, really. Except maybe that choker she's wearing. That's kinda sparkly and keen! Still, I bet it would look even better on the actual Miss Liliana.

The bejeweled choker featured a large central amulet at the woman's throat with a sizable sapphire of a rich, dark blue. There was something kinda mesmerizing about it, and Rat found she had to tear her eyes away.

And not just *because it's sparkly!*

Rat was on Mistress Vess' right, staring directly at her, studying her close. Then she noticed the hostess' left hand was tapping on a bound volume. Dodging the two zombies, Rat whipped around the back of the mistress' chair to the other side and peered down at the book in the candlelight. It was a printed copy of something titled *The Fall of the House of Vess*. Moreover, though this faux Mistress Vess might not look much like the true Miss Raven-Hair, she did look *exactly* like the illustration of Miss Liliana Vess on the cover of the book. She double-checked this two, three, four times. *Exactly* like the illustration. Even the hairstyle and the dress were the same. The only difference was the choker with its blue gem.

And speaking of gems . . .

Beside the book was another even more interesting item partially covered by a cloth napkin. Rat was quite sure it was the egg-shaped gem that had belonged to the Elder Dragon Bolas.

The one he had used to absorb the Sparks of so many Planeswalk-ers. Rat distinctly remembered that when the dragon disinte-grated, his gem had fallen atop the pyramid. And she remembered that Miss Liliana—the *real* Miss Liliana—had picked it up just before planeswalking away. Now here it sat, beside Mistress Book Cover, the candlelight sparkling on its almost liquid sur-face. Rat's pockets were currently stuffed with diamonds, but she found she'd be willing to trade them all for this prize.

Just then, Mistress Book Cover tapped her crystal goblet with her spoon to get everyone's attention. The murmur of pleasant-ries and the consumption of dessert quickly settled into near si-lence, and all eyes looked her way (Rat's included).

She stood and spoke. "Gentlemen and ladies, I am honored that you have joined me here at my home. I know for some of you this reunion of the Cabal is not a happy occasion . . ."

She let the sentence and the sentiment hang, and on cue a round of protests circled the table to the obviously pre-assumed gratification of the hostess.

She went on: "Until *very* recently, all of you held sway over vast territories when the Cabal was at its peak under Belzenlok. And most of you believe the Cabal's time has passed now that the demon is gone. But as I hope you've seen here tonight, there's another option. For let's be honest, my new friends, *you* did all the work. *You* kept the people in check. *You* kept the coffers flow-ing. The demon didn't do that. *You* did. *You* are the true heroes of the Cabal."

This also met with general approval. Rat had no idea what this Cabal was, but she had a pretty good idea it must be fairly horrible.

I mean "Cabal" is not a word that inspires happy feelings, right?

"So what's missing? What did Belzenlok actually provide?" asked Mistress Book Cover. "He wasn't just a figurehead, of course. It's not enough to simply *inspire* fear. You need a leader who can back that fear up with actual power. Enough power to keep the peasants in line. Enough power to protect the Cabal from the Benalish and the Serrans and anyone else who might seek to once again bring down our great works. And yes, I did say *'our.'* Because before I made my presence known in the Caligo, I infiltrated—yes, *'infiltrated'*—the Cabal to see if I found it worthy. And I did. The only problems, as I saw it, were the whims of Belzenlok, which actually served to hold us all back. And those problems no longer exist. Now only one difficulty remains. Who shall take the demon's place?"

She paused again. The room was dead silent.

Lord Valois swallowed hard, cleared his throat and proposed, "The Curse of the House of Vess."

She gave another small bow of her head as he took up her cause: "It makes sense, my friends. She has a name and a story that is the stuff of every child's nightmare. Do you know of a single household in all the land that doesn't have a copy of that book? And yes, I know we all think of it as a children's tale. But every adult was a child once, and the best fears hew back to those early days. If we were all being honest, everyone at *this table* fears the necromancer Liliana Vess. And fear her they should."

Rat thought that this impromptu speech of the lord's sounded very well rehearsed.

"And it isn't just the name. Liliana Vess has the *power* to back it up. You see what she's done here . . ." He stood unexpectedly and grabbed a tight hold of a collared servant—an old man with an elegantly trimmed white beard—palming the back of his head. "These people cower before her. They've rebuilt this home—*her* home—in a matter of *weeks*. They serve her night and day. They know they can do nothing to defy her. Should they speak even a *single* word of treason . . . They. Will. Burn."

A tear began to roll down the old man's cheek. Rat was half inclined to leap up onto the table, run down its length and stab Lord Valois in the throat.

The lord released the old servant and pushed him away before taking his seat and resuming. "That's two criteria down. What remains? Trust. Yes, trust. We want a leader whom we can trust to put the Cabal above his or her own petty grudges. Belzenlok invited his fall by playing cat and mouse with some ancient sorceress from his past. A sorceress who gathered allies to help her. If I might ask Mistress Vess . . . do you have old enemies that should be of some concern to us?"

"I do not."

"And why is that, if I'm not too bold?"

"Not too bold, Lord. It is a reasonable question. *Perfectly* reasonable. I have no old enemies because every enemy I've *ever* had is dead. And the only way they could come back to interfere with the Cabal is if I myself raise them. And frankly, I'm simply not enough of a fool to ever make that mistake. When I raise the dead, I control them completely and absolutely." As if to prove the point, Mistress Vess waved her hand at the two zombies that stood behind her chair.

It was only then that Rat made another—perhaps obvious— discovery. Close as she was to the two undead guards, it suddenly occurred to her that neither had any scent. She'd seen plenty of zombies among the Golgari and Rakdos, and she'd never known one not to *"completely and absolutely"* stink of rotting flesh.

Something smells very wrong here, and it's not these zombies.

Lord Valois was saying, "So you see, my friends—my old comrades—the Cabal can rise again."

Mistress Book Cover corrected him, "The Cabal *will* rise again."

Then, led by Lord Valois, the rest of the guests took up the chant: "The Cabal will rise again. The Cabal will rise again. The Cabal will rise again!"

Meanwhile, on a hunch, Rat reached out to touch the zombie closest to her—and as she suspected, her hand passed right through the creature . . .

It's an illusion!

Unfortunately, Rat's attempt caused the sapphire at Mistress Book Cover's throat to glow. Blue smoke poured forth from the amulet into both zombies, rendering them solid enough to smash their fists against the wall, leaving dents that the poor servants would later have to repair. Simultaneously, Mistress Book Cover shot to her feet and looked around. Rat stepped back, momentarily fearful. But the mistress' eyes passed right over her as the hostess addressed her guests: "We have an intruder here. A trespasser. Some sorcery hides this spy from our vision. But the spy exists and must be caught. Now."

Around the table, many of the guests rose to their feet. They began casting counter magic of all sorts, but this hardly terrified Rat. For years, when she was younger, her parents had sought to find a spell to cure her condition.

None of that stuff ever worked.

Still, she figured she had better get going . . .

But not before I scoop up that shiny on the table.

Rat grabbed Bolas' gem. But as soon as she touched it, multiple shouts rang out: "There!" and "I see her!" and "It's just a girl!" and "A thief!" and worst of all, *"Get her!"*

Mistress Book Cover waved her zombies forward and said with a voice like ice, "Take her. Now."

A panicked Rat dropped the gem and ran.

More voices echoed across the room as Rat scurried out of it: "Where'd she go?" and "I've lost her again!" and "Which spell revealed her?" and "Secure the perimeter!"

Mistress Book Cover screamed in fury.

Rat fled, but wasn't afraid. Quite the reverse. She knew down to her soul that none of the Cabal's spells had revealed her to the room.

It was the gem. The gem of Nicol Bolas. Holding it made me . . . significant. *Holding that gem . . . that's the cure to my Curse!*

FIFTY-ONE

LILIANA VESS

Liliana emerged from her fog, only vaguely aware that the boy crouching beside her now had *hurt her*! Her neck burned. Her hands were raw and bleeding. She reached over and grabbed him by the collar and growled, "What in Urza's name do you think you're doing?"

He fumfered out something about "your collar," and she instantly released him to grasp at her throat. She was wearing the metallic collar of the prisoners of this place, and he had put it on her! She squeezed both her hands into fists and summoned a spell to reave his soul. Spectral clouds of purple-tinged black mana gathered as he scrambled backward. She aimed and unleashed the magic, which rushed toward the boy—only to be blocked by Gideon's white aura!

Gideon?

No. Not Gideon. The boy had raised a diamond-shaped shield of white light. Perhaps there was a certain coincidental resemblance to Gideon's aura of invulnerability—or perhaps Gideon was just on her mind. But she now remembered where she had seen this boy before. On Ravnica. She had seen him fighting her Eternals.

Not my Eternals! Bolas' *Eternals!*

And not just him. His female companion, too. The one with her daggers out, ready to kill.

From behind his shield, the boy said, "I was just trying to remove your collar."

"Really?" Liliana said darkly. "So the two of you *didn't* come from Ravnica to kill me?"

Their quick exchange of a stunned glance told the story. Her memories were still hazy from whatever spell they had already attempted to place on her—or maybe from the collar—but she wasn't going to die at the hands of these two incompetents. The boy was fairly well protected but clearly inexperienced. So Liliana would take down the woman first by summoning up more of the purple-black coalescing mist between her bleeding fists. The death magic burned where her raw skin had been cut, but she could fix that later when her enemies lay dead. She sent the dark, rippling energies forward. The woman dodged. But this was not a bolt of fire or lightning, soaring on past ad infinitum. The mist swirled back around to strike the woman from behind—only to be blocked once again by another of the boy's shields.

"Sphere," the woman said. "Over her."

"But—"

"Do it, Teyo! Now!"

The boy nodded and dropped both his shields. Liliana saw her moment. Once more she gathered the dark power. And just as she unleashed it, she found herself completely surrounded by a dome of bright-white light. Her magic crashed against the wall of the boy's construct and nearly doubled back on her; she was barely able to block her own power to save her life, and in any case, it knocked her back on her ass.

Shaking off the impact, and with her palms resting flat on the earth, she reached down, down, through the dirt and soil, past roots and earthworms and other detritus, until she found what she was looking for. She issued her summons, then struggled to find her feet, pushing herself to stand. The purple-black mist was just clearing, and through the white glow of the hemisphere, she saw the woman approaching with her long knives out. They glowed violet with their own spectral energy.

Liliana smiled grimly. They were coming, working their way up. Just a few more seconds . . .

"When I say *now*, drop the sphere," the woman commanded. "And I'll do the job I was sent to do."

"I'd rather not," the boy said.

"Teyo . . ."

"I think it might be best if I keep you both separated, at least until everyone calms down."

Liliana's mind was still foggy, but it almost seemed as if the kid was trying to protect her.

But that makes no sense. No one who'd survived the fighting on Ravnica would protect Liliana Vess, right?

The question instantly became moot as three undead corpses tore their way up through the ground and attacked Liliana's two assailants.

The boy looked scared out of his wits, though he managed to retain enough of them about him to keep extant the hemisphere of light surrounding Liliana. He backed away as a rotting woman with considerable meat left on her bones shambled toward him, her jaw distended and hanging loose, her skeletal hands looking more like claws, ready to rend him to pieces.

The woman, meanwhile, stabbed her blades deep into the

chest of the large decomposing man that had rushed her. Straightaway, Liliana felt her connection to and control of the zombie severed. It fell face-first like the corpse it was.

But Liliana pressed her final thrall forward, and this one presented the zombie-killer with more difficulties. It had clearly been feeding the worms for quite some time and was little more than a skeleton. The woman stabbed at it, but the blades swept through an empty rib cage. It reached for her, and she suddenly turned violet and ghostly, its hands passing right through her with no more effect than her knives had had on it.

The boy continued to back away while raising a diamond-shaped shield to block the female zombie. But by this time, he had been maneuvered into position. A skeletal hand burst forth from the dirt of the vegetable patch and grabbed his ankle tightly. He let out a little scream and tried to shake the hand off, but Liliana reinforced its power and strength, essentially staking the man-child in place. As the hand's grip tightened, the shield holding back the undead female began to shimmer and waver.

In front of Liliana, the woman with the knives solidified and kicked out, snapping the shin of her attacker, who dropped to one knee but kept advancing, dragging the broken leg behind it. But the woman simply circled wide around the creature, racing back toward the hemisphere and Liliana.

"Teyo, get ready!"

Liliana knew she'd have to time this perfectly. If she brought up her magic too soon, the besieged boy wouldn't drop his. She'd have to be prepared for the dome of light to fall—and then strike quickly, before the woman could strike first.

The woman said, "Now!"

Liliana rapidly brought up another dark cloud.

But the boy hadn't dropped the shield. It had been a feint, a trick to lure her out. Although if it had, it seemed to have fooled the woman, as well. For even as Liliana's dark mist again crashed uselessly against the inner wall of the hemisphere, the woman was already turning to the boy, saying "Teyo, I said *'Now!'*"

The female zombie broke through the boy's failing diamond-shaped shield. It was all but upon him, and yet he still maintained the hemisphere around Liliana. Only when the mist dispersed—when neither Liliana nor the woman was quite at the ready—did the boy Teyo drop his shield.

Caught off guard, both women belatedly tried to renew their attacks, but before her opponent could bring her spectral knives to bear and before Liliana could bring up more spectral energy of her own—something struck Liliana from behind, sending her into darkness . . .

FIFTY-TWO

DOVIN BAAN

It was hardly surprising when the gorgon returned to Baan's safe house and informed him that his plan had worked perfectly.

Equally unsurprising was his response: "Of course."

He could practically *hear* her scowl.

He went on. "I should warn you it is only a first move upon the chessboard, the first step toward my solution to your problems. A dangerous fragment that could easily backfire without my further assistance. I have not yet given you the plan in its entirety, in order to prevent you from executing it—and then executing me. So I ask you quite simply, Queen Vraska, do we have an agreement?"

She paused, which was hardly surprising. But he knew the length of the pause would be very telling. Five-point-seven seconds or more, and it meant that she was still seriously considering his death. Five-point-six seconds or less, and it meant she was only pausing so as not to seem too eager. He waited, counting the ticks in his head.

"We have an agreement," she said in exactly five-point-five seconds.

Baan allowed himself a small smile and then, with a mystic gesture, clarified the terms for the binding mystic record: "You agree to secretly keep me alive in exchange for my ongoing service?"

"Yes," she said, as he had known she would. The gorgon was willing to risk the consequences, choosing Baan and the Golgari over everything else.

"You do know," she said, "that I'll still need proof of your demise for the guilds."

"Of course," he said again as he crossed the room confidently. He opened a closet door. A veiled figure stood within. He removed the veil to reveal a statue, a perfect replica of himself with a look of terror etched upon his face.

"Impressive work," she said. "Not much in the way of art, and the expression borders on cliché, but it's very realistic. Very convincing. Who's the sculptor?"

"I am," he said. "And I apologize for the expression. I had to create it in a mirror, and emotion does not come naturally to my face."

"It might have been the perfect proof—before you were blinded. You must know it's useless now. No one will believe I petrified a blind man."

"Indeed. I showed this to you merely to demonstrate how far ahead I have planned my contingencies. This was created in this studio weeks before Lazav blinded me. For although I will admit I had not planned for such an injury, our meeting here today, on the other hand, is one that I fully anticipated as an eight-point-nine percent possibility."

"And is that really the only reason you have presented this effigy for my perusal?" She seemed to be altering her style of diction to match his—though whether consciously or unconsciously was not yet clear.

Still, he seriously considered her question for two-point-eight seconds before responding: "No, I believe you are right. There is an element of vanity to this display. I felt *someone* should see it."

"I understand."

"Good. We understand *each other*."

"And the problem of proof?"

"I have been working on an alternative. We'll need witnesses. Well, *one* witness, in particular. Chandra Nalaar."

FIFTY-THREE

KAYA

Rat was standing over Liliana, holding the tree branch she had used to render the necromancer unconscious. The girl looked fairly proud of herself, but Kaya wasn't in the mood to offer praise. "You should have used your daggers, Rat. You should have killed her."

"I didn't want to."

"No? Look around you. She was using the undead to kill your friends."

"But I stopped that. You know, by clonking her."

With Liliana unconscious, the three zombies were inert on the ground, which hardly made them less terrifying; each seemed capable of rising again at any moment.

Teyo, meanwhile, was *still* struggling to pry open the grip of the skeletal hand around his ankle.

An exasperated Kaya turned on him, barking out, "And you didn't follow orders."

"I'm sorry, but—"

"That doesn't cut it, Teyo. You didn't drop the sphere when I told you, when I was ready. Then you dropped it later, when I wasn't. That could have gotten both of us killed."

"I dropped the hemisphere when *Rat* was ready," he said, finally freeing his leg. "With that log."

"A good thing, too," Rat said to Kaya, "because when *you* were ready, *she* was ready. And *that* could've gotten all three of you killed—and I would have been stranded here . . . forever. Besides, you don't really want to kill her now, do you?"

"Oh, don't I?" Kaya said, striding toward the unconscious woman with her blades out. Kneeling before Liliana, Kaya held one of her long knives to the woman's throat, just above the golden collar.

"Wait, mistress!" Rat called out.

"I'm not going to have a better opportunity," Kaya stated, though she remained still—neither putting the blade away, nor slicing it into skin.

"Maybe not, but I know—*I know*—you're not thrilled about the idea of killing a defenseless woman."

"You'd be surprised."

"Just listen, at least. Listen to what I found out."

So Rat told her story, of the party and the "servants" and their mistress and her book and the Cabal and the zombie-illusions that became zombie-solids after the sapphire in the amulet had emitted the blue smoke.

Throughout the telling, Kaya kept her dagger poised at Liliana's throat, while Teyo approached slowly, sniffing the air, as Rat finished her tale: ". . . So then I grabbed for . . . I mean . . . well, see, basically, after the zombies solidified—and Mistress Book Cover and the others figured out someone was there— I figured I better get out and come back to report to you two."

"You did the right thing," Kaya said, feeling slightly calmer and very tired.

Rat's head bobbed up and down. "Yep. Yep. That's what I did. The right thing."

Teyo walked right up to Rat and sniffed at her. She gave him a look, but he stepped back and slapped his forehead with the heel of his hand. "Of course! It's a djinn! This fake 'Liliana Vess' has a *djinn* in her power. *That's* what I've been sensing and smelling: djinn-smoke. It's in the air, all around us, present but diffuse. But you were close enough that I can smell it on your clothes and hair."

"I'm infected with djinn-smoke?" She sniffed at herself and made a face. "Mistress Kaya, can we go back to Orzhova so I can take another shower?"

"Wait, wait, wait," Kaya said. "What's a djinn?"

Teyo and Rat stared at her. Then Rat turned to Teyo and said, "There's something you know that she doesn't? You barely know anything."

Kaya said, "Stop it."

Teyo nodded, saying, "No, no, it's true. I barely know anything."

Rat said, "He'd never seen a viashino or a vedalken before two days ago."

Teyo was still nodding. "Or a leonin. Or a gorgon. Or an elf. Oh, or an angel!"

"Or a pegasus. Or a griffin. Or a goblin."

"Well, at least I'd heard of goblins. We have goblins on Gobakhan. I'd just never met any. But—"

"All right, I get the point," Kaya said crossly, poking the air with the dagger that *wasn't* still flush against Liliana's throat. "Teyo's ignorant, and yet I'm the one who doesn't know what a . . . what a . . ."

"What a djinn is," Rat said. "Although to be fair, I've never seen a djinn."

"Really?" Teyo said, stunned. "There's something I've seen that the Rat hasn't?"

"I'd never seen a diamondstorm before yesterday, either. Or was that today? I've completely lost track of time."

"Me, too."

"*Enough!*" Kaya shouted. "What's a djinn?"

Teyo crouched down before Kaya to explain. "Well, see, there are djinn on Gobakhan. Small spirits of fire or air that emerge sometimes from the Western Cloud or the Eastern Cloud, respectively. If you catch one, like inside your geometry, it has to grant you a wish to be released."

"Did you ever catch one?" Rat asked, excited.

"No, I was never fast enough, and my three-dimensional geometry was pretty awful—really, until I came to Ravnica. But Arturo caught one once. He wished for a hot meat pie, and the abbot later said Arturo was lucky he didn't wind up baked *inside* the meat pie. Anyway, djinn don't have a lot of magic. You can't, say, wish for the Eastern Cloud to vanish or anything like that. I mean you can, but it's not gonna happen. And the djinn are tricksters, too. So you have to phrase your wish *very* carefully."

"And what makes you think there's one here?" Kaya demanded.

"Well, all djinn—fire-djinn *and* air-djinn—smell vaguely of smoke. Sweet smoke, like incense. But none of the djinn of Gobakhan are quite this potent. That's why I didn't put it together at first. I saw Arturo's fire-djinn up close. But I didn't smell anything from just outside the sphere the djinn was trapped in. I only smelled her smoke after she conjured up the meat pie for Arturo and he let her go. And within a minute of the djinn disappearing, the smell had dissipated, too. But here, it's, well . . . everywhere—and it's strong. Whatever djinn this 'Liliana' is using is big and very powerful. My guess is she has him or her trapped in that sapphire amulet."

Kaya took all this in and was silent for a long time. Finally, she said, "None of this is any of our business." She turned her attention back to the knife at Liliana's throat. Liliana lay there, still unconscious and unmoving. Kaya began to apply pressure, and a single drop of blood dripped down between her skin and the servant's collar around her neck.

Teyo and Rat both shouted, *"Wait!"*

Kaya hesitated, though she wasn't quite sure why.

Rat said, "We need to help all these people first—the servants. I promised them."

Kaya shook her head. "We came here to kill Liliana Vess, not free the prisoners of Caligo." But still she hesitated.

Rat pounced. "But you took an oath to protect people. *'Never again.'* Remember?"

Of course I remember. But . . .

"There's no reason why we can't free them *after* we've killed Vess. The real Vess."

Teyo pointed at Liliana's face. "Maybe *she* has a reason."

Kaya looked down again. Liliana's eyes were open and staring daggers at the ghost-assassin. And *still* Kaya hesitated.

Vess didn't move. She took no action, defensive or otherwise. She simply stated, "No reason. Just a request. One last request before you kill me."

FIFTY-FOUR

RAL ZAREK

Ral and the Wanderer made their careful way through Tezzeret's base. They weren't trying to be stealthy.

It's not like he doesn't know we're here.

They were simply trying to avoid the inevitable ambush.

Let's face it, we're not going to avoid anything. We just don't want to be taken by surprise. Or, in any case, not so much surprise that we wind up dead before we can even get to Tezzeret.

But there wasn't a single ambush.

There were three.

If Ral thought he'd taken out all of Tezzeret's gargoyle forces save their leader, he was dead wrong—and almost dead because of it.

He and the Wanderer entered a high-ceilinged chamber full of polished stone staircases, immense circular glass windows and large, rotating clockwork gears—all of it decorated by delicate metal filigree. Ral spent a second or two trying to discern the purpose of the machinery, and quickly came to the conclusion that the clockworks controlled an actual clock: a Multiversal Clock, with each circular window actually a clock-face, showing the time of day on numerous worlds, including Alara, Ravnica, Dominaria, Amonkhet, Innistrad, Kaladesh, Fiora and others.

Seeing his face, the Wanderer asked, "What's wrong?"

"Wrong? Nothing. It's a masterpiece . . ."

"What are you talking about?"

So enthralled was he, and so confused was she, neither noticed at first as the largest of the gears rotated slowly around bearing etherium statues—right up until the point when those statues came to life with glowing eyes and echoing roars.

The gargoyle leader was there, living stone and mutable etherium, but he left the battle to his six fellows. Two smaller gargoyles quickly took flight, as two hulking gargoyles leapt down from the revolving gear to charge the Planeswalkers.

Ral's Accumulator was switched on and fully charged, but he was determined not to use even a joule more than necessary at least until he faced Tezzeret himself. So he left one of the leaping gargoyles to the Wanderer and blasted the other with just enough juice to shear off its etherium head.

For her part, the Wanderer used the long reach of her broadsword to achieve the same end.

But the two now headless gargoyles were only a feint to give the two fliers their opportunity. Each scooped a Planeswalker into the air and attempted to dash his or her brains against the stone.

Ral lay hands upon his captor and blew a massive hole in its chest that exploded out its back. Trouble was that by this time, Ral was high enough above the floor that his brains could still wind up dashed. But as the deceased gargoyle fell away, Ral created multiple small concussive thunder blasts beneath him. They slowed his descent enough so that he hit hard against the stone floor—but not hard enough for any brain dashing.

The Wanderer, meanwhile, trapped in the other creature's grip, planeswalked away, gargoyle and all. Three seconds later, she planeswalked back unencumbered.

They were separated now. Ral was on the ground floor. The Wanderer was atop one of the staircases on the other side of the clockworks.

"Where'd it go?" Ral asked, calling out from across the chamber.

"Torn apart within the Blind Eternities," the Wanderer called back.

The gargoyle leader still did not attack. He nodded to his last two minions, both of whom advanced, leaping down off the clockworks.

Ral fired another precision strike, but the gargoyle leapt above the blast and came down behind him. One etherium arm was shaped like a scimitar, and the creature swung it at Ral's Accumulator. Ral barely managed to dodge. He toppled and fell on his back. The gargoyle advanced, red eyes glowing, scimitar on the upswing.

The other gargoyle rose up on its wings and fired projectile-like claws from both hands. The Wanderer parried most of them with her sword, but one struck her in the shoulder. She hissed inwardly but otherwise ignored the pain and leapt off the staircase, catching the gargoyle off guard. The sword came down and cut the gargoyle in twain. As the Wanderer tumbled toward the ground far below, she planeswalked away and reappeared a foot or two above the floor. She still hit hard—but not as hard as if she had fallen the whole distance. She quickly struggled to her feet, pulled the claw out of her shoulder and turned her sword toward the gargoyle leader.

Meanwhile, Ral was still on his back, an overturned tortoise weighed down by his heavy Accumulator. This was the second time in pretty much as many days that this had happened, and he made a mental note that he'd have to do *something* about the Accumulator's balance. But there wasn't exactly time for that now. The gargoyle's scimitar-arm was swinging down, and Ral fired off twin blasts from his hands that sheared off its feet at the calves while simultaneously thrusting him back a good ten yards out of its reach. The gargoyle came crashing down to its knees but extended its wings and took to the air. Still on his back, Ral made a slashing move with one hand, and five slim electrical bolts radiated off his five fingers to cut through the air. The gargoyle corkscrewed to avoid them—and it did avoid four of the five, but the thumb-bolt caught the edge of one wing and blew the wing apart. The gargoyle augered in on its remaining wing, attempting to take Ral Zarek out with its final act. But he'd been rocking back and forth, finally building the necessary leverage to roll out of the way. The gargoyle crashed down where Ral no longer was. He rolled back, slapped a hand on it and fried the creature until its etherium began to melt.

Ral found his feet in time to see the lead gargoyle shake his head and disappear back into the clockworks.

"Your shoulder okay?" Ral asked.

"It's fine."

They entered a circular chamber of no great size. Low ceilings. Nowhere to hide. And every surface seemed to be covered in dark burnished glass.

Low conductivity. This chamber was practically made to contain me. If not actually made to contain me.

A panel slid open in the curved wall. Then another and another. Three massive squat etherium golems with hammerlike heads and clamping serrated metal jaws emerged equidistant from one another. They stomped forward on pincer arms and legs. Their craniums barely cleared the ceiling. Once they'd closed in, there'd be no getting past them.

Ral and the Wanderer took positions, standing back-to-back. Ral shook his head.

What's the point of putting me in a non-conductive room if you're going to send highly conductive opponents to kill me? Or in other words . . . what's the catch?

He found out soon enough.

As the golems advanced, Ral fired a test blast at the closest one. It hit the creature, ricocheting off to strike one of its fellows . . . then the third . . . then back to the first, creating a circuit among all three. The power kept flowing in circles between them, causing no damage whatsoever.

"We may have a problem," Ral said.

"It's all right. I can handle them."

"Is your sword made of metal?"

"Of course, it's made— Ah. Yes, I see."

"Hand it to me. Quickly."

"It won't work for you the way it works for me."

"I understand your reluctance, but unless you see another option . . ."

The golems were almost upon them. "Here," she said. "Better use two hands."

He took her advice and still could barely keep the sword aloft. "Krokt, this thing is heavy!"

"I tried to warn you."

He rushed forward and swung it down diagonally, adding a little charge to propel it faster. It slashed across the golem's chest and cleaved a pincer arm in two. (Ral's own electricity flowed from the golem-circuit back down the sword into his hands. It would have electrocuted the Wanderer, but to Ral Zarek it was practically mother's milk—plus the power replenished his Accumulator just a bit.) Missing an arm now, the golem's own weight caused it to buckle and crash to the floor.

The Wanderer had to dodge the second golem and then the third, but with the circuit broken, Ral was able to heave her sword back over to her. Within seconds she had carved up one, and within a few seconds more the other.

"That was different," he said.

"I didn't like it," she responded. He assumed she was scowling, but as usual he couldn't see her face.

Randomly choosing one of the three open panels, they moved on.

Now they entered an immense workshop with even higher ceilings than the clockwork room had offered. Ral couldn't even see the upper limit of the chamber. Thick black support columns disappeared up into shadow.

He was on the alert for trouble, but he couldn't help noticing the sheer scope of the place and the sheer quantity of works-in-progress scattered across the dozens of metal worktables. As the Izzet guildmaster, Ral Zarek prided himself on his ability to quickly size up, evaluate and identify almost any machine one could imagine. But the quantity of unrecognizable technology in this room alone—this room that Tezzeret didn't seem to mind them seeing—was *not* making him happy. Every item on every table looked both mysterious and dangerous, and he hesitated to think how each might be used against Ravnica and the Multiverse. Ral had been right about Tezzeret developing into a significant threat. The storm mage was more than ready to find the artificer and finish him off once and for all.

But the artificer had other plans.

When the two Planeswalkers reached the center of the chamber, something dripped down on Ral's head. He looked up toward the shadowy ceiling and barely managed to dodge another glop of a tar-like substance falling from above. Yet another glop marred the Wanderer's wide hat.

He felt the goop dripping down his scalp and reached up to wipe it away before it dripped down into his eyes. Instantly he found that his hand was stuck to his forehead.

More of the sticky goop was falling now, missing them but hitting the floor.

"Don't step in it!" he shouted.

"Yes, I got that!"

That's when the chamber's columns started to move.

Ral didn't know what to make of it at first, until the creature's thorax and head descended from above. The columns weren't columns, but the long thick legs of a huge spidery strider, dripping sticky sludge from its slavering jaws to entrap its prey.

Hampered by having one palm stuck idiotically to his forehead, Ral used his free hand to aim a bolt straight up toward the creature's abdomen, while the Wanderer rushed forward to swing her mighty blade at one of its column-thick legs.

These swift, brave actions nearly got them both killed.

The monster's stomach split open and a torrent of the sludge came flooding out—hitting the floor and splashing over them both—even as it lost a leg and toppled over to crush them under its weight.

With one boot stuck to the floor by the splash of sludge, Ral wasn't able to dodge or duck or roll—and wound up trapped, his own legs pinned beneath another of the monster's buckled limbs. That's when he noticed the stinger. It rose up from behind the creature, ready to strike.

The Wanderer—now barefoot, having lost her footwear to the sludge—raced forward and intercepted it, slicing it off before it could pierce Ral's chest. Instead, it twisted and landed flat across the side of his face, sticking there. The injured strider swung its head fast enough to knock the Wanderer off her feet and knock the wind out of her, too. She bounced and rolled into another puddle of sludge. She held on to her sword, but the blade also dipped into the goop and, winded as she was, she was having trouble extricating it.

The strider's jaws descended toward her. Ral, who still had

one hand free, blasted the monster right between its eight eyes. It reared back, screaming, and then collapsed completely dead.

But the victors weren't exactly out of the woods. Both were stuck to the tile floor. Ral was pinned under a leg and still had one hand stuck to his forehead and the monster's stinger stuck to his cheek. And the Wanderer couldn't lift her sword.

At which point, a door opened, and Ral raised his head to see a small humanoid creature—blue-skinned, female and almost spherical—emerge. She peered in, saw the two trapped Planeswalkers and shouted, "Yes, yes. Now, now. Go!"

She stepped back, and half a dozen similar homunculi raced into the room holding simple daggers. Normally, this group wouldn't represent much of a threat, but given the Planeswalkers' current straits, the little creatures and their sharp knives might be very dangerous indeed.

So Ral didn't take any chances. He blasted the closest one with a bolt. The Wanderer managed to channel the kinetic energy from the strider's last head-slam into her sword; she twisted the blade and was able to slice through the hardening sludge and free the sword in time to stab a second creature. Ral blasted three more, and the sixth tripped, face-planting into a pool of the black goo. Unable to free himself, the homunculi struggled and struggled and then struggled no more as it apparently suffocated—or perhaps drowned—in sludge.

The original spherical homunculus said, "Oh, dear," and ran back through the open door, not even bothering to close it behind her.

No new threat appeared, but there was still the battle to extricate themselves. It took considerable effort and way too much time than made either of them comfortable, but they managed it. Once more, the Wanderer planeswalked away. She was gone for much longer, at least a long minute or two. But she finally returned and crossed to Ral, pushing the strider's leg off his legs and cutting him out of the clothing that was stuck to the floor. She very carefully cut the stinger off his cheek, managing to do it without cutting off any skin. But Ral had to fry the sludge on his forehead to free his hand. The frying pitch left behind a sizable burn mark and the stench of roasted flesh, and it was extremely painful, but once this was all over and Tezzeret was dead, a healing spell would fix it up fine. He caught his reflection in a metal table and saw that his hair was a sticky disaster, too. He'd probably have to shave his head when he got back to Dogsrun.

But hair grows back.

Still, it was all a bit of a blow to his vanity. He had to lose one boot. So he ditched the second one, as well. By the time they were done, they were both barefoot and dressed in sliced-up rags. It was a minor miracle that none of the sludge had gotten in or on Ral's Accumulator. They looked toward the open door, then exchanged a glance.

"Ready for the next ambush?" he asked.

She shrugged resignedly.

They walked through the door together. But there were no more ambushes.

They entered an immense open-air arena, filled with towering machines of unknown purpose. And standing in the center of it all was a smiling Tezzeret, flanked by the lead gargoyle and the little spherical homunculus. The artificer made an expansive gesture with his etherium arm and declaimed, "Welcome to my Grand Laboratory, Zarek. I thought you'd never get here."

Ral smiled, too.

No more sideshows. Time for the main event.

FIFTY-FIVE

LILIANA VESS

Liliana Vess—the *real* Liliana Vess—calmly faced down her two would-be assassins, the boy and the woman, with the latter's knife to her throat. With every passing second, the spell that had befogged her mind was beginning to clear. She was starting to remember . . .

Against the advice—even the pleading—of Karina Témoin, Liliana had, with no plan or preparation, marched into her old home to confront this second "Liliana," this *forgery*, in front of her assembled guests, in the house's refurbished grand salon, as all were being served wine and hors d'oeuvres.

Before Liliana had been able to get a word out, the new mistress of the House of Vess had taken some offense: "How dare this peasant come before the great Liliana Vess uninvited?"

"*'Peasant'?*" Liliana growled.

She was ignored. The mistress waved a lazy hand in the direction of her two zombie bodyguards. "Out of my presence, wench, or suffer the wrath of my undead."

Scoffing, Liliana attempted to take necromantic control of the two zombies but was stunned to find she could not. It suddenly occurred to Liliana that the two creatures were mere illusions. And she said as much. Shouted as much. As a result, for a second or two, the mistress' guests seemed suspicious of their hostess, turning to her for an explanation.

Unfortunately, Liliana's accusations also resulted in a change to the sapphire amulet around Mistress Vess' neck. It began to glow and smoke poured forth, rushing into the "bodies" of both "zombies."

Suddenly they were solid enough to grab Liliana, drag her over and force her to kneel before their mistress. Though the smoke should have been a clear signal of deceit, the zombies' obvious solidity served as a decided answer to any of the guests' questions, and they laughed at the sight of the strange madwoman being manhandled by their hostess' servants. Thus, Liliana found herself at the mercy of two supposedly undead creatures that she could not influence with her extremely powerful necromancy.

As her knees slammed to the floor, Liliana looked up at the woman who had taken her name, but her eyes instead focused above and behind the new Mistress Vess. Unnoticed by the rest of the assembly, ravens were gathering indoors on the balcony. The black birds quickly converged into the form of the Raven Man.

Speaking in a voice that only Liliana could hear, he asked, *Is this the true Liliana Vess on her knees?*

Liliana glared up at him while making an effort not to respond in any way, shape or form.

Are you trying to get yourself killed? he thought to her. *Have you truly lost, not just the will to live, but any semblance of self-respect? Even now, you suffer this indignity and take no action? Put this woman and her laughing friends on their knees. You have the power! Use the Veil! That's why I arranged for you to receive it. So that you could always protect yourself.*

Protect myself and serve you! she thought-screamed back at him.

Now, as Kaya allowed Liliana to rise to her knees (without ever removing the blade from her throat), the irony seemed quite clear: The Raven Man had in fact unintentionally driven Liliana closer to a kind of suicide because she knew he only wanted her alive in order to use her.

"This one will need more than just the threat of a collar," Mistress Vess had commented—seemingly to the air. "Bind her mind," she had commanded.

Again, the Raven Man had urged Liliana to act: *I warn you, girl, do not permit this! Do you truly want to spend your life under this woman's thrall?*

But to prevent herself from falling under *his* thrall, Liliana did nothing to prevent herself from being befogged and swiftly collared.

Safe from him. I'm safe from him now . . .

It was only then that Mistress Vess noticed the Spirit-Gem in her new servant's hand. Liliana saw the woman's tongue circle her mouth acquisitively. "Hand that to me," she commanded.

Like an automaton, Liliana held it out, and her mistress greedily grabbed it. Instantly the façade of the dark-haired beauty—the image that so exactly matched the picture on the cover of the book in Mistress Vess' other hand—fell away, revealing an old woman with ratty gray locks.

There was a gasp from the crowd, and the old woman (who was nevertheless considerably younger than the true age of the true Liliana) threw the egg-shaped gem to the floor, immediately returning to her prior appearance. Her panicked look was brief. She pointed to the Spirit-Gem, which had rolled to a stop a few feet away, and said, "Beware, my friends. Do not touch that cursed thing. It creates an illusion of your greatest fear. I hesitate to say it, but now you know mine. Though I have been young and beautiful for centuries, I still dread the passage of time. A shallow fear, I freely admit—especially since I am immune to that passage. But there you have it. Even Liliana Vess has her vanities. You, there." She pointed at an old collared servant. "Get a napkin and pick that up."

The white-bearded servant nervously obeyed, hesitating only briefly before using the napkin to lift the egg. Nothing seemed to happen to him, and he heaved a sigh of relief. His mistress nodded with thin lips. "Yes, a potent if petty bauble, easily thwarted by a mere napkin. We might someday find a use for it."

Another servant entered then and said, "Dinner is served, mistress."

"Excellent," Mistress Vess replied, having fully regained her composure. "Ladies. Gentlemen. Please." She indicated the door to the dining room, and the assembly began making its way within.

All but one. A single guest, a young kor woman in an elegant red velvet gown, hung back while the rest filed in. Her hostess eyed her with smiling hostility. It was a look this guest returned in equal measure.

Mistress Vess turned to the white-bearded servant and nodded toward the napkin-wrapped Spirit-Gem. "Take that to the dining room. Stand by my chair and wait for me."

"Yes, mistress."

"I assume I don't need to tell you what will happen to you if you lose your grip on the thing."

"No, mistress."

"Good. You may go. Now."

He departed quickly, leaving his mistress with the two zombies, the kneeling befogged Liliana, and the pale-blue-skinned Red Velvet, who approached and whispered, "You know, my dear Liliana, your fear of old age is familiar to me."

"But you yourself are so young, child. I find it hard to believe you know such a fear already."

"Maybe not the fear . . . but the *image* of that fear: the old woman that you so briefly appeared to be."

"I'm not sure I understand, dear girl."

"She reminded me of an initiate of the Cabal. Someone I worked beside on occasion. We had the honor of tallying the mystical items that the demon Belzenlok collected and hoarded before his demise."

"Did you now?"

"We did. This initiate and I. She was many years my senior, and yet I was a trusted priestess of our order, so I had authority over this rather pathetic functionary. And it's odd. Among the items we inventoried was a lamp."

"A lamp?"

"Yes, an old oil lamp. One wouldn't think it had the slightest value, except that the lid of the thing was actually a large sapphire, not unlike the one you wear at your throat."

"How fascinating."

"This one is much lovelier, of course. Though maybe that's merely the result of your beauty reflected upon it. Otherwise, it could be an exact duplicate."

"And what special magics did this *lamp* possess?"

"We never knew. Back then, so many items came across our desks, we barely had time to log them in our register. The intent was for the initiate to discern their natures at a later date. But she abandoned her duties some weeks ago. I don't believe I ever saw her again. Then, of course, Belzenlok fell, and chaos descended. Many items of the inventory were lost, and it's hard to say what disappeared before and what was misplaced after. Fortunately, I managed to preserve the register itself. I have it, you see. Hidden away."

"Does anyone else know of this hidden register?"

"Only myself. I made certain that only I have the power to remove it from its hiding place and reveal it to whomever it might concern—*about* whomever it might concern."

"A wise and prescient move. Quite unlike what you're doing now."

"Excuse me?"

Mistress Vess' eyes went very cold. "Silence her," she commanded in a harsh whisper.

The sapphire flashed briefly blue, and in that instant Red Velvet found that she no longer had a mouth. Panicked noises gargled in her throat but found no outlet from the now smooth blue skin of her lower face. And there was no one close enough to hear her muted cries, save the illusory zombies and the befuddled true Liliana, who observed all of this with no objective interest.

None of my business . . . What my mistress does is none of my business . . .

"You miscalculated, dear," said the false Liliana. "If you're the only one who can produce the register, then ridding myself of you rids me of any concern over it surfacing. Any reasonable concern, in any case."

There were more murmured, fearful noises.

She's scared. But I'm not. I have nothing to be scared of any longer. For nothing more can be taken away from me, as long as I serve my mistress faithfully.

"I'm tempted to collar you," her mistress said to the mouthless kor. "A little payback for the way that pathetic old functionary you mentioned was treated by a trusted priestess. But unlike you, I don't take foolish risks."

Tears were shed. Muffled pleading.

But a smiling Mistress Vess seemed to take some pleasure in Red Velvet's desperation. Up to a point. Then the smile vanished abruptly, and she issued another whispered command: "Drown her in the bog. Don't forget to give her back her mouth. If they find her in the morning, we will all think it quite the tragedy that she chose to go for a stroll alone along the morass before dinner."

Was that command directed at me? No, I am ignored for now. It is well.

Red Velvet shook her head vehemently and tried to scream. But her hostess merely patted her on the head, said "Goodbye, dear child," and snapped her fingers.

Red Velvet disappeared in a puff of blue smoke.

Only then did "Liliana" deign to look down upon Liliana. "Let's see. What to do with you? I know. Go to work in the dirt of the garden. See if you can make something grow . . ."

Now that it had all come back to her, now that she was fully aware again, a part of Liliana was enraged at having been enthralled and used, forced into servitude by her imposter . . .

And yet . . .

And yet part of Liliana was also in despair to *be* fully aware again . . .

Aware of all my crimes. And of the punishments I deserve for them. Tortures far worse than "making something grow."

Still, the rage over her indignities was something she could hold on to. So hold on to it, she did.

For now, at least, Liliana wanted vengeance on Mistress Vess.

She slowly turned her eyes to face the woman Kaya and spoke calmly and coldly: "Here's my one request, my proposition. Help me take down the woman abusing my name for her petty ends. Help me free the people of my homeland, and I'll *let* you cut my throat. You have my word." As she spoke, the collar around her neck began to heat up. It was somewhat painful, but it was still only a warning.

She saw the woman's expression change to one of shock. She stumbled over her response: "I—I don't know that I can take a woman like you at your word. And I still don't know if this is any of our business."

The boy Teyo jumped in. "But shouldn't it be?"

The woman didn't respond. She and the boy turned to look behind Liliana and waited.

Then Kaya shook her head. "No, that's *not* the priority. And whatever promises you made, I took no oath to honor them."

Teyo said, "You took an oath on Ravnica. We can't leave these people to the mercy of the djinn and its mistress."

Liliana said, "That's all I'm saying." The collar became hotter still, but she almost relished the pain.

Again, the two assassins paid her no mind. They looked behind her, silent and attentive.

Eventually, Kaya muttered, "Goddess, spare me from the ideals of the young."

"Is it your goddess you consult with?" Liliana asked with some contempt.

The boy smiled and tried to stifle a laugh. Kaya rolled her eyes.

Liliana couldn't quite make out what was going on, so she cut to the chase: "Do we have a deal or don't we?" Now she could feel her neck burning. She was impatient to have this over with—one way or another. But to Liliana's increasing fury, they continued to ignore her in favor of this goddess.

Teyo looked suddenly hopeful. He said, "If Rat does steal the amulet, we can undo everyone's imprisonment and decide what to do with the real Liliana after."

Liliana scowled. "Your goddess is a rat?"

Kaya said, "Teyo, let me make this clear. The decision about the real Liliana has already been made." But she returned her knife to its sheath and turned to her captive, saying, "We accept your deal. For the time being."

"Wonderful," Liliana replied flatly. "Now my only problem is this collar. I need to remove it to be effective." She could smell her flesh burn.

"Wait—" Kaya protested.

"This will only take a moment." Liliana focused on the top layer of the epidermis beneath the collar, turning the scorched skin necrotic. The smell was rather unpleasant, but the pain subsided and the horrified faces of the woman and the boy somewhat made her evening. "There," she said. "The collar has no use for what it registers as a dead woman. Help me remove it. Then I can steal life energy from the garden to heal myself."

"I said wait. You're sure the collar won't work on you when your neck is . . . in that condition?"

"Quite sure, but that doesn't mean I want to suffer this indignity for a moment longer."

"Too bad," Kaya said. "I have a plan to bring down your imposter, and you'll need to be wearing a collar to execute it."

FIFTY-SIX

TEYSA KARLOV

Tomik wasn't exactly a boy accustomed to making a scene, but there he was, trying his damnedest to storm into her suite of rooms, all in an outrage, saying, "Which strategy are we working on now? Plan E?"

Teysa smiled. There was a steaming pot of tea on the side table and two empty cups. She said, "Would you pour the tea?"

He ignored the request. "I know you sent Zoltan to seduce me, sent Morov to bribe me and sent Maladola to intimidate me. And I want you to know that all three have failed."

Teysa responded: "As I knew they would."

This stopped him for a beat. Belatedly, he rolled his eyes and said, "Oh, please."

"It's quite true, Tomik. I sent them to you to prove a point."

Flummoxed, he fumfered out, "I have no idea what that *point* might have been. But whatever it was, I still won't help you take the guild away from Kaya."

Teysa sighed and said, "Well, you really *did* miss the point. There's no need to take the guild from Kaya."

"Then what's this all been about?"

"Let me remind you that we both know Kaya doesn't want the job. She wants to be free to planeswalk the Multiverse. And if the late, *late* unlamented Obzedat has taught us anything, it's that there are advantages to having an out-of-reach or absent guildmaster."

"What?"

"Oh, come now, Tomik, I know you're brighter than this. Let's set Kaya free to planeswalk as she likes, returning *when* she likes to perform ceremonial functions. Let Kaya—in her absence—take all the credit for the work of the Syndicate."

And all the blame, as well.

Teysa continued, "If Kaya wants to forgive the *occasional* debt, that's fine, too. She can be the hero . . . as long as *you* keep things running as acting guildmaster. As *permanent* acting guildmaster."

"Me? I'm not qualified to do this permanently."

Teysa laughed. "Tomik, I'm very fond of you, honestly. And do you know why? Your unrelenting humility. You serve the Orzhov and believe that's all you are. A servitor. But sometimes all that humility does get in the way. Your way. My way. The Syndicate's way."

"I don't see what—"

"I knew you would doubt yourself, which is exactly why I sent the Triumvirate—in order to *prove* to you that you're immune to seduction, bribery and intimidation. On top of that, you have the backing of Bilagru and the Orzhov armed forces. Best of all, there is no one who is more efficient and competent than you, my young friend. How long has Kaya been offworld? And look at what you've already accomplished."

"But the politics. I have no standing. No ancestors. The oligarchy will eat me alive."

Grabbing her cane, Teysa struggled to her feet. Forgetting his former ire, Tomik rushed to help her, but she waved him off. She said, "I don't want to sound immodest, but you have *me*. I know the players. I can control the Triumvirate and all the interests they represent. And I have the Karlov name and all *it* represents. The respect it commands. The respect it *demands*. Tomik Vrona, I am willing to offer all of that in service to your tenure as permanent acting guildmaster."

For nearly a minute, he just stood there looking dumbfounded. Then his eyes squinted at her suspiciously, as though he might know her mind by observing her face with more care. "If this is some ploy to take command . . ."

Teysa sighed again. "Tomik, I don't want to be guildmaster. Does this surprise you? Frankly, I don't want that target on my back. You know—you more than anyone else know—that I have spent years in detention because of my past ambitions. Now like Kaya, I'd like my freedom—but of a different kind." Balancing herself on her chair's armrest, she held up her cane. "I want to be able to limp my way down the street and breathe the open air. I want to be able to eat a meal without fear of poison."

Not to mention, I don't need the weight of a few thousand debtor contracts crushing my soul.

She slammed the cane down on the carpeted floor. It didn't quite make the loud crack she had hoped for, but the soft thud was still mildly effective. "Damnit, Tomik, all I want—all either of us wants—is a strong, well-run Orzhov Syndicate."

She could already tell he was considering her offer.

She pressed a bit, appealing to his nostalgia. "Haven't we always worked well together? We can do this, you and I, with only a little cooperation—as it pleases her—from Kaya."

Tomik swallowed and said, "If I take you at your word, I want you to know that I'm determined to follow Kaya's lead and create a kinder, gentler Orzhov."

"And I'm all for that. No one wants a return to the bad old days of the Obzedat. Remember, I suffered under their rule, too."

"And Kaya would have to agree to all of this."

"Of course, but honestly, don't you think she'll be *thrilled* with this solution?"

He mused for a bit. Then Tomik Vrona smiled and nodded.

Teysa reached out with her free hand, and he shook it.

He stood there grinning for a few moments, looking foolish and very sweet.

She smiled at him and said, "*Now* would you pour the tea?"

"Actually, I suppose I have Orzhov business to attend to."

"I suppose you do, Permanent Acting Guildmaster Vrona."

They shook hands again, and he was gone.

When the door clicked shut, Lazav emerged, as before, from the shadows, saying, "So was that Plan F or G?"

"Plan A," Teysa said as she eased herself back down into her ebony chair. "That was *always* Plan A."

"So Tomik Vrona will be the true power behind Kaya's throne . . . and Teysa Karlov will be the true power behind Tomik Vrona's throne. You're twice insulated, twice protected."

Teysa shrugged and smiled.

"And how will the Triumvirate take this news?"

"Well enough, once I assure them that our plan hasn't changed. I will wield behind-the-scenes power—keeping our hands close to our vests—until they *unanimously* agree which of their number should become guildmaster."

Lazav smiled, too. "And as they'll *never* unanimously agree . . ."

"Exactly. Moreover, I expect Slav will be just fine with this arrangement. I believe he has become somewhat seduced by the subtle and unintentional charms of our new acting guildmaster. Even Maladola might come around, with Bilagru working on her. They're both big on guild strength, and the giant sincerely believes Tomik will make the Orzhov stronger."

"What about Morov?"

"By the time Armin realizes his support from the others has been undercut, I'll have groomed Lazlo Morov to make a move on his cousin. In the old families, new blood is always appealing . . . to new blood."

"What of Tomik's kinder, gentler Orzhov?"

"What of it? I'm quite eager for Kaya and Tomik to promote that image. One of the biggest problems under the Obzedat was that the Syndicate had grown too infamous. Ravnicans had become afraid to take out even the smallest loan with the Orzhov. But once the populace hears that a few worthy debtors have been released from debt, they'll *line up* for loans. Because every idiot believes in the power of her, his or their own luck. They all think they'll be able to pay their loans off quickly or else they'll be among the chosen few whose loans are forgiven. So they'll take the risk. And then we'll have them. We'll have them all."

"Their purses."

"No, no, no. I don't want those. I don't care about that. Coins are just a means to an end. I'd tell Tomik to forgive every debt this minute if I thought it would give the Orzhov true power. Instead, we'll use their debts to bring them to the guild. We'll eventually offer to trade *interest* on their zinos for an *interest* in the divine."

"So not their purses. Their souls."

"That's where the true power lies, my friend."

"So will Tomik Vrona change the Orzhov as he believes . . . or will the Orzhov change Tomik Vrona?"

"That's a false dichotomy, Lazav. We all take different paths as we advance our spirits."

"And you reveal this to me, why?"

She sat back in the chair and laid her cane down horizontally across her lap. "Simply because you're very good at what you do.

Just as Tomik is very good at what he does. Think of it as a sign of respect. If I tried to keep my plans from you, you'd eventually learn them anyway, but along the way you might do much damage. Instead, I offer you clarity, an open alliance. You trade in information. The Orzhov now trades in coin. But in time, we will trade in the hearts and minds of the people of Ravnica, which is the source of all information on this world. So I ask you, is there a better path to achieve your goals than by helping me achieve mine?"

"Now I see: *'We all take different paths as we advance our spirits.'*"

"Exactly. Do we have a deal?"

"We do."

"Lovely. Would you pour the tea?"

FIFTY-SEVEN

RAT

Rat watched and waited.

In groups of two or three or more, the guests departed, all seemingly in very good spirits, all presumably assured that the Cabal would rise again. Rat had a good memory and was good at faces. By the time Lord Valois took his warm leave of his hostess on her porch, Rat was fairly certain that all the guests—and most of the servants—were now gone.

It's time.

Her first little incursion had clearly put Mistress Book Cover on the alert. Zombies—or the illusions of same—now stood guard at every door and window. They weren't real, of course, but Rat knew that if she came in contact with any of them, it would alert the amulet (or, in theory, the djinn trapped within the sapphire) and its mistress.

Rat watched as Mistress Kaya avoided that problem by ghosting her way in through a wall drenched in shadow. Then, as the current mistress of House Vess offered up one last wave to Lord Valois before heading back inside, Rat made her move. She was small enough to easily sneak between the legs of the zombie guarding the still-open front door without coming into actual contact with the faux creature.

Mistress Book Cover was standing in the grand salon addressing the old servant with the white beard: "Tell Karina to come to me. I want her to draw me a bath. The rest of you can go for the night."

"Yes, mistress. But . . . um . . . where do you want this?" He held up Bolas' gem wrapped in a napkin.

She considered the question for a time. Then she ordered him to close his eyes. He obeyed. She cautiously took the item from his hand, careful to touch only the napkin and not the gem itself. Satisfied—and quite relieved—she said, "Keep your eyes shut tight unless you want to lose them."

"Yes, mistress. No, mistress," he replied nervously.

She reached out and touched the surface of Bolas' egg with one finger. Instantly she transformed into an old gray-haired woman, wearing decidedly less elegant attire. She quickly took her finger away, and just as quickly she was the Mistress Vess of the Book Cover once again.

Rat was more convinced than ever that she wanted that egg. *It'll change everything! My whole life . . .*

Its current owner inhaled and exhaled deeply, nodded to herself and spoke. "You may open your eyes, now, Georges. And you may go. Don't forget to send Karina."

"Yes, mistress. Yes, mistress. No, mistress."

Moving quickly, the old man walked right past Rat, exiting through the front door and closing it behind him. Mistress Book Cover slid the bolt home to lock it. Rat quickly unbolted it, and unsurprisingly no one noticed.

Knowing what to look for, Rat spotted Mistress Kaya amid

the shadows, upstairs on the balcony overlooking the salon and her new target, Mistress Book Cover.

The latter mistress sighed with satisfaction and turned toward the stairs, just as the real Miss Liliana entered through the front door with Teyo.

Hearing this, Mistress Book Cover wheeled back around and strode forward. "I know I locked that door." She stopped short upon seeing Miss Liliana and Teyo. Outraged, she shouted, "What are you doing here, wench? Who gave you permission to leave my garden? Who told you it would be all right to track that dirt into *my* house?"

This'll be the test . . .

Miss Liliana passed it. She stood there with blank eyes, pretending—per Mistress Kaya's plan—that she remained enthralled to the djinn's spell. It had taken some effort on Mistress Kaya's part to convince Miss Raven-Hair to go along with her plan, but the necromancer was now playing her part. She said nothing—even after Mistress Book Cover tucked *The Curse of the House of Vess* under one arm and stepped forward to slap Miss Liliana across the face.

The new Mistress Vess stared at the original, who, in turn, stared at nothing.

With a dismissive and frustrated wave, Mistress Book Cover turned from the seemingly befogged Miss Liliana to take in Teyo Verada. Rat couldn't help noticing—even if the mistress did not—that Teyo already had a small white glowing circle at his right ear, meaning he was ready for action. "And who are you?"

"My name is Teyo, mistress."

"And what are *you* doing in my home?"

"I—I'm not sure, mistress. I'm a poor itinerant monk. Well, an acolyte, really . . ."

Poor Teyo. He can't even lie about being a full monk!

Rat, who was slowly moving in closer to Mistress Book Cover, thought Teyo was a pretty feeble excuse for a con artist—but he looked appropriately nervous, which seemed to be doing the trick.

He said, "I walked up to this woman and asked for some bread. She wouldn't speak to me, but she took my hand and brought me here."

Now Mistress Book Cover looked pleasantly surprised. She turned back to Miss Liliana and said, "So you brought me a potential new servant? Good, good."

Rat giggled and shook her head. Mistress Vess was arrogant enough not to even question Miss Liliana's befuddled loyalty.

Teyo said, "I think there's been some misunderstanding, mistress. I'm simply passing through these parts. I'm not a servant, though I am of course willing to work for my supper."

"Certainly. I don't suppose you have anything of value to *trade* for your supper?"

"No, mistress," he said, shaking his head, embarrassed.

Is he actually *embarrassed? I should let him hold some of my diamonds. Although, really, he wouldn't appreciate 'em, you know?*

Holding the bound volume in one hand and the napkin-wrapped gem in the other, Mistress Book Cover put both down on an end table. It took all Rat's willpower not to make a grab for the egg right there and then. But she knew better than to touch the thing—napkin or no napkin—before the djinn and its mistress had been neutralized.

Mistress Book Cover approached Teyo. Roughly, she grabbed his chin between her index finger and thumb, turning it back and forth to examine his features closely. "Hmphf," she huffed. She seemed quite unimpressed.

Well, what does she know? He's adorable!

"All right, boy-who's-willing-to-work-for-his-supper. I don't suppose you have any useful skills, such as carpentry or masonry? I'd like to put an addition on my house."

"I worked in the garden in the monastery."

Still not lying . . .

"That should be satisfactory. You can work in the garden with this one." She offered Miss Liliana another dismissive wave. She also blinked several times and pressed two fingers against her temple.

Rat knew why. By this time, she was standing right in front of Mistress Vess, reaching for the amulet at her throat. And although the woman couldn't see the young thief, Rat was partially obscuring, blocking, interfering with the false Liliana's view of the real Miss Liliana and Teyo. Rat was well aware from prior experience (and the prior testing of her abilities over the years) that Mistress Book Cover's mind was filling in the blanks, compensating for what she could no longer see directly. But the added effort was making her edgy. Somewhere in her subconscious, the woman could sense something was wrong, so Rat knew she had to act fast. She got a solid grip on the amulet, right when her target said, "This boy will need a collar."

And thus, just as Rat snatched the sapphire away with one good tug, smoke began to flow out of it.

"Teyo, look out!" Rat shouted in warning.

But Teyo was ready. He might not have been fast enough to capture a djinn back on Gobakhan, but with one sweep of his hand, he captured the small cloud of blue smoke within a sphere of light.

The smoke clearly did not like being trapped, slamming against the inside of Teyo's sphere. Teyo's cheek twitched with each individual impact, but he maintained the sphere.

"Can you hold it?" the real Miss Liliana asked, a faux servant no longer.

"Yes," Teyo answered firmly, with enough confidence to make Rat proud.

Only as Rat moved out of the way did Mistress Book Cover react. First to Teyo trapping the smoke: "What is—" And then, when her hand moved to her neck and found the amulet gone: "My sapphire!"

But before she could say another word, Mistress Kaya had leapt down from the balcony to hold a dagger to Mistress Book Cover's now naked throat, hissing: "Don't speak. One wish, one word, and you're dead."

Rat was still eyeing Bolas' egg-shaped gem on the little table, but she knew the job wasn't yet finished. Forcing herself to turn away from the temptation, she held up the sapphire and asked Teyo, "Okay, now that I've got whatever what this thing is, whatever what do I do with it?"

Teyo, focusing on maintaining the sphere around the still-pounding smoke, called out, "Destroy the jewel! That'll set the djinn free of its mistress' control."

Despite Mistress Kaya's earlier threat, Mistress Book Cover shouted, *"No!"*

But Mistress Kaya pressed her knife against the woman's throat, drawing a little blood and silencing her.

Rat looked around for something to break the amulet. All she could find was the hard wooden end table currently sporting *The Fall of the House of Vess* and the egg. So Rat reached back and with all her strength slammed the sapphire down against the table. She held it up and studied it. The dark-blue jewel was now cracked, but it hadn't broken.

Teyo said, "Once more."

Miss Raven-Hair said, "Who are you talking to? What am I missing here?"

Mistress Book Cover whispered, "You fools, you're going to get us all killed."

"Once more," Teyo repeated.

And Rat slammed the amulet against the table again . . .

FIFTY-EIGHT

RAL ZAREK

Ral unleashed another lightning bolt at Tezzeret, exploding the makeshift shield of metal that the artificer's magnetism had gathered in front of him. Tezzeret was blasted back. Though the storm mage had his opponent on the ropes, Ral wasn't taking any chances. Tezzeret had miscalculated by allowing their final battle to take place in the open air. As Ral fought, he was also subtly and slowly raising a major lightning storm overhead. If necessary, he'd soon be able to bring down a strike that would completely incinerate Tezzeret, leaving only his smoking etherium arm.

Just the proof I'll need for the guilds.

Ral smiled grimly and threw another bolt.

The Wanderer, meanwhile, was covering Ral's back against the lead gargoyle. Out of the corner of his eye, Ral noted that the creature was proving to be a much worthier foe than any of his fellow minions—gargoyle or golem, homunculus or even strider—had been. The others had been dangerous, certainly, yet all had been dealt with rather swiftly by either Ral's lightning or the Wanderer's sword. But this behemoth of a gargoyle was fast, agile and extremely strong. He was giving the Wanderer a serious challenge, flying over every swing of her sword, wheeling about in the air, forcing her to quickly turn or be raked across the back with his razor-sharp claws. So far, neither combatant had been able to do any real damage to the other, but Ral thought the fight could easily go either way.

If Ral could just finish Tezzeret off quickly, he could come to his partner's aid. In fact, if Ral could just finish off Tezzeret, the gargoyle might flee and no aid would be necessary.

Ral was also on the lookout for the little homunculus. She had disappeared from sight shortly after the battle was joined. She wasn't much of a physical threat, but if she came back with some of her master's technology, that could—in theory—change the course of the conflict, and Ral didn't want to leave anything to chance.

Tezzeret was slowly backing away from Ral across the sand floor of the arena. Suddenly he raised his arms, and two metal pylons rose up out of the sand on either side of the storm mage. Instantly they began to drain the power from his Accumulator at a steady pace.

But that's a tip-off.

"Your machines want my power," Ral called out. "Let's see just how much power they can take!" He reached out with both arms and blasted out a massive flow of electricity. The pylons absorbed the power at first, but soon enough they were sparking. Ral kept pouring it on. One pylon exploded! The other caught fire and died.

"Is that the best you've got?" Ral said.

"They did well enough. We both know you just used up most of what was stored in your little backpack."

"True," Ral said, still smiling. "Whatever will I do now?" Of course, by this time, the storm was ready. He summoned up a lightning bolt from the sky that Tezzeret barely managed to leap clear of.

Unfortunately, the bolt also caught the Wanderer off guard. As the ground shook from its impact, she turned her head at just the wrong moment, and the gargoyle struck with an etherium-and-stone fist that dropped the Wanderer to the ground, unconscious. And since she was no longer consciously trying to stay on Alara, she instantly planeswalked away to who-knew-where.

Ral felt bad about that, but he felt fairly confident she'd return as soon as she recovered.

And by that time, I'll have this all sewn up.

Tezzeret was on one knee, wiping his mouth with his flesh hand. He said, "Crucius' Spleen, I thought she'd never leave."

Ral was prepared for the gargoyle to attack. "I can handle both of you," Ral said. Instead, the creature landed far away, near the top of the arena.

"I don't require any help to defeat the likes of you, Zarek."

"Really? Have you been fighting the same battle I've been fighting?"

"No."

Arrogant bastard. Fine, let him go down smirking. Time to end this.

Ral raised both arms and brought down from the skies his most massive bolt yet.

In response, Tezzeret raised his etherium arm and, using it as a lightning rod, appeared to absorb every last erg into his chest.

When the lightning faded and his eyes readjusted, Ral was stunned to see Tezzeret standing there, smoking and crackling with power—but unharmed.

The artificer's chest had irised open, revealing the void, the Planar Bridge technology, within. It projected outward, creating a huge circular hole in space. The change in air pressure knocked Ral back a few steps. And then the meteorites flew through the portal and knocked him off his feet.

He scrambled back up, barely dodging the huge rocks crashing out of the bridge all around him. When one got too close, he shattered it with a bolt of lightning, but another smaller rock got past him, clipping him in the side.

Ral couldn't even see Tezzeret anymore—he was somewhere on the far side of the portal—but Ral could hear him laughing. Laughing and shouting, "Did you really think I wouldn't be prepared for you, Zarek? All those times we fought—all those times I pretended to be on my last legs, barely escaping your wrath— did it never occur to you that I had your number? You're a one-trick pony, boy. It's a great trick, most of the time, I suppose, with most folks. But not against me. Why do you think we're fighting out of doors? So that you'd be fool enough to do exactly what you did. Bring a storm and fuel my power with it."

"Fight me!" Ral yelled, ignoring the pain in his side while dodging another huge boulder that flew out of the portal and very nearly crushed him.

And then—just like that—the Planar Bridge vanished, sucked itself up into itself to reveal Tezzeret behind it, his chest irising closed.

"Fine," he said. "Let's fight. Shall we use fists? Or do you want to throw more power my way?"

Taking the chance that like the pylons, Tezzeret could only absorb so much, Ral blasted the artificer with everything he had while simultaneously bringing down the most intense barrage of lightning he'd ever attempted to control. It had taken less than this to shear the arm off the God-Eternal Kefnet.

The conflagration was spectacular.

And 100 percent ineffective.

When it was over, Tezzeret stood there. Static danced all around him. His metal arm smoked. The aperture in his chest was again irising shut, revealing that any excess power was simply channeled away to another plane.

He stalked toward Ral, saying, "Got that out of your system? Good. So *now* we'll try fists."

Ral had been in plenty of street fights in his youth on Ravnica. Sometimes against several opponents at once. And pretty much every time, until he learned to control his powers and became something of a street thug himself, he had gotten his ass kicked.

This was no exception.

If anything it was even more brutal. Tezzeret had seven inches on him and seventy pounds, more or less. He had a longer reach, a metal arm, a metal fist, and very few fleshy targets for Ral to strike back against.

Within a few minutes—minutes that seemed an eternity—Ral was doubled over on the ground, bleeding from his mouth and nose. Both eyes were swelling shut, and he was pretty sure he had a broken rib or two. He was definitely having trouble breathing. He had no choice. He had to get away. He tried to summon the will to planeswalk—when Tezzeret raised both hands into the air and backed off a few steps, saying, "Wait, wait, don't go just yet. I'm finished; I'll stop. Really, it's your fault, Zarek. You barely managed to lay a hand on me, but you *do* get under my skin. So I may have overdone it. Sorry if I got carried away."

Through swollen lips, Ral told him what he could do with his apology.

Tezzeret laughed again. And then apologized again for laughing. And then he knelt down before Ral and said, "Look, the fight's over. So let's talk about what happens next." With his flesh hand, he reached over and detached his etherium arm from the rest of his body, which might just have been the most disturbing thing Ral had seen all night, as flesh and metal retracted to release the thing. The sound alone made Ral gag.

Or maybe that's the blood in my mouth.

Tezzeret dropped the metal limb in the bloodstained sand in front of Ral, before standing and walking away.

"Krzntch," he called out. Or something like that.

The little homunculus came running, carrying another etherium arm. This one was pristine and shiny with who-knew-what fresh technological horrors already built in. The diminutive creature held it aloft, saying, "Here, boss!"

The gargoyle landed beside the homunculus and took the arm from Krzntch. He then proceeded to install it on his master's body with no more fanfare than if he were clicking a rotor into place on a mizzium flier. Tezzeret said, "Thank you, Brokk. I've been eager to give this a try." Then he nodded toward his old arm and said to Ral, "That's yours now. I don't need it, and you can use it as proof of your 'success' today. As proof of kill."

"What?" Ral murmured. He was so confused at this point, he thought he might have a concussion. In fact, he was pretty confident he had a concussion.

Tezzeret sighed, and when he spoke again, his words came out with exaggerated slowness, as if he were instructing a young child in something just a little too complicated for the tyke to understand. "I don't need the arm. And I *really* don't need thirty or forty Planeswalkers hunting me in your place. I mean they can't all be as ineffective as you, can they?"

Ral cursed again.

Tezzeret ignored it. "I have long-term plans, Zarek, and I prefer to avoid distractions. So go back to Ravnica. Be the hero. Tell them it was a tough fight, but in the end, you triumphed. And by all means, show them the arm and tell them I'm dead. You do that, and we both win. Or tell me again what I can do with the mercy I'm showing, and I'll kill you now. Then I'll offer the same deal to the next great big hero who comes my way."

Left with the choice of dying or leaving, Ral reached out with a muted groan—and a scraping sound from somewhere within his chest cavity—and laid a hand upon Tezzeret's abandoned arm. Then, summoning up all that remained of his strength, he planeswalked—*planeslimped*—back to Ravnica.

FIFTY-NINE

TEYO VERADA

Teyo struggled to maintain his focus on maintaining his geometry against the pounding of the smoke within. "Once more," he told Rat urgently.

Liliana, who couldn't see or hear Rat and wasn't at all sure what was going on—save for the fact that she knew she was missing something—said, "Who are you talking to? What am I missing here?"

Teyo just barely heard the false Liliana whisper, "You fools, you're going to get us all killed."

Teyo repeated, "Once more."

And Rat slammed the amulet against the table again, shattering the sapphire into fragments.

Immediately the faux zombies disappeared, and "Liliana" transformed into an old woman. But the most significant result by far was the tremendous quantity of smoke that poured forth from the shattered jewel.

It was only then that Teyo realized the full extent of his miscalculation. He thought he had been holding the djinn in his sphere. But he now knew he was only holding a fragment of the entity's essence. He now knew that this djinn wasn't simply larger than any he'd ever encountered (or even heard of in stories) on Gobakhan—it was flat-out huge and hugely powerful.

The only saving grace was that the djinn couldn't fully re-form yet because Teyo was holding a fraction of itself within his geometry.

But that was not a saving grace destined to last for very long.

The big smoke cloud began forming lightning *inside* the house.

Teyo's eyes went wide, and he struggled to raise a four-point shield while simultaneously maintaining the sphere.

But just then, an older woman—a collared servant—entered the room from the back of the house and screamed in response to the tableau before her.

That scream distracted Teyo just enough. A bolt of lightning struck his weak four-pointer. It shattered like the sapphire, and Teyo was sent flying.

He heard Rat call out his name—*Or was it Kaya or Liliana?*—as he struggled to clear his head.

"I'm okay, I'm okay."

"Not you," Liliana called out. "Your sphere!"

Teyo looked up, realizing he'd lost the geometry on his sphere. The smoke within was merging with the smoke without, and the great djinn was re-forming: blue skin, glowing blue eyes, pointed ears, tattoos, black hair, black eyebrows and a long, thin black mustache—or sometimes his hair was hair and sometimes it was just dark smoke, swirling and dancing alongside the blue smoke that comprised his spirit.

The djinn stared down at Teyo as his voice boomed out,

"ZAHID WILL HAVE VENGEANCE! VENGEANCE ON YOU ALL!"

Through the smoky haze and his hazy grasp on consciousness, Teyo spotted Rat tossing what appeared to be . . . *Bolas' Spirit-Gem* to the real Liliana. For reasons he couldn't begin to explain, this gave him hope . . .

SIXTY

TOMIK VRONA

Tomik was just unlocking the door. He had been hoping against hope that Ral would be here in their apartment waiting for him, fresh from his victory over Tezzeret.

I won't—I can't—think about the alternative.

The reality was somewhere in between.

Before he'd taken two steps inside, before he'd put down the bag of groceries or even closed the door, Ral Zarek planeswalked home—he seemed to be on his hands and knees in the air, two feet above the floor. He promptly fell that short distance and landed hard, bouncing a little on the hardwood floor.

Tomik dropped the grocery bag and rushed to his side, tripping over something that sent him stumbling into Ral, who groaned painfully upon impact.

"I'm sorry; I'm sorry," Tomik breathed out.

He'd never seen his man like this. Beaten. Bloody. Bruised.

Maybe broken. His entire face was swollen almost to the point of being unrecognizable. There was a nasty burn on his forehead, black goop matting down his hair, and he began hacking and coughing up blood.

"Karlov's Ghost, Ral, what happened?"

Ral looked up at him. Tears were forming in his black, bruised and swollen eyes. He didn't, maybe couldn't, speak.

"No, shhhh, sorry. Never mind that now. Let me get you into bed. Then I'll summon a healer."

He tried to lift Ral, but his lover was like dead weight in his arms. It took all his strength, and he nearly tripped over the same damn metal whatever he'd tripped over moments before. He took a second look and realized . . . *it was Tezzeret's arm!*

"You did it!" he said with forced enthusiasm, trying to buck his lover's spirits up. "You took out Tezzeret! He got his shots in. But you got him!"

Ral didn't respond—but Tomik realized he was struggling just to breathe. He lowered him onto the bed where they'd made love the night before. Blood soaked into the sheets.

Tomik was working very hard not to cry. At least not in front of Ral.

Sucking it up, Tomik said, "It'll be all right. It's over now. You won."

Ral just looked up into Tomik's eyes and said nothing.

Tomik wanted to kiss him. But there didn't seem to be a square inch on his face where a kiss wouldn't cause him more pain.

"I'm proud of you, Ral. I'll get the healer." He rushed away from the bed so that Ral wouldn't see him break down completely.

SIXTY-ONE

LILIANA VESS

Forming out of the smoke, the massive djinn seemed to *fill* the grand salon from floor to ceiling, from wall to wall to wall to wall. The fact that there was still space in the room for the forgery, the woman Kaya, the boy Teyo, the servant Karina and herself seemed like a minor miracle to Liliana Vess.

The djinn glared down at Teyo and boomed, *"ZAHID WILL HAVE VENGEANCE . . . !"*

And just then, someone called out, "Miss Liliana, over here!"

Liliana turned. A few feet away stood a girl where there had been no girl before. She was holding Bolas' Spirit-Gem and tossed it, vanishing even as the egg left her hand. Instinctively, a confused Liliana caught the mystic bauble . . . and suddenly someone else was there that hadn't been there before. For a brief horrifying moment, she thought it was Nicol Bolas, back from the dead. Or maybe Bolas' ghost, as the dragon hovering before her was decidedly transparent.

But no, the horns are wrong. The expression, too, thank the gods.

Whomever the creature was, he did bear a striking resemblance, however, to her former tormentor.

There's something dangerous in the smile that he and Bolas have in common. And if this smile seems kinder, that should make me want to trust it less . . .

But somehow she didn't trust it less. She tried to get her head around what she was seeing.

Is this his astral form? Or maybe just a vision . . . or a hallucination? Maybe I've finally lost my mind completely.

A voice sounded telepathically in her mind, saying, *Perhaps, it is all of these things.* Again, the voice sounded kinder and infinitely more benign than Bolas.

Yet there is an undeniable similarity, as well.

It's less than surprising, sent the dragon. *My name is Ugin. A Spirit Dragon and Nicol Bolas' somewhat-less-evil twin.*

As reassuring introductions go, that one is less than compelling, a suspicious Liliana sent back, with Bolas, her four demons, the Onakke spirits, the Raven Man and all their attempts to use and manipulate her circling her consciousness.

I understand your caution. But you'll see I have no desire to be numbered among your manipulators.

Said every manipulator ever.

True.

Just get to it—or end . . . whatever this is.

As you wish. The Spirit-Gem in your hand was made from my essence and has summoned my spirit to you.

It belonged to Bolas.

Bolas took what did not belong to him. That cannot come as a surprise.

No, I suppose not . . .

The Gem has established a link between us. Know that the child who gave it to you sacrificed much to put it in your hands. Do not squander the opportunity.

What opportunity?

The Spirit-Gem, now cleansed of Bolas' influence, has the power to help you become your true, best self, Liliana Vess. But you must want that. You will have to choose.

Choose what?

Perhaps what Gideon Jura believed you merited?

Don't— Don't you bring him into this! He's done enough!

What would he want for you, Liliana Vess?

Stop . . .

Ugin remained silent, waiting.

He'd . . . he'd want me . . . to . . . to try . . .

Ugin nodded once and slowly faded from view.

Wait, WAIT! Where are you—?

"*. . . VENGEANCE ON YOU ALL!*" Liliana's eyes swept back to the djinn. It was as if no time whatsoever had passed during her conversation with the transparent—and perhaps imaginary—dragon. The djinn still loomed over the groggy, recovering boy. This Zahid wanted vengeance and didn't seem too particular about whom he took it out upon: "*AND I WILL START WITH YOU, LITTLE MAN!*"

Then—as if she hadn't already faced more than enough psychic meddling for any one lifetime—something or someone in Liliana's mind, like a psychic voice but less distinct, urged her to save *Teyo.*

She glanced down at the Spirit-Gem still in her hand and was surprised to find that she *did* want to save him, to save one of the Planeswalkers sent to kill her—even if she didn't quite know why.

Am I being influenced? By the quiet voice? By Ugin? By the Gem?

She took half a second to clear her head, to evaluate and separate all external influence from Liliana Vess.

No. The boy talked Kaya out of killing me. He tried to save me. I want *to save him.*

So that took care of the why but didn't exactly reveal anything about the how.

"YOU WILL SUFFER FOR THE CRIME OF TRYING TO CONTAIN THE MIGHTY ZAHID!"

That's when she heard yet more inner voices, moaning, *Vessel . . .*

SIXTY-TWO

KAYA

"*ZAHID WILL HAVE VENGEANCE! VENGEANCE ON YOU ALL! AND I WILL START WITH YOU, LITTLE MAN! YOU WILL SUFFER FOR THE CRIME OF TRYING TO CONTAIN THE MIGHTY ZAHID!*"

Seeing Teyo in imminent danger, Kaya pushed the former faux Liliana aside and leapt. Her daggers plunged into the djinn's back, and he was just solid enough in that moment to cry out in real pain. But he instantly transformed into smoke, and she tumbled right through him, unable to ghost fast enough to avoid a very solid—and very large—fist that batted her across the room.

She slammed into a love seat that flipped backward on top of her. As she struggled to push the piece of furniture off and clear her head, Kaya looked up. Both the servant and her former mistress were cowering before the djinn's wrath. Liliana stood stock-still. But Rat was now next to Teyo, struggling to shake *his* head clear. As always, the young acolyte responded valiantly. Reaching out with one hand, he attempted to contain Zahid in another large sphere.

But a small percentage of the djinn's smoke remained uncaptured, and *both* the djinn and the smoke began fighting back, pounding upon the construct from within and without, as his voice echoed throughout the house: *"AGAIN? YOU SEEK TO BIND ME AGAIN? NOW YOUR TORMENTS SHALL LAST AN ETERNITY!"*

Extricating herself from beneath the love seat, Kaya could see cracks forming in the sphere, and it seemed clear Teyo wouldn't be able to hold Zahid for long.

Then Liliana—*the real Liliana*—called out: *"Let him go!"*

Liliana turned toward the djinn, and Kaya could now see her in profile, wearing the Chain Veil she had used to control the Eternals.

Is that a good sign or bad?

Liliana's voice reverberated from behind the Veil: "Release the djinn, Teyo."

Teyo, for obvious reasons, seemed reluctant to comply with Liliana's command: "I don't know. He won't let me grab him a third time."

Rat said, "It'll be all right."

Teyo looked Rat in the eyes, nodded with implicit trust and dropped his hand.

The sphere evaporated, and immediately Zahid reached for Teyo—only to find himself blocked by the Veil's Onakke spirits. Hundreds of them. Maybe thousands.

Holy Ancients . . .

The spirits prevented the djinn's hand from reaching Teyo. Zahid transformed his entire arm into blue smoke, but they blocked that, too, sucking the smoke in through their open shrieking mouths. They surrounded him, encircled him, rotated around him like a planetary ring with screaming faces.

Then the djinn himself began to scream.

Kaya moved toward Liliana, calling out, "What are you doing?"

Liliana's reply was cold as a midnight crypt: "I'm doing what every necromancer is born to do. I am draining the life force from my enemy."

Rat asked, "*You're* doing it or the Veil?" Then she nudged Teyo to repeat the question for Liliana.

He did. "Are you doing this or is it the Veil?"

Again, the cold voice responded, "The Chain Veil and the Onakke spirits are increasing my power, but the sorcery is mine."

Rat prompted Teyo, "Tell her to stop . . ."

He repeated what Rat told him, practically word for word: "Stop. The djinn was just another victim here. Angry, lashing out. He does not deserve to die."

Kaya approached Liliana tentatively. Beads of sweat had formed on the necromancer's brow. The muscles in her face were taut. She was straining against something, but whether it was the Onakke or Zahid or her own worst impulses was impossible to say.

But Rat's words—via Teyo—seemed to be getting through to her. "We cannot right a wrong with another wrong," the two teenagers said consecutively. "There has to be a way for us to show mercy."

Liliana spoke in that sepulchral voice: "Do you hear the boy, Zahid? We are not your enemies but your saviors. We offer you freedom. Freedom and mercy. But we have one condition, one *wish* before we release you: Leave Caligo and its people—and us—alone."

Fighting through the pain, the djinn glared at Liliana, then nodded. *"I AGREE TO YOUR TERMS—WITH ONE EXCEPTION. I WANT LILIANA VESS."*

Kaya, Rat and Teyo all turned toward Liliana. Her face behind the Chain Veil revealed little, but Kaya was close enough by this time to hear her inhale and exhale softly, close enough to see the slight nod of acquiescence. The necromancer said, "You and these others may not deserve to die, but Liliana Vess certainly does."

She walked forward then with lowered head, a willing lamb ready for slaughter, saying, "You may have—"

But just then the *other* Liliana shouted in protest, *"You can't let him have me! I am the great Liliana Vess!"*

It was only then that the real Liliana—not to mention Kaya, Teyo and Rat—realized whom Zahid was actually referring to. Liliana took a step back, and Kaya could almost sense the cruel smile on her face. She removed her collar, revealing the blackened dead skin underneath. Then she crossed to "Liliana" and spoke low enough so that only her imposter and Kaya could hear. "You fool . . . *I* am Liliana Vess."

The faux Liliana stared back at her uncomprehendingly. Then incredulously. Then finally the truth began to sink in—as did the terror: "No, no! I'm sorry! Please."

But Liliana had already turned away from the woman whose true name none of them would ever know. With a tremendous effort—a grasping of her hands and an unholy roar—the original Liliana wrenched the Onakke spirits away from the djinn and forced them all back into the Veil.

Free of pain, the djinn's posture finally . . . relaxed.

He looked around the room, at Liliana, at Kaya, at the old servant, at Teyo and said, *"YES. I HAVE THROWN MY NET TOO WIDE. THERE ARE VICTIMS HERE I WAS FORCED TO HURT. SAVIORS HERE WHO HELPED ME ESCAPE. YOU HAVE MY APOLOGIES. AND MY THANKS, MORTALS."*

Rat called out, "Don't mention it!"

But Zahid didn't hear and, in any case, wasn't quite done. *"BUT THERE IS ONE,"* he said, turning toward the spare Liliana, *"ONE WHO DESERVES NOTHING BUT WRATH . . ."* Fast as flame he took up the imposter in his smoking, fiery fist. She screamed as he began burning her alive. *"ONE I WILL NOT SOON RELEASE."* He laughed.

The real Liliana didn't seem to mind, watching the torture with burning eyes.

But Rat cried out, *"No!"*

Belatedly, Kaya leapt toward the djinn once again with her long daggers brandished. She stabbed "Liliana" to put the woman out of her misery, doing her a favor she hardly deserved by at least ending her suffering.

The servant woman gasped, and Zahid roared, swinging at Kaya again. But this time she was ready, this time his hand passed right through her ghosted form.

Liliana seemed to snap out of her own bloodlust, then. She said, "I warn you, Zahid, do not reignite this conflict. You've had your vengeance, brief though it was. The woman is dead. Now leave while you still can."

Zahid brooded for a few seconds, the blue and black smoke roiling around his scowling face. Then, without warning, he departed, *rocketing* away as a comet of flame and smoke—creating a massive hole in the roof he had only recently helped repair. Smoking wood and plaster fell down upon Rat, Teyo, Liliana, Kaya, the servant and the charred, smoking corpse of "Liliana Vess." All but the latter covered their heads with their hands as the debris fell, leaving the House of Vess in something of a ruin once again.

After standing there in silence for some brief but endless amount of time, Rat said, "Tell Liliana to take the Veil off now."

Teyo swallowed and said. "Take the Veil off now . . . *please?*"

Another pause ensued. Then, with what seemed like another difficult internal struggle, Liliana removed the Veil from her face.

Kaya could only wonder aloud: "Now what?"

SIXTY-THREE

CHANDRA NALAAR

She planeswalked back to Ravnica . . . because she wasn't sure where else to go.

She returned to Tenth District Plaza and the ruins of her former home in the Embassy of the Guildpact for the same reason.

She could go home to Kaladesh, to her mother. She could go find Nissa on Zendikar. She supposed she could do a lot of things. But for the moment, she sat down on a block of fallen marble and stared into the middle distance, trying to clear her mind. Trying, if such a thing was possible, to cleanse her soul.

She had no idea how long she'd been sitting there amid the dust and debris. She wasn't even sure what day it was anymore.

Nothing had been fixed; nothing had been settled. But eventually—mostly because her back was stiff and her ass was sore—she stood.

"Chandra!" It was Jace. "I've been looking everywhere for you."

"All right," Chandra murmured, barely responsive.

"You were offworld." It wasn't a question.

"Uh-huh."

"Were you on Kaladesh?"

She shook her head.

"Well, where then . . . ?"

In fact, she had been on Ravnica, lying across the long wooden bar, long after the tavern, whose name she couldn't quite remember, had closed. The ogre bartender had taken some pity on the "tiny girl" and had hoisted her up and left her there to sleep off her drunk.

Now someone was splashing water on her face. She sputtered and muttered, "Stop it, stop . . ."

"Get up, Chandra. I need your help."

Chandra opened one crusty eye and looked up. She had to search through the gloom to squint at what eventually turned out to be Vraska.

"Get up," repeated the Golgari queen.

"Why?"

"I told you, I need your help."

"For what?"

"I've found Dovin Baan."

In an instant Chandra was on her feet. Within a few seconds of that, she was actually able to resist the need to vomit. She swallowed back the bile and choked out, "Where is he?"

"Someplace called Zinara on a plane I've never been to called Regatha."

"I know it, but . . . why would Baan go there? And how do you know?"

"I may not know Regatha, but I know Ravnica. Here, the Golgari know everything, for here, we are *everywhere*, just beneath the surface."

"I thought that was House Dimir."

"I have been known to trade for information with the spies of Dimir, as well. We are one of their major sources, and when necessary they are one of mine."

"And how does that lead you to Baan being in Zinara?"

"Baan kept a safe house there. He had notes in his office, showing notations about how to improve security for the place. The notes were in code. But after my people recovered the papers, the Dimir were able to break the code. It was an exchange of information for a common cause. Cost me less than I would have thought."

Chandra shook her head. "Baan's not that sloppy, believe me. Code or no code, he'd never leave any papers behind that could track his movements."

"Maybe not. But I wonder . . . how confident was he when he went to guard the Immortal Sun? How desperate was he when he was blinded? You were there. What do you think?"

"I don't know."

"I tracked him to Kaladesh with Vivien Reid. He had been there, and he was hurt. But he planeswalked away again."

"That's what we figured. But Regatha? It's hard to believe he'd choose to hide on a world where I'm actually . . . *someone*."

"Someone?"

Chandra sighed. "I was once the Abbot of Keral Keep, which isn't far from Zinara."

Vraska smirked. "You were an abbot? You?"

"It's not *that* funny."

"If you say so. Is there a reason why Baan might go there?"

"Well, I suppose he might have decided it was the last place I'd look for him. Plus, the bastard might fit in well with the Order there. Still . . . he just wouldn't leave clues behind, no matter how confident he was. No matter how desperate he became. No clues he didn't want us to find, at least."

"Look, it's possible Regatha could be a feint. Even a trap. But I have to try. I don't know if you've heard, but I've been tasked by the other nine guilds to kill him. And it wasn't a request."

"Yeah, I may have gotten wind of some of that."

"Then you see my dilemma."

"Yeah."

"I could use someone who knows Regatha. Someone to watch my back. We both know how insidious Baan can be. Plus, he's injured. Cornered. Dangerous."

"If he's there."

"And if he's not, it's a wasted trip. Do you have something better to do?"

Chandra thought about that for a long time. "No," she said finally. "There is literally nothing better for me to do than kill Dovin Baan."

"Don't get *too* enthusiastic. Remember, Baan is *my* kill. Has to be if I'm ever going to cement my truce with the other nine guilds. Are we clear on that? Because if we're not, you're not coming."

Chandra found herself extremely reluctant to agree to those terms.

I don't need her permission, damnit!

Her vehemence actually caught her off guard.

Wait . . . This is exactly what everyone keeps asking me. Am I the type to hunt down a blind man and assassinate him in cold blood? Even if it is Dovin Baan? Jace, Ajani, Kaya and the rest are right. That's not me. Or is it? No, no. No.

Before her disturbing mental pendulum could swing back the other way, Chandra quickly promised that she'd let Vraska finish Baan off.

Minutes later, they were both on Regatha. Vraska did look a little lost. But Chandra knew the city, and it wasn't hard to locate the only blind vedalken—or really the only vedalken at all—in Zinara. He was, in fact, holing up in a house provided by the Order—or so multiple sources confirmed.

"It's still too easy," Chandra warned Vraska. "I don't know if he's really here or not, but if he is, it's definitely a trap."

"For anyone, or just for you?"

Chandra shrugged. She really wished she had brushed her teeth. A shower wouldn't have been a bad idea, either.

But I suppose I don't have to smell fresh to confront Baan.

"Are we going or not?" Vraska said. "Or rather, are you coming with me or not?"

"Yeah, I'm coming. Of course."

The supposed safe house overlooked a lake of molten lava. They watched it for an hour from a hundred yards away, using a telescopic spell to maintain a clear view. But the door never opened and the windows were shuttered, so they still hadn't confirmed Baan's presence, when a tiny plume of smoke briefly emerged from the chimney.

"Well, *someone's* in there," Chandra said. "No guarantee it's Baan."

"Guess it's time to find out. How do we approach this?"

They discussed their options. There was much back and forth, but eventually they agreed on a plan.

It began with Chandra walking right up to the front door and unleashing a fireball big enough to blow the portal wide open. She stepped inside through the flames.

And Baan was there, standing behind a kitchen counter with the rear door of the house at his back. The white bandage around his eyes gave him a look of permanent surprise, but his voice belied his appearance: "It took you rather longer to find me than I anticipated, Nalaar."

"So this *is* a trap," she said, casually unconcerned.

"Not the kind you mean. As usual, you assume that my feelings toward you are no different than your feelings toward me.

And as usual, that is not the case. For I have *no* feelings toward you. Unless, perhaps, *contempt* counts."

Chandra could feel her anger rising already. And not just her truly righteous anger toward Baan. This was anger that had been building for days. Anger toward Bolas. Toward Liliana. Even toward *Gideon*—for the crime of dying. Her hair was already aflame. Her eyes burned brightly.

"If it's not a trap, then what?" she growled.

"It is a place where I hope to teach you a lesson about how fruitless it is for you to hunt me. If I cannot convince you here, I will planeswalk to another world and seek to convince you there. And if not there, a third world. Or a fourth. My options are limitless, because unlike you I do not enter any scenario unprepared. Especially since you are so ridiculously easy to prepare for."

He whistled, and multiple flying thopters—Baan's signature mechanical tool for doing his dirty work—emerged from the rafters. Chandra blasted half a dozen, at least. But others got in close enough to poke her with electrified prongs. Multiple shocks dropped her to her knees before she was able to burn them all. Furious and in pain, she fired a blast at their maker, but Baan ducked behind the fireproof stone counter. She fired another blast at the ceiling above him, causing flaming debris to fall. She half expected him to planeswalk then, but she saw that the back door was now slightly ajar. She scrambled to her feet and raced across the burning room.

Outside, more thopters waited. With more space to work, she was able to blast nearly all of them, but the flying devices had more space, too, and once again, a few managed to prod her with their electric stings. She screamed and burned them.

Baan, meanwhile, slowly backed away, putting some distance between himself and Chandra. She noted to herself that if he went too much farther, he'd step off the edge and into the lava lake behind him. But blind or not, he somehow knew exactly how far he could retreat, pausing beside a stone bench that Chandra guessed was as fireproof as his kitchen counter.

"Are we finished for now?" he shouted. "Though it is clear you have learned no lessons today, perhaps I've planted a seed that will bloom upon our next confrontation. Even someone as thick as you, Nalaar, must have the capacity to comprehend her own inadequacies eventually."

An enraged Chandra threw a fireball but was hardly surprised when he ducked down behind the stone bench for protection.

No, it was Baan who was surprised, because, per their plan, Vraska was crouching behind that bench, cutlass drawn. As the fireball dissipated, Chandra saw Vraska lunge toward her prey. At the last second, Dovin extended his right hand to unleash a tiny thopter that shocked Vraska with enough juice to stagger her. Still her sword came down, slicing off that extended hand. Baan screamed and grabbed his bleeding wrist with his remaining hand. A stunned Vraska collapsed over the bench. Baan stepped back and raised his leg to kick Vraska off the ledge and into the lava.

Chandra threw a white-hot ball of fire right at him. There was one last scream and when the fireball was gone, so was Baan. Completely gone. She had expected to see a body, so she grimly concluded he must have planeswalked away at the last second.

Chandra ran to the bench to grab and steady a teetering Vraska. The pyromancer was still so hot, Vraska flinched away from her touch. Chandra was about to apologize when something over the gorgon's shoulder caught her eye. A body. Charred to a crisp and still aflame. But there was a glimpse of blue skin and white bandage . . . before the corpse of Dovin Baan sank away into the molten lake.

A dazed Vraska had turned to follow Chandra's gaze. Now the furious gorgon wheeled back on her partner with eyes glowing golden, ready to petrify Chandra into stone. "You! Took! My! Kill!"

For reasons Chandra couldn't explain, she didn't bother to close or cover her eyes.

"Worse," Vraska shouted, though the glow began to fade from her eyes, "you incinerated and lost the body—and with it the proof I needed. I came prepared with a spell that would have calcified his corpse, allowing me to carry it back across the Blind Eternities. But now I'll have no end of trouble with Niv-Mizzet and the guilds. They already don't trust me!"

Somewhat chastened (though perhaps not quite as chastened as she should be), Chandra said, "I'll vouch for you with Niv and everyone. I promise. And look . . ." Chandra pointed at Baan's severed right hand, lying on the ground at their feet. ". . . Magics must exist that can identify that as Baan's."

Vraska looked *somewhat* mollified. Grumbling to herself, she picked up the hand and cast her calcification spell upon it. "This better work," she said.

"Looks like it's working."

"I don't mean the spell. I mean using the hand as proof."

"It will," Chandra said.

"They're still not going to like it that I didn't take Baan out personally."

"I'll make them understand. He was always mine to kill. For you it was a job. For me . . . it was very, very personal."

"I never should have brought you along," she groused, before planeswalking away.

Chandra hesitated.

I did it. I killed Dovin Baan. I wanted him dead, and I killed him.

She stared out at the red lake.

So why doesn't this feel better?

She wasn't sorry he was dead. Wasn't sorry she was the one to kill him.

But it doesn't feel the way I thought it would.

Was it because Baan hadn't tried to kill *her*? That their enmity, much as she had wanted it to be, wasn't mutual?

Doesn't matter. I didn't have a choice. This wasn't cold blood. Baan was about to kill Vraska. He could have just planeswalked away, but instead he was going to kick her into the lava. I had to kill him to save her.

It didn't sound convincing even in her own head. She had sought this out, sought *him* out. For Kaladesh. For Ravnica. For men like her father and Gideon. Baan might not have been personally responsible for either of their deaths, but it was the officiousness and heartless efficiency of men like him that paved the way for others to do the killing. She had wanted revenge for all that.

And I got it.

And it tasted of ashes.

She planeswalked back to Ravnica alone.

"Where then . . . ?" Jace was asking.

"I had to make a quick trip to Regatha."

"Why? Wait, never mind. It doesn't matter. I've thought about this long and hard, and I finally came to the conclusion that we—or at least I—need to *save* Liliana."

Chandra nodded. "That sounds right," she said. And she meant it.

Revenge is not the way, not the answer. I'd rather be a Gideon who wants to redeem Liliana than a killer who wants vengeance on a former friend.

"So you're in."

"I'm in."

"Thank you. Now we need to hurry. I don't know how far along they are in this plan."

"Where do we go?"

"I didn't mention it, but when I read Exava, I learned that Jaya was leading Guildmaster Kaya to find Liliana."

"Jaya?"

"Yeah."

Why would Jaya do that without telling me?

"Do you know where she is?" Chandra asked, trying to keep her voice neutral.

SIXTY-FOUR

RAT

Teyo and Mistress Kaya helped the woman Karina remove her collar. They told her to spread the word that "Liliana Vess" was dead. She rushed out of the damaged house, as eager to escape their presence as that of the corpse of her former mistress on the floor.

Leaving the body amid the debris, Rat, Teyo, Mistress Kaya and the real Miss Liliana stepped outside into the cool night air. Looking across the grounds from the porch, it was already clear that word was spreading fast. Former "servants" were pulling off their collars and running away, presumably returning to their own homes.

Rat noticed ravens gathering in the trees and wondered if the carrion birds could sense the late Mistress Book Cover within the mansion. She looked back toward the front door, and thought the House of Vess already looked like a ruin once again. It wasn't just the hole in the roof or the damage caused by the djinn. A decay was setting in. The Caligo Morass was already reclaiming its own.

She turned back to mention this to her friends when she saw Mistress Kaya and Miss Liliana studying each other, somewhat dangerously. Immediately Rat stepped between them, saying, "You cannot kill her, mistress. You must not."

She looked to Teyo for support. He was eyeing Miss Liliana nervously, but he piped in, "She's right, Kaya. You can't kill her. It's simply not right."

Miss Liliana's eyes darted from Teyo to Mistress Kaya.

The latter spoke carefully: "I'm not so sure."

Miss Liliana said, "Excuse me. I'm standing right here."

In response, Mistress Kaya pushed past Rat to confront the object of their discussion: "Yes, you are. So, all right, we had a deal. We've saved 'your people.' Are you ready to die?"

Miss Liliana looked stunned for the briefest of moments, but then a look of contempt passed over her face. She stepped off the porch and onto the lawn. In a matter of seconds, the grass beneath her feet withered and died while the skin around her neck healed. Then she turned to face Mistress Kaya and said, "I am now. Assuming you're ready to kill me."

"I'm not sure why I shouldn't be," Mistress Kaya said. "We all saw how much you enjoyed the djinn's torment of the other Liliana. To me, you seem evil enough to kill."

"Somehow," Miss Liliana said, with her head held high and a haughty air, "I can't bring myself to disagree."

Rat stepped off the porch to join her. "Please, Mistress Kaya, you're looking at it the wrong way. No one said she's perfect, but she could be a lot worse."

"That's hardly an argument for keeping her alive."

"Who's arguing with you?" Miss Liliana said.

Rat pointed at the small purse on Liliana's belt that contained the Chain Veil. "She could have used the Veil to kill Mister Zahid.

She probably could have used it to kill us all. But she didn't. We had to talk her down, but she made the right decision every time, um, you know, in the end. Just like she made the right decision with the dragon in the end. She's on a path to redemption. I know it."

Mistress Kaya shook her head. "Rat, how could you possibly *know* that?"

"ZAHID WILL HAVE VENGEANCE!"

They were still in the thick of it, but Rat just couldn't resist any longer. The egg—her chance at a cure—was *right there*! On the end table. Right next to the book and the shards of sapphire. Right there. Just begging to be snatched up.

So Rat snatched it up.

Since they could see her anyway, neither Teyo nor Mistress Kaya noticed that anything had changed. And Miss Liliana wasn't looking her way. But she saw the looks on the faces of Mistress Book Cover and the old servant. They weren't looking through her. She *knew* what that looked like.

No, they're looking at me! They see me! It works!

Yes, they do, child, said a new unfamiliar voice, sounding deep in her mind.

Rat's eyes swept the room. For a second, she thought the voice might belong to the djinn. Then she looked down and somehow knew the gem was the source. But to be sure, she thought back, *Did you just speak to me, Mister Egg?*

I did. I am the essence of the Spirit-Gem.

That's great! I love this Gem! Though it's kinda hard to believe that something this wonderful used to belong to that awful dragon, you know?

He stole it. He never appreciated or understood its true power. But it affected him, nevertheless.

It revealed him for whatever what he was, right?

Exactly, child. The Spirit-Gem can reveal its possessor's true, best self. For Bolas, his was still a nightmare. But for you . . .

It's cured me!

For the moment.

Meaning it's going to wear off?

Meaning somebody else needs it more.

Somehow Rat knew Mister Egg meant Miss Raven-Hair. That she needed the Gem to find *her* true, best self. Rat stared down at the bauble she held in her hands. The bauble that in turn held all her hope for a normal life. *You want me to give you up? But . . . you're so shiny. And with you . . . with you . . .*

The decision must be yours, given freely. What does your true, best self tell you to do?

Rat was silent for what seemed like a very long time—but probably wasn't very long at all.

You sure play dirty, Mister Egg.

She turned and called out, "Miss Liliana, over here!" Then she tossed her the egg.

I guess she needs it more.

Mistress Kaya shook her head. "Rat, how could you possibly *know* that?"

"I . . . I just have this feeling, you know? A *strong* feeling."

Wheels were turning behind Miss Liliana's dark eyes. "All right," she said, crossing her arms. "I gather the two of you have an invisible friend. Where is she then? Here?" She squinted in Rat's direction. And then suddenly her eyes went wide, and she gasped, "It's you! The girl who gave me back Ugin's—who gave me back the Spirit-Gem."

Rat was thrilled. She attempted a fairly awkward curtsy and then, pointing at the Gem, said, "I call it Mister Egg."

Teyo said, "Wait, she can see you?"

"I can see her," Miss Liliana whispered.

Rat was so excited, she started jumping up and down, jingling her bells. "That's pretty amazing. Not a lot of people can do that on their first try. Not a lot of people can do it at all, really. My name's Araithia Shokta, but you can call me Rat. Everybody does. I don't mind it at all. Rat. The name kinda fits me, you know? I'm from Ravnica, and I'm not a Planeswalker, so it's also pretty amazing that I'm here, right? But Mistress Kaya brought me, and when I think about it, I think maybe I was brought here for a reason, maybe? And maybe that reason's you, miss. Maybe. The fact that you can see and hear me seems like a good sign. Doesn't it seem like a good sign, Mistress Kaya?"

All eyes looked to the ghost-assassin. She appeared stunned. But she nodded slowly, and when she spoke she sounded suitably impressed. "As Spearmaster Boruvo said, *'Anyone with the good taste to take notice of our Araithia deserves our full consideration.'*"

"Is that what he said?" Teyo asked, stepping off the porch.

Rat punched him in the arm. "Shush, you."

"Ow. The same spot. Always in the same spot."

Mistress Kaya faced down Miss Liliana: "I have questions. If I don't like the answers, we go back to the original deal, the original plan."

"And you kill me? So kill me. I won't be interrogated."

"Be interrogated," Rat said. "What's the harm?"

This seemed to stump Miss Raven-Hair. She turned a dark glare from Rat to Mistress Kaya but then said, "Fine. Ask your questions."

"You were Gatewatch."

"Is that a question?"

"No. You were Gatewatch, but you went to work for the dragon. Why?"

"He had taken control of the contract on my soul. Defying him meant my certain death."

"See?" Rat interjected. "And she *still* defied him!"

"Hush, Rat, I mean it," Mistress Kaya said, still glaring at Miss Liliana. "So you traded other lives for your own?"

Miss Liliana didn't even pause. "Yes, I did. Though . . ." Now she paused. Or . . . no. She didn't pause. She simply stopped talking.

"Though?"

"I don't want to make excuses. I traded other lives for my own."

"Though?"

She looked down, addressing the turf. "Though I tried to mitigate the . . . the carnage. Bolas insisted I use the Eternals to kill. But I gave them as little agency or guidance as I could manage without disobeying his orders, as disobeying would have resulted in my death. And I stopped them from entering any buildings. Nine Hells, why didn't every non-combatant just stay inside?"

Teyo said, "That's true. The Eternals didn't go inside. That helped us, Kaya, you know it did."

"It did, yes. But the Elderspell? Did you know that was coming?"

"I learned about it that morning, yes."

"But you let Planeswalkers die . . ."

"Rather than die myself. Haven't we covered this?"

"After the Elderspell was cast, Eternals did follow Planeswalkers into buildings."

"That was the spell, not me. The Sparks drew the Eternals in. I didn't encourage it, but I couldn't—or rather I *didn't* stop it, either."

"So why *did* you turn on Bolas? It wasn't a late change of heart, was it?"

"Not really." There was another long pause. Mistress Kaya waited. Miss Liliana inhaled and exhaled twice. Then she looked up. "When the day began, I kept waiting for my moment. Thinking that at some point—if I lived long enough—I could turn the tables on Bolas. I suppose you could call it *hubris*. Something Gideon always warned us against. Just another thing about him I didn't take seriously. Or not seriously enough, anyway. I convinced myself that if I bided my time and did the dragon's bidding—killed on his orders—I'd live long enough to bring him down."

"Seriously?"

"That was how I rationalized it. But that's all I was doing. Rationalizing. Making excuses. I believe that deep down I even knew that at the time."

"And is that what happened? You finally saw your moment? *After* Blackblade shattered and Gideon fell? *That* was your moment?"

"No. That was the moment when I saw that no moment was ever going to come. I didn't turn on the dragon to stop him or even to end the slaughter. I was still being selfish. I turned on Bolas because I didn't want to live as his slave for all eternity. Even my death was preferable to that. So I turned on him in order to die with some measure of . . ."

"Dignity?" Rat asked.

Miss Liliana didn't seem to hear her. "Myself."

"Only you didn't die; Gideon died," Mistress Kaya stated.

"I won't talk about that."

"You brought him up."

"Even so."

"You don't get to decide which questions I ask."

"Yet I very much get to decide which questions I answer. How you respond to my responses—or lack thereof—is your business. What I choose to say or not say is mine."

"Then answer this: Did you plan on living through your attack on Bolas?"

"I did not. I'm honestly not sure I plan on living through this conversation."

"I appreciate your candor."

"While it lasted. I'm done now." Miss Liliana turned back toward Rat, saying, "I hope you're satisfied . . ." She looked immediately confused. "Wait, where'd the girl go?"

Teyo said, "She's still in the same place. You have to focus on her. If you lose focus, even for a moment, she'll disappear. At least to you. Kaya and I can always see her." He sounded pretty darn proud of himself.

Miss Liliana concentrated. It didn't take her long. Rat promptly appeared and said, "Hi. Ready to live again?"

Miss Raven-Hair scowled. "I gather you believe I should."

"I *know* you should!" Rat shouted. And then more quietly said, "I also know *you* don't think so. But here's the thing: It's like some big cosmic irony, right? Mistress Kaya brought us here to kill you, but we're all gonna save you instead!"

Miss Liliana balked: "I don't need saving. I don't want it."

"Hah! You just lied twice. Question is, are you lying to us or to yourself?"

She couldn't answer.

Mistress Kaya spoke instead, with considerable hesitation, "I believe . . . I believe Rat is right about you, Vess. Or . . . in any case . . . I believe it's worth giving you the opportunity to find out."

Rat's grin widened, and she pushed on: "See? I *am* right about you, Miss Liliana. You need to come with us. With Mistress Kaya and Teyo and me."

Now Mistress Kaya and Miss Liliana *both* balked.

"Wait a minute, Rat—"

"I'm not going anywhere with—"

Rat glanced at Teyo. He didn't object. He just looked overwhelmed (and adorable).

But Rat was on a roll, pointing at herself, Teyo and Mistress Kaya: "See, the three of us are together because we made such a great team dealing with the crisis on Ravnica. And the *four* of us made an even better team dealing with the crisis on Dominaria!"

"I wouldn't call this a crisis—"

"You can't possibly compare a con artist with a djinn to Nicol Bolas—"

Teyo said, "I'm not sure we actually did *anything* as a team, Rat."

Rat smiled again. "We will. Trust me. I'm a little bit psychic."

SIXTY-FIVE

JACE BELEREN

Dawn was breaking on Dominaria as Jace, Chandra and Jaya planeswalked in. The first two had tracked down the third to find out where Kaya had gone to kill Liliana Vess. Thus confronted, Jaya had reluctantly agreed to show them the way to Liliana's ancestral home in Caligo.

Jace could tell Chandra was still mad at her mentor. Chandra understood what Jaya had been trying to do, how she'd been trying to protect Chandra—but she didn't like it one bit.

"I expected more trust from you at this point," Chandra had said. "More respect."

Jaya had not responded.

Now the three of them arrived at the mansion in time to find a number of peasants gathered around a funeral pyre. Jace shouted at his companions, "Stop the fire!"

He'd caught a glimpse of Liliana's distinctive dress.

Jaya and Chandra quickly absorbed the flames, extinguishing the pyre—and the already charred corpse.

For it was a corpse. Jace did a quick telepathic read. There was no brain function. She had been dead for at least an hour.

But maybe it's not her . . .

Upon witnessing the pyromancers' power, most of the crowd had scattered. But an old man with a white beard and an old peasant woman rushed forward.

"What are you doing?" he demanded frantically.

"You must let us burn Liliana Vess' body to prevent her from rising again!" she pleaded.

Minutes later, the three Planeswalkers had learned the whole story from the old couple, Karina and Georges Témoin. How Liliana had returned to Caligo and forced the locals into servitude. How the "servants" had been rescued by Kaya and Teyo and a young woman.

Young woman? Jace asked Jaya telepathically.

Kaya's friend, Rat, Jaya explained. *Not everyone can see her. I couldn't see her. But I gather some people can.*

Karina Témoin continued, "When Liliana's power turned against her, she was revealed to be an old woman made young by magic. I saw it with my own eyes. And at the end there, her power . . . it was tormenting her, torturing her. That's when Mistress Kaya stabbed her—as a mercy."

A suspicious Chandra asked, *Do we believe this?*

Jace responded darkly: *They believe it. Sincerely. I'm reading both of them, and they're telling the truth—at least the truth as they know it.*

And Jaya: *So you have doubts? Why?*

Excuse me if I'm having a little trouble accepting that Liliana is actually—

Suddenly Jace rushed over to the unlit pyre. To the only partially burned purse on Liliana's—*on the corpse's*—belt. It was empty.

Hah!

Smiling now, he turned back to Karina and Georges with an air of triumph: "Where is it?"

"You mean that fancy gold-link veil?" Karina asked, perplexed.

"Yes!"

"Mistress Kaya and the others took it with them. The boy Teyo had it trapped inside a glowing sphere of light. They said they'd need it as proof."

Jace literally staggered backward. He turned around and stared at the charred remains of Liliana Vess.

Because this is *her. Liliana is dead.*

He knew she'd never willingly part with the Chain Veil. The phrase *over her dead body* came involuntarily—and heartbreakingly—to mind.

Chandra said aloud, "Liliana couldn't give it up without dying. Those were the rules, right?"

"The rules wouldn't matter if she was already dead," Jaya said grimly.

Jace saw Chandra take this in. Watched as it slowly became a reality for her as it just had for him. A couple of tears ran down her face. He wondered why there were none running down his own.

Karina seemed to take offense. Forgetting her fear, she reprimanded the pyromancer: "How can you shed tears over the Curse of the House of Vess?"

Chandra wheeled on the woman, flames dancing about steaming eyes. "Don't tell me who to mourn!"

Karina took a few steps back, and her husband wrapped his arms around her protectively. There was a moment of danger, a possibility of things turning ugly fast.

But Chandra's wrath seemed to simply drain away. As if she no longer had the energy to sustain it. The fire in her eyes died. "I'm so tired," she said weakly.

Jaya attempted to put an arm around her. "Chandra . . ."

But her protégée pushed her off, snapping: "If I want comfort, I'll get it from my real mother, thank you very much."

Turning her back on a stunned Jaya, Chandra said to Jace, "I'll see you back on Ravnica. I have one more thing I promised to do there."

Then to the accompanying gasps of the Témoins, Chandra planeswalked away in fire.

Jaya sighed. She was tired, too. "Well. My work here is done," she said sardonically. "I think I'll go to Regatha for a few days to rest before meeting up with Teferi, Ajani and Karn. If you need me, that's where I'll be." Then as an afterthought, she added, "But don't need me."

What could Jace do? He nodded. And then she, too, planeswalked away in flames.

By this time, the old couple was quite literally shaking in their shoes. Jace said, "Not to worry. You've done nothing wrong. Go ahead. Reignite the funeral pyre. It's time."

Jace watched Liliana burn, staying to the bitter end.

He found he couldn't cry for her—or for himself.

He was just . . . numb.

When only ashes remained, Jace telekinetically spread them across the morass.

You're free Liliana. Finally free, finally home.

Jace desperately needed Vraska. He returned to Ravnica.

SIXTY-SIX

ANA IORA

She trudged up the lane in ill-fitting shoes.

If I get a blister, someone's going to die for it.

There was the sign, hanging from the roof. The Fiddler's Inn. No actual words, of course. Just a crude wooden carving of a goblin child playing a violin.

Underwhelming.

She went up to the gate and took a deep breath before entering. Then she unlatched it and proceeded across a small courtyard, containing a few empty wooden tables and benches and a bit of broken glass. At the inn's front door, she took another deep breath, turned the knob and proceeded inside. The door slapped across a dented bell hung from the doorpost by a thin strip of iron. Its off-pitch ding summoned an old goblin from the back room. He honked his large nose into a handkerchief—and by this time, the woman felt mildly blessed the goblin used one at all.

Still, try not to touch anything.

Without a word, he climbed up onto a stool behind the front desk and handed her the registry to sign. She noticed that most of the other signatures were simply "X."

Obviously, it's a high-class joint with a high-class clientele.

Of course, given how she was currently dressed—*like a Caligo peasant*—she probably fit right in. With some reluctance, she picked up the frayed quill, dipped it in the leaky inkwell and signed the registry, "Ana Iora."

Ana Iora?

The goblin stuffed the soiled handkerchief behind his large pointed ear, stuck two ink-stained fingers in his mouth and whistled. Minutes later Ana was being escorted up the stairs to her room by a small yellowish-green goblin. She had no luggage.

Not a Spirit-Gem or a Chain Veil to my name.

She did have a minuscule diamond, allowing her to tip the young goblin well . . . but not so well as to attract any undue attention. The door soon shut, leaving Ana alone with her thoughts, which weren't exactly fantastic company at the moment. She wondered why she'd picked that name. *Ana,* of course, was the given name of her former mentor, back when Liliana was a child on a path to becoming a healer. But she had no idea where *Iora* had come from; it had just popped into her head. In any case, "Liliana Vess" was dead and must remain so. And *Ana Iora* was as good a name as any.

So Ana Iora looked around her new room and was not impressed. But she needed to lay low for now, which meant lowering her expectations.

Besides, this particular inn wasn't exactly my choice . . .

She remembered the ravens gathering on the roof of the House of Vess, making her anxious. She waited for the proverbial other shoe to drop. For the Raven Man to make his unwanted appearance. Meanwhile, Liliana had again lost sight of the strange young girl known as Rat.

Where had she gone?

Liliana quickly realized Rat hadn't gone anywhere. As the boy had warned, when Liliana's thoughts had wandered (to the Raven Man), she'd lost focus on the girl, causing her to fade from consciousness. Liliana concentrated again on where she knew the girl should be, and Rat came back into focus. Liliana had a flash of recognition then, realizing that she had actually—in those few short seconds—forgotten what Rat had looked like. Even the sound of Rat's voice was tinged with a sense of recovering something Liliana had misplaced within her mind. The girl was saying she was positive that Liliana belonged with their small group. She had convinced Teyo—not a difficult task, as he gazed at Rat the way Jace once gazed at Liliana. But Rat had even convinced the older, worldlier Kaya.

Nine Hells, she's even halfway to convincing me.

Liliana felt a strange connection to Rat for some reason. Perhaps it was merely that the girl had tossed her the Spirit-Gem that had connected her to the Spirit Dragon. Or maybe it was that Rat believed in Liliana with such *preposterous* certainty.

But maybe there's more to it . . .

Liliana had to admit—to herself, at least—that she'd held the Spirit-Gem before, and it hadn't sent or linked Ugin to her until *after* she had received it from Rat.

Had the girl activated *it, somehow? What did Ugin say—that the child sacrificed something?*

Kaya intruded on Liliana's thoughts then, saying, "We need to think this through. I was contracted by the guilds to kill Liliana Vess, and—"

Rat piped in: "Well, you already killed *a* Liliana Vess."

Kaya and Liliana both rolled their eyes at that—then noticed their similar reactions. They perhaps had more in common than either would prefer to admit.

And neither of us knows quite what to do with that knowledge.

Kaya shook off that concern and said, "I don't care about the money the guilds were paying for the hit." Then she qualified her statement, "Or I don't care about it much."

"We don't need money. Think of all the diamonds," Rat said.

"Diamonds?" Liliana asked, feeling a bit at sea.

Kaya waved off the question. "The point is, it's not about the money. Not killing Liliana could hurt the Orzhov. Besides, if I don't return with proof of her death, the guilds'll simply hire another Planeswalker assassin to do the job."

Liliana admitted, "There are plenty of those . . . and plenty of other Planeswalkers who'd love to kill me for their own reasons. Even free of charge."

Teyo hesitantly cleared his throat and suggested, "What if—what if we used the Chain Veil as proof? I couldn't help noticing that you were much . . . *darker* when you put it on. Maybe it isn't good for your redemption?"

Liliana found herself jumping to deny that: "The Chain Veil is a minor tool for focusing my power. I have no reason to give it up."

Rat stated simply, "That's not true."

Liliana remembered that the girl was psychic—and in a more intuitive, less intrusive way than Jace Beleren.

Which makes her less powerful . . . and more dangerous.

Rat looked Liliana straight in the eye. "It's not a mere tool, is it?"

Liliana again found herself struggling with her answer. Finally, she blurted out, "No. It's cursed and very dangerous. Perhaps keeping the Chain Veil is my penance."

Rat gave her the stink-eye and said, "Or is that just your excuse to hold on to its power?"

Which, of course, is perfectly true.

Almost inevitably, the Onakke spirits began whispering to her then: *Vessel, this is not the time to part with us. Do not surrender* the Veil, but rather surrender yourself to the Veil. Surrender your-self to us.

That was bad enough, but then the ravens in the trees cawed, followed by the voice of the Raven Man: *Do not be a fool, Liliana Vess. You cannot seriously be considering this.*

"Are you all right?" Teyo asked.

She turned to the boy. He was staring at her with what might have been real concern.

Would I know real concern if I saw it?

Kaya also stared at Liliana. Rat, too, once Liliana managed to refocus her back into existence. It seemed clear they couldn't hear either the Raven Man or the spirits. The former warned, *There are dangers ahead, Liliana. I can see them even if you cannot. Without the Veil, you will surely perish.*

"With the Veil," Liliana said out loud to both the Raven Man and her new companions, "I was *ready* to perish." With some-thing akin to physical pain, Liliana began to mentally divest her-self of the Chain Veil, which suddenly seemed like a clear first step on her path of choosing redemption over power.

They were still staring at her.

She said, "You're right about one thing. The Veil would make excellent proof of my death: No one would ever believe that Lili-ana Vess would give up its power except over her dead body."

"Plus," Rat pointed out, "if anyone comes to Dominaria to check, they'll learn Liliana Vess did die here."

Liliana removed the Chain Veil from the purse at her side. Even now, the temptation to don it was palpable, intense. She croaked out, "I have to admit I've never been able to get rid of it before. When I've tried, it felt like I was dying."

Rat said, "I think you have to *want* to, you know?"

Do I want to?

No, Vessel, drink us in . . .

Liliana, don't be a fool . . .

Yes, damnit, I do want to!

And just then the Spirit-Gem in her other hand began to glow, brighter and brighter and brighter. They all shielded their eyes. In fact, Liliana involuntarily raised the Veil itself to shield her eyes. Then with a last bright *FLASH*, the Spirit-Gem disappeared from her hand, startling Liliana so much that she actually dropped the Veil onto the patch of dead grass at her feet.

And somehow Liliana knew that she had indeed detached herself from the Veil—but only after she herself made the choice to get rid of it.

And yes, admittedly I had a little help from the Spirit-Gem.

Rat was staring at Liliana's empty hands.

"I did it," Liliana said to reassure her. "I'm no longer connected to the Veil. I can feel the difference."

And thankfully, I can't hear the Onakke anymore!

Rat said mournfully, "But . . . where's Mister Egg?"

"What? Oh. I don't know. It just . . . disappeared. Perhaps it returned to Ugin."

"Ugin?"

"Never mind."

"Never mind. Right."

Strangely, the girl looked positively crushed. It occurred to Liliana that maybe Rat had felt the power of the Spirit-Gem when she had held it in her hands, and maybe she liked that power a bit too much. It was probably a good thing that "Mister Egg" was gone.

Last thing I want is for Rat to go down that path. My path.

Even now, Liliana hardly felt like she was off the path.

But maybe, just maybe, I took a step in the right direction . . .

She hadn't been fixed. She was still very, very broken. But her soul did feel . . . *lighter?*

All four of them were now staring down at the Veil in the grass.

Kaya started to reach for it. "Well, if this is going to be the proof—"

Liliana grabbed her hand. "You can't touch it, or you'll risk its curse."

"Well, then how—?"

"Let me try," Teyo said. He cupped one hand, spread out his fingers and created a hemisphere of light about the size of a rubber ball. Or half the size of one, anyway. With it, he scooped the Veil (and a little bit of dead grass and dirt) up off the ground and then proceeded to complete the sphere, sealing the Chain Veil within.

Briefly—just before the sphere had fully encircled the Veil—Liliana heard the Onakke one last time—*screaming*. They clearly didn't care for the white mana flowing through Teyo's magic.

Liliana warned, "I wouldn't even keep it in your sphere for too long, lest it corrupt your magic."

With a quick frightened nod, Teyo acknowledged her warning.

Right then, en masse, the croaking ravens flew away. All four humans turned to look, but only Liliana could hear the voice of the Raven Man echo in her mind: *Our work together isn't finished, Liliana. You'll see me again. And soon.* Then he/they was/were gone.

"So now what?" Rat said cheerfully. Liliana thought the cheerfulness was perhaps a bit forced. That the girl was perhaps still mourning the loss of the Spirit-Gem but had made a conscious decision to move on. Liliana admired her for that.

Kaya said, "Teyo, Rat and I have to return with the Veil to Ravnica and the guilds."

"Obviously, I can't go with you," Liliana stated. And then, looking around, "Nor can I stay here, on Dominaria."

Kaya asked, "Do you know the plane of Fiora?"

"I've been there once or twice over the last century."

Rat asked, "How old *are* you?"

Liliana smiled thinly and said, "That's not a polite question."

It was then that Kaya told her of the Fiddler's Inn in the Lowlands.

"Lowlands?" Liliana asked.

"The lower city of Paliano on Fiora. The three of us will meet you there in a day or so. But let me be clear. In letting you live, I have made myself responsible for anything you now do. So I warn you, Liliana, you had better be at the Fiddler's when we arrive. Because if you're not, I'll know you weren't serious about seeking any kind of redemption . . . in which case I *will* hunt you down and kill you for your crimes against Ravnica. Is that understood?"

Now, standing in her mediocre lodgings, Ana Iora tried to understand why she had come to Fiddler's Inn in the Lowlands of Paliano on Fiora. It certainly *wasn't* because Kaya's threat had frightened her. Honestly, Liliana was more afraid of herself . . . and what she might do without these three to help her.

And does that make any sense?

After all, the Gatewatch had tried to redeem her. Gideon and Jace and Chandra had tried to redeem her. They had all failed.

Well, maybe Gideon succeeded just a little. Maybe.

How could Liliana Vess—or Ana Iora—possibly think these three strangers had any chance at helping her?

Not three strangers, really. Four *strangers.*

She was forgetting to include herself. And without a doubt, she felt like a stranger to herself right now.

Looking out the window, Liliana spotted a single raven in a tree. It abruptly flew off.

No whispers, no threats, no cawing even.

She attempted to shrug it off.

Not every raven in the Multiverse is a harbinger of the Raven Man. For all I know, it might've just been a crow.

She shut the heavy curtains on the daylight. She suddenly felt a desperate need for sleep.

SIXTY-SEVEN

TEYO VERADA

As Teyo, Kaya and Rat planeswalked back to Ravnica and Orzhova, Teyo was focused on yet another new thing he'd never attempted before: maintaining his geometry around the Veil *while* planeswalking.

He barely managed it—but he *did* manage it.

He was more than a little proud of himself and turned to get a little validation from Kaya and Rat. But as usual, the two women had collapsed after their shared journey through the Blind Eternities.

Madame Blaise rushed to help her mistress and, before Teyo could warn her, wound up tripping over the unseen (by her) Rat. Teyo tried to help Rat—while still maintaining his sphere of light around the Chain Veil—allowing a flustered Blaise to focus on getting Kaya to bed.

Teyo, in turn, helped Araithia to her room and helped her into her bed, which embarrassed him a bit—though he tried to hide that.

It wasn't clear whether or not Rat noticed.

She notices most things.

But right now she just seemed grateful. "You know," she told him, "my life has opened up in so many ways since meeting you. I think you're my good-luck charm . . ." Then she added quickly, "And Kaya, too, of course,"

"I feel exactly the same way about you." Then he added quickly, "And Kaya, too, of course."

He left her to rest, coming out of Rat's room just as Blaise was exiting Kaya's and calling for more servants.

Per her mistress, Blaise ordered one servant to inform Acting Guildmaster Tomik Vrona that his true guildmaster was back. A second servant was sent to inform Chief Bilagru. A third was to go to Niv-Mizzet to inform the Living Guildpact that Guildmaster Kaya was calling for the Firemind to assemble all ten guilds in the morning. Then, glancing over at Teyo, Madame Blaise summoned forth a fourth and commanded, "Bring a grounder so that young Master Verada may safely stow that presumably dangerous artifact for the night."

Once the servants were dispatched, Blaise then took a deep breath and took a few steps toward Rat's room, to see "if I can be of any help to the poor girl."

"I'm happy to . . . *interpret* for you, madame," Teyo offered.

"I appreciate that, but I am determined to learn how to be of some assistance to the child, which means I am equally determined to learn how to *see* the child."

Teyo said, "Well, she's in the bed. Focus on her there."

Blaise nodded and entered.

Teyo waited, assuming that he'd in fact be needed.

But after a brief pause, Blaise came back out, stating definitively that "Mistress Rat is gone."

Teyo smiled and told the servant, "She's there. You just can't see her. But don't feel bad. Most people can't."

Blaise squinted at Teyo, who realized that he had, perhaps, sounded *slightly* condescending. But before he could apologize, madame handed him a note:

> Going to see my mother. Be back tomorrow. Don't leave without me.
>
> Rat

Teyo found himself rushing into the room. Rat was indeed gone, and the balcony door was now open.

"Don't leave without me." Look who's talking.

He sighed, apologizing profusely to Madame Blaise and—still carefully maintaining his geometry around the Veil—exited back into the corridor.

A servant was waiting there with something called a grounder made of something called watersilver. (A typical grounder, he was told, was designed to trap ghosts, but this model had been modified to contain cursed objects.) Teyo carefully lowered the Chain Veil into the grounder and then released his sphere back into the aether. The servant sealed the grounder, and Teyo gingerly carried it into his room.

Standing in the doorway, Madame Blaise asked, "Can I get you anything, my boy?"

"I could use a pot of chokra."

"I'm afraid I don't know what that is."

"A hot drink, strong and bitter. Helps you stay awake."

How am I going to get through the night without chokra?

She said, "We have coffee. Sounds much the same."

"Coffee then, please, madame." He sank with a groan into an overstuffed chair. He knew he wouldn't be getting much sleep this night, not with the Chain Veil to guard, but he could at least take a load off his admittedly aching feet.

SIXTY-EIGHT

ATKOS TARR

A tkos Tarr was happy to be useful to Lazav, who hadn't given him an assignment in two or three days, at least. Atkos hated letting his skills rust for even that long.

What good is being Dimir's top assassin if the boss doesn't want anyone dead?

Fortunately, the boss now had someone who indeed needed to die.

But the Dimir guildmaster had made himself *very* clear: "The hit must take place in the morning, *during* the meeting of the Living Guildpact and the ten guilds." As an afterthought, the spymaster had added, "And don't drink *any* blood. No one must know that a vampire was behind this kill."

That was disappointing of course, but there would be other opportunities to feed when the job was done.

So Atkos simply took up position and settled in for the long night and the longer wait . . .

Blaise smiled and nodded and closed the door behind her.

Teyo stared at the grounder, but his thoughts were all on Araithia Shokta.

"Don't leave without me." Like I'd ever go anywhere without her ever again.

SIXTY-NINE

TOMIK VRONA

Madame Blaise came out of Kaya's bedroom and said, "She will see you now." Despite feeling fairly confident Kaya would be pleased with what he had to tell her, Tomik was nevertheless a great big ball of nerves.

He and Bilagru exchanged a quick look and entered.

Is the giant nervous, too?

Kaya was in bed, eating breakfast from a tray. She looked tired.

Still, she looks better than my poor Ral did.

It had taken the healer half the night to repair Ral's injuries, and even when she was finished, Ral still looked like one big bruise. One big bruise with a shaved head. Tomik had been forced to shave it to remove all the black gunk stuck there.

That doesn't matter. Hair grows back.

Still, it left Ral looking particularly raw and . . . vulnerable.

But he was sleeping now; he'd be all right. Tomik had placed Tezzeret's arm in plain view, so Ral could see it when he woke and remember his victory.

Kaya said to Tomik, "You look tired."

"Me? No, I'm fine."

"I know the Orzhov contracts must be a burden on you."

"No, really, I'm growing used to them, and—"

"You must think I'm taking advantage of your generosity, and I am truly sorry about this, but I need to take one more planeswalk after the guild meeting this morning before I can take those burdens back."

"Actually," Tomik said, feeling a little victorious, "that won't be necessary." He proceeded to explain the new plan for Syndicate leadership, and she listened with an expression that he couldn't quite read.

Somewhere between dubious and relieved, maybe?

She said, "So I'd remain guildmaster in name only, while you continue to act as . . . as acting guildmaster—as de facto guildmaster."

"We'll need to come up with a better title for me to sell the idea to the faithful, but, essentially . . . yes. I mean—if *you're* all right with it . . ."

She didn't answer right away, and Tomik's nervousness returned. He started to defend the idea and hoped he wasn't simply babbling: "I'm not much for tooting my own horn, but I believe I accomplished quite a bit in the short time you were away, not the least of which was making progress, even *peace*, with both Teysa Karlov and the Triumvirate."

Kaya's gaze fell upon the giant, and Bilagru quickly confirmed that Tomik still had his support and the support of the Orzhov armed forces.

Kaya asked, "Are you sure about this? Because I have to admit, I love this plan so much, I feel extremely guilty about accepting it."

"Do not feel even a little bit guilty. I'm glad you love the plan, because, well . . . simply put, *I love my guild,* and I believe that I . . ." He glanced up at Bilagru and corrected himself. "That *we*—can follow the example you've set, the work you began, to make the Orzhov better. We'll still keep charge of Ravnica's financial interests—its necessary regulations, loans and collections—but we'll do it without breaking the faithful for generations."

"I certainly can't think of anyone better qualified for the task," Kaya said—which was a great relief to Tomik.

"Neither can I," said Bilagru. He "gently" patted Tomik on the top of his head in a vaguely paternal manner that felt a bit like a hammer was driving Tomik's skull down into his chest cavity.

Trying not to look too pained for the giant's sake, Tomik reiterated to Kaya, "I'll still need you to stop by Ravnica occasionally for ceremonial functions . . ."

"I'm *happy* to do that. I like Ravnica." She reached out her hand. Tomik approached the bed and held out his own. She squeezed it. "I've made good friends on this world—including the two of you. Besides, Rat will want to come home periodically and see her parents, I'm sure."

Tomik still felt the need to confirm: "So you're *really* all right with this?"

"I am if you are."

They squeezed each other's hands again.

Then a smiling Tomik departed with Chief Enforcer Bilagru, proud to be the Permanent Acting Guildmaster of the Orzhov Syndicate. (Or whatever his new title turned out to be.)

SEVENTY

VRASKA

The statue/corpse of Isperia still loomed over the proceedings at the Azorius Senate House, where once again Niv-Mizzet had called a meeting of the ten guilds. Vraska believed the venue continued to be chosen on purpose to embarrass her or intimidate her with evidence of her great crime.

Vraska resented the lack of respect for the Golgari and its queen, but in fact, the more time passed, the more Vraska reveled in her decision to kill Isperia for *her* great crimes. The gorgon wasn't sorry she'd killed the damned sphinx. Nor was she embarrassed or intimidated.

And let's face it, Lavinia is a much more reasonable choice for Azorius guildmaster than Isperia or Baan ever was. In the final analysis, I did all of Ravnica a great favor.

It was a much bigger crowd than at the previous meetings. Clearly some guild officials had been told of the assassination plans for Baan, Vess and Tezzeret as a fait accompli, when it was too late to change course. Niv-Mizzet was there, of course, glorying in his new role as a glorified master of ceremonies. Lavinia stood on one side of Isperia to represent Azorius, while Aurelia waited on the other, representing Boros.

Hekara had replaced Exava as the Rakdos representative. When asked why by Lavinia, Hekara said Exava was under the weather. "Also under a trapeze act, being used as their living net. Not sure why. The boss said something about her embarrassing the Cult by losing a talent competition against a couple of amateurs."

Kaya, Teyo, Tomik and Bilagru were all there, representing Orzhov. But so were the Triumvirate *and* Teysa Karlov. Vraska was a bit surprised everyone in the Syndicate was so chummy all of a sudden. Much as she liked Kaya, and generally wished her well, she found she preferred it when the other guilds had more internal disarray. It kept their eyes turned inward, keeping the Golgari out of their sights.

Vorel and Vannifar were there for Simic. Borborygmos and Gan Shokta represented the Gruul Clans, while Selesnya was covered by Boruvo and Emmara. A scowling Maree and a dour Ral stood for Izzet. The latter had shaved his head, making him look more like a prisoner of war than a guildmaster.

A few offworld Planeswalkers were also present, including Vivien Reid, the Wanderer and, of course, Chandra. Vraska nodded knowingly to Chandra, who looked slightly confused before nodding back, which gave Vraska pause. Then, unsurprisingly, another Chandra arrived, forcing the first Chandra to shapeshift into Lazav. Vraska wondered why the Dimir guildmaster bothered with this repetitive charade, but she supposed it made him feel important and powerful. Or perhaps it taught him something. After all, he now knew there was some understanding between the pyromancer and the Golgari queen.

Well, fine. The truth behind that will be revealed soon enough, anyway.

Per Dovin Baan's stingily provided advice, Vraska had brought Huntmaster Myczil Savod Zunich—or simply Myc, as he preferred to be called. The elf had been surprised and gratified to be chosen over Storrev, Azdomas, Varolz or Cevraya. It was an easy concession to the young Myc's vanity, further cementing his loyalty to Vraska over Izoni.

Baan was right, as usual.

Vraska saw that Teyo had the Chain Veil in a sphere of light, while Ral had Tezzeret's arm. It was clear the other two assassins had done their jobs.

For a moment, she considered what she was about to do. The part of her that loved Jace knew their lives would be less complicated if she took another path today. But the part of her that loved the Golgari believed this was the best way forward for her people, and thus her decision was confirmed, made and solidified.

Looking around, Vraska half expected Jace to show, but so far he was staying away—which was just as well. Best to keep him at some distance from this aspect of her life.

The aspect that might hurt him . . .

When all had assembled, the Living Guildpact nodded to Kaya, who stepped forward into an Azorius Verity Circle: "I killed the woman known as Liliana Vess. As proof of kill I offer this . . ." As Vraska had presumed, Kaya indicated the Chain Veil in Teyo's sphere.

A clearly relieved Teyo "handed" it over to Niv-Mizzet, who had the boy lower it into some kind of puzzle box, which the dragon then sealed for safekeeping.

But who'll keep it safe from the dragon? I'd best look into that.

Vorel asked, "Can an *artifact* be used as proof that the woman is dead?"

Lavinia stated, "The Liliana I knew would only give up the Veil over her dead body."

To Vraska's surprise, Chandra stepped forward, too. "Liliana *is* dead. Jace, Jaya and I saw her corpse on Dominaria." She nodded toward Kaya, who scowled, perhaps not appreciating that she was being checked up on. Chandra concluded by saying, "We received a Jace-tested report from an eyewitness who confirmed that Kaya stabbed Liliana in the back with her daggers." Vraska didn't know Chandra well, but she had never heard the woman sound so cold. It seemed especially strange, since she knew from Jace that Chandra had once cared a great deal for Liliana. Jace was an even bigger concern. Vraska didn't like that he'd had to go through all that, even down to seeing her dead body, the body of a woman he'd once loved. And she *really* didn't like that her witness Chandra was also acting as an after-the-fact witness for Kaya, as well.

It seems . . . too convenient.

But there was nothing to be done about that now.

As soon as Kaya stepped out of the Verity Circle, Vraska stepped into it and produced—brandished, really—Dovin Baan's calcified hand. "This is—or rather *was*—the right hand of Dovin Baan."

Without a word, Lavinia held out her hand for Vraska's proof. The Golgari queen gave it to her and Lavinia performed a brief arcane ritual over it. A small spectral image of Baan appeared over the stretched skin and bones of the severed appendage. Lavinia nodded and stated for the crowd, "This is indeed the hand of Dovin Baan."

The Firemind said, "State for the record that you killed Baan."

With a dark glance at Chandra, Vraska begrudgingly stated, "I am forced to confess that I did not."

There was a brief murmur of surprise from the crowd as Vraska removed herself from the Verity Circle, only to be quickly replaced by a stone-faced Chandra Nalaar. The gorgon caught Ral's look of sympathy—*pity, most likely*—but looked away.

Chandra said, "I killed Baan—over grudges old and new. But I believe Vraska should be credited for the kill, as she was prepared to do your will and slay Baan herself when I acted. Besides, I never would have been there if Vraska hadn't brought me along."

Vraska was briefly anxious over that last detail.

Again, too convenient.

But no one else seemed concerned, and Niv-Mizzet offered, "The Living Guildpact is willing to credit Vraska with the kill. What say the guilds of Ravnica?"

The nine other guilds all said, "Aye."

Vraska waited a dramatic beat, then nodded to Myc, who piped up with, "The Golgari also says aye."

"Then it is unanimous," the dragon said.

Chandra turned to Vraska and asked, "Satisfied?"

Vraska nodded. She didn't like that Chandra was making it seem like they had some kind of arrangement between them.

Even if we did.

And somewhere in the back of her mind, Vraska also didn't like Chandra's changed demeanor. This was one of Jace's best friends. Someone he viewed as a younger sister. She was clearly in pain, a pain that ran deep, which was a kind of pain Vraska well understood. The gorgon berated herself for involving Chandra in her schemes . . .

But when Chandra planeswalked away in flame right then and there, Vraska mostly just felt relief. She was glad Chandra wouldn't be sticking around to overthink what took place on Regatha. So ultimately, Vraska indeed felt *very* satisfied. The Golgari was at peace with the other guilds, freeing up Vraska to consolidate her power within the Swarm . . . at which point she would lead its ascent over all of Ravnica.

All thanks to the death of Dovin Baan.

SEVENTY-ONE

DOVIN BAAN

Dovin Baan was alone in his Ravnican safe house, waiting for Vraska to return. Not that he wasn't keeping busy in the meantime. He was using his thopters to fashion a mechanical right hand to replace the hand the gorgon had taken. After that, he would set to work on creating some magical-mechanical devices to replace his lost eyes. His thopters all had optics, so he believed it should not be too difficult once he figured out the interface.

Baan was mildly annoyed with Vraska for cutting off his hand—it had not been part of his plan—but he could not deny the wisdom of her action. Hard evidence of his demise would certainly lend credence to Vraska and Nalaar's story, and if the Golgari queen had told him of her intent in advance, he *might* have been reluctant to comply. Baan was in fact slightly embarrassed that his own fear of further mutilation had blinded him to the need for such an action. And in any case, learning to perfect himself with no eyes and only one hand would be an interesting—if brief—challenge.

Beyond that, Regatha had gone exactly as he had expected it to go. For Baan, it was child's play to get Nalaar to attempt to incinerate him and simple enough to let the conflagration hide his planeswalking, while a pre-planted thopter projected an illusion of light, depicting his charred corpse sinking into the lava.

Now his safety was assured, and his mind would be occupied, as raising the unruly Golgari to perfection presented an intriguing and tantalizingly complex puzzle.

Baan noticed a slight rise in temperature in the room.

Is someone here?

"Vraska?" he called out. There was no response.

Baan listened for a breath, for a heartbeat.

Nothing.

No one was there.

Dovin Baan decided it was the inconsistent Ravnican weather combined with the shoddy construction of the building. He would have to create something to regulate the temperature of his domicile.

The thought of making his new home more efficient brought a smile to his face . . .

SEVENTY-TWO

RAL ZAREK

A tense Ral knew it was now his turn. He had been hoping against hope that either Kaya or Vraska might have failed, too.

But no.

Inhaling deeply and running one hand over his shaved head, he stepped forward into the Verity Circle, holding Tezzeret's arm. With a nod to the Wanderer, he described in a clear voice their journeys and battles.

"All true," she confirmed. "Although I am forced to admit that I lost consciousness and planeswalked away. I did not witness Tezzeret's end."

All eyes in the Senate House turned back to Ral Zarek, still holding Tezzeret's etherium arm. Niv-Mizzet and Tomik and everyone else expected him to regale them with the tale of his opponent's demise.

Ral hesitated . . . then, despite the fact that the Firemind had long ago taught him a spell that could thwart an Azorius Verity Circle, Ral told the absolute truth: "Tezzeret beat me. He could have killed me easily. Instead, he gave me this arm to use as false proof of his death. He assumed I would be too vain or too frightened to reveal that I had failed. I am neither."

Everyone was too surprised to gasp or murmur.

Thus, the silence allowed Ral to actually hear the Wanderer breathe a sigh of relief. This revelation clearly tallied with her assumptions. She said, "After recovering consciousness, I planeswalked back to Esper. The fortress was completely deserted. And too little time had passed for that to be the result of Tezzeret's forces meandering off on their own. It was an organized abandonment, which suggests that Tezzeret himself was behind it and used his Planar Bridge technology to execute it. Moreover, that technology, which had previously made it so easy for me to follow him, was no longer registering upon the Blind Eternities at all. I suspect that I had previously been overestimating my own skills—that Tezzeret had been *intentionally* leaving a trail for me. Now that he believes himself '*dead*' to the Multiverse, he has made certain that trail has run cold."

Ral dared a look at Niv-Mizzet, whose expression revealed acute disappointment in his protégé. Ral looked at Maree, who was smiling more broadly than Ral had ever known her to smile in her life. Finally, Ral looked at Tomik, whose face was full of pity for his lover.

And somehow that's even worse . . .

SEVENTY-THREE

CHANDRA NALAAR

Chandra leaned against a tree, chewing on a mint leaf and waiting.

She was on Zendikar to see Nissa. Chandra had no idea where on this plane Nissa was, but she felt confident the tree would tell Nissa where *Chandra* was.

That sounds ridiculous, but I bet it works.

In times past, the anticipation, the desire, the *need* to see Nissa Revane made Chandra's heart flutter a little bit. Or a lot.

Not today. Or . . . not tonight, *I guess.*

It had been early morning when she'd left Ravnica, but here on Zendikar, it was night, with a sliver of a moon hanging above the forest.

So under that moon, leaning against that tree, Chandra waited for Nissa—with a decided lack of anticipation—filling her time by confronting her various demons.

Despite what she had told Jaya, Chandra had not let her mom comfort her. Truthfully, she hadn't even seen Pia, let alone told her what was bothering her. In part, because Chandra hadn't quite pinpointed exactly what *was* bothering her.

It wasn't Jaya. Chandra hadn't liked what Jaya had done— keeping information from her and facilitating things so that Chandra wouldn't have to make tough choices or feel difficult feelings—but deep down, Chandra knew Jaya had meant well. In fact, if anything, Chandra felt the need to *apologize* to Jaya, while making it clear that this *former* protégée didn't want her former mentor to "protect" her that way ever again.

So what *was* troubling her?

Is it Liliana's death? Or Gideon's?

In part, it was both. Chandra knew she'd miss each of them terribly. She had loved them each in not dissimilar ways. The big sister she never had. The big brother she never had. Gids at least went out on his own terms, but it seemed especially sad that Liliana had in the end been completely unable to follow or find her true, best self. Still, Liliana and Gideon had saved Ravnica and probably the whole Multiverse from Bolas, so Chandra was determined to make *that* her last memory of them.

No, the main thing bothering Chandra was Dovin Baan. She still wasn't sorry he was dead. Nor even sorry she had killed him. But killing Baan has taught her something about who she wanted to be. Or at least who she *didn't* want to be . . .

I'm not a hunter. Not a killer. That's not me. And I can't simply be a survivor, either. That's not enough . . .

Before she could quite crystallize what *might* be enough, the ground beneath her feet began to stir. It felt a little like an earthquake, but Chandra knew better. She'd been looking down at her feet; now she looked up. The turf before her had all but liquefied, as it roiled toward her like a wave. And riding that wave?

Nissa Revane.

"Chandra," she said.

"Nissa," Chandra said, hoping that for just a moment, for just one little moment, the sight of the elf would make the pyromancer's cheeks burn, make her heart skip a beat, give her those flutters.

But no.

Chandra had never been into girls. Her crushes—and she'd had her fair share—were mostly the brawny (and decidedly male) types like Gids. But there had always been something about Nissa Revane specifically, something the two of them shared in that great chemical mix—arcing between them like one of Ral Zarek's lightning bolts—that had thrilled her. From the moment they first met.

Now everything's different.

It was over. Before it had ever had a chance to begin. Maybe, maybe they had missed their moment. A time when if Chandra had demonstrated more courage or more self-possession, she might have told Nissa how she felt. A time when if Nissa had acknowledged even the slightest hint of interest or self-knowledge, they might have found their way to each other.

But that was oversimplifying things, and Chandra knew it. And she was fairly certain that Nissa knew it, too.

On Ravnica, in the wake of Gideon's death and Bolas', they had admitted to each other that they loved. But both of them knew deep down they were only speaking platonically.

And in any case, sometimes love isn't enough.

As usual, Nissa said nothing. Chandra finally understood that words were simply not the elf's native tongue. She was uncomfortable with them. They overwhelmed her. Now that this simple, simple fact was finally clear—now that it was way too late—Chandra understood, and that understanding granted her tremendous sympathy for Nissa Revane.

All this time . . . I'd been trying to force her to speak to me in my *tongue. And all this time she'd been all but* begging *me to speak in* hers. *And neither of us understood each other because we had no shared language.*

"I'll always love you," Chandra said, after they had been looking into each other's eyes for she had no idea how long.

"And . . . and I . . . I love you," Nissa struggled out in response.

Present tense. Immediate. Nissa doesn't change; she doesn't evolve. She just . . . is. She exists in a state of Is. But that doesn't work for me. Because I have changed. I've changed more in the last seventy-two hours than I have since I first discovered I was a Planeswalker. Gideon's death. Liliana's death. Baan's death. They have changed me. Changed me and changed what I want.

"But . . ." Chandra began.

"Yes," Nissa said with the slightest of nods.

"You can tell me I'm wrong." Chandra was trying to help her, trying to translate Nissa's language into her own. "Correct me with a tiny shake of the head. But the truth is that I *exhaust* you, don't I?"

Nissa's eyes closed. There was no tiny shake of the head. She tried to speak then, tried for once to translate her language into Chandra's own. "I . . . I could never keep up. With you. With your . . ."

"Emotions."

"Yes," she said.

We're meeting each other halfway. It's good, even if it is sad.

"You care for me," Chandra said.

Nissa's eyes opened again, opened wide as if Chandra had accused her of some horrible crime—the crime of not caring. "Of course."

"And there was even some attraction. And I will always— always be very fond of you. I will always love you," Chandra repeated. Repeated because she needed the words on her side of this broken equation. She needed to hear herself say them out loud. "But I exhaust you, and I understand that now. I'm big and loud and awful and needy and too damn much. I can't ask you to change yourself for me. And I can't change myself for you. I can't be with someone that . . . that I have to *stifle* myself to be with, stifle myself to make you comfortable just to be around me."

"No," Nissa agreed.

"Neither of us would want that for the other."

"No," Nissa agreed, and she stroked her hand across Chandra's cheek, brushing aside a tear that Chandra hadn't realized she'd shed. The elf's touch was sweet and tender and, oh, so very gentle. Lovely as anything Chandra had ever experienced in her long short life.

And it's not enough. And that's sad, a bit. But it's not a tragedy. Not a tragedy to finally know, after all the will we or won't we of it all, that it isn't going to be. We did—we are. But only Nissa lives in the State of Is. I can't live with her in the State of Are. That's not who I am or ever was.

Nissa stepped back, and Chandra did the same. They came up for air, so to speak, not gasping or frantic. It was very much like a midnight swim under a sliver of moon, where their heads sink ever so briefly beneath the surface, and long before their lungs might have begun to struggle and burn, they break through the liquid plane, barely disturbing the mirror of the crescent in the water—and certainly not disturbing it for very long—so that each could take her cleansing, easy breath.

And say goodbye.

"You have your work here on Zendikar," Chandra said.

Nissa didn't even bother nodding this time. She knew that Chandra now understood her language. The language of silence. Neither of them had to struggle anymore.

But Nissa did want to learn Chandra's language, too. Or at least a few words. "What will you do?" she asked.

Which brought Chandra back to her earlier questions.

What will I do? What do I want? Who do I want to be?

A hunter like Vraska? A killer like Kaya? A mere survivor like Ral? No. No. No.

I want to be a hero. *I want to help people. Frankly, I want to be Gideon-freaking-Jura.*

So Chandra Nalaar decided right there and then that Gideon was who she'd strive to be. She knew she might not always succeed, but the important thing was that she tried and kept trying, no matter the odds. *That's* what Gids would do.

And even that *is an oversimplification . . .*

Because she *was* a hunter; she *was* a killer; she *was* a survivor, and there was guilt—tremendous guilt, *soul-crushing* guilt— attached to all three of those truths. But she thought Gids might have felt that guilt, as well.

So if I can evolve into him, there's a chance I can find a way through it, find a way past it . . .

She'd return to Kaladesh and to her mother's home. She could make that her base of operations. But then she'd 'walk and 'walk and 'walk, looking for trouble, looking for people in need. Looking to be a one-woman Gatewatch to solve as many of the Multiverse's problems as she could.

Or die trying.

She spoke none of these things, revealed none of these feelings out loud, elucidated none of her plans or goals. Literally none of them. And she thought Nissa looked both a little grateful and like someone who understood.

Nissa took her hand and squeezed it. Chandra squeezed Nissa's back. That was all the goodbyes they needed. Maybe they'd see each other again. They both certainly hoped they would.

But maybe not. And if not . . . I can imagine a lot worse endings than this.

Feeling determined, if not exactly happy, Chandra planeswalked away from the State of Is—and from former dreams of the State of Are—and returned to the evolving reality of Chandra Nalaar and that woman's new home base on Kaladesh.

SEVENTY-FOUR

JACE BELEREN

Jace was in Vraska's quarters, feeling like the walls were closing in.

He opened the door and stepped outside to check with Storrev one more time.

"Is she . . ." There wasn't even much point in finishing the question.

"I am sorry, no. Queen Vraska has not yet returned from the Council of the Guilds. If the queen's royal consort would prefer—"

"Please don't call me that." Liliana had once referred to Jace as her consort, and he hadn't been too thrilled with the title then, either.

"Perhaps you'd prefer to be called the Former Living Guildpact?"

"Jace will do just fine, thanks."

"As you wish . . . Jace." Admittedly, the lich's whisper-thin voice lent itself to formal titles, and her calling him Jace had really just made things awkward for the both of them.

"Mister Beleren, perhaps?"

"That would be preferable, thank you."

"But shouldn't the guild meeting be over by now?"

"I'm sure I don't know, Mister Beleren."

"I probably could have gone," he said, more to himself than the Erstwhile. "I probably *should* have gone."

But truthfully, Jace hadn't wanted to hear anything more about Liliana's death. He'd barely been able to get his head around the fact that she was gone. He knew he hadn't even begun to mourn her yet. Or Gideon, for that matter.

Both their deaths are going to hit me soon. And hard.

More than that, however, he had skipped the meeting because he was afraid to hear what Vraska was going to tell the others. He felt in his bones that the Golgari queen was keeping things from her allies—and that Jace Beleren's lover was keeping things from him. And he simply had no idea what he was going to do about it.

What I'm going to do about us.

SEVENTY-FIVE

VRASKA

Once the guild meeting was satisfactorily concluded—and after making sure she wasn't being followed—Vraska went to see Baan to tell him that all had gone as planned.

Unfortunately, Baan wasn't prepared to hear it—or anything. She found him in his safe house, with a smile on his face and an even wider smile slit into his throat. There were no signs of a struggle. But his *left* hand had been removed, though from the lack of blood around the wrist, it had apparently been removed postmortem.

For a moment, the Golgari queen wondered if the body was a fake—more of Baan's wheels within wheels.

But truthfully, she knew better. Dovin Baan was dead. Killed by someone who had known exactly where to find him. Killed by someone who knew Vraska had lied about his death. Killed before Baan could give Vraska the rest of his plan to secure her rule over the Golgari.

Vraska would still have trouble from Izoni and the devkarin, and now, potentially, from the other nine guilds, as well. Vraska had lied to everyone, including lies of omission to Jace—and she had done it all for nothing.

She looked down at Dovin Baan's body with its gloating expression and its *screaming* irony. Now Vraska had all the proof of kill she needed. Only now she couldn't use it. In fact, she'd have to destroy the body herself to make sure no one else could use it against her. Still, disposing of a body was the Golgari's bread and butter.

Taking a deep breath, she set about that grim task.

SEVENTY-SIX

RAT

Easily avoiding both living and mystical security with her insignificance, Rat returned to the Cathedral Opulent.

She had spent a fun night with her mother Ari, and even got to see—and be seen—by her father Gan Shokta and by Borborygmos when they returned from the guild meeting. They told Araithia and her mother that Master Dovin Baan and Miss Liliana Vess were dead, but that the Bolas minion Tezzeret was still at large in the Multiverse.

Of course, Rat didn't tell any of them that Miss Liliana was still alive, too. But she told a *version* of what occurred on Gobakhan and Dominaria, the summation of which amounted to: *"I have grand adventures—and friends!"*

All three seemed to enjoy her tale. They expressed their pride in her and told her they were happy for her. Rat promised to come home and visit periodically. No one protested her going to other worlds for long stretches.

One good thing about the Gruul: They're not exactly precious with their children.

Climbing in through her Orzhova window now, she raced out of her assigned room to check in with Teyo and Mistress Kaya. The guild meeting had gone well from their point of view, as well. No hitches. They'd all leave for Fiora early the next day.

Madame Blaise entered with a tray of tea and nearly smashed into Rat, who blithely dodged out of the way. When informed of this by Teyo, the loyal servitor got quite flustered. A somewhat giddy Rat stole the sugar bowl off Madame Blaise's tray and held it up right in front of the woman's face, as the loyal servitor berated herself for forgetting it in the kitchen. Rat then replaced it on the tray, and the old woman wondered if she was losing her mind . . . before realizing that Mistress Araithia—whom she absolutely refused to call Rat anymore—was playing a little prank "on old Blaise." Fortunately, the motherly woman didn't seem to mind the little joke at her expense. She was able to laugh with the others. Rat apologized through Teyo, and Madame Blaise accepted her apology and, moreover, swore that one day she *would* find a way to see her young mistress in order to "serve the poor girl better." Her determination almost brought a tear to Rat's eyes. Or might have. Except that right now Araithia Shokta was too happy for tears.

Happy as she was, Rat was still a bit sad over the loss of Mister Egg and what it might have meant to her.

Still, you gotta admit, sometimes it's a lot of fun being the Rat.

SEVENTY-SEVEN

BLAISE

Still chuckling to herself, a bemused Blaise left her mistress with Teyo and Araithia.

Really, they're all so charming together. And young Master Teyo's obvious crush on the girl is very sweet.

Moving along Orzhova corridors, she snapped out commands to various minor servitors in order to assure that her three charges would be well provided for and comfortable. Food brought (the two teens especially liked Selesnyan plums), fireplaces stoked, beds turned down, et cetera, et cetera.

Snug as three bugs in a rug.

Honestly, there were few things more satisfying to Madame Blaise than a job well done for people who were grateful for her service. For mistresses and masters who could have a little fun and bring an honest smile to an old woman's face.

Off duty for the time being, she practically sauntered out of the cathedral's porticoes and into the open air—still carrying the sugar bowl.

Walking down the broad street, still in view of the Cathedral Opulent, she passed many a member of the Syndicate, from the lowliest and the poorest to the highest and the mightiest. She knew them all, and they all knew her, all acknowledged her with—at minimum—a polite nod of the head. Yes, even the biggest of big shots offered signs of respect to Madame Blaise as she passed. In the little pond that was the great cathedral, she knew she was a very big fish. Someone who could get things done. Someone, frankly, that you didn't want to cross. So they all courted her—at least to some degree—and certainly none would ever think to slight her. (The last one who did wound up with a broom closet for an office and a near-constant shortage of toilet paper, no matter which lavatory the now pathetic advokist attempted to use. And the best part about that man's misfortunes . . . was that Blaise wasn't responsible for any of them. Other parties had arranged the young fool's travails, either because they didn't like the way the arrogant little snot had treated madame—or because they sought to curry madame's favor. Or more likely both.)

When she was some distance from Orzhova, she turned down an alley and turned into someone else entirely, a tall male stranger.

This stranger cast a quick spell and the illusion upon the sugar bowl faded away, revealing it as Dovin Baan's severed left hand. The stranger exited the alley, now looking like a minor Rakdos demon. Soon the demon—or some fourth or fifth shape—would be home at Duskmantle, the House Dimir guildhall, where he, she, it or they could safely morph into Lazav.

Whomever he might be.

As his demon form loped down a busy thoroughfare in full view of many a Ravnican soul, Lazav contemplated Araithia "Rat" Shokta, who could only be seen by her mother, her godfather, Teyo, Kaya . . . and Lazav himself. Of course, Lazav had known about Rat for over a decade and a half, since shortly after the girl was born. Right away he had realized that her unique condition would be extremely useful to himself and House Dimir. So unsurprisingly, he had been—and continued to be— determined to exploit it. The girl wasn't the first child Lazav had "recruited" (or perhaps a better word would be *collected*); nor was she likely to be the last. Why, just before Bolas had arrived on Ravnica, Lazav had added the infant Merritson to his collection, a child of obvious potential—though perhaps not nearly as much potential as young Araithia had possessed since birth.

Hers was a truly special case. As soon as his spies had told him of her, Lazav had made his way to Gruul territory in the form of the centaur Boruvo—and had quickly been forced to shift into a somewhat generic minotaur when he found that Boruvo was already there. Boruvo and the girl's mother could see the babe. But even her own father could not. Nor could most anyone else. Approaching the crib, Lazav had been prepared to perceive it as empty. And then had quickly been forced to pretend that he *did* perceive it that way. For in fact, he could see the young Araithia and hear her start to cry. Her Curse of Insignificance did not affect him.

Never for a moment was Araithia Shokta insignificant to me.

And of course that had made things much easier. As time passed and she grew from a baby to a little girl, he would approach her periodically—in one form or another—and have his kind little talks with the girl-who-was-so-grateful-to-be-seen, before using his mental prowess to cause her to forget those chats seconds later. More often, he was extremely careful to pretend he couldn't see her at all. It had almost become a game the way he was constantly *trying* to bump into her or mow her down unawares. Besides, it helped train her to be on her toes, aware of her surroundings and quick. Plus, it was just a little bit funny.

Funnier than her prank with the sugar bowl, certainly.

To this day, Rat believed she was Gateless, though she had secretly been inducted into Dimir years ago—before being made to forget that, as well.

In fact, Lazav had brainwashed the girl into his perfect little secret assassin, creating an entirely different identity for Rat: Atkos Tarr. The Dimir guildmaster was a bit embarrassed by the clumsy reverse spelling of the name of Rat's alter ego. But Araithia had been so young when Lazav started working with her—*on her*—that such simplicity had been necessary. And surprisingly—though rumors of the deadly Atkos being one of Dimir's very best assassins ran the length and breadth of Ravnica—it hadn't occurred to anyone that Atkos was Rat. Probably helped that Atkos believed he was a male vampire and behaved that way. Or perhaps that didn't even figure into it. So few people knew about Rat at all (more had heard of Atkos, frankly) that it could hardly occur to them to make the connection. Lazav wasn't sure which was the real reason and didn't much care.

As Blaise, Lazav had entered Rat's room the night before and had pretended not to see the girl to put her at ease. Then Blaise had addressed her as Atkos Tarr, for her name was also her trigger word, one that placed her into a suggestive trance. Lazav/Blaise had given Atkos quick instructions, thought-strands, via compressed telepathy. Then Blaise had walked back into the hallway to show Teyo a pre-prepared note. (Lazav had long ago learned to fake Rat's handwriting, though he was fairly certain Teyo had no idea what her handwriting looked like.)

Of course, Lazav sent Atkos to kill Dovin Baan, whose secret safe house had never been secret or safe from Lazav, who'd had spies watching it from the moment Baan had established it, long before Bolas arrived on Ravnica. Thus Lazav had known Baan was there from the moment he returned to Ravnica from Kaladesh. The vedalken—like all of Atkos' victims—never stood a chance against a killer too insignificant to notice.

Rat had been programmed to go to her mother's after and

then return to Madame Blaise with Baan's hand concealed under a spell of illusion. The girl remembered nothing; she wasn't even aware her prank with the sugar bowl had simply been a means of handing the hand over to her handler.

She executed everything perfectly, and to his embarrassment, it was Lazav who nearly slipped up—*did slip up, frankly*—by referring to her as Mistress Araithia, despite the fact that Blaise had never been told the girl had any other name save Rat.

No one noticed, of course.

But that's no excuse. I can't afford to grow complacent now. Not at this crucial juncture.

Lazav turned a corner and turned into a striking young elven woman, partially inspired by Emmara Tandris, as his thoughts turned to Vraska. The gorgon might not know it yet, but she and the Golgari already belonged to Lazav and Dimir. The shapeshifter would wait for his moment, letting the Golgari queen stew, and when the time was right, he'd bring forth Baan's left hand and reveal that her lies had placed her squarely under the Dimir guildmaster's thumb.

Lazav contemplated Rat a little more. It was a shame there hadn't been the time or the opportunity to debrief her, gleaning every morsel of knowledge and intelligence she had gained while traveling to other worlds with Kaya.

But that will come.

At first, Lazav had been unhappy about Araithia leaving Ravnica for prolonged and ill-defined periods of time. Both Rat and Atkos were extremely useful to the shapeshifter, and initially he didn't relish losing their services. But the more he thought about it, the more he warmed to the idea. Rat's alliance with Kaya extended Dimir's reach beyond the spymaster's own world.

And in a Multiverse full of planeswalking enemies and (temporary) allies, Atkos Tarr might have considerably more work to do in his future . . .

SEVENTY-EIGHT

RAL ZAREK

Ral Zarek walked slowly home, taking the long way back to the Dogsrun apartment he shared with Tomik.

As soon as the all-guild meeting was adjourned, Chamberlain Maree had called an emergency conference of the Izzet League. Every high mucky-muck in the Izmundi and the League (from Mizzix of the Izmagnus to Chief Chemister Varryvort) had flocked there like vultures, and even Niv had been allowed—perhaps encouraged—to attend by Maree, since Ral had been the dragon's own choice to succeed him as guildmaster.

Within seconds of the conference being called to order, Maree had launched her attack on Ral's leadership qualifications, quoting back his own words to him (and all assembled): *"Ravnica needs to know it can trust its leaders to defeat would-be conquerors and to bring its enemies to justice."*

Now that it was clear Ral had failed to do that, reason

dictated—or so the chamberlain suggested—that Ral must step down as Izzet guildmaster. Ral had seen this coming but had held out some hope that others in the guild might be more sympathetic. They were not. When Maree had demanded his resignation, some seconded her motion, while others remained silent. No one spoke up to support him.

Of course, Ral did not resign. After all, as he made clear to the gathered Leaguers, there was no way Maree would or could ever have the chance to fail the way he had. Maree wasn't a Planeswalker, and Tezzeret wouldn't show his face on Ravnica again. So unless the chamberlain had a plan for taking down the artificer offworld, she might as well back the Krokt off.

Maree, of course, had no such plan, so Ral took advantage of her somewhat embarrassed silence to remind her and everyone that he could have lied about killing Tezzeret but had refused to betray his guild and his world in that way. He then did something particularly bold—even reckless—insisting on a vote of confidence in his leadership. To Maree's chagrin (and in stark contrast with the lack of support he had garnered only minutes earlier), Ral won near-unanimous approval from those present.

Still, I wish it hadn't come to that.

Glancing at Niv-Mizzet, who had remained silent throughout the conference, Ral had initially felt confident the dragon understood the unfairness and raw ambition behind this attack on his former protégé. Perhaps the Firemind even felt bad about Ral nearly losing his hard-won position. Ral understood that the Living Guildpact could not interfere in the internal workings of any one guild, not even the guild he had founded. Yet the more Ral stared at the dragon—shiny and reborn—the less certain Ral became that Niv's famous Firemind had been paying any attention whatsoever to his successor's predicament. For all Ral knew, Niv was thinking about neural core-weavers . . . or maybe about his supper.

With the leadership question settled in his favor, Guildmaster

Zarek had consciously taken on a generous air, making a show of recognizing and acknowledging Chamberlain Maree's many skills and talents, assuring her she still held a prominent place within the Izzet League. Then he dismissed everyone for the time being, ordering Maree to nominate and convene his new scientific cabinet, something that Ral, in his brief tenure as guildmaster, had not had the opportunity to do until this time.

What with the evil megalomaniacal dragon to defeat and everything . . .

Ral had won, reconfirming his ascendancy, but the whole thing had been stressful and draining and had briefly made him question whether he even *wanted* to be Izzet's guildmaster.

Now, as Ral approached his apartment, he did see one silver lining in all this: Tomik. With Kaya back on Ravnica, Orzhov's acting guildmaster could step down. He'd still have his work as her advisor and assistant, but he'd now have considerably more free time for Ral. And it was clear that Tomik's time, love and support were things Ral would very much need.

He opened the apartment door, calling out his lover's name.

But Tomik wasn't there. Just a note:

Guild business. Home late. Love you.

—T

SEVENTY-NINE

TEZZERET

Tezzeret planeswalked into the small room in a shower of blue and silver sparks, unfolding himself from the void within his chest. Immediately the artificer felt . . . not claustrophobic but cramped. A small cabinet like this couldn't, or at least shouldn't, contain him or his plans anymore. He found himself actually resenting the space.

Still, he had always been pragmatic. If this was the most secure location for the rendezvous, so be it.

He looked about him. The room was empty except for a full-length wall-mounted mirror and two large, soft leather-backed chairs. Tezzeret cleared his throat, and within a few seconds, the Wanderer stepped out of the liquid surface of the mirror to join him.

Tezzeret asked: "Did it work?"

The Wanderer replied, "Unfortunately, no. It's disappointing, but Ral actually confessed his failure. I didn't think he had it in him."

"Honestly, neither did I."

"He has the love of a good man. Or at least he thinks so. That belief seems to have changed him."

Tezzeret rolled his eyes. "Funny how weakness can occasionally and accidentally result in strength. Where does this leave us?"

"If Ral had not confessed," said the Wanderer as she morphed into Lazav, "I had, per our plan, been prepared to blackmail him. That's no longer possible, as I don't have anything else on him . . . yet."

Tezzeret scowled and growled, "Is it all bad news?"

"Not at all. I have my hooks deep into the Golgari; Vraska has put herself completely at my mercy."

"Does she know?" Tezzeret asked, feeling slightly less grumpy. *Slightly.*

"She knows she's in trouble. She doesn't yet know from where the trouble will spring."

"What exactly do you have on her?"

"I'd say that's not your concern—"

"I'd insist it's very much my concern. Our agreement dictates—"

"Yes, yes, I know. Which is why I was about to answer your question before you so rudely interrupted."

Tezzeret exhaled. "Apologies."

"You seem tense, my friend. It's the fortress, isn't it? The Wanderer—the *real* Wanderer—mentioned you had abandoned it."

"Exactly. It was a worthwhile sacrifice in exchange for granting you control of Zarek and the Izzet. Now it feels like I gave up a perfectly good headquarters for nothing."

"You can probably reclaim it."

"You think so?"

"Who'd ever think to look for you there now?"

"Huh. Maybe. We'll see. In any case, we were on the subject of Vraska . . ."

"Have a seat, and I'll gladly reveal all."

Tezzeret nodded, and both of them sat down. The chair was surprisingly comfortable. So comfortable, in fact, that Tezzeret was convinced a comfort spell had been placed on the thing— one designed to lull Lazav's guests into a false sense of ease. But Tezzeret didn't *do* ease.

Lazav thinks he's handling me. But when the time comes, he'll learn the opposite was true all along.

He gripped the arm of the chair with his (now even more perfect) etherium hand and gave it a little crunch, damaging the chair slightly and breaking the spell. He was instantly less comfortable, which was just fine with Tezzeret, who asked again about, "Vraska?"

"Yes, Vraska. Well, despite her claims to the Living Guildpact and the ten guilds, I know and have proof that neither Vraska nor Chandra killed Dovin Baan. So obviously, when the time is right, I'll hold that knowledge over her head, forcing her to side with Dimir on transguild matters or else risk revealing to every guild— including her own—that she's a liar who cannot be trusted. Better still, Vraska doesn't even have full control of the Golgari, as Baan didn't have the opportunity to reveal his full plan to her."

"Good. Good. Chaos within the Golgari will be useful to the both of us."

"My thoughts exactly."

"And the Orzhov?"

"We have the inside track there, too. Having three leaders— Kaya the figurehead, Vrona the functionary and Karlov the power behind the throne—may have appeared clever to our dear Teysa, but the current Orzhov structure that she's created is ripe for us to exploit."

"So three down; seven to go."

"Don't forget Simic."

"Ah, yes. Four down; six to go."

"Exactly. Our plans proceed apace."

EIGHTY

ANA IORA

Ana woke with a start . . . desperate to remember her name. But it all came back to her soon enough.

Amnesia isn't one of my gifts, unfortunately. Where's Jace with a good brain wipe when you really need him?

Jace . . .

Well. Enough of that. She is Ana Iora. And Ana Iora is on Fiora. Iora. Fiora. That must be where I got the name. It bloody well rhymes, which makes it a pretty asinine choice. But she wrote it down. Too late to change it now. At least not at the Fiddler's.

She rose to wash. The bathroom was down the hall. This wasn't Liliana's kind of place.

But maybe she can learn to make it Ana's kind of place.

The water came out brown at first.

No, this will not be Ana's kind of place. No matter how humble Ana waxes, she will demand better than this. Eventually.

Eventually, the water cleared, and she splashed it cold across her face. She looked for soap and found none.

Minutes later, she was back in her room. She pulled open the curtains with some trepidation, half expecting the tree opposite her window to be occupied with hundreds of ravens, weighing down every limb, bough and branch. But there were no ravens. No birds, even. So she opened the window, allowing a cool breeze to play across her damp, somewhat tangled hair.

Ana, it seems, doesn't have the same self-respect—or vanity— that Liliana once possessed. That will have to change, too. Eventually.

She dragged a heavy wooden chair over to the window, sat down and stared down the road leading up to the inn. Waiting. Waiting. Waiting at the window. Rapidly growing more and more impatient, antsy, anxious. She kept thinking about how Kaya, Teyo and Rat had come to Dominaria to kill her—but had wound up saving her instead. They were no Gatewatch, but they might in fact be better for her.

Works-in-progress, like I am. Like Ana Iora is.

The thought occurred that they'd be easier to manipulate, since by this time the Gatewatch pretty much knew all her tricks.

No, damnit, stop that!

She was right to reprimand herself. She didn't want to *be* that person anymore. She didn't want to be Liliana Vess, at least not for the time being. She knew she was still damaged goods, still in need of a redemption she hadn't yet achieved. She barely believed she was capable of it, let alone deserving of it.

Really, it's not fair to the three of them. They shouldn't be burdened with keeping her secrets, with guiding her course, with . . . well . . . with Liliana Vess.

She was practically ready to bolt.

Take off. Planeswalk to somewhere obvious. Innistrad, probably. Let Kaya hunt me down there and take me out as she vowed.

Let her kill Liliana Vess for crimes against the people of Ravnica and for the crime of not wanting to be saved—or not wanting to be saved enough, *not wanting to be* Ana *enough.*

The idea sounded fairly appealing, and honestly, the only thing stopping Liliana from bolting was that she wasn't exactly sure *why* she was bolting.

Or maybe I do know. I'm too tired, too broken to gut it out, to do the work, to make myself into someone else, someone new, to turn Liliana into Ana.

Damnit, I hate introspection.

She stood. It was time to leave. To planeswalk. She was ready. She'd go. Unless they came. Unless they came now. Or now. Or now.

What are you doing? Since when are you an indecisive twit? Since now, apparently. Another difference between Liliana and Ana.

She wondered absently how long she had slept.

She wondered absently where she could buy a decent wardrobe or summon the magic to transmogrify her current clothes into something presentable.

She wondered absently about how long it had been since she had eaten anything, and if it *had* been as long as she suspected, why she wasn't hungry.

She wondered absently when exactly she had resumed her seat—and how any chair could be *this* uncomfortable.

Then she spotted Kaya and Teyo walking up the lane toward the inn. Without conscious thought, she was out the door and out of her room, down the stairs and outside, ridiculously thrilled to see them.

"Is she here?" she asked, semi-desperate.

Teyo nodded and said, "She's right here between us."

For some reason, Ana needed more reassurance and looked to Kaya, who put her arm around air and said, "Here."

Ana focused, focused . . . and there, with Kaya's arm around her shoulder, was Rat, smiling and happy to see her. Happy to be seen *by* her. "Hello, Miss Ana," she said.

"How did you—?"

"I'm a little bit psychic, remember? Everything about you just screams Ana now. Or Miss Ana. Sorry."

"No, it's fine. It's fine." Liliana discovered she was wiping her eyes and quickly chastised herself.

I don't care if you are Ana, you are not *that sappy.*

But she had to admit that it warmed the atrophied stone that passed for her heart to see that this innocent child was happy to have Ana Iora of Fiora in her life.

Yes, being with these three will definitely be better than being with the Gatewatch.

Besides, the Gatewatch must all continue to believe Liliana Vess was dead. She could never see any of them again.

I can never see Jace again . . .

EIGHTY-ONE

JACE BELEREN

Lying in bed together, wrapped in each other's arms, Vraska had told Jace everything.

He had tried not to scowl when she described how she had used a vulnerable Chandra in her ploy to fool the guilds. Vraska wasn't proud of herself—and obviously not thrilled that the whole plan had backfired horribly—but she still felt, given what she knew at the time, that the risk had been worth the cost.

But Jace could tell Vraska was waiting to see whether that *cost* now included him. Desperate to reassure her (and himself), Jace shoehorned his thoughts into a further betrayal of Chandra with a promise to keep his lover's counsel, saying, "We all have secrets."

She had kissed him then.

Wonder if she'd have kissed me if I had said, I'm telling.

He ruefully decided it paid sometimes to have a somewhat loose alliance with the concept of integrity.

She laid a hand on his chest. He pulled her closer. They were silent for a time. But this wasn't an easy, comfortable silence. Both were waiting for the next shoe to drop, the next revelation, the next crisis.

Or just for one of us to take a risk and speak.

So he spoke: "Will you still come with me to Vryn . . . just for a little while?" She didn't answer instantly, and so he kept talking to fill the brief silence. "I mean, now that I have all my memories back, I need to rediscover my past. I guess I told you that already."

"Mm-hmm."

"And I'd very much like to share that rediscovery with the woman I love. But I guess I told you that already, too."

"It's all right. I like hearing it."

He waited.

Finally, she sighed and said, "I want to go with you, Jace. Sincerely. By Krokt, I'd love to go. I'd love to leave all this behind and be with you, be there as you found yourself, for better or worse."

"But . . ."

"But someone out there killed Baan. She, he or they know the truth and could use it to destroy me. And if it were *just* about me, I'd still go with you. I'd risk that for you, certainly for one short week."

"But . . ."

"But the Swarm is vulnerable—I've *made* them vulnerable—and I simply can't leave now."

Jace nodded. "I understand. I do." But deep down he knew she'd always choose the Golgari over him. And maybe that wasn't even wrong. Maybe it was exactly how she should be choosing. But maybe he also knew what that meant.

She'd commit any sin for the Golgari—then confess her sin

after, so that I either bless her fait accompli or reject it and destroy us. Vraska and I, we . . . we aren't going to make it as a couple.

Still, he wasn't quite ready to let go. He said, "I understand why you have to stay. Do you understand why I have to go?"

"I do."

He kissed her gratefully.

She kissed him back, passionately. They made love again, grasping at each other, desperate to hold on.

Then he showered and put on the clean clothes Storrev had laid out for him earlier. She watched him from the bed, naked and enticing and a little . . . frightened, perhaps?

Well, I'm scared, too.

He kissed her lips gently. "I'll be back soon," he said. "Soon as I possibly can . . ."

"I'll be here," she said. "I'll be waiting."

He kissed her one more time. Then Jace summoned up a hazy memory of Vryn and planeswalked away . . .

PROLOGUE

EIGHTY-TWO

KAYA

Araithia's newly founded and newly reunited team of four sat on hard wooden benches around a wobbly wooden table in the courtyard in front of Fiddler's Inn as a little yellow-green goblin child served them their supper—or in any case, served Kaya, Teyo and "Ana" their supper. (Teyo ordered double to accommodate Rat.) It was humble fare, beans with bits of ham and toast, which Ana absently pushed around with her fork, but which the other three enjoyed well enough. Madame Blaise would be appalled, but Kaya had eaten worse on her travels.

And the wine's fairly decent.

Once the goblin walked away, Liliana Vess leaned forward and said, "Listen, I am who I am. Don't expect wholesale change. I'm a necromancer. Death *is* and will continue to be my stock-in-trade."

Kaya thought Liliana sounded overly confrontational, overly

cynical . . . but was trying a little *too* hard to sound that way. Kaya wasn't psychic like Rat, but she could sense Liliana's vulnerability and need.

Or Ana's vulnerability and need, anyway.

Kaya also noticed how hard Liliana was working to focus and *maintain* focus on Rat, desperate to keep Araithia in her consciousness, almost as if Liliana was feeding off the girl's innocence and optimism. And Kaya couldn't immediately decide if that was good or bad. Then she remembered it was how she herself had felt just a few short days ago. Like she was feeding off both Rat's and Teyo's light. She could hardly condemn Liliana for wanting and needing what she herself had wanted and needed.

What I still want and need from them, honestly.

So Kaya was determined to give Liliana a chance. After all, she'd shown up here on Fiora at the Fiddler's and waited for them, just as Rat had known she would. That seemed a good sign. Maybe the four of them might work as a team.

Besides, if our next stop after Fiora goes as I expect, I'll need their help. All their help. Maybe Liliana's help, especially. Beyond that, I could use the company, not to mention the moral support.

It was strange. Kaya had spent the last six years as a solo act. The lone assassin, 'walking from plane to plane, sending phantoms, haints, ghosts and spirits—plus the occasional zombie or vampire—to her or his or their final rest. She hadn't thought it bothered her to live a life of itinerant solitude. It was only now, with this sudden acquisition of two good friends (and one dangerous question mark), that the lone assassin realized what a *lonely* assassin she had become. She relished her time with Teyo and Rat, genuinely enjoying their companionship.

She didn't feel parental toward them exactly. More like a big sister, which carried its own responsibilities, she supposed.

Though truth be told, she didn't feel burdened at all. To the contrary, she felt tremendously unburdened. Tomik had lifted those blasted Orzhov contracts from her soul. The two teenagers had brought her joy and friendship, and last night, she'd even managed to finally have that good cathartic cry she'd been needing and wanting ever since the War of the Spark had ended. She had cried for Gideon Jura, for Dack Fayden, even. She had cried for Hekara—both for the razor-witch's tragic death and for her stunning resurrection, which had clearly cost Hekara some piece of herself, not to mention her friendship with Rat.

And Kaya had cried for herself. The grief had—as she had predicted—caught her unawares, in bed just after she had blown out a last candle, generating great heaving sobs for over an hour as she mourned people she loved and people she barely knew, as the enormity of Ravnica's tragedy and loss finally hit her. She eventually cried herself to sleep and woke up . . . grateful. Only a few days ago, she had felt numb: not a ghost-assassin but a ghost herself. Now . . .

I can breathe again.

All these thoughts raced through Kaya's mind in a flash. She downed an entire glass of wine and poured herself another. Belatedly, she realized that Ana was still looking at her, expecting some kind of response. She had to mentally turn back the clock even to remember what it was the woman had just said to her— and filled the time by busying herself with the drinking of more wine. Finally recalling Ana's last defiant statement, Kaya shrugged and said, "I'm still a ghost-assassin. Our powers are our powers. I don't expect you to become a creature of sunshine and light. I expect you to use what you have to redeem past sins. If it helps—or at least puts things in perspective—that's what I'm trying to do, as well."

Rat said, "Oh, yeah, me too."

The other three all looked at her with cocked eyebrows—even Teyo.

"I've done bad stuff," Rat said defensively. "I'm a thief, after all."

Teyo said, "I bet you've never once stolen anything from anyone who couldn't afford to lose what you took."

"Of course not. That would be awful. And mean. Very mean. Plus, why would I do that, when I can steal from someone who *could* afford the loss, you know?"

With perfect deadpan delivery, Ana said, "You're a monster, all right."

The Rat pointed at her: "See, *she* gets me." Then the young woman started to giggle.

It was an infectious sound. They were all chuckling soon, even Ana, who caught herself and abruptly stopped, staring at her half-empty wineglass and murmuring, "I must be intoxicated."

A still-chuckling Teyo asked, "Where will we go next?"

Kaya took another sip and then put down her glass, steeling herself for what she knew she had to do. She said, "There's a situation I've been avoiding for months. Nicol Bolas was supposed to help me with it, but obviously that's not happening now."

Ana said, "Help from Bolas never helped anyone *but* Bolas."

Kaya nodded. "Agreed. In fact, I've come to suspect the dragon may have instigated the problem himself in order to force me into trading favors with him. In any case, it's time I faced this thing head-on. We'll rest here at the inn tonight. Because tomorrow we're planeswalking to Tolvada, my homeworld . . ."

ACKNOWLEDGMENTS

As always, I had significant help on both *Ravnica* and *Forsaken* from a vast number of people, including—but not limited to— the following . . .

At Del Rey, I'd like to again thank my editor Thomas Hoeler, who held my hand through two books on very tight deadlines. He believed I could handle the gig when I myself was less than convinced. I'd also like to thank Elizabeth Schaefer, who walked me along the yellow brick road through Emerald City, when Tom decided to go to Middle Earth instead. Thanks also to Scott Biel, Keith Clayton, Alex Davis, Nancy Delia, Elizabeth Eno, Ashleigh Heaton, Julie Leung, David Moench, Tricia Narwani, Erich Schoeneweiss and Scott Shannon. On the audiobook side, thanks to Catherine Bucaria, Robert Guzman, Nick Martorelli, Nicole Morano and the narrator of *Ravnica*, Robert Petkoff. And I cannot thank Magali Villeneuve enough for both books' amazing covers and for her visual creation of our Rat.

At Wizards of the Coast, my thanks go out to the always invaluable Nic Kelman, and to loremaster and backstop Jay Annelli. Thanks also to Doug Beyer, Richard Cornish, Chris Gleeson, T. C. Hoffman, Lake Hurwitz, Daniel Ketchum, Liz Lamb-Ferro, Ari Levitch, Mark Rosewater, Steve Sunu, Gerritt Turner and Jeremy Jarvis. I also want to thank the amazingly talented Django Wexler and other Magic storytellers who came before (or sometimes during) my time among the Planeswalkers, especially Nicky Drayden, Kate Elliott, Jenna Helland, Adam Lee and Alison Luhrs.

At the Gotham Group: J. D. Cisneros, Tony Gil, Ellen Goldsmith-Vein, Julie Kane-Ritsch, Gavin Laing, Julie Nelson, Alicia Rose, Matt Shichtman, Joey Villareal and, of course, Peter McHugh.

For putting up with my split focus, I'd like to thank my *Young Justice* family, in particular Melissa Lohman, Amy McKenna and Brandon Vietti.

Last but not least, I'd like to thank my actual family for their support. My in-laws, Zelda & Jordan Goodman and Danielle & Brad Strong. My nieces and nephews, Julia, Jacob, Lilah, Casey and Dash. My siblings, Robyn Weisman and Jon & Dana Weisman. My cousin Brindell Gottlieb. My parents, Sheila & Wally Weisman. My wife and personal photographer, Beth, and my amazing poppers, Erin and Benny. I love you all.

ABOUT THE AUTHOR

GREG WEISMAN has been a storyteller all his life. He's best known as the creator of Disney's *Gargoyles* and as a writer-producer and show-runner on multiple animated series, including *Gargoyles, W.I.T.C.H., The Spectacular Spider-Man, Star Wars Rebels* and *Young Justice.*

In addition to writing the *New York Times* best-selling *War of the Spark: Ravnica* and its sequel *War of the Spark: Forsaken,* Greg wrote the first two books in the *World of Warcraft: Traveler* series of novels—plus two original novels, *Rain of the Ghosts* and *Spirits of Ash and Foam.*

He's also written several comic book titles, including the *New York Times* bestseller *Star Wars Kanan,* as well as *Captain Atom, Gargoyles, Young Justice, Mythic Legions, Mecha-Nation* and *Starbrand and Nightmask.*

Greg lives in Los Angeles with his wife Beth and his own somewhat twisted imagination. Erin and Benny, his two wondrous kids (and Planeswalkers in their own right), are fully functioning grown-ups. Thus Greg's proudest achievement is that he didn't mess them up—too much.

ABOUT THE TYPE

This book was set in Aster, a typeface designed in 1958 by Francesco Simoncini (d. 1967). Aster is a round, legible face of even weight and was planned by the designer for the text setting of newspapers and books.